## The kidnapper hu

For about ten second̶s̶ ̶ ̶ ̶ ̶ ̶ ̶ ̶ ̶ ̶ ̶shock
kept Duncan p̶ ̶ ̶ ̶ ̶ ̶ ̶ ̶ ̶ ̶ed into action.
Fifteen minutes! ̶ ̶ ̶ ̶bastards were giving him no
leeway at all. Perhaps they didn't know that he didn't
own a car. Thank God he'd been planning to jog some
time this morning, and he was already wearing sweats
and sneakers. The Crossroads Shopping Plaza was a
mile and a half away, about ten minutes if he ran at his
absolute top speed. Fortunately, he knew the bookstore
they were talking about, so at least he wouldn't have to
waste time searching for it.

He grabbed his keys and wallet, then remembered his
cell phone and spent a few more precious seconds
zipping it into his rear pocket. He'd call Gordon as soon
as he'd retrieved the kidnapper's instructions. Even
though it meant a delay before an investigation could
be launched, he didn't dare risk taking the time to make
any calls until he actually had those instructions safely
in his hands.

The guy on the phone had sounded as if he was just
looking for an excuse to kill Summer.

"An entertaining read."
—*Publishers Weekly* on *Secret Sins*

# THE
# DISAPPEARANCE

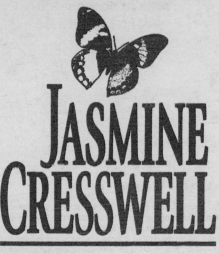

# JASMINE
# CRESSWELL

MIRA

ISBN 1-55166-486-0

THE DISAPPEARANCE

Copyright © 1999 by Jasmine Cresswell.

All rights reserved. Except for use in any review, the reproduction or utilization of this work in whole or in part in any form by any electronic, mechanical or other means, now known or hereafter invented, including xerography, photocopying and recording, or in any information storage or retrieval system, is forbidden without the written permission of the publisher, MIRA Books, 225 Duncan Mill Road, Don Mills, Ontario, Canada M3B 3K9.

All characters in this book have no existence outside the imagination of the author and have no relation whatsoever to anyone bearing the same name or names. They are not even distantly inspired by any individual known or unknown to the author, and all incidents are pure invention.

MIRA and the Star Colophon are trademarks used under license and registered in Australia, New Zealand, Philippines, United States Patent and Trademark Office and in other countries.

Printed in U.S.A.

For Yolande Corinne Steger,
with affection

# *Prologue*

Joseph Malone had been expecting death for the past six months. Only a fool wouldn't have recognized the danger, and he was an idealist, not a fool. Most of the time he was too busy with the final stages of his research to wonder exactly how they'd kill him, but when the nights were especially hot and sleep wouldn't come, he'd lie in his hammock and wonder. A bullet in the back was their usual method—except that they didn't yet know where to find him. Their willful ignorance of the rain forest was his major protection, and it was a powerful one. As long as he remained deep in the forest he was safe, guarded by the exuberant extravagance of nature and the ferocious loyalty of the Xuaxanu tribe.

Unfortunately, he couldn't stay in the rain forest forever, not if he wanted to achieve his goals. So, with great care, and even greater reluctance, he'd made plans for a trip to the United States. Fernando had offered his personal protection weeks ago, but Joseph had rejected it. Not because he didn't trust Fernando. Oddly enough, after years on opposite sides of the fight to preserve the rain forest, Joseph had developed a degree of respect for Fernando's abilities that bordered on affection.

No, it wasn't lack of trust that had caused him to

reject Fernando's offer of help, it was lack of confidence. He simply didn't believe Fernando could make good on his promises. Fernando might be one of the richest and most powerful men in the world, but even he was helpless to impose his will on the seething mass of corruption and exploitation that passed for law enforcement in Amazonia. So, realizing that he was courting danger, Joseph had left the hidden village headquarters of the Xuaxanu tribe and made his way by canoe and motorboat to Manaus, the city that served as gateway to Brazil's vast Amazon territory and as jumping-off point for travel to the rest of the world.

He tried to keep his journey secret. Even so, at the airport he was on full alert, constantly anticipating attempts to kill him, smelling conspiracy every time he was forced to confront a sweat-soaked, underpaid official of the faraway central government. But nothing untoward happened. He traveled from Manaus to Recife, changed planes and boarded the jumbo jet bound for the United States. His ultimate destination was Washington, D.C., and a rendezvous with Fernando, but he'd chosen to fly into Miami simply because it was the closest point of entry and he thought he might feel marginally safe once he was on U.S. soil.

America. His father's country. Land of the brave, and home of the free. As a teenager, he'd been cynical about the lazy patriotism of most Americans, scoffing at their arrogant belief that the United States was the best country in the world. But after three years of living in Brazil, he was more willing to be impressed by what the United States offered its citizens. In comparison to the institutionalized corruption he'd witnessed in the shantytowns scattered along the Amazon River,

Americans lived under a political system that was a model of honesty and efficiency. No wonder so many of them were pioneers, willing to take huge risks. It was easy to learn the habit of bravery when you enjoyed the security of genuine freedom.

The flight north from Recife was typically long and boring. So uneventful, in fact, that Joseph began to feel faint prickings of hope. Hope that he'd make it safely out of Brazil. Hope that he and Fernando might both live long enough to meet in D.C. as arranged. Hope that Summer Shepherd would never have to decipher the secrets contained in the disks he'd mailed from Recife airport.

But twenty minutes after landing in Miami, he realized that he'd allowed himself to hope much too soon. He wasn't even out of Customs yet, and already he was in trouble. Paralyzed with frustration, Joseph watched as a U.S. Customs official rummaged around in his suitcase with determined thoroughness. This was no routine search, Joseph thought grimly. He'd been set up.

The official gave a satisfied sigh when he picked up a large, sealed plastic bag, stuffed with white powder. He was careful to hold the bag by the edges, presumably so as not to contaminate any fingerprints that might be on the surface of the plastic.

Cocaine, Joseph thought bitterly. At least a kilo. And I'll bet the bastards found some way to make sure my prints are all over the damned Baggie.

All the signs indicated that Customs had been tipped off to expect him. The man who'd rifled through his suitcase was a senior officer, and there were two younger, more junior officials hovering close by. Although it was useless, Joseph made an automatic protest of his innocence. The officials listened with undisguised skepticism.

Too late, Joseph realized that he'd underestimated his enemies. Of course they weren't planning anything as clumsy as murder. They hadn't been waiting for him to come out of the rain forest so that they could kill him; they'd been waiting for him to emerge so that they could squeeze information out of him. They wouldn't murder him; they'd torture him until they got what they wanted: not his life, but his research notes.

The formula.

Despite the air-conditioning, Joseph realized he was drenched in sweat. He fought back a sickening wave of fear. He was a scientist, not a soldier, and although his years in the jungle had given him a high tolerance for discomfort, he doubted if he would have the stomach to withstand the infliction of intense, calculated pain. What, precisely, were the bastards planning? How many of the U.S. officials had they bought off? All of them? None? Was he going to disappear from the Customs hall, never to be seen again?

He swallowed, his palms wet and his mouth bone dry with fear as the Customs officer read him his legal rights. Even though he knew it was useless, he made another protestation of innocence. The officials all ignored him.

Wild-eyed, Joseph looked around the Customs hall, desperately seeking an escape route. Sensing that he was planning to run, the agent must have given some silent signal, because suddenly Joseph was surrounded by burly officials, all with drawn weapons.

It was automatic to resist when they dragged him off to an interrogation room, but that achieved nothing except to get his arms nearly wrenched out of their sockets and handcuffs slapped on his wrists. The agents hauled him into a bleak, windowless interrogation room that smelled of stale cigarette smoke and human fear. His own fear, maybe. God knew, he was scared. So much was at stake, and not just for him, but for hundreds of thousands of other people.

He slumped deep into his chair and refused to answer questions or to acknowledge the presence of his interrogators. Buried deep within the protective wall of silence, his brain raced. All right, he had to accept the fact that he'd miscalculated. His enemies must have tracked him down when he stopped his boat for refueling at one of the ramshackle towns along the banks of the Amazon. Which confirmed that, at least for now, his enemies didn't want him dead. If they'd known enough about his movements to plant cocaine in his suitcase, they could certainly have arranged for him to be murdered before he ever left Manaus.

Instead, they'd arranged for him to be arrested. In the United States, of all places. Okay, so they wanted information—information that they could only get from him. No real surprise in that, but there had to be a reason, both for the time and the place of his arrest. The fact that they'd let him leave Brazil meant that they wanted him to get as far as the United States. Somehow they believed that by having him arrested and thrown in jail here, they'd be able to get information that couldn't be squeezed out of him in Brazil. So torture—easy to arrange in Manaus and more difficult in the United States—probably wasn't going to be their preferred method.

Joe wasn't as reassured by that insight as he should have been. What the hell did they need him here for? On U.S. soil, headed for an American jail? For the life of him, he couldn't fathom what they were planning to do. He only knew that he'd better figure it out fast if he wanted to save his life.

And his work.

# *One*

"Ms. Shepherd! Summer! What a pleasure to see you here."

Summer turned around and recognized a distinguished Brazilian physicist who had been one of the most influential scientists contributing to the success of the 1997 environmental summit in Japan. She held out her hand, smiling warmly. "Dr. Pelem, what a nice surprise."

"I'm surprised to be here," he said. "I'm not quite sure how I made such an exclusive guest list. I believe your esteemed vice president must have put in a good word for me."

"Possibly, but the fact that you've just been appointed director of the Brazilian Academy of Sciences might also have something to do with it. Congratulations, Dr. Pelem."

He waved his hand. "You know how it is with academic honors," he said, smiling. "Once you are too old to produce any more worthwhile work, they appoint you director of everything imaginable to keep you out of mischief."

She laughed, accepting his proffered arm and letting him escort her toward the entrance to the John Quincy Adams State Drawing Room. "Then the system has failed miserably with you, Doctor. I read your report on last year's environmental summit, and it's by far the most intelligent and succinct summation of what happened there. And I noticed a couple of well-deserved zingers slipped in there amid all that bland United Nations prose."

"Then we can join each other in mutual admiration," he said, his eyes twinkling. "I read your paper on ozone depletion over the Antarctic in *Nature,* and I was extremely impressed, not just with the science, but with the good sense of your conclusions."

"Thank you. I'm sincerely honored. Approval from you is a real compliment."

"You're welcome. And now, since we're in this happy mode of mutual compliments, may I take the liberty of a very ancient man and tell you that you are looking especially lovely tonight? You are a dazzling combination, Ms. Shepherd. Brains and beauty in one most delectable package."

She laughed. "Thank you again, I'm sincerely flattered. Although, these days, I'm sure even ancient scientists aren't supposed to notice how their colleagues look."

"To which I say, Ms. Shepherd, thank God I am still a man first and a scientist second. Ah! There is the ambassador making not-so-discreet hand signals at me. I must take my leave and hope that we will speak again later."

Dr. Pelem bowed over her hand and disappeared into the crowd. Summer drew in a deep breath, steeling herself to greet her stepmother, who was welcoming guests in front of the magnificent fireplace. She walked forward with grim determination.

"Summer, my dear, you look so…frazzled. I hope nothing's wrong?" Olivia Shepherd kissed the air next to her stepdaughter's cheek, then stepped back, allowing her flawlessly made-up face to wrinkle into a faint suggestion of a worried frown.

Summer resisted the urge to tug at her dress and smooth her hair. "No, I'm fine, thanks, Olivia. Everything's just hunky-dory."

She winced at the gaucheness of her reply, wondering why she could never think of witty comebacks to her stepmother's jibes until their meetings were over and she was home in bed. The ability to undermine Summer's self-confidence was one of Olivia's best-honed skills, and she used it ruthlessly.

"Hunky-dory?" Olivia repeated the phrase with mocking relish. "My dear, I'm glad you're so... upbeat."

"Why wouldn't I be?"

"I heard that you're in danger of losing your job. The powers-that-be at the university obviously aren't as convinced as you are that the polar ice caps are about to melt and float us all into the ocean."

Summer gritted her teeth and decided not to waste her breath attempting to explain—for the zillionth time—exactly what her careful, statistical research into the thinning of the ozone layer was really about. "It's true that the university briefly lost funding for my project, but we found a replacement sponsor without too much difficulty."

She blushed at the lie. Replacement funding had been almost impossible to secure, and her postdoctoral fellowship had less than six months left to run, at which point she would be unemployed. But she sure as hell wasn't going to admit that humiliating truth to her stepmother. "My job's secure," she said defensively.

"I'm glad to hear it." Olivia made no effort to sound sincere. "I know how wrapped up you are in your causes, Summer. Your father and I often wonder where you'd hide yourself if you didn't have that lab to bury yourself in."

"I'm sure I'd find somewhere suitably obscure." Summer gave herself a mental shake, angry that she was allowing her stepmother to manipulate her emotions so successfully. "Speaking of Dad, where is he?" she asked, glancing around the crowded room.

"Over by the windows, talking to the Brazilian foreign minister." Olivia's mouth twisted into a tiny, patronizing smile. "I don't think they'd appreciate being interrupted right now, but I'm sure Gordon will find five minutes to chat with you before the evening's over."

"Yes, I'm sure he will." Summer had eleven years of experience dealing with her stepmother, and after an initial skirmish, she could cope quite well with this sort of routine bitchiness. She flashed a smile as false as her stepmother's. "After all, an enterprising journalist might notice if the entire evening passed and the secretary of state never even said hello to his own daughter."

Olivia's nostrils flared slightly, the only sign of anger she allowed herself. "Your father is a busy and important man, Summer. You need to get over the idea that he can drop everything and come running as soon as you walk into the room."

"Since my father and I haven't spent more than twenty minutes alone together for at least a year, I guess I've managed to figure that one out all by myself."

"Good. And while we're on the subject of your

relationship with your father, please remember that he's depending on you to behave appropriately tonight. He persuaded me to add your name to the invitation list against my better judgment. So for God's sake, don't corner the Brazilian foreign minister and start haranguing him about his country's destructive policies in regard to the Amazon jungle. Or whatever tiresome environmental cause is at the top of your list right now."

"Gee, I'm glad you mentioned that, Olivia. Otherwise, of course, I'd have rushed right up and asked the old guy if he'd hugged a tree today."

"Your attempt at sarcasm is entirely misplaced, Summer. The fact is, you have absolutely no sense of moderation where your causes are concerned."

"That's because I know the world is running out of time to make vital changes—"

Olivia didn't let Summer finish. She turned abruptly and walked toward a group of new arrivals. She loved celebrities, and her smile warmed into genuine welcome as she greeted one of television's most famous journalists. "Ted, thank you for coming tonight at such short notice. You're looking simply wonderful! I don't need to ask if you enjoyed your trip to Fiji! I can see you did."

Summer slipped away, swiping a glass of wine from the tray of a passing waiter and gulping it down fast enough to lower her temper from high boil to medium simmer. She conquered the urge to retreat into the nearest rest room, even though she badly wanted the reassurance of checking her appearance in the wake of Olivia's cutting remarks. To hell with worrying. Her long, midnight blue dress was new, she'd pinned her hair up in a stylish French twist—at least, she hoped to God French twists were still stylish—and she'd spent ten minutes putting on makeup, which was about nine-and-a-half minutes longer than usual. She wasn't going to reward Olivia's malice by obsessing about whether or not she really looked frazzled.

Summer helped herself to another glass of California merlot—Olivia made sure that only the finest of American products were used at her parties—and exchanged polite conversation with a dozen people she didn't know but who all seemed to recognize her. By necessity, Summer had gotten better at chatting with strangers recently. Among the many unexpected results of her father's appointment as secretary of state had been the reflected glare of celebrity that illuminated her at functions like this dinner in honor of the Brazilian foreign minister. Washington insiders, the real movers and shakers, knew that she and her father weren't intimate. But hangers-on who weren't privy to the inside scoop liked to chat with Summer and foster their delusions of being close to the center of power.

Making her way through the throng of designer-clad bodies, she was accosted by one of her father's colleagues, then by an editor from *Vanity Fair.* Shedding *Vanity Fair,* she was captured by the international editor for *U.S. News and World Report.* Having learned by bitter experience that nothing she said to a journalist was ever off-the-record, Summer refused comment on a recent TV biography about her father, even though the program in question had made her dead mother sound like a radical flake who had narrowly escaped confinement in a mental institution.

Finally, to her relief, she ran into Rita Marcil, the senior environmental reporter from the *New York Times* and the closest thing to a friend she was likely to find at this party. Rita had been invited, she informed Summer, so that aides to the Brazilian foreign minister could brief her "informally" on the great strides Brazil was making in controlling the commercial exploitation of the Amazon rain forest.

"Did they convince you?" Summer asked. "It would be a real coup for them if you wrote a positive story about what's happening in Amazonia."

Rita shrugged. "I believe the Brazilian government is making belated efforts to develop the region in a more responsible way, but it's too little, too late. Right now, it would take a hell of a lot more than a puff piece at a dinner party to convince me that we're not already looking at the first major ecological disaster of the twenty-first century."

Summer shook her head. "We hear so much about what a small planet we live on nowadays, and how we're all interconnected, and yet people in this country don't seem to give a damn about what's happening to the environment in most of the developing world."

Rita gave a cynical smile. "Honey child, if the smartest, best-paid PR firms in this country can only get a third of the adult population to vote in a presidential election, we don't have much chance of keeping Joe Citizen interested in an arcane topic like agricultural techniques in the Amazon rain forest."

"But that's way more important than Washington politics—"

Rita laughed, genuinely amused, and Summer reluctantly joined in the laughter. "Okay, so maybe I'm the only person at this party who believes that Washington, D.C., isn't the source of every significant event in the universe, but it makes me crazy when reputable scientists can't get anyone in our government to pay

serious attention to hard data about the connection between rain forest destruction, ozone depletion and
global warming.''

"Come on, Summer, get real. You've been around
long enough to know that official Washington never
allows scientific data to interfere with its policy decisions.''

"I guess. But I keep hoping something will wake
the politicians up before it's too late—''

"Offer a politician the choice between winning his
next election and saving the planet for future generations and guess which one he'll go for. No prize for
guessing right.''

"I know." Summer sighed. "I'm so damn tired of
politicians paying lip service to the cause, and then
passing legislation that makes a bad situation worse.''
She and Rita joined the crowd of guests making their
way into the dining room. "Going anywhere exciting
for your vacation this year?" Summer asked as they
waited for instructions on how to find their assigned
places in the massive Benjamin Franklin State Dining
Room.

Rita perked up at the mention of a vacation. "The
opposite of exciting, I hope. My brother's renting a
cottage in Maine for the entire month of August. It's
twenty miles from the nearest town, and there's no
television in the house. He's planning to write the
great American novel and cook fabulous meals, and
I'm planning to sail every day and not answer my
E-mail. How about you?"

"I have three weeks scheduled in Alaska next
month—''

"Sounds great, but knowing you, it's probably
work-related.''

"Well, yes, but I've built a few days of downtime into my schedule. This summer I swear I'm going to read fashion magazines every weekend and learn important stuff like whether yellow nail polish is in or out, as opposed to worrying about trivial things like whether it's too warm for emperor penguins to breed in Antarctica."

Rita took her printed seating instructions from one of the attendants. "I'll call you after Labor Day to check up on the answer."

"About the penguins?"

"No, the nail polish. I already know the penguins are in trouble. The polar ice is melting so fast that there aren't enough ice floes left for them to make nests on." She glanced down at her place card as they walked into the dining room, past a phalanx of Secret Service officers. "I'm sitting at table twelve. How about you? I guess you're at your father's table with the VIPs."

"Are you kidding? My stepmother isn't convinced I'm housebroken, much less that I'm suitable company for the Brazilian foreign minister and his wife." Summer was dismayed to hear a note of hurt in her voice, and she quickly checked the instructions she'd just been given. "I'm at table sixteen."

A masculine voice spoke right behind her. "The same table as me. What an unexpected pleasure. How are you, Summer?"

Duncan Ryder. She barely managed to stop herself groaning out loud at the sound of his voice. Duncan was Olivia's brother, and one of her least favorite people in the world. She should have realized he would be here tonight, since he worked at the State Department and had just been promoted to the rank of counselor—almost unheard of for someone who was still on the low side of forty.

Her father and stepmother both considered Duncan to be God's gift to American diplomacy—not to mention the single women of the world. Every so often Gordon would point out to Summer what an excellent husband Duncan would make for her, which would have annoyed Summer more if not for the fact that Olivia nearly went into an apoplectic fit at the mere suggestion of her brilliant brother getting involved with her useless stepdaughter. If she'd wanted to ease Olivia's mind, which of course she didn't, Summer could have told her stepmother to quit worrying—that she was more likely to marry Fidel Castro than Olivia's brother. There were few people in the world who made her feel more uncomfortable than Olivia, but Duncan Ryder was one of the select few.

Fighting a strong urge to flee for the nearest exit, she turned to greet him with a pointed lack of enthusiasm. "Hello, Duncan, how are you? I haven't seen you in a while."

"I've been out of the country. Trying to persuade a group of American companies to invest in various development projects in Recife." He looked at her with faintly sardonic amusement. "Of course, I caught the first flight back to D.C. when I heard that you were coming to this party."

"Oh, of course. I know how much you love spending time with me."

"And you with me."

"Oh, sure, you're my dream man. In fact, I turned down a date with George Clooney just on the off chance that Olivia would put me at your table."

He inclined his head in mocking acknowledgment. "I'm deeply flattered. Thank you."

She bit her lip in frustration. It was infuriatingly hard to get Duncan to rise to the bait. "I'm surprised you know who George Clooney is," she muttered. "I didn't know you ever watched television, except for C-SPAN."

"Sure I do. Watching television fills in the idle moments when I'm not helping money-grabbing commercial developers buy up pristine wilderness."

Summer pretended not to notice his sarcasm. "Is that what you were doing in Recife?"

"There isn't any pristine wilderness in Recife," Duncan said with sudden curtness. "Just a lot of decaying nineteenth-century architecture and thousands of hungry people."

Rita cleared her throat. "I hate to interrupt, but this is my table. It was nice seeing you, Summer. I'll catch up with you in New York before I leave for Maine."

Summer had completely forgotten about Rita, who was gazing at Duncan with the sort of rapt appreciation he inspired in most women. She made belated introductions, wishing there was some way to convey the message that Duncan's stunning good looks masked a personality with all the charm of an alligator suffering from toothache.

"Rita, this is my stepmother's brother, Duncan Ryder. He's a counselor at the State Department, in charge of U.S. commercial relations with Latin America. Duncan, this is Rita Marcil from the *New York Times*. She heads up their environmental reporting team."

"I recognize the name from your byline," Duncan said, shaking hands with Rita. "It's great to meet you.

I was very impressed by the article you wrote last month about the effects of foreign investment on India's environmental regulations. Your insights gave me a lot to think about when I was preparing the agenda for my meetings in Recife.''

Rita smiled, pleased by the compliment. ''It was an interesting article to research, and some of the conclusions weren't what I'd expected.''

''I can see why. It was a truly enlightening piece—shocking in the way really good journalism sometimes is.''

''Thank you.'' Rita, the supposedly cynical journalist, actually blushed. Summer, recognizing the dreaded first signs of infatuation, repressed a sigh. Duncan's average affair lasted about a month, at which point he invariably lost interest, and—all too often—she found herself in the bizarre position of explaining to his discards that she was the last woman in the world to have insider tips on how to revive Duncan's flagging interest.

She flashed him a look of fulminating dislike, which, naturally, he didn't notice, since he was busy arranging a meeting with Rita for the following week. To discuss her research on India was the pretext, although Rita looked as if she'd have been more than ready to discuss hair transplants or the problem of hog-carcass disposal if that was what it took to get a luncheon date with him. She couldn't understand Rita's reaction, especially since she'd been dating another man quite seriously.

The luncheon arrangements made, Duncan said goodbye to Rita and put his arm under Summer's elbow to guide her to their table, where the other eight guests were already seated. They barely had time to introduce themselves before the Marine Corps band played the national anthems of Brazil and the United States, and a line of white-jacketed servers paraded out of the kitchens carrying laden silver trays.

Summer was seated between Duncan and a Japanese businessman who spoke almost no English. Mr. Fujito tried valiantly to get his tongue around the stubborn American consonants, and Summer did her best with sign language, but by the time chilled cucumber soup had been replaced by lobster ravioli, Summer's jaw ached from smiling, and she actually felt a spurt of gratitude when Duncan asked her if she would like to dance.

"Thanks for rescuing me," she said as they glided around the floor in time to the brisk pacing of the Marine Corps band. "Things were getting distinctly sticky on my side of the table. Mr. Fujito either told me that he has a subsidiary company in São Paulo that manufactures batteries, or he told me that he manufactures ladies' brassieres. I was trying to decide if there was any polite way to clarify which one by means of sign language."

Duncan laughed, twirling her expertly past a short, perspiring gentleman and a tall, thin lady in a mustard yellow dress. "Mr. Fujito's company manufactures the batteries for about two-thirds of the cars built in Brazil."

"Whew, that's a relief. I can manage a sign language conversation about cars a lot more easily than one about underwear."

"You could try speaking Portuguese," he suggested.

She rolled her eyes. "What a great idea! First, I'll recite the days of the week and count to ten. And then, for my grand finale, I can say *please, thank you* and *goodbye.* At which point I'll have demonstrated my total command of the Portuguese language.''

"I thought you might have picked up some Portuguese when you were in Brazil last year."

"I was only there for two weeks, and I don't inhale languages in my sleep the way you do. Besides, I went with an old friend whose mother is Brazilian, and he acted as our interpreter when we needed one."

"What did you think of Brazil?" Duncan asked. "We never had a chance to discuss your impressions, and I'd be interested to hear them. Recently, I've begun to feel that the more so-called facts I learn about the people and their history, the less I understand what truly makes the country tick."

She and Duncan had been forced into each other's company at least a dozen times since her trip with Joe Malone, so it wasn't quite accurate to say that they'd had no chance to discuss her impressions of Brazil. The truth was, when she was with Duncan, she was too busy scoring mental points against her stepmother to devote much time to having a real conversation with him. Summer was surprised to feel a momentary twinge of regret at the abortive pattern their encounters had fallen into.

"Brazil's too vast to sum up in a couple of slick sentences," she said. "But for what it's worth, I was overwhelmed by the vitality of the cities, the richness of the history and the sheer beauty of the scenery. As for the Amazon rain forest..."

She broke off and Duncan prompted her. "Go on."

She shook her head. "It's been more than eight months, and I still can't find words to describe what it felt like to see so much natural abundance coexisting with so much manmade destruction. One minute I wanted to weep because vast swaths of rain forest are still so magnificent and so untouched. The next minute I wanted to scream with rage at the way the land had been violated.''

She regretted replying honestly the moment she had spoken, expecting to precipitate one of their typical arguments about the relative merits of conservation versus economic development, but Duncan surprised her by agreeing that the highway built through the heart of the rain forest had come at an unacceptably high price in terms of brutalized natural resources.

Relieved not to have spoiled their unusual harmony, Summer chatted quite amiably with him for the rest of the dance. His years as a diplomat had certainly turned him into a great dancer, at least of the sedate ballroom variety, and she actually found it rather pleasant to be whisked around the floor to the pulsing rhythms of the *Emperor Waltz* by Johann Strauss. No wonder nineteenth-century chaperones had been so alarmed at the introduction of the waltz to polite society, Summer thought. There was something distinctly erotic about the swooping, swirling movements, and she was having a hard time remembering that it was Duncan Ryder holding her in his arms and causing these unexpected twinges of awareness. Her love life definitely required some urgent attention if Duncan—of all people—could have her thinking wistfully about cool sheets and hot sex.

Gordon Shepherd had been dancing with Senhora Nabuco, the wife of the Brazilian foreign minister, and their paths crossed as Summer and Duncan came off the dance floor. Her father made introductions all around, and Senhora Nabuco—an elegant, rail-thin woman in her early fifties—succumbed to Duncan's charm and good looks with almost as much speed as Rita had earlier. The two of them were soon deep in conversation about a Brazilian composer that Summer had never heard of, but whom Senhora Nabuco and Duncan apparently both admired.

Her father watched Duncan's skillful handling of the older woman with smiling approval before turning to exchange a few words with Summer. "How are you, my dear?" he asked, escorting her toward the side of the room for a few moments of private conversation. "It's been much too long since we had a chance to chat, but my schedule has been quite ridiculous recently. I sometimes feel that I ought to make a notation in my daybook—take five seconds to breathe."

"It's okay, Dad. I understand that your job has to be the top priority for the next eighteen months. We'll have plenty of time to catch up when your stint as secretary of state is over. After all, there's an election coming quite soon, and once the new administration is in place, you'll be a free man again."

"True." Her father frowned and seemed to hesitate for a moment, then he smiled, patting her hand somewhat awkwardly. "You're looking very lovely tonight, Summer. I'd forgotten how attractive you can be when you're properly dressed."

"Thank you." She decided to take that as a compliment and not probe too deeply into the subtext of disapproval. "You're looking pretty darn handsome yourself, Mr. Secretary. Not a gray hair in sight and no new wrinkles. Hard work and impossibly tight schedules seem to agree with you."

He chuckled, obviously pleased, and tugged at his

hair. "Not a bad crop for a man who's just turned sixty, is it? I'm lucky enough to find all the hard work invigorating, and as you know, I never needed much sleep."

"No, you were always late to bed and early to rise. Not like Mom. Do you remember how she used to be up until all hours and then sleep until noon? I came downstairs on a couple of occasions and found her baking bread at three in the morning!"

He frowned, uncomfortable with the reference to his former wife. "Your mother wasn't very good at organizing her time, I'm afraid. Her inability to keep to a schedule was a constant bone of contention between the two of us. However, that's over and done with, and best left in the past, where it belongs. Let's talk about you instead. How's life treating you, Summer? Are you still enjoying Manhattan? And your job?"

She accepted the change of subject, realizing the reminiscences about her mother had been out of place. "Yes, I'm enjoying it very much. New York is a great city once you get used to the crazy level of noise, and I've made some good friends. Although I'd like it even better if I could afford an apartment bigger than a broom closet." She smiled wryly. "It's tough to make ends meet on a post-doc fellowship."

He looked concerned. "My dear, if you need some extra money for rent, you know you have only to ask—"

"No!" she said so sharply that he flinched. "Sorry, Dad, I didn't mean to sound rude, but I'm almost thirty years old, and there's no reason for you to even think about subsidizing my rent."

"There's every reason in the world. You're my daughter."

"And you paid for a great education so that I could earn my own living."

"You've always been so fiercely independent," he said regretfully. "You wouldn't even let me help you out when you couldn't get a job after graduate school."

"I had the money Mom left me," she said. "Dad, I was fine. I am fine. Don't worry. I'm not going to go broke and cause a scandal."

"As if you would." He smiled, patting her on the arm. "I see that Olivia did as I asked and put you and Duncan at the same table. Now, there's a young man after my own heart—"

"Yes, Dad, I know how much you like him—"

"He's a real achiever. Great brains inside a cool head. Just the sort of man who would make an ideal husband for you. In my opinion, you couldn't do better than to think seriously about marrying Duncan...."

Summer held on to her temper. Just. "Fortunately, there's zero chance that Duncan will ever ask me to marry him, so we don't need to fight about this."

"Certainly not here," Gordon said, glancing at his watch. "I have to get back to my table. I've been away from the foreign minister much too long. Are you going to be in town tomorrow? If so, why don't you call Brian—he's my new assistant—and ask him to find a gap in my schedule when we could meet. Come for coffee, or tea, if you prefer. I'm sure there must be fifteen spare minutes somewhere in my day that could be squeezed out for you. You are my daughter, after all."

Summer ignored the churning in her stomach and managed a cool smile. "Thanks for the generous offer, Dad, but I have business meetings scheduled all day tomorrow. A seminar with a group of scientists visiting from Australia.''

"Another time, then." Gordon didn't ask whether Summer planned to stay in Washington for the entire weekend. He didn't invite her to spend Saturday night at his house. "Can you make your own way back to your table?''

"Of course. Goodbye, Dad. I'll be in touch."

"Goodbye, Summer. I'm so glad you came tonight. It was wonderful to see you." Gordon walked swiftly back to the head table, smiling and shaking hands with a dozen people en route, a quip at the ready for everyone. Admiring glances followed his passage and Summer heard a woman murmur, "He's a handsome devil, isn't he?''

"He is indeed," her male companion replied. "This administration is damn lucky to have him on board. And his wife's another winner. Thank God he divorced that outdated hippie he was married to when he was in Congress. Do you remember her?''

"Deborah? How could anyone forget her? And Gordon didn't divorce her, she died.''

The man grunted. "Deborah, that's right. Well, dying before Gordon came into the national spotlight is the only useful thing she ever did, if you ask me.''

Afraid to move and draw attention to herself, Summer stood rooted to the spot until Gordon took his seat next to Senhora Nabuco. Then she turned and walked blindly toward the nearest exit. The ladies' room was empty, an unexpected bonus, since she was shaking so hard that she needed to lean against the marble counter to support herself. Her mother had been the kindest, warmest person Summer had ever known, and one of the smartest, too. It pained her that so many people in her father's circle had been unable to look beyond the homespun clothes and unfashionable hairstyle to see the valuable woman beneath.

When the shaking stopped, she leaned forward to look into the mirror, applying color to her lips with intense concentration. Her relationship with her father had been going steadily downhill for eleven years, ever since he'd abandoned Debbie, her mother, and moved in with Olivia. Add to that the pressure of his duties as secretary of state and it wasn't surprising that he had so little time for her. Their lack of intimacy was sad, but hardly the stuff of high tragedy. Half the women she knew would probably claim that they had a less-than-perfect relationship with their fathers. She snapped her purse shut and straightened her shoulders. Time to get back to Mr. Fujito and Olivia's annoyingly perfect brother. Oh, joy! For the rest of the evening she could look forward to cross-examination by Duncan or sign language with Mr. Fujito. What a terrific choice.

"I told the waiter to take away your ravioli and leave the rack of lamb," Duncan said when she returned to their table.

"Thanks. Sorry to have been absent for so long." She smiled brightly. "Where's Mr. Fujito?"

"Dancing with Mrs. Fujito." Duncan looked at her steadily. "What happened that upset you so badly you couldn't trust yourself to come back to the table?"

"Nothing." She could have done without Duncan's irritatingly acute powers of perception. "This lamb is delicious, isn't it?"

"Yes." Duncan leaned forward and put his hand over hers, forcing her to stop eating. "Who am I, Summer?"

Startled, she put down her fork. "That's a bizarre question. What do you mean? You're Duncan Ryder, Olivia's brother."

He gave an angry laugh. "Duncan-Ryder-Olivia's-brother. You make it sound like a one-word, all-purpose condemnation."

"Well, you are Duncan Ryder, and you are Olivia's brother," she said defensively.

"Yeah, sure, but as far as you're concerned, the fact that I'm Olivia's brother defines everything there is to know about me. My sister married your father and you wish she hadn't. End of Duncan's biography."

"I know lots about you that has nothing to do with Olivia," Summer protested.

"Name one thing."

She racked her brains. "You work in the State Department and you're assigned to the South American section. There, that's one thing."

"Right. Great going. Eleven years of forced acquaintance and all you know is that I'm Duncan-Ryder-Olivia's-brother and I work for the State Department."

What else did she know about Duncan? Surely she must know a lot. After all, the guy had been driving her nuts for years. But right now, she was drawing blanks on every front. Except...she could work out how old he was. Olivia was forty-five, and Duncan was seven years younger. She calculated rapidly. "You're thirty-eight years old and you've never been married," she announced triumphantly.

"Thirty-nine," he corrected her with silky smoothness. "I had a birthday last month. And I was married and divorced by the time I was twenty-seven."

"You were married?" She stared at him in astonishment. "I never knew that."

"Why would you? You never asked."

"How long were you married? Do you have any children?" Summer was forced to acknowledge that it was ridiculous to be asking such basic questions of a man she'd supposedly known for eleven years.

"Four years and no children, thank God. That was one of the few mistakes my ex-wife and I managed to avoid."

"You think having children is a mistake?"

"It would have been a disaster for Irene and me. Between the two of us, we had enough emotional maturity to take care of one well-adjusted goldfish. Maybe."

She smiled, forgetting she was annoyed with him. "That bad, huh?"

"Worse. But let's be kind and just say that Irene and I married too young."

She leaned back in her chair, sipping ice water. "What else don't I know about you, Duncan?"

He shrugged. "Just about everything that matters."

"So pretend we've met tonight for the first time and tell me a few important things about yourself."

He pulled a face. "That sounds like the beginning of the worst sort of job interview. Good morning, Mr. Ryder. Please tell us why we should hire you in five sentences or less."

She put her glass of water back on the table, laughing. "All right, here's a specific question for you. Your father was a three-term senator, and your mother was one of the leading lights of the Republican party in Michigan. You obviously like being involved in government or you wouldn't work for the State Department, so why didn't you choose to follow in your father's footsteps and run for elective office? Isn't that where the action really is for political junkies?''

"Maybe, but I've seen from the inside what a terrible toll running for political office takes on your personal life, and I have no interest in getting involved in that particular rat race. Besides, the Ryder family has lived in the same rural Michigan community for five generations. It was time for somebody to be born with itchy feet, and I got lucky.''

"You've been posted overseas three times since I've known you.'' Summer wondered why she remembered that. Probably because she'd been so delighted to have him out of the country for months at a stretch. "Hasn't all that travel cured your itchy feet?''

He shook his head. "Not yet. So far, it just seems to have confirmed that I have a chronic itch.''

"Don't you ever get homesick for the States?''

"Yes, quite often. But any time the homesickness lasts for more than a day or two, I request some vacation time and pay a visit to my parents' home in Michigan. The first week, I'm so happy to see old friends and family that I can't understand why I ever left home. By the end of the second week, I'm ready to hitch a ride on the back of the municipal dump truck if that's what it takes to get me out of there.''

Summer was surprised to realize that she understood the feelings he was describing, and even shared them to a certain extent. "I guess I suffer from a touch of the same itchy-feet syndrome,'' she said. "Fortunately, living in Manhattan is the next best thing to moving every year. The city constantly reinvents itself around you, so you can never get bored.''

"Which is the opposite of Washington. Here, people move in and out, depending on the results of the latest elections, but the institutions are so entrenched that they defeat any attempt to change them.''

"Don't you find all that institutional weight oppressive? I think I would.''

"Sometimes. But a sense of continuity and tradition in a changing world isn't always bad. I actually like Washington quite a lot. It's a more livable city than you'd imagine.''

*"Livable* is the last word I'd use to describe it. This town always strikes me as high-gear obsessive-compulsive, badly in need of a few calming sessions with a good shrink.''

He grinned. ''It's certainly filled with people, including me, who are nowhere near as important as we think we are. But it's also a genuine center of world affairs, with an atmosphere that's a heady mixture of bullshit and raw power.''

"If bullshit and power happen to be what turn you on.''

"Yeah, well, I'm willing to admit to being a power junkie. As for the bullshit…sure, it can be annoying. But then again, there's a special pleasure when you manage to demolish other people's carefully guarded piles of manure.''

She smiled at the image, conceding mentally that Duncan was probably one of the more successful people in Washington at cutting through rhetoric to get to the heart of an issue—and then acting on it.

"You're staring at me as if I have gravy on my chin,'' Duncan said, reaching for his napkin.

"I'm sure no gravy would dare to land on such a prestigious chin,'' she said, embarrassed to realize just how intently she'd been studying him. ''Let's see, what else do I need to know about you, besides the fact that you're Olivia's brother?''

His eyes met briefly with hers, his expression both amused and sympathetic. She had the disconcerting impression that he understood exactly why she'd mentioned Olivia's name—that he understood how difficult it was for her to reconcile these new insights into his character with the preconceived images that she'd harbored since their first meeting. Which happened to have been less than six weeks after Summer's mother died, on the day his sister married her father. No wonder she'd been so resentful of everything and everybody in Olivia's family, Summer thought. Her impressions of Duncan—and her stepmother, for that matter—were inevitably colored by the fact that she'd been deeply grieving for her mother when Olivia married her father.

"Okay, here's the rest of my biography," Duncan said. "My hobby is underwater photography, and I like to go to the movies at least once a week. My ex-wife lives in California with her third husband, and my most recent girlfriend just ditched me after complaining that I'm a workaholic who avoids emotional commitment by burying myself in my work—"

"Was she right?"

"Probably, at least the workaholic part. Even though the Cold War is over, when you work at the State Department, it's easy to get caught up in the delusion that the fate of the world rests in your hands."

"God knows, I empathize with that feeling," Summer said. "The statistics I'm collecting right now point conclusively toward the fact that the destruction of the ozone layer is progressing more rapidly than anyone predicted even three years ago. And nobody seems to care. You just have to mention the words *ozone layer* and the average person's eyes glaze over with boredom."

"Perhaps because people feel there's not much they can do about it and we have only so much energy to spare for remote causes."

"If enough individuals change their behavior, it makes a huge difference. And our government could achieve miracles if they'd only treat the scientific evidence seriously."

"You can't expect the government to act until the scientific community is more in agreement—"

"Ninety-five percent of the scientific community is already in agreement." Summer sighed. "Every so often I fantasize about what a scientist like me would need to do to attract the attention of our government before it's too late."

"And what have you concluded?"

"That I need God to float down on a cloud and order Congress to listen."

He raised his wineglass in a sardonic salute. "And your second option?"

She laughed ruefully. "Outside of divine intervention, there's nothing I can do except keep plugging away, compiling data and trying to get the facts out in front of the public any way I can. Realistically, I don't think the politicians will sit up and take notice until the ocean is lapping at the basement of their office buildings. And then they'll probably order new sump pumps in the hope they'll do the trick until the next election is over."

Mr. and Mrs. Fujito returned at that point, and conversation became general around the table once more.

She and Duncan didn't speak to each other again until the master of ceremonies announced the final dance. As the lights dimmed very slightly on the dance floor—security concerns kept the periphery of the room bright—Duncan stood up and extended his hand with formal courtesy. "Summer, would you dance with me again?"

Something curiously like desire flickered in the pit of her stomach.

He escorted her to the dance floor, deliberately giving a wide berth to Olivia and Gordon, who were partnering each other for this final dance. His arm went around her waist, his hand resting lightly on her back, his thumb just grazing her bare skin above her zipper. She drew in a tiny involuntary breath when their eyes met, her lungs so constricted that she had to look away. Without saying anything, Duncan stepped forward, leading her into the opening steps of the dance.

Summer reminded herself that this was Duncan-Ryder-Olivia's-brother, and that it was bizarre—disorienting—to be feeling such an acute sensation of arousal just because he was holding her. She concentrated on the movements of the dance and studiously avoided looking at him. She was doing quite well until his hand moved higher up her back to guide her past another couple. Then, to her embarrassment, she trembled in reaction to his touch.

He gazed down at her, and she knew she hadn't imagined the flash of emotion she glimpsed in his eyes. Even so, she was astonished when he spoke in a voice that was not quite steady. "Did I ever tell you that you're the most desirable woman I know?"

Her mouth was so dry she could scarcely answer him. "No, you never told me."

"I should have. I've wanted to many times."

She shook her head. "That's impossible. You despise me."

His expression became rueful. "You're confusing your feelings with mine."

"I've never despised you. How could I when you're so damn perfect?" She acknowledged the truth. "You intimidate me."

"Then the feeling's mutual."

"I intimidate you?" She would have laughed if she hadn't been too astonished to express any other emotion.

"Sure. You always have." He gave her a wry smile. "Do you think we have the basis for some kind of a deep and meaningful relationship here? Mutual intimidation seems like a real nineties kind of bond."

The concept of starting a "relationship" with Duncan left her speechless. What did he mean by "relationship," anyway? Could he possibly mean affair, as in sexual relationship? The possibility was mindblowing. Mind-blowing, but amazingly—incredibly—tempting.

Summer was still trying to think of how she wanted to answer him when her father and stepmother waltzed past. Olivia gave them a puzzled look, as if she couldn't fathom why the two of them were dancing together for the second time in a single evening. Summer wasn't sure she knew the answer to that question herself. She had the ignoble thought that if she really wanted to infuriate her stepmother, she couldn't find a better way than starting a prolonged and passionate affair with Duncan.

The realization of exactly what she was contemplating brought her to her senses. She could find plenty of ways to mess up her love life without starting an affair simply to annoy her stepmother. In fact, based on past experience, messing up her love life seemed to be one of her special talents.

With a feeling of regret that surprised her by its intensity, she returned her gaze to Duncan. "I don't think a relationship between the two of us could ever work out," she said. "There's just too much family stuff that would keep getting in the way."

"Only if we let it."

"How could we keep it away from us?" As if to prove her point, the music stopped and Gordon came hurrying up before Duncan could say anything more.

"Duncan, we need you. Come with me, please. Senhora Nabuco is asking for you." He gave Summer a swift, impersonal kiss on the cheek. "Goodbye, my dear. I know you'll understand why I have to rush. Senhor Salazar Nabuco is not a patient man." He strode off, not looking back, a man of great consequence, with important things to do.

Duncan took her hand and clasped it for a moment between both of his. "I'm sorry I have to go, because we're not done with this conversation. I'll call you, Summer."

She felt a glow of pleasure that she tried to quell. "My phone may expire from the shock."

He was already following her father across the room, but he looked back and smiled, with his eyes as well as his mouth. "It's sturdier than you think. Thanks for a great evening, Summer."

"You're welcome."

He was swallowed up in the milling crowd before she had time to say anything more. Which was just as well, since Summer had no idea what to say next to Duncan-Ryder-Olivia's-brother, who, in the course of this evening's dinner, had somehow been transformed into plain Duncan Ryder, sexy and interesting man.

# *Two*

The seminar given by the Australians produced so much fascinating debate on the causes of ozone layer destruction that Summer decided to wait for the continuation of the informal discussions after lunch, even though it meant missing the three-thirty train she was scheduled to take back to New York. Since it was Saturday, she didn't anticipate any problems in changing to a later train, but when she arrived at Union Station in the early evening she discovered her mistake. The only way for her to get back to Manhattan without a twenty-hour delay was to pay a hefty surcharge and upgrade her ticket to first class.

Spending the night in a hotel would cost even more than the upgrade, so Summer handed over her credit card, mentally composing a memo that she hoped would persuade the authorities at Columbia to reimburse her for the excess. Fat chance, she decided, bumping her wheeled suitcase up the steps and onto the train. The guardians of the departmental budget would expect her to spend the night on the platform and catch a train in the morning.

Even in first class, the train was crowded, although she had somehow gotten lucky enough to be assigned a window seat. The balding, middle-age man occupying the place next to her appeared eager to start a conversation, but Summer wanted to organize her notes while they were still fresh in her mind, so as soon as her luggage was stowed she pulled out her file of papers from the seminar and started to read in forbidding silence.

Her seatmate took the hint and found a crossword in his magazine, leaving her free to work. Her seat was spacious and comfortable, an agreeable reward for maxing out her credit card, and Summer gradually relaxed, enjoying the unusual sensation of luxury travel. The data compiled by the Australian scientists was so mind-blowing that she quickly lost track of her surroundings, and the train was almost an hour into the journey when her attention was caught by a tinkling ripple of laughter that sounded both familiar and ominously nearby.

Summer's head jerked up from her notes. Good grief! She must be mistaken. Why in the world would her stepmother be taking the train to New York? Since the day of Gordon Shepherd's inauguration as secretary of state, Olivia had shunned public transport. Her preferred method of travel was military jet whenever she could swing it, followed by a distant second best— her husband's stretch limo with full Secret Service escort.

But one brief glance was enough to confirm that it was indeed Olivia seated just across the aisle, her back toward Summer, only three rows down, and without a sign of a Secret Service agent anywhere nearby.

Great, Summer thought gloomily. Olivia decides to slum it on the only occasion I've traveled first class for years. Just what she needed, two encounters with her Wicked Stepmother within the space of two days. She huddled deeper behind her files, sneaking glances at Olivia as her stepmother leaned forward to speak to the man seated opposite her.

Olivia looked her usual stunning self in a sage green suit of silk shantung, demonstrating a degree of travel elegance that most women had abandoned a quarter of a century earlier. Summer, by contrast, guessed that she looked about as elegant as the wreckage of last year's Thanksgiving dinner, and her nose was probably shiny enough to qualify as a stand-in for Rudolph.

She should be thankful that her stepmother hadn't already noticed she was on the train, Summer thought, rising hurriedly to her feet. At least she could spruce herself up a bit before their inevitable confrontation. Ducking her head, striving for invisibility, she climbed past her seatmate and scrambled down the aisle to the rest room.

Astonishingly, the makeup purse in her briefcase contained lipstick, powder and mascara, a sign that the Fates were willing to show some benevolence now that they had pulled their dirty trick of putting Olivia and Summer into the same compartment on the same train. Scowling into the narrow mirror above the sink, Summer scraped her hair into a ruthlessly tight braid, applied makeup and shook out her linen jacket, hoping to get rid of at least a few wrinkles. Combed and groomed, her reflection stared back at her, neater than before, but still a hundred light-years away from her stepmother's casual elegance.

Summer felt a surge of familiar irritation when she realized she was once again allowing her stepmother's mere presence to throw her into a wallow of self-criticism. It had occurred to her some time during the sleepless hours following her parting from Duncan that there could be few things in the world more pathetic than a thirty-year-old woman who allowed her self-image to be shaped by her stepmother. For the past eleven years she'd been so busy waging war with Olivia that she hadn't noticed how many casualties were piling up on the battlefield—her relationship with Duncan Ryder, among them. Duncan might well be the total pain in the butt Summer had always imagined. On the other hand, he might be a great guy. She had no way of knowing, simply because, until last night, she had never allowed herself to see Duncan as an individual, a person in his own right, separate from Olivia.

"Time to lighten up and get a grip," she told her reflection, and pushed open the rest room door, striding down the aisle to her seat without making the slightest effort to be quiet or inconspicuous. There was almost no chance that she would be able to escape Olivia's attention for the remainder of the journey, and she might as well get their encounter over and done with.

Naturally, since she made no effort to hide, Olivia didn't notice her. There had to be a life lesson in there somewhere, Summer decided. Shrugging, she returned to reading her notes, but the once-fascinating Australian statistics had lost their appeal, and she soon found herself casting covert glances in her stepmother's direction, wondering what had prompted this trip to New York.

Olivia was traveling with a companion, that much was clear. She was speaking animatedly to the man seated opposite her, and he leaned forward from time to time to take her hands, clasping them between his cupped palms. Summer found it strange that her stepmother tolerated his touch. Olivia liked the adulation of important or famous men, but only at a safe distance. She was a woman who always stood on her dignity, a tendency that had increased in the eighteen months since Gordon Shepherd became secretary of state. Oddly enough, her aloofness made her the ideal hostess for her position, since many foreign dignitaries appreciated Olivia's rigid adherence to tradition and protocol.

Who was the man? Summer wondered. Not someone Olivia had chosen for his good looks, that was for sure. He was dark, his complexion swarthy, with features that were commanding but not in the least handsome, just as his body was stocky and strong rather than graceful. Despite the fact that he was smiling, he was surrounded by an indefinable air of authority, an aura of command too powerful to ignore, even though he was doing nothing more than sitting in a train, flirting with an attractive woman.

And he was flirting, Summer realized with another shock. He must be somebody amazingly important for Olivia to tolerate his encroachments into her personal space. Summer was sure she'd seen him before, but she couldn't put a name to the slightly familiar face. Was he one of the more obscure cabinet members? Or maybe an undersecretary at the State Department? Summer watched, hypnotized, when the man took Olivia's hand and pressed a kiss against her knuckles, before turning her hand over and pressing another kiss into her palm.

She held her breath, expecting her stepmother to snatch her hand away. But Olivia just laughed, the sound coy, and so soft that Summer would never have registered it if she hadn't already been watching with hypnotized fascination. Olivia's back was still turned toward her, so Summer couldn't see her facial expression, but her stepmother's body language plainly indicated that the man seated opposite her was more than a friend. They were both trying to be circumspect, but their hands kept coming together, almost as if their need to touch each other was overcoming their self-control. The man eventually reached out and rested his hand against Olivia's cheek in a brief, betrayingly intimate caress. In return, she traced the outline of his mouth with her fingertip before regretfully shaking her head and letting her hand fall into her lap.

"I want you," the man said, the low murmur of his voice combining with the movement of his lips to make the words crystal clear. "Thank God you managed to arrange things so that we have all night together."

At such revealing words, Summer felt a complicated mix of emotions even though she couldn't hear—or see—Olivia's reply. She had convicted her stepmother of a hundred sins over the years, but the one she'd never suspected, even for a moment, was the sin of infidelity. Olivia and her father had always seemed to enjoy a close, loving and entirely faithful relationship. In fact, if she was totally honest with herself, the closeness between her father and stepmother was one of the reasons Summer disliked Olivia so much. Her stepmother had found the secret to attracting and keeping Gordon's mercurial attention, a secret that Summer and her mother had sought for years without success.

Summer cast her mind back to the previous night and tried to visualize how her father and stepmother had behaved at the banquet. They had seemed as affectionate and devoted as ever, she decided. Had that been a pretense, at least on Olivia's side? Or, incredible thought, perhaps Olivia's devotion to her husband had always been a sham and this man was just the most recent in a long line of lovers?

Summer shook her head, rejecting the trend of her own thoughts. She had no right to leap to the conclusion that Olivia was being unfaithful on the basis of nothing more incriminating than a couple of affectionate gestures in a public place and a murmured comment that she might have misheard. Olivia was one of the most controlled women Summer had ever met, and it seemed unbelievable that she would risk her marriage and her important position simply for the sake of some torrid sex.

*Fernando de Something Something*—that's who he was. The name flashed across Summer's mental screen, but she knew it wasn't quite right. The man was Brazilian, so it wasn't de Something, but da Something. She searched to pull up the memory. Fernando Autunes da Pereira—yes, that was it. She finally remembered where she'd met this man before. It had been as recently as last night, at the dinner for the Brazilian foreign minister. Barry Jensen, the chairman of General Motors, had made the introduction. He'd mentioned that Fernando was one of Brazil's most successful businessmen, the president of a vast family-owned conglomerate called…

Summer's memory drew a stubborn blank regarding the name of the company, although she did remember that Fernando had paid her several charming and quite unbelievable compliments.

Still, even if Fernando was blessed with a surplus of Latin charm, and came draped in the dazzling mantle of great wealth, a Brazilian industrialist was an odd choice of lover for Olivia, who was a bit of a xenophobe beneath her superficially sophisticated manners. If Duncan was the first Ryder in five generations to be born with itchy feet, Olivia was the opposite: a chip off the old Ryder block, who thought that the United States was the greatest country in the world, and Michigan the greatest state within the union. Olivia rarely accompanied Gordon on his official overseas trips. She much preferred to limit her contacts with foreign dignitaries to American soil, where she could make sure that they didn't expect her to eat sheep's eyeballs, or get dirty and sweaty touring children's hospitals in the middle of the jungle.

But despite all the reasons why a relationship between her stepmother and Fernando Autunes da Pereira seemed unlikely, the longer Summer watched the pair of them, the more intimate they appeared, until she was forced to the incredible conclusion that they truly must be lovers.

Olivia, the supposedly perfect wife, was having an extramarital affair.

Having reached that amazing conclusion, Summer spent a blissful half hour imagining various scenarios where she strolled over to the couple and devastated her stepmother by threatening to reveal the affair to Gordon Shepherd. In all these fantasies, Olivia was gratifyingly tongue-tied, and Summer eloquently witty, a role reversal she relished to the full.

Fortunately, sanity returned before she did anything as stupid as attempting to turn her daydream into reality. Gordon Shepherd would be devastated to learn that his wife was being unfaithful and—despite her horrible relationship with Olivia—Summer had no desire to be the person who ruined her father's illusions of marital bliss. Grimacing, she shrank deeper into her seat, hiding her face behind a magazine, determined to do all she could to avoid alerting Olivia to her presence.

When the train pulled into the outskirts of New York City, Olivia and Fernando were still so wrapped up in each other that neither of them glanced in Summer's direction. She collected her belongings and scooted for the exit, with her seatmate following close behind. They were almost the first passengers to disembark, and thanks to her seatmate's bulk and height, she was able to get off the train undetected and make her way to the exit without having to exchange a single word with either her stepmother or Fernando.

Summer heaved a sigh of relief as she emerged into the cool, clear Manhattan night and hailed a passing cab to take her uptown. Fortunately, it was likely to be several weeks before her next meeting with Olivia took place—plenty of time to get used to the idea that her father's perfect second marriage wasn't quite as perfect as she had always assumed.

As the cab made its way through the heavy traffic on Sixth Avenue, she deliberately put her stepmother out of her mind and turned her attention to the more pleasant task of deciding whether she was going to read one of the juicy-looking new novels she'd bought in Washington, or indulge in a long, scented soak in the tub, with the stereo turned up full blast. Maybe she'd do both, Summer decided.

The one thing she wouldn't do was sit around her apartment wondering if Duncan Ryder would call some time before the weekend was over.

There was a message from Duncan Ryder waiting on her answering machine when she got home. It wasn't a very long message, or a very significant one, except that he'd never called her at home before. He just said how much he'd enjoyed spending time with her on Friday and that he would be in touch when he came to New York next week. Summer played the message four times, and was still mulling over her reaction to his message when she arrived next morning at the section of the Columbia University campus that housed her office—a nine-by-twelve cubicle that an administrator with a sense of humor had classified as a laboratory, presumably because there was a gas pipe connected to a rusted-out Bunsen burner tucked away in a corner of the room.

The morning was gray and overcast, not raining, but decidedly chilly for May, and Summer thrust her hands into the pockets of her jeans as she walked across campus, wishing she'd worn something warmer than a cotton sweatshirt. Even though it was a Sunday, and almost the end of the academic year, the usual scattering of students and visitors hung around the various buildings and courtyards.

Summer moved through the chattering groups of people without really seeing them, her thoughts meandering from determining how best to clear the administrative clutter from her desk to wondering what she would say to Duncan if he actually followed through on his phone call. Was she nuts even to consider going out on a date with him next week? Quite apart from the complication of his being Olivia's brother, there was the undeniable fact that she had a track record of screwing up important friendships by introducing sex into the equation. Look at what had happened to her relationship with Joe Malone, which had been strained almost to the breaking point by their fatal decision to go to bed together while they were vacationing last year in Brazil.

Still, the situation with Duncan was different, she decided. Even if she went out on a disastrous date with him, she wouldn't be in danger of screwing up their friendship, for the simple reason that they weren't friends. On the contrary, they had an eleven-year history of intense mutual dislike. So if Duncan turned out to be the self-satisfied, egotistical prick she'd always assumed he was, then she wouldn't have lost anything, except a few hours of her time.

Cheered by that thought, Summer smiled as she passed a cluster of students sitting on the low stone wall that surrounded the Climatology Department building. Heck, what was she worrying about? Her opinion of Duncan had always been so low that it would be a major upgrade to classify him as an egotistical prick.

Rummaging in her pocket for the key to her office, Summer climbed the shallow flight of stairs leading to the building's imposing entrance, a relic of art deco opulence. One of the students broke away from the group and ran up to her just as she found the key. "Sorry to bother you, miss, but we're looking for the Edith B. Stroud Geology Library. Do you know where it is?"

The student who'd asked the question wore thick-lensed glasses and had a dark curly beard that was so bushy it not only obscured his features, it looked almost fake. Summer tried not to grin. She never ceased to be amazed at the lengths some undergrads went to in the name of self-expression. "Edith B. Stroud?" she repeated, wrinkling her forehead and trying to avoid staring at his beard. "I don't think I've heard of tha—"

She never finished her sentence. She felt a prick like a bee sting in her upper arm and instinctively jerked away. Or she would have jerked away if a pair of strong arms hadn't reached out from behind and grabbed her. A piece of cloth was thrown over her head and she heard a scuffle of foot movements, also from behind, as her wrists were swiftly and efficiently tied.

She was being kidnapped.

The thought was so crazy—why would anyone want to abduct her?—that it took a couple of vital seconds to sink in. When she opened her mouth to scream, it was already too late. The cloth had been taped tightly around her head, sealing her mouth, and she was being half dragged, half propelled toward some unknown destination.

How could this be happening? There had been more than one group of students hanging around, hadn't there? Not just those five or six lounging by the steps. Surely somebody would notice that she was being dragged away against her will.

Summer tried to struggle, to kick out at her captors, but whatever drug they'd injected her with was swift-acting and already taking effect. She felt faint and terrifyingly woozy. She closed her eyes in an instinctive effort to block the horrible sensation of vertigo even though it was already dark behind the hood.

Her foot bumped up against something solid. A car tire, maybe. She barely assimilated the information before a heavy hand pushed down on the crown of her head, shoving her forward. Her forehead bumped against another hard object. The frame of a car door?

She couldn't think anymore; it hurt way too much. Pain, nauseating in its intensity, exploded behind her eyes, spreading out to push against her skull.

She gagged, and colored light danced across her retinas, but only for an instant. Blackness descended in a thick shroud, cutting off air, making it almost impossible to breathe. Fear grew until it was a giant pouch, suffocating her, sealing her inside its lethal embrace.

She was fading fast, but—dammit—she wasn't going to go quietly. She tried to force a scream through her vocal chords. She managed a feeble whimper.

Struggling to the end, Summer fell into the waiting darkness.

# Three

Duncan rubbed his unshaven chin and stretched contentedly, shoving with his heels to move his chair out of the sun streaming in through the kitchen window. Life didn't get much better than a fine spring morning in Washington, with a pot of coffee at your elbow and your favorite sections of the newspaper stacked on the table waiting to be read. It had been weeks since he had had a Sunday completely free, and he intended to enjoy every last lazy minute. He chewed the final bite of his cinnamon bagel, licked cream cheese from his thumb and reached for the sports section. What had the Orioles done yesterday when they played the Indians?

It seemed that Cal Ripken, Jr., had hit a home run in the bottom of the ninth and saved the day for Baltimore. All right! Duncan grinned and punched the air. He was pouring himself a second cup of coffee when the phone rang. He ignored it, rifling through the rest of the sports section in search of the latest European soccer scores, which always seemed to get buried in an obscure spot on the back pages. He'd developed an un-American passion for professional soccer during his tour of duty in Portugal, and he had a polyglot list of teams he supported.

When the phone rang for the second time, he barely

registered the sound. He only half heard his answering machine click on and pause for a few seconds before clicking off without recording any message. Probably an aborted telemarketing pitch, Duncan thought, congratulating himself on ducking the calls.

He found the soccer scores from Saturday's European games, but he'd barely read the first column of results when the phone rang yet again. He yawned, listening as the answering machine clicked on, ran for several seconds without anyone saying anything, and then clicked off.

Duncan frowned, putting down the paper and sitting up a little straighter. There had been an odd waiting quality to all three silences that bothered him, even though he realized that the pregnant pause before the caller hung up was probably nothing more than a glitch in some computerized telemarketing program. He picked up the paper and turned back to the chart of soccer scores, but before he could find the place where he'd left off reading, the phone started to ring for a fourth time.

He snatched the receiver, irritated by the repeated interruptions to his supposedly peaceful Sunday morning. "Yes, what do you want?"

"Your attention, Mr. Ryder." The voice was heavily accented. "I speak to you on behalf of the Brazilian Justice League."

"You've called on a personal phone line, at my home," Duncan said crisply, wondering how the hell they'd found his unlisted number. "If your group wants to make a statement about a United States government policy toward Brazil you should call me at the State Department. My number there is—"

"Mr. Ryder, you will not interrupt me again, since

I do not plan to speak long enough for this call to be traced. Your government has chosen to harass and persecute the Brazilian Justice League by arresting our leader, Dr. Joseph Malone. He is currently imprisoned in Miami, denied bail and awaiting trial on trumped-up charges that he smuggled cocaine from Brazil into the United States. We intend to make sure that your government releases Dr. Malone and allows him to return to Brazil to complete his humanitarian work."

Joseph Malone. Duncan stirred uneasily as he recognized the name. Joseph Malone was an old friend of Summer's, and he knew the two of them had vacationed together the previous fall.

"Who are you?" he demanded. "What's your name, and why are you calling me? I'm sorry if you feel that the arrest of Dr. Malone is unjust, but the United States government doesn't arrest people on trumped-up—"

"You were told not to interrupt."

"I didn't interrupt. I was simply responding—"

"This is your third and final warning, Mr. Ryder." The caller sounded both cold and contemptuous. "If you interrupt again, this conversation will be terminated. We are calling you because the phone lines of your brother-in-law, Gordon Shepherd, the secretary of state, are monitored by official security services, whereas yours are not. You should inform Mr. Shepherd that the Justice League believes the United States has committed an act of war against the Brazilian people. Consequently, the Justice League has taken Summer Shepherd into captivity as our prisoner—"

"Jesus Christ! Are you telling me that you've kidnapped Summer—"

A click warned him the phone had been disconnected and Duncan was left listening to dead air. He jumped to his feet, staring in horror at the silent phone. He'd blown it, big time. Supposing they didn't call back? He let rip with a couple of choice expletives and dashed to the counter where he'd left his cell phone recharging. He tried to get his mind around the fact that some group of political crazies had kidnapped Summer. Summer, of all people, who had probably never entertained a political thought in her life unless it affected the environment. He grabbed his cell phone to call Gordon Shepherd, leaving the regular phone line open in hope that the kidnappers would call back. Jesus, what was he going to say to Gordon? How did you find words to inform a man that his daughter was being held captive by a bunch of political crazies?

Duncan had barely started to dial the secretary of state's private number when the regular phone rang again. He flipped off the cell phone and seized the regular one, forcing himself to wait a couple of seconds before speaking. No need to let the bastards know he was sweating bullets. He sucked in a gulp of air. "This is Duncan Ryder."

The rasping foreign voice spoke into his ear. "You were warned to remain silent, Mr. Ryder. You disobeyed. I hope you now understand that I am serious in my threats. If so, you will also understand the wisdom of listening to me instead of wasting precious time asking stupid questions."

The caller paused, but Duncan didn't fall into the trap of responding.

"Very good, Mr. Ryder. For a government bureaucrat, you learn quickly."

Duncan leaned over and depressed the record button on his answering machine. He held his breath, but the kidnapper continued speaking, apparently not hearing the faint click as the tape started to turn. Or possibly not caring if his threats were recorded. Perhaps he had good reason to believe that his calls weren't going to be traced in time to cause him any problems?

"As I started to tell you, Mr. Ryder, the Brazilian Justice League is holding Summer Rain Shepherd hostage. We consider her a prisoner of war, complicit in the crimes of her father, and totally expendable. If the secretary of state wishes to see his daughter alive, he will follow my instructions precisely. Failure to comply with any of our demands will result in the immediate execution of the prisoner of war."

The kidnapper paused again. Duncan gripped the receiver until his knuckles turned white, but he didn't speak.

"You have learned your lesson, Mr. Ryder. Very good. Your behavior bodes well for the continued safety of Ms. Shepherd." The kidnapper didn't attempt to hide his mockery. "You will find instructions outlining our terms for releasing Ms. Shepherd at the bookstore that is located in the Crossroads Shopping Plaza. To receive enlightenment, I recommend that you study the books in the section devoted to political science. You have precisely fifteen minutes to get to the store, and fifteen minutes more to find our communication. At the end of this half-hour period, if you are not seen leaving the bookstore with our printed instructions prominently displayed in your hands, the Justice League will assume that you have no interest in continuing negotiations for the release of Ms. Shepherd and we will act accordingly."

The kidnapper hung up. For about ten seconds after the line went dead, shock kept Duncan paralyzed.

Then he exploded into action. Fifteen minutes! Christ, the bastards were giving him no leeway at all. Perhaps they didn't know that he didn't own a car. Thank God he'd been planning to jog some time this morning, and he was already wearing sweats and sneakers. The Crossroads Shopping Plaza was a mile and a half away, about ten minutes if he ran at his absolute top speed. Fortunately, he knew the bookstore they were talking about, so at least he wouldn't have to waste time searching for it.

He grabbed his keys and wallet, then remembered his cell phone and spent a few more precious seconds zipping it into his rear pocket. He'd call Gordon as soon as he'd retrieved the kidnapper's instructions. Even though it meant a delay before an investigation could be launched, he didn't dare risk taking the time to make any calls until he actually had those instructions safely in his hands. The guy on the phone had sounded as if he was just looking for an excuse to kill Summer and make headlines for whatever loopy cause the Justice League supported. If the kidnappers intercepted an unauthorized phone call from Duncan to Gordon Shepherd, that could be more than enough to trigger Summer's execution.

Duncan had been embassy point man on enough violent kidnappings when he was in South America to have a vivid mental image of what Summer might be going through right at this moment. Those images scared the hell out of him. He was grimly aware of the fact that if they didn't recover Summer within the first forty-eight hours, their chances of finding her alive went down exponentially. Not to mention the fact that every hour in captivity increased the likelihood that she'd be physically and psychologically scarred, even if she wasn't murdered.

Of course, it was always possible that the call had been some sick form of practical joke, and that Summer was alive and well and relaxing in her New York apartment. No time to check that out now. Duncan sprinted for the elevator. Jesus, how come he'd never noticed that it took an eternity for the damn elevator to travel between floors? He glanced at his watch as the doors finally opened and he stepped inside. It was 10:34. Was that good or bad?

He'd forgotten to check the time when the kidnapper issued his ultimatum, and he could only guess how far he was into his allotted fifteen minutes. One minute? Three minutes? Not more, surely.

Duncan drew in another deep breath and forced himself to stop conjuring up nightmare pictures of Summer being raped and tortured. His task now was to focus on getting to the bookstore in the minimum amount of time possible. In other words, he needed to stop reacting with knee-jerk panic because the kidnap victim was Summer, the woman he loved, and start reacting like the trained professional he was.

The elevator doors opened onto the ground floor. Duncan ran outside, scanning the sidewalks as well as he could without slowing down too much, hoping to identify any passersby who looked as if they might be members of a radical political group like the Justice League. After a half mile, he gave up and concentrated on running. Trying to scrutinize bystanders was losing him speed for no good purpose. This morning, everyone looked suspicious, even the woman pushing a baby in a stroller. Especially the woman with the baby stroller. That was a favorite disguise for bad guys and good guys alike, since even the most hardened criminals were rarely willing to attack a baby carriage without checking to make sure that it was empty.

The designated bookstore was called the Bookworm, and he passed it every day on his regular jogging route. Duncan's stomach cramped, and he wiped a trickle of sweat out of his eyes with his forearm. He was fit, but he didn't usually run with a hundred-pound weight of fear churning around in his gut. He pushed himself to his limits, running with fierce concentration, keeping just inside the line of total exhaustion. It wouldn't do any good if he arrived at the Bookworm and collapsed. When he jogged, he normally ran eight-minute miles for five miles, forty minutes total. It was almost comforting to know that if he was feeling this stressed after only a mile, he must be hitting a hell of a pace.

He turned into the shopping plaza, wiping more sweat off his face with the hem of his sweatshirt. He didn't want to appear so wild-eyed and frantic that they tossed him out of the store. Crossroads Plaza was a strip mall, and the Bookworm was located more or less in the center. He checked his watch again. It read 10:43. Nine minutes since he'd first noted the time and safely within the fifteen-minute limit imposed by the kidnapper.

Duncan walked into the store, all his senses on red alert, and encountered a scene that was jarring in its tranquillity. Browsers strolled the aisles, the aroma of fresh-brewed coffee permeated the air, and there was a pleasant Sunday-morning somnolence to the atmosphere. Despite the idyllic peacefulness, it seemed safe to assume that at least one of the kidnappers was in here, watching him. Possibly inside the store itself, but if not inside, then certainly not too far from the entrance. Otherwise, how would they know if he successfully retrieved the instructions?

Making his way around an elderly man who was autographing a book on gardening, Duncan passed front tables piled high with the latest bestsellers, then made a rapid tour of the store. His tension mounted when he reached the children's area in the back of the store and realized there was no section devoted exclusively to political science. That was what the kidnapper had said, wasn't it? If he wanted enlightenment, he should check out the political science section.

Duncan grabbed a sales assistant, interrupting her as she tried to help another customer. "Where do you shelve your political science books?"

"If you could wait a moment, sir, I'm helping another customer—"

"Where...are...the...political...science...books?" He ground out the question, barely able to refrain from shaking her.

She glared at him, tugging her arm out of his grip. "In the philosophy and religion section. Over there."

"Thank you."

The assistant didn't reply. She turned her back, rigid with hostility, and Duncan zigzagged across the store, the weight of anxiety in his stomach getting heavier by the second. He scanned the shelves in the philosophy section so fast that the titles were a blur. Good God, there had to be a thousand books here, everything from Plato's *Republic* to journalistic accounts of the collapse of communism, with no clear division between the tomes on economic theory and pop biographies of politicians and religious leaders.

The son of a bitch was deliberately making it as

difficult as possible. Well, to hell with that. The kidnapper had more or less indicated that the instructions were printed on a sheet of loose paper shoved between the pages of a book, so he needed to work fast if he was going to find it. A thousand or so books to check in less than fifteen minutes made for truly lousy odds.

Duncan started with the first book on the top shelf, pulling it out and flipping through the pages, looking for a message. Nothing. Grimly, he moved on to the second book, and the third and the fourth. Nothing, nothing, nothing. Duncan started to sweat again, although the bookstore was air-conditioned to a temperature barely warmer than a refrigerator. No way he could check every single book before his time limit ran out, so that meant he had to narrow his search. But how? How the hell was he supposed to second-guess the thought processes of a political terrorist who claimed to have kidnapped the only daughter of the secretary of state?

He'd never seen so many books on angels. Surely he could discount them, since angels could hardly be considered a subcategory of political science. The same applied to all the other religious titles. And then there was a row of first-person accounts by citizens who believed that they'd been abducted by aliens. Why were they shelved here? Alien abductions had nothing to do with philosophy and less than nothing to do with political science.

About to move on, Duncan suddenly pulled up short. Alien abductions. *Abduction* was another word for kidnapping. That sounded like the sort of twisted connection that might appeal to a bunch of crazies like the Justice League. He fought back a wave of hope and reached for the first of the alien abduction books,

this one written by twin brothers who believed their
cancer had been cured by seven-fingered alien doctors.
Nothing. He checked a collection of tales by people
who'd been raped and/or impregnated by aliens. Nothing. Grimly, he rifled through the pages of a self-help
book on how to heal your psychic wounds after being
abducted by aliens. Nothing. Duncan swore under his
breath. He didn't have time to make too many more
wrong guesses.

The final book on the shelf was stacked in multiple
copies. *The Roswell Catastrophe: What the Government Doesn't Want* You *to Know.*

Duncan had seen the author on TV, explaining how
he'd gained top-secret information about the landing
of several alien spacecraft at Roswell, New Mexico,
in 1947. The author was a full-blown conspiracy freak,
who not only believed he'd been kidnapped by aliens,
but also believed he'd been kidnapped and held prisoner by rogue elements of the United States Air Force
to prevent his leaking the truth about Roswell to the
general public.

The premise of the book sounded antigovernment
enough to appeal to the Justice League, Duncan decided. One of the copies of the book was turned face
out. He pulled that copy from the shelf and quickly
flipped through the pages. A sheet of bright pink legal-
size paper, densely covered with typing, fell into his
hands. Mouth dry, palms sweating, he read the first
few lines just to make sure he'd found what he was
looking for.

These are our conditions for the return of the prisoner of war, Summer Rain Shepherd, daughter of
the reactionary tyrant, Gordon Shepherd, so-

called secretary of state for the corrupt regime of the United States government.

We protest the brutal desecration of the Amazon rain forest for no purpose beyond feeding the insatiable profit demands of the American military-industrial complex. Without American money, the Brazilian government would not have been able to destroy the rain forest by means of reckless construction of unnecessary roads, so the violation of our nation's greatest treasure could not have occurred.

We also condemn your government's illegal persecution of Dr. Joseph Malone, who has devoted his life to the cause of true justice for the oppressed people of Amazonas.

Duncan was swept by a wave of such intense anger that he had to stop and suck in a couple of deep breaths before he could continue reading. It was so bitterly ironic that Summer—of all people!—was being held hostage by people protesting the destruction of the Amazon rain forest. God knew, the rain forest couldn't have a much more passionate defender than Summer Shepherd.

It struck him that the language of the note was oddly outdated for the post-Cold War world, but maybe he shouldn't be surprised. The Brazilian Justice League sounded like an organization that would provide a cozy home for aging Marxist guerrillas with nowhere else to turn in a world that suddenly worshipped at the altar of the marketplace. The fact that Marxist ideals weren't winning many converts these days didn't make the Justice League less dangerous. On the contrary. Few people were more dangerous than true believers whose ideals had been defeated in the court of public opinion. Duncan wondered what Summer might now be enduring, all in the name of some doomed-to-fail revolution, waged by fanatics who didn't seem to have noticed that the communist governments of Eastern Europe had done more to destroy the environment than even the most profit-hungry of Western corporations.

"Did you find what you were looking for, sir?"

Duncan blinked, returning to the reality of the bookstore. The sales assistant he'd interrupted with his question about the location of the political science section was standing right next to him.

He nodded. "Yes, thank you. I got what I needed."

He started to move past her, and she held out her hand. "Are you buying that book, sir? Can I help you at the center island cash register?"

Duncan stared at her with attention that was suddenly sharply focused. Why was she being so persistent when he'd been downright rude less than ten minutes ago? "Yes, I'll take the book, but this is what I really came in here for."

Holding up the sheet of distinctive pink paper, he looked at her in open challenge, and she returned his gaze with a mixture of bewilderment and wariness. "Is that one of our flyers?" she asked, stepping up to the cash register.

He hesitated for a split second before answering. "Not exactly," he said. "It's a leaflet from the Brazilian Justice League."

"I don't believe I've heard of them. Are they autographing in the store today?" She smiled apologetically as she aimed her laser scanner at the price code on the back of the book. "I should know which authors are going to be here, I guess, but I've been away for a week on vacation.''

If she was acting, she was turning in a world-class performance. "No, they're not autographing, but I heard they'd be in the neighborhood," Duncan said, handing over his credit card. "By the way, what's your name? You've lost your name tag."

She glanced down at her forest green apron, where there were two empty holes prestitched for a name tag. She patted her apron pocket. "No, it's not lost. The pin broke and I haven't had time to get it fixed." She handed over the book in a bright plastic bag. "Here you are. I'm Donna—"

"Hey, Donna, can you help out over here?" A young man walked toward them, looking frazzled. "There's a kid in the children's section who wants to buy a picture book for his baby sister." The assistant rolled his eyes. "He's got all of five bucks to spend."

"Sure, I'll be right over. If there's nothing else you need, sir?"

"No, thanks." Duncan shook his head and hurried toward the exit. The half-hour deadline to show the kidnappers he'd retrieved their instructions was looming very close.

On the way out of the door, he stopped to speak to the woman at the main cash register. "What's the name of the assistant over there in the kids' section?" he asked, remembering to smile. "She was real helpful and I'd like to put in a good word for her with the manager."

The woman chuckled. "That's Donna Kieferman, and she *is* the manager."

"No wonder she's so good at her job. She's been here a long time, I guess."

"Three years, ever since the store opened. I guess that is pretty long these days."

If she'd been there three years, it was extremely unlikely that she was a plant for the Brazilian Justice League. Duncan saluted the cashier with his book bag. "Thanks. See you later."

He walked outside, holding up the piece of distinctive pink paper as he'd been ordered to do. He scanned the parking lot, trying to spot anyone who might also have been outside his apartment building earlier on. There was nobody he recognized, but, of course, that didn't mean there was nobody watching him. It just meant the kidnappers were good at working undercover.

He had to be right on the cusp of the thirty-minute time limit, and he decided to read the rest of the letter before he did anything else. For all he knew, there might be some more time-related orders for him to follow. Besides, he wanted to give the League operative—whoever he or she was—plenty of time to see him. There was no point in making the kidnappers nervous. Nervous criminals tended to get violent.

He skipped a second reading of the opening propaganda and went straight to the outline of the League's demands.

You may, if you wish, waste time and resources attempting to find where we have hidden Summer Shepherd. We guarantee that you will not succeed in finding her. The only way you will secure her safe return is to follow our instructions precisely.

You will immediately make arrangements for the release of Dr. Joseph Malone from custody. You will then select two representatives of the

United States government who will present themselves at the federal prison in Miami no later than 0500 hours on Tuesday, May 20. They will carry documentation sufficient to insure the release of Dr. Malone into their custody.

These two U.S. government agents and Dr. Malone will drive immediately to Mason Airport, which is located between Jacksonville and Orlando in Florida. At 0900 hours on Tuesday, May 20, the People's Army of the Brazilian Justice League will exchange Summer Shepherd for Dr. Malone.

Aside from the two agents escorting Dr. Joseph Malone, no other U.S. government personnel will be permitted on the grounds of Mason Airport. The presence at the airport of military or police personnel loyal to the oppressor government of the United States will result in the death of Summer Rain Shepherd.

To reassure you that she is both alive, and in our hands, a videotape will be delivered to you soon. And, as a guarantee of our intent to negotiate in good faith, no announcement concerning the capture of Summer Shepherd will be made to the world's media. For your part, you will signify your willingness to comply with our terms by inserting an advertisement in the classified section of tomorrow's *Washington Times*. Your advertisement will state that Gordon Shepherd seeks help in finding a lost treasure.

> The Brazilian Justice League

The willingness of the kidnappers to keep silent about Summer's abduction sent a chill of foreboding down Duncan's spine. The people behind this kidnapping might be political crazies, but it seemed they were well-informed political crazies. They obviously knew about the American government's stated policy of never negotiating with terrorists, and they were, to all intents and purposes, offering the government a way to break its own rules. By promising secrecy, they gave the government a window of opportunity to comply with their demands. Dealing with fanatics who understood the legal limitations on the negotiating powers of the American government was going to be like walking across a field you already knew was planted with a hundred land mines....

Time to call Gordon Shepherd and relay the news. Duncan pulled out his cell phone and keyed in the private home phone number of his brother-in-law. To his relief, the phone was answered right away, and not by a machine.

"Hello."

"Olivia, it's Duncan—"

"Duncan, what a nice surprise! What's up? You don't often call us on a Sunday. In fact, come to think of it, you don't call us nearly often enough—"

"Olivia, this isn't a social call. Is Gordon there? I need to speak to him right away."

"He's in the shower, but talk to me for a couple of minutes and he'll be finished. Or he can call you back—"

"I'm sorry, I can't wait. This is urgent. You need to get him right now."

"Out of the shower? Have you any idea how much he hates that?"

Duncan gritted his teeth. "Get him, Livvy. Now."

It was a couple of minutes before Gordon Shepherd

came to the phone. "I have shampoo dripping into my eyes, Duncan, and the air conditioner is blasting freezing cold air at my wet ass. This had better be a national emergency, or pretty damn close."

"It is a national emergency."

Duncan's hand tightened around his cell phone. "Gordon, I'm sorry, there's no easy way to break this to you, so I'll give it to you straight. You have to prepare yourself for some bad news...."

"Yes, yes, get on with it."

Jesus, this was worse than he'd even imagined. He took refuge in official formality. "I'm sorry to have to tell you, Mr. Secretary, that I have good reason to believe your daughter may have been kidnapped."

"What! What the hell are you talking about?"

"I'm sorry, sir, but we need to authorize a check on Summer's apartment in New York right away to confirm that she's missing."

"Summer has been kidnapped." Not surprisingly, Gordon Shepherd sounded dazed.

"Yes, sir. She's been seized as a hostage by a group calling themselves the Brazilian Justice League—"

"Why do you know this and not me?" Gordon Shepherd's voice was harsh.

"The kidnappers called me, sir. They said that they didn't call you because your phone lines can be monitored, and for obvious reasons, they didn't want their call traced."

"Where the hell are you? What's that noise I can hear in the background?"

"Traffic. I'm at the Crossroads Shopping Plaza. It's a strip mall near my condo where I just picked up the instructions for negotiating Summer's release. Her kidnappers don't want money. I'm afraid it's more complicated than that.''

''Any chance we can comply with their demands? Or even come close?''

Duncan hesitated. ''I'm not sure, sir.'' Gordon was reacting as a father, not as the secretary of state, and he prodded him with a tactful reminder. ''I believe you need to contact the directors of the CIA and the FBI, sir. And they'll probably want to notify the president. There are procedures we'll have to follow—''

Gordon Shepherd drew in an audible breath. ''How long will it take you to get over here with the ransom demands?''

''Ten minutes to jog over to the nearest Metro station. Fifteen minutes on the train. Ten more minutes to get to your house. It's quicker than calling a cab or waiting for you to send a limo.''

''Do it,'' Gordon said. ''And for God's sake, be as quick as you can.''

# Four

The silence terrified Summer even more than the preternatural darkness, or the difficulty of breathing through the hood that still covered her head. Where could she be imprisoned that was so totally devoid of sound? She'd called for help repeatedly ever since she regained consciousness—an hour ago? two hours? four?—but there had never been any reply, not even curses or an order to keep quiet. She spoke again, more to hear the comforting sound of her own voice than because she expected a reply.

"Hello, is anyone there?"

The response, as always, was silence. Panic washed over her, churning around in her stomach until she was afraid she would vomit on her own fear. Where were the kidnappers? It was so creepy to imagine them standing and watching her but refusing to speak. Or was she alone? Summer strained to hear the telltale sounds of human breathing, or the rustle of involuntary moving. But nothing broke the deadweight of silence unless she herself made a sound.

She had never realized until now that silence could be such an effective form of torture. She racked her brains, trying to find an explanation for the silence, but the only one she could come up with was almost too horrible to consider. Summer tried to push the thought away, but it remained stubbornly front and center of her fears.

*Have I been buried alive?*

There, she'd said it, and the terrible possibility was a fraction less terrible now that she'd spoken the words, not exactly out loud, but at least inside her head. Could you be buried alive and continue to get enough air to breathe? She remembered reading about a group of college students who kidnapped a little boy, imprisoned him in a wooden crate, dug a pit, then stuck a pipe into the crate near his head so that air would filter in from above ground, keeping him alive until they collected the ransom money.

Burial would certainly be a supereffective method of hiding her, so she couldn't rule out the possibility that was what the kidnappers had done to her. If she was buried, would the kidnappers be able to locate her again? What if they were relying on some marker like a tree that might get blown over in a storm? Summer tried to swallow, but her mouth was too dry and she gagged instead. Supposing they couldn't find the burial spot when they came looking for her...*if* they came looking for her. Maybe they'd always planned to kill her and wanted the pleasure of torturing her first.

Summer fixated on images of a lingering death by starvation, or by suffocation as the breathing pipe clogged with leaves and the air in her coffin slowly ran out. In the nick of time, just as full-blown hysteria was about to set in, she managed to get a grip on her too-vivid imagination.

*Quit with the neurotic mental movies or you'll drive yourself nuts. If ever there was a time to keep your cool and think rationally, this is it.*

Good advice, but could she follow it? Well, she could sure try, instead of lying around, wallowing in her own fear. She couldn't see, and there didn't seem to be anything to hear, but she could touch and feel. So what could she deduce about her surroundings? She could move around a little, and the surface she was lying on felt like a thin pad of foam rubber laid over a hard surface. There was a cotton hood tied over her head, but she could breathe fairly easily, which must mean that she was lying somewhere well-ventilated and fairly spacious, not buried underground, her body destined to become brunch for worms and rodents.

Summer forced her thoughts to move on before she could detect too many flaws in her own logic. Enough already with the worries about being buried alive. Positive thinking was the way to go; her mother had always believed that. Except that it was so damned hard to focus on the positive when your mind kept drifting into a state of terror, like fog blanketing the side of a mountain, concealing the safe pathway down.

*So get back to defining your physical surroundings.* Summer obeyed her own command and rocked tentatively from one side to the other. Rolling to her left, she hit a solid surface. A wall? She waited for a spasm of pain to pass. Her whole body ached, as if it were bruised right down to the level of individual cells, and the slightest movement hurt, despite the fact that she was lying on a padded surface. Was she in a bed? Probably not. The cushioning wasn't as thick as a mattress, but perhaps she was lying on a cot?

On the other hand, she might be stretched out in a coffin with a fancy padded interior.

Summer slammed the door shut on that returning nightmare. No way she was going to walk herself back down that destructive mental path. Instead of imagining herself into a state of paralytic dread, she would devote her energies to sitting up and taking stock of her surroundings.

It was one thing to tell herself to sit up, another to actually do it. Her muscles not only ached, they were limp and useless, refusing to respond to signals from her brain ordering them to move. She was crying silent tears of agony and frustration when she finally managed to roll herself over onto her right side and hunch forward in a position where she had enough leverage to swing herself upright.

She sat up, weak and panting. And unspeakably relieved to discover that there was space enough for her to do so. Then she had to rest against the wall—or whatever the surface behind her was—while she willed herself not to throw up. She flexed the various parts of her body as well as she could, testing to see if anything was broken. Nothing seemed to be, and her muscles started to work marginally better as soon as she used them. Drawing on her willpower as much as on her reserves of strength, she scooted gingerly forward on her bottom, feeling with her bound feet to make sure that there was a solid surface in front of her.

She'd covered only a very short distance—no more than a foot—when her progress came to an abrupt halt. It seemed that not only was she hooded and bound, she was also tethered at the waist by some sort of restraint, like a dog leash. Oddly, the leash reassured her just a bit. After all, why would the kidnappers want to tether her, except to stop her moving around? And if they didn't want her to move, that surely meant they were keeping her in a normal room, not locked in a closet, much less buried in a makeshift grave.

Summer was sufficiently heartened by the likelihood of being in a regular room that she could almost forgive the humiliation of the dog leash.

She'd just reached this marginally more cheerful state of mind when multiple pairs of hands reached out and fastened roughly around her upper arms, forcing her onto her back. She'd had no awareness of anyone approaching, and the instinct to fight was reflexive. She struggled in bitter silence, trying to knee her invisible captors even though the rational part of her brain knew there was no hope of evading them, and that she was wasting strength she might be wiser to preserve. She felt a human body loom over her, its face pressing close to hers, hands groping at the waistband of her jeans. In a moment of utter despair, she wondered if she was going to be raped before she was murdered.

The threat of rape gave her a burst of adrenaline that renewed her strength. Struggling for air behind the enveloping hood, she redoubled her resistance, but it was only a few moments until lack of oxygen left her too exhausted to fight anymore. Gasping for breath, she cringed away from the encroaching hands, hating her own weakness, but unable to resist any longer. One captor pinned her down, then rolled her onto her stomach and held her immobile while a second captor reached behind her. Oh, God, why couldn't she hear anything except the hideous, snorting sounds of their breathing? Was this going to be a double rape? Was this what sexual arousal sounded like when you couldn't see the other person?

Except it wasn't her kidnappers' raunchy breath that

she heard, it was her own, Summer realized. Humiliatingly, the snuffling, moaning and groaning she was hearing all came from her. And the kidnappers weren't trying to rape her, or even to inject her with more drugs. They were simply unfastening the tether at her waist and removing the tape from her feet so that she could walk.

Summer shivered. She ought to feel reassured by the fact that, so far, nobody had beaten or raped her, but all she felt was consuming dread. She stumbled when she tried to stand, because her legs had gone numb and her hands were still tied behind her back, which kept her off balance. The two guards supported her on either side and half dragged, half carried her for a distance she judged to be about fifteen feet, before pushing her down into a wooden chair with armrests.

Despite their close body contact, she couldn't determine if the guards were male or female. And since they managed to walk without making any sound, she got no relief from the weight of silence that felt as if it had been pressing in on her for half a lifetime. Still, silent and sexless as the kidnappers might be, they were living, breathing people walking at her side, and that was a definite improvement over the worms and rats her imagination had been providing for company so far.

The hood was torn from her head and a knife slashed through the tape binding her hands. Despite the pain as her circulation returned, it was such a blissful release to be able to bring her hands in front of her body that it took a few moments to register her surroundings. When she did look around, she discovered that she was sitting in front of a video camera, mounted on a tripod, in a room that was covered from floor to ceiling in black cloth, with a floor that was padded by the sort of foam rubber mats that she'd seen in studios that taught tae kwon do and other martial arts.

At least the padded floors and cloth-draped walls explained the smothering, all-enveloping quality of the silence, and it also suggested that the kidnappers were keeping her someplace where they were afraid their activities might be overheard. Maybe even in an apartment building, since they seemed so anxious to muffle sounds in every direction.

Her captors seemed to have melted into the ether as soon as they untied her. Even as Summer had that thought, a figure stepped out from behind the video camera, stepping with careful silence in rubber-soled shoes, bolstering her guess that the kidnappers might be trying to avoid the sound of tramping feet being carried to neighboring residents. Robed in black like the state executioner for a medieval king, he—or she—wore gloves and a hooded mask over his face. Summer wanted to convince herself that he looked ridiculous, like a Halloween ghoul, but found herself shuddering instead. In a low-budget movie, he'd be funny. In real life, he was terrifying.

A second similarly sexless and black-robed figure peered into the camera viewfinder and fiddled with a few knobs and dials before straightening and nodding to indicate that he was satisfied with his preparations.

Summer had grown so accustomed to silence that her stomach lurched when a disembodied voice spoke from out of the darkness. "Pick up the newspaper from the stool to your left."

She turned reflexively, only regretting her immediate compliance when it was already too late. The paper was the *New York Times,* and it was dated Monday, May 19. Which meant that even if this was the very earliest edition, it was already more than twelve hours since she'd been seized from the university campus. Did the choice of newspaper mean she was still being held somewhere in the New York area? Possibly, although not necessarily. With satellite printing plants, the *Times* was distributed across the nation in the early hours of each morning.

The disembodied voice spoke again. "Read the article headed President To Address The United Nations."

She stared into the darkness, not quite sure if the hooded figure in front of her was the person speaking. "Why should I?"

"Because your life depends upon it, Ms. Shepherd. Hold the newspaper in front of you, so that your father can see you were alive on the nineteenth of May. Then start reading at the beginning of the article."

She tossed the newspaper onto the floor and stared scornfully into the camera, saying nothing. She suddenly realized that if all her captors were so intent on keeping silent, she ought to make as much noise as she could. She sucked in a gulp of air, expanded her lungs and screamed as loudly as she could. She had no idea what her defiance would achieve, but she sure as hell wasn't going to comply meekly with every demand the kidnappers made. She might be terrified, but she wasn't going to give them the satisfaction of instant obedience.

Her captors reacted swiftly. One of the hooded figures walked over to her side and backhanded her across the head with sufficient force to cut off her scream and topple her from her chair. The blow was so hard that she lost consciousness before she hit the floor.

When she came to, she was still on the floor by the chair, her head pounding with a throbbing pain that felt intense enough to split her skull open if she moved. So much for challenging her captors, she thought sickly. She'd really achieved a whole lot.

With extreme care, she hauled herself into a sitting position and waited for the room to stop dancing the macarena. It wasn't until she managed to stand up, after several failed attempts, that she realized she was alone and that the kidnappers hadn't bothered to tie her up again when she passed out. Excitement made her heart beat faster. Maybe her kidnappers had gotten careless. If she could find a door, she could at least confirm her suspicion that she was being held in an apartment building....

Her fantasies of escape lasted less than ten seconds. She hadn't taken more than a couple of shaky steps forward when she heard a door open and close with well-oiled quietness behind her. She whirled around just as one of the kidnappers appeared at her elbow and another squatted next to the video camera and checked the settings.

The same disembodied masculine voice spoke again. "Sit on the chair," it instructed. "If you scream again, Ms. Shepherd, there will be consequences you will regret."

"Worse than being tied up like a dog with a hood over my head?"

"There are many worse fates than being tied up and left to lie on a comfortably padded mat. I do not intend to continue this conversation. Are you now ready to proceed with the filming, Ms. Shepherd?''

''No.'' Since she wasn't sure who was speaking, she stared challengingly into space. ''I need a drink and to go to the bathroom.''

''You can do both. But only after you have read a paragraph from the front page of the *New York Times* as I requested earlier.''

Summer wanted to be brave. She wanted to hurl further defiance at her captors. But her entire body shimmered with pain, she was scared she might throw up at any minute, and most of all, she desperately needed access to a bathroom. The closest she could come to defiance was to hang her head and say nothing.

''Ms. Shepherd, I don't understand why you feel this need to resist my simple request. What do you hope to achieve? Don't you think your father would like to hear your voice and be reassured that you're alive, as we have promised him?''

The voice had a very slight foreign accent, almost imperceptible unless you listened really attentively. Summer stared at her hands and wondered what her father was feeling right now, this minute. What had the kidnappers demanded as a ransom for her safe return? she wondered. They were too well organized to have captured her by mistake, and so they must be aware that her father didn't have much money. He was comfortable financially, but he didn't have access to the sort of serious fortune that would make a kidnapping operation of this size worthwhile. Which meant that these people wanted something other than money. Something important, since they were prepared to go to such lengths to get it. Given her father's position in the government, it seemed safe to assume they were going after some favor they believed only the American secretary of state could grant. And that meant something to do with international politics.

With all the kooks and fanatics roaming the world, their demands could range from the outrageous to the comically absurd. Unfortunately, whatever they wanted, there was almost zero chance that her father would actually have the freedom to negotiate a deal for her release. The government had strict rules forbidding negotiations with terrorists, and they weren't likely to suspend those rules for her or they'd be opening the floodgates to a security nightmare that would affect every family member of every cabinet official.

Great, Summer thought gloomily, she was totally screwed. Her life most likely hung in the balance, and it was *real* depressing to know that there wasn't much her father could throw into his side of the bargaining scale. She allowed herself to wallow in self-pity for a few moments before pulling herself back from the brink. Okay, so her father couldn't negotiate a deal for her release. Well, that meant it was her job to keep herself alive as long as possible so that the FBI would have a better chance of finding her.

The mere idea of having a definite goal in mind bolstered her self-confidence slightly. No more offending her captors or making pitiful attempts to escape. Staying alive was the key. That, and trying to discover some clue about the motives of the people who had abducted her.

"What do you want from my father?" she asked, finally looking up and staring straight into the eyes of the hooded figure in front of her. Weren't kidnappers supposed to keep their victims alive longer if you established a personal connection? "What deal are you trying to negotiate with him in exchange for my freedom?''

''It's better that you don't know.'' Even though she was now looking at him with maximum attention, she still wasn't sure if the voice she heard came from the kidnapper she could see, or another one who was hidden.

''Just do as we ask, Ms. Shepherd, and refrain from trying to discover who we are. If you reflect for a moment, you will realize that we wear these concealing robes as much for your protection as for our own. If you wish to live, obviously you must remain ignorant of who we are. Now, read from the newspaper and let your father know that you are alive. Doesn't he deserve that much peace of mind? And you can give it to him so easily.''

She knew she was being manipulated, just as she'd tried to manipulate her captors. But what the kidnapper said was true. The fact that they were taking such elaborate care to conceal their identities probably meant that they wanted to release her alive.

And, realistically, the bottom line was that they could starve and terrorize her into cooperation, or she could agree to their demands right now, while she was still in relatively good shape and there was some hope that she could survive long enough for the FBI to trace her. After all, what harm could it do if she read a few lines of text from an American newspaper? Even if these people were terrorists, plotting to blow up hundreds of innocent people if her father didn't cooperate with them, she couldn't see how reading a passage from the *New York Times* was going to further their aims. All it would do was prove to her family and friends that she'd been alive on May 19. And the government's forensic labs were so sophisticated that the tape itself might provide tons of information to the FBI agents who were presumably scouring the country trying to find her.

Still, she wasn't going to give in without negotiating first. She needed to bargain while she had some leverage, however tenuous. "I'm not reading anything until I've been to the bathroom," she said. She needed to retain some tiny shred of physical dignity if she was going to make it through.

The man considered for at least a minute. "All right," he said finally. Again without any signal that Summer could see, two more black-robed and masked figures instantly emerged from out of the shadows, where they had been hidden by the folds of the black, fabric-draped walls. That made at least four guards right here with her in this room. No surprise there, not really. She hadn't paid attention to the group of "students" lounging outside her office building, but there had been at least five of them, maybe as many as seven.

The two guards escorted her, one on either side, to a washroom containing a sink and a toilet but nothing else, not even a bar of soap or a wall mirror. Summer didn't care. She used the facilities and splashed water all over her face and hands, cleaning herself up and restoring circulation, before sticking her head under the tap and drinking what seemed like gallons of tepid water. She felt so much better afterward that she decided to wait until she was rescued before worrying about whether or not the water had been safe to drink. She didn't allow herself to notice that she felt very hungry now that she wasn't thirsty anymore. *Ignore the rumblings in your stomach. They're just a minor discomfort, nothing more.* Somebody strong and healthy like her could live for a couple of weeks without food, provided she got plenty of water.

Her courage bolstered by the simple pleasure of no longer craving either a drink or a rest room, she returned to the armchair in the spotlight and picked up the newspaper.

"What do you want me to read?" she asked, settling into the wooden armchair and refusing to look intimidated. "I've forgotten."

"Read the article on the front page headed President To Address The United Nations."

"Why do you want me to read that particular article? What's so important about it?"

"Just read, Ms. Shepherd. Don't waste your energy attempting to establish a bond with us. Believe me when I say that no such bond can be forged."

So much for her plan of constructive engagement, she thought wryly, and started to read. Her head still ached so badly that it was difficult to develop profound and intelligent thoughts, but try as she might, she couldn't imagine any double meaning that could be affixed to this short, straightforward account of the president's forthcoming pledge to reduce America's share of the world's total carbon emissions by the dawn of the twenty-first century. She supposed it might be possible to take isolated words, then cut and paste them into a totally new message, but the FBI had plenty of experts who would know instantly that the tape had been tampered with. Moreover, the kidnappers would undermine their own purpose if they tampered with what she was saying. To prove that she was alive, they needed to have her on tape reading the article exactly as it appeared in today's newspaper.

Summer felt reassured that her decision to cooperate was the right one. Much as she dreaded being used as a propaganda weapon against her father and her country, she really didn't see any way that the kidnappers would be able to utilize this video, except as proof that she was alive.

She stopped reading after a couple of paragraphs. Whatever their intentions, there was no point in providing the kidnappers with anything beyond the minimum. And from the FBI's point of view, she couldn't see how increasing the length of the tape would be of much benefit.

"Very good." The man she had begun to think of as the Chief Executioner stepped briefly into the circle of light and indicated to his sidekick to stop rolling the videocam. "Thank you, Ms. Shepherd."

"You're welcome," she said sarcastically. "Now, how are you going to reward me for being such a cooperative prisoner? Personally, I think a hearty steak dinner would be great."

It was all she had time to say. She felt the now-familiar sting of a needle inserted into her upper arm. The hood was tossed over her head and tied once again. Arms grabbed her on either side and she was marched back to whatever corner of the room they had been keeping her in.

She tried to protest when she felt them start to tie up her ankles, but she was already losing consciousness. By the time they had her on the floor, with her hands pulled behind her back, she could no longer hold a thought long enough to put it into words.

A dark blanket covered her. Whether it was real or only in her mind, she couldn't tell.

The silence reclaimed her.

# *Five*

The president had flown back to the White House from Camp David within an hour of receiving confirmation from the FBI field office in New York that Summer had not returned to her apartment, but on Monday morning when the task force reconvened in the Situation Room at the White House, he could only stay long enough for a quick update. The need to keep Summer's kidnapping secret required the president to stick to his previously planned schedule, and that meant he would start his morning by breakfasting with a deputation of grade school students from Mississippi.

Lack of sleep might be making him cynical, but as far as Duncan could tell, the need for absolute secrecy was about the only thing the members of the task force had agreed on. Official contingency plans for dealing with the abduction of cabinet officers, or members of their families, provided few guidelines that were directly applicable to Summer's case, and although certain security precautions and investigative procedures swung into operation with well-oiled precision, there were other decisions that needed to be made on a case-specific basis. Duncan had spent a lot of time yesterday sitting on his hands and biting his tongue. He'd reminded himself at frequent intervals that yelling at a roomful of administration dignitaries wouldn't achieve anything except to get himself tossed out on his ass. And being cut off from the latest information about the search for Summer would have been even worse than keeping his mouth shut while the FBI director and the head of the CIA fought a full-scale war over which department had ultimate jurisdiction over the rescue operation.

Duncan had spent the night with his sister and brother-in-law. He hadn't managed to sleep, and judging by his appearance this morning, Gordon Shepherd hadn't slept, either. He was haggard, his complexion tinged with gray, and he looked so emotionally and physically ravaged that Duncan thought the risk of a heart attack had to be very real.

The president, notoriously bad at keeping to a tight schedule, was reluctant to leave the reconvened meeting even though his chief of staff was trying to chivvy him from the room. The president always reacted with strong emotions to family crises, and he paused in the doorway to put his arm around Gordon's shoulders.

"We're going to get your daughter back, Gordon." The president then wrung Gordon's hand, his eyes misty with tears. "Our government has the finest investigative resources in the world, and we're damn well going to find her."

"I hope so, sir, but right now we don't seem to be turning up any good leads." Gordon's voice was hoarse with fatigue and worry.

"We'll turn up something soon, you can count on it." The president glared at his chief of staff. "Harry, I want updates sent to me every hour, on the hour. And if anything breaks, I want to be informed no matter where I am or what I'm doing."

"Yes, sir. We'll keep you fully informed." The chief of staff held open the door, glancing at his watch for the third time in as many minutes. "Sir, you really have to leave now. The students from Vicksburg will be arriving at the Oval Office in nine minutes."

"I know my schedule. Dammit, Harry, give me a moment here." Turning to Gordon again, the president spoke with fierce determination. "I'm not going to allow the foreign policy decisions of this country to be influenced by terrorists, but we'll do whatever it takes to get your daughter back. And then we're going to nail the bastards who took her, you can count on it, Gordon."

Duncan tried not to feel cynical, but right off the top of his head, he couldn't see how the administration was going to do whatever it took to get Summer back from a bunch of foreign terrorists without compromising the government's ability to make unbiased foreign policy decisions.

Gordon was too upset to detect flaws in the president's logic. "Thank you, sir. I appreciate your concern. I'm grateful.... My wife and I appreciate..." Normally the master of smooth diplomacy, Gordon couldn't finish his sentence.

The president gave him a final sympathetic pat on the shoulder before rushing off to his appointment with the grade school kids, thus narrowly saving his chief of staff from death by apoplexy.

Gordon stood for a moment, staring at the door where the president had left, his hands hanging limply at his sides. When he finally snapped out of his trance and walked back to his seat, he stumbled and would have fallen if Duncan hadn't steadied him by placing an unobtrusive hand under his elbow.

"Duncan?" Gordon stared at him bemusedly, as if surprised to find him there. Then he gave his head a quick little shake and sat down at the table, pouring himself a glass of ice water and visibly taking hold of himself. "Shall we begin, gentlemen? We have a lot to get through in the next two hours. First, I decided to comply with the Justice League's demand that I should put an advertisement in the personal columns of the *Washington Times*. I asked Duncan Ryder to take care of that on my behalf. Did you manage to reach Harvey Fochs at the number I gave you?"

Duncan nodded. "Yes, sir. Mr. Fochs promised to get the advertisement inserted into the late editions of this morning's paper."

"Thank you." Gordon made a notation on the legal pad in front of him and turned to the director of the FBI. "Julian, you next. What do you have for us? Your technical people have been listening to the tape recording Duncan made of the call from the kidnappers. Have they come up with any useful insights?"

"They've got some preliminary data for us." Julian Stein, the director of the FBI, opened a file and read from a single sheet of notes. "I'm afraid most of it's either negative, or merely confirms what we already know. The man who called isn't using a voice distortion device and his accent is that of a Brazilian national who has spent considerable periods of time in the United States."

"No surprises there," Gordon commented.

"No," the director agreed. "As to background sounds on the tape, we could detect none, and certainly none that might help in pinpointing a location from which the call was made. The complete absence of identifying features does suggest that the people behind Ms. Shepherd's abduction have some experience with abductions. It's possible that they've kidnapped prominent people before and ransomed them for money to support the activities of the Justice League."

Bram Cooper, head of the CIA, grunted. For once, he seemed in agreement with his arch rival. "We all know that kidnapping for profit has reached epidemic levels in parts of South America."

"How about the ransom note?" Gordon asked, looking disappointed. "Did you have any better luck there?"

The FBI director shook his head. "Not much. The paper the ransom note was written on is standard stock, obtainable at any office supply store, nationwide. The only identifiable fingerprints on the note are those of Duncan Ryder. There is some biochemical residue, but that analysis isn't yet complete. The book where the note was found is covered in prints, including Mr. Ryder's, but none makes a match with any prints that we have on record."

"Any reason to suppose the bookstore is involved in the kidnapping?" the chief of staff asked. "Other than as a place to hide the ransom note, I mean."

"Not that we've been able to uncover," Julian Stein said. "We've interviewed store personnel who were working at the Bookworm on Sunday morning and we've run preliminary checks on all their employees, but we haven't turned up anything surprising. For now, we're assuming the Bookworm was chosen because it's the closest bookstore to Duncan Ryder's apartment, and not because one of the employees is a Justice League sympathizer."

The pencil Gordon had been playing with snapped, although he didn't seem to notice.

"What I'm hearing you say, Julian, is that the kidnappers haven't made any mistakes thus far, so we have no immediate leads."

"Unfortunately, that's correct."

"The note was written on a computer?" The question came from Bram Cooper.

The director nodded. "Yes. Which again is no help at all, I'm afraid. It's not like the good old days when criminals used typewriters and we could pinpoint the machine they used by examining the typeface."

"How about a psychological profile of the person who wrote the ransom note?" Gordon asked. "Have your people come up with anything on that?"

"This is more promising. First, as several of you pointed out yesterday, the overall tone of the ransom note is strangely outdated.

"Rick Buglione—he's our senior profiler—suggests that some of the phrases sound like propaganda lifted straight out of an antiwar protest of the Vietnam era."

"There are still plenty of Marxist true-believers left in South America," Bram Cooper pointed out. "Just because we Americans have decided the Cold War is over, that doesn't mean every village revolutionary in Brazil has gotten the message."

"True, but having established a tone that suggests the writer is politically motivated, the note then switches gears and complains about rain forest destruction in the Amazon region of northern Brazil."

"It's a strange juxtaposition," Bram Cooper agreed, scratching his chin. "You could argue that the United States has participated in some controversial development projects, but Amazonia has to be one of the places where we've interfered least. For good or ill, neither the American government nor American private industry played much of a role in building the Trans-Amazon Highway.''

"So, bottom line, what are we dealing with here?'' The president's chief of staff paced the windowless security room, tension in every line of his body. ''Are we facing a bunch of former left-wing guerrillas who've given up politics and become environmental fanatics instead?''

The FBI director shook his head. ''I'm not saying anything definitive right now because my people are still working on the details. But Rick Buglione is the best profiler in the business, and in his opinion, at least at this stage, we would be smart to treat the whole ransom note as a scam.''

Gordon Shepherd looked up, startled. ''What the hell does that mean? My daughter's disappeared, and that's certainly no scam.''

"No, I'm sorry, Gordon, I'm tired and I spoke loosely. I didn't mean to suggest that the kidnapping of your daughter hadn't taken place. It's the motive behind the abduction that Rick Buglione questions. In his opinion, the writer of this ransom note doesn't give a damn about American involvement in the destruction of the rain forest, much less the oppression of starving peasants by the so-called military-industrial complex. In Buglione's opinion, the high-flown rhetoric is so much flimflam.''

"Then what is the motive behind the kidnapping?'' Bram Cooper sounded both impatient and skeptical.

"According to Buglione, the only thing the letter writer really cares about is getting Joseph Malone released from jail.''

Of course! Duncan thought. How the hell did I miss that? Then he went cold, his body freezing into stillness while he absorbed the shocking implications of what the FBI director had just said.

*The writer of the ransom note only cared about getting Joseph Malone released from jail.*

Summer and Joseph Malone were old college friends who had spent weeks last fall touring Brazil, ending their vacation by traveling together deep into the Amazon rain forest without the benefit of any professional guides. According to Olivia, who always seemed to know this sort of thing, Summer and Joseph weren't just friends, they were longtime lovers. Now Joseph Malone was in an American jail, waiting trial on charges that could bring him multiple years in a federal prison. How would Summer have reacted to that news?

She must have been distraught when she heard Malone had been arrested. Duncan had always suspected that when Summer loved, she would love with her whole heart; that she would be uncompromising and utterly loyal in her devotion. Did she love Joseph Malone with that sort of intense, uncompromising loyalty? Duncan hadn't thought so. To him, Summer still had a naive, sexually unawakened quality. But he could be dead wrong, since his judgment was seriously defective where Summer and love were concerned, chiefly because his opinions were always infused with a hefty dose of wistful optimism. Optimism that—one day—she might notice that he was an anatomically correct adult male with fully functioning body parts. And even a few empathetic and functioning brain cells.

How far might Summer be prepared to go in order

to rescue Malone from jail? Duncan wondered bleakly. Would she be willing to arrange for her own kidnapping? With a sinking sensation in the pit of his stomach, he recalled a snippet of their conversation on Friday night. He'd asked Summer what she thought it would take to get politicians to pay attention to the problems of global warming. And she'd laughed, and made some joke about needing a direct message from God. Was this kidnapping Summer's substitute for a divine warning? A way of winning freedom for Malone and simultaneously drawing attention to the environmental causes that were so important to her?

Duncan searched the other faces in the room, which were curiously blank. Perhaps deliberately? It was impossible to tell what anyone was thinking except Bram Cooper, who was looking annoyed.

"There's no conflict between wanting to save the rain forest and wanting to spring Malone from jail," Cooper said irritably. "I've had my people pull up everything we've got on the Brazilian Justice League, and our records show that Dr. Joseph Malone was identified as the head of the League as far back as 1993. He even donated funds from a patent he owns to swell their bank balance. He's not just their leader, he's their money man."

"I didn't know that," Julian Stein admitted. "I'll make sure the information is passed on to Buglione and see if that changes his opinion about the note."

The CIA director looked smug. "It should do. That's why the Justice League is so damned anxious to get Malone out of jail. He's not only their head honcho, he's their paymaster. With him in jail, the troops have no income. Once you know that, the demands in the ransom note all tie together and make perfect sense. No conflict there.''

Gordon Shepherd reached for a glass of water and discreetly swallowed three Excedrin. Duncan wondered if Gordon was reacting to general stress, or whether he'd just made the same connection between the demands in the ransom note and Summer's friendship with Malone that Duncan had made earlier.

''Is there anything more you can tell us about the Justice League, Bram?'' Gordon's voice betrayed no hint of what he was feeling, but his desire to keep the CIA director talking suggested to Duncan that his brother-in-law was well aware of the fact that Julian Stein had been on the brink of heading the meeting in a very frightening direction.

''Plenty,'' Bram Cooper said. ''They've been causing trouble one way or another since 1979. And as far as my people are concerned, there's nothing off-key about their ransom note. It's written exactly the way you'd expect, two parts bullshit and one part hard-core demand.'' He glared at the FBI director. ''As for the left-wing political tone, that's not surprising, either. How many environmental fanatics do you know who are also members of the Young Republicans?''

''You have a good point.'' The president's chief of staff cleared his throat, taking center stage. ''Tell me, is there any evidence that the Justice League has staged violent international protests before? Is there a pattern we can follow here that might give us some guidance on how to handle this?''

''Wish there was, but no.'' Bram Cooper shook his head. ''On the plus side, the League has worked for years to get meaningful land reform for Brazilian peasants, especially peasants living in the northeast region, and they've sometimes operated like a charity, feeding starving children when there's been a particularly severe drought. On the other hand, they have no respect for other people's property. They've protested against the roads being built through the rain forest since day one, and the local authorities blame them for a lot of sabotage of expensive construction equipment. The League has also protested the transfer of peasants to Amazonia, claiming the peasants had no training in land management and that they would starve.''

"They were right about that in a lot of cases,'' Duncan said.

"Yes, they were,'' Bram Cooper conceded. "There's no denying that there's a lot of truth in what the Justice League is claiming. The trouble is, they aren't content to campaign peacefully for change. They turn to violence instead. The Justice League got mad when nobody listened to them and started blowing up buildings to get attention for their cause.''

Gordon Shepherd winced at the reminder of the violence his daughter might be facing. "Have they killed a lot of people?''

"The good news for us is that they've been careful to avoid killing anyone, which might be why they barely got any media coverage in Brazil, let alone the rest of the world.'' Bram Cooper leaned forward, emphasizing his point. "In my opinion, they got frustrated with the ineffectiveness of their no-kill policy and decided to make a play for the really big time. And that's why they snatched the daughter of the American secretary of state. Maximum publicity, but no need to kill anyone, if everything goes according to their master plan.''

The FBI director broke his silence. "You think

they've kidnapped Ms. Shepherd strictly to publicize their cause?''

"Yes, that's exactly what I think," Bram Cooper agreed. "That, and to get back Joseph Malone, their moneyman. Killing two birds with one stone, to use a cliché."

"There's just one flaw to that logic," the FBI director said, sounding testy. He was normally a mild-mannered man, but Bram Cooper always succeeded in rubbing him the wrong way. "The kidnappers have said that they won't contact the media, and they've kept their word. So much for the idea that they've snatched Ms. Shepherd to get worldwide media exposure for their cause."

"It's early days yet—"

Julian Stein barely contained a snort. "Take my word for it, the people who wrote that ransom note just want Malone out of jail. They don't care about media attention for the cause of rain forest preservation."

Bram Cooper bristled. "And what do you think will happen when we release Joseph Malone? I'll tell you. The Justice League will inform the entire world that they held the United States government up for ransom—and that we paid."

Gordon Shepherd rose hastily to his feet. "Gentlemen, we had this discussion yesterday and it's counterproductive to go over the same points again. Let me sum up the situation as I see it. We are deploying the full resources of the government in the hope that we will find my daughter.

"However, we are in the fortunate position that if we can't find any trace of her, we can negotiate for her release. Joseph Malone has not yet been convicted of any crime. You all heard the attorney general yesterday when he assured us that the charges being brought against Dr. Malone can be quietly dropped. Charges are reduced by the prosecution all the time, for a variety of reasons. And if Joseph Malone is not facing charges of smuggling cocaine, we are free to negotiate an exchange of my daughter for him—''

The FBI director followed Gordon to his feet. ''Before we proceed down this path, I need to talk with Joseph Malone. That would clearly seem to be my most important task right now.''

''That makes sense,'' Gordon agreed. ''Although Malone is not likely to cooperate with us, do you think?''

''We'd better hope like hell that he does, because we can't force his cooperation.'' Julian Stein spoke grimly.

Gordon sat down with a bump. ''You surely can't be suggesting that if Malone refuses to be handed over, we have to sit on our hands and wait for the Justice League to execute my daughter?''

''Don't worry, I don't believe it will come to that.''

Julian Stein hesitated, then drew in a short breath, apparently deciding that he had no choice but to speak plainly. ''I'm sorry, Mr. Secretary, but there's another aspect to this kidnapping that I have to bring up. The fact that your daughter knows Joseph Malone personally—that she vacationed with him in Brazil just last fall...''

''I fail to see the relevance,'' Gordon said icily.

Julian Stein looked away. ''I believe, Mr. Secretary, that you're speaking as Ms. Shepherd's father at the moment, and not as a senior cabinet officer in the United States government. Your daughter's prior friendship with Joseph Malone is a factor we simply can't ignore when we're deciding how best to handle this very delicate situation. To put it bluntly, there is at least a possibility that your daughter is not entirely an innocent victim—"

Gordon Shepherd sprang to his feet again. His face flushing scarlet with anger, he drew himself up to his full six feet two inches. "I cannot believe that you are suggesting what you seem to be suggesting, Mr. Director. The fact that my daughter once attended the same university as Joseph Malone, along with thousands of other students—"

"And vacationed with him in Brazil—"

"No, Mr. Director. She merely allowed him to act as her tour guide. A sensible decision on her part, since he's bilingual and well-informed about the region. That doesn't mean she was an accomplice in her own abduction."

Julian Stein leaned forward, about to make an angry response. At the last moment, he drew away. Having made his point, he was willing to back off, at least temporarily. "At the moment, Mr. Secretary, I'm still gathering information and drawing no firm conclusions. However, it's my job to consider all the possible facts before we rush into negotiating with these kidnappers. And right now, since Ms. Shepherd isn't available for interviews, I need to talk to Joseph Malone and find out what information he can give me about his relationship with your daughter, and his own relationship with the Brazilian Justice League."

The angry flush of color had already drained from Gordon's cheeks. "And if Malone says he's... involved...with Summer? Are you going to accept the word of a drug dealer? A man who is a voluntary exile from his own country and has spent the past several years as the leader of a group that isn't much better than a gang of political terrorists?''

''No, Mr. Secretary. I won't accept Joseph Malone's word without checking it against all other possible sources. But I will evaluate any information he gives me to insure that we protect the national security interests of this country as well as the safety of your daughter.''

If Gordon Shepherd had looked haggard at the beginning of the meeting, he now looked to be teetering right on the verge of collapse. Somehow, though, he recovered himself and met Julian Stein's gaze with dignity. ''Yes, I can see that you need to reassure yourself of the facts of the case, Mr. Director. That being so, I'll look forward to hearing your report after you've spoken with Joseph Malone. I rely on you to be in touch with me as soon as your interview with him is concluded.''

''You'll hear from me as soon as I've spoken to Malone,'' the director promised. ''Now, my plane is on standby at Andrews, and if there's nothing else you need me for, Mr. Secretary, I'd like to be on my way to Miami.''

After the director left, there was an uncomfortable silence, broken only when Gordon Shepherd asked the remaining participants to outline the immediate next steps they planned to take in the search for Summer. The meeting continued for another thirty minutes and then broke up, leaving Gordon and Duncan alone at the table.

''Don't go,'' Gordon said as Duncan stood up and started to put his notes through the shredder.

"Of course not, if you need me. Do you want me to come home with you?"

"I don't know if I should go home." Gordon rubbed his forehead distractedly. "Olivia is so upset that we only made it worse for each other last night. When I'm here, at least I feel that I'm doing something to find Summer." He paced the soundproof, windowless room as he spoke, his steps hesitant and uncoordinated, as if he was too busy thinking to have spare brainpower to direct to his feet. His face was so pale that it appeared bloodless. Only his eyes had color, and they burned with febrile intensity. Finally, he stopped pacing and sat down again, resting his head on his hands.

"Did she do it?" he asked bleakly, with no preamble. "I can't be objective anymore. Did she arrange her own kidnapping? Is she capable of torturing us all like this?"

"She's capable of it," Duncan said, his voice sounding curt because he was reluctant to acknowledge the truth. "If she loves Malone enough, and if she's convinced that he's been framed for a crime he didn't commit. Which is what the note said, remember?"

"Oh, God." Gordon's shoulders slumped. "Do you think she's in love with Malone?"

"I have no idea, sir. It's not a subject she would discuss with me."

"Julian Stein believes she's involved, doesn't he?"

"Stein is the director of the FBI. He's paid to think the worst about everyone." Duncan hooked a chair and sat down next to his brother-in-law. "But you're her father, Gordon, and that means you have to believe in her one hundred percent right up until the moment that you're presented with incontrovertible proof that she's a co-conspirator, not a victim."

"I'm also the secretary of state," he said tiredly. "How do I know when I'm entitled to react like a father and when it's my duty to react like the man who is responsible for the foreign policy of the United States government?"

"Right now, there's no conflict between the two," Duncan said, resting his hand on his brother-in-law's arm. "Right now, the most important thing is to find Summer. The longer this situation goes on, the more dangerous it becomes for everyone, both on a national and on a personal level. So we have every reason to assume she's an unwilling victim and to stay focused on finding her."

"That's true." Gordon lifted his head and tried, not very successfully, to smile. "You have an enviable knack for shoveling through the muck and grasping hold of the core issue, Duncan."

Duncan wished he was half as sure of his opinions as he sounded. The trouble was, when you'd spent six years hopelessly in love with a woman who considered you about as exciting as dental floss, your judgment of her motives didn't exactly operate at peak efficiency. He thought back to Friday night and wondered if Summer's unexpectedly mellow mood had been nothing more than a ploy designed to soften him up for what she knew was ahead. He had to concede it was a possibility, even if he would never admit that to anyone except himself. Why else had she radiated signals of sudden sexual awareness, when for years she'd conveyed the unmistakable message that his absence was a great deal more desirable than his presence? With any other woman, he couldn't imagine being played for such a complete sucker. But with Summer, all she needed to do was smile and he was lost.

In the circumstances, Duncan decided, he and Gordon weren't going to achieve very much by spending the rest of the day together. They were more likely to drive each other crazy than to reach any useful conclusions. "There's one thing I know for sure," he said. "You need to go home and take a nap. You won't do Summer or anyone else a favor if you make decisions when you're too tired to think straight."

Gordon shook his head. "I ought to stay here. There must be something I can do...."

"There's nothing you can do that's more useful than taking a nap. You've been worrying about Summer nonstop for twenty-four hours. Let me call for your car." With the stepped-up security that had gone into effect the moment Summer's kidnapping was confirmed, Gordon was no longer allowed to drive his own car or to go anywhere without a full Secret Service escort.

"I wish to God I could sleep," Gordon said. "I'd like to go to bed and wake up when this nightmare is over."

"If you're serious, I'm sure we could find a doctor who'd be willing to prescribe something to knock you out cold for a few hours."

"No, of course I wasn't serious." Gordon stood up, managing a shaky smile. "I'll be fine after a nap. I'm anxious to hear what Julian Stein will have to tell us when he gets back from Miami."

The Secret Service escort arrived and Duncan walked with his brother-in-law to his official limo, which was parked in a locked underground facility, with military guards posted at the only entrance. Even so, the Secret Service agents were obviously on edge, anticipating trouble. "Can I give you a ride home?" Gordon asked, getting into the car.

Duncan shook his head. "No, but thanks for the offer. Olivia lent me one of her cars this morning, and it's parked five or six blocks away. I'll enjoy the walk."

"When you've had a chance to rest, come to the house and spend some time with Olivia, will you? She's really taking this hard, and there's nobody for her to talk to."

"Of course I'll come." Duncan shook his brother-in-law's hand. "Now, go home, get some rest yourself and try to stop worrying."

Gordon gave a wry smile and got into the car. "Well, I can manage the part about going home. I guess one out of three ain't bad."

Duncan watched his brother-in-law's limo roll out of the parking facility. He discovered when he got outside that the day was overcast and breezy, with the threat of rain lurking in the low, dark clouds. He walked briskly, trying to analyze everything that had been discussed at the meetings. He discovered that his brain stubbornly refused to do anything except fixate on images of Summer as he'd last seen her. God, she was so damn beautiful it made his throat ache just to think about her. Beautiful, smart, dedicated to her work—and desperately in love with Joseph Malone? Maybe he'd been kidding himself for the past six months, imagining that her feelings for Malone were more friendly than passionate.

He reached his borrowed car just as it started to rain in earnest. The meter had expired two hours earlier, so it was no surprise to see that he had a parking ticket shoved under his windshield wiper. He stuffed the ticket into his pocket, simultaneously springing the door lock with the remote. Pulling the door open, he leaned inside and tossed a package from the driver's seat onto the passenger side of the car.

He'd latched the seat belt and was about to turn on the ignition when he gave a sudden strangled yell. Jesus, where had that package come from? Unfastening his belt, he leaped out of the car and flung himself onto the pavement, waiting for the explosion.

Nothing happened. Several passersby stared at him, then circled warily, giving him a wide berth. He hauled himself to his feet, dripping wet and splattered with mud. He turned back to the car, approaching this time from the passenger side, where he'd carelessly tossed the package wrapped in brown paper and sealed with masking tape.

The package that hadn't been there when he'd left the car three hours earlier.

He rubbed off raindrops with his sleeve and squinted through the window. The package lay innocently in the middle of the passenger seat. If it was a bomb, it certainly didn't have a delicate trigger. It was addressed to him by name, in large letters, but without any street address. How had somebody known that he was going to drive Olivia's car this morning? The hairs on the back of his neck prickled at the realization that somebody must have been watching Gordon and Olivia's house.

Across the top of the wrapper, in heavy black marker, someone had written *Videotape. Property of The Brazilian Justice League.*

The ransom note had promised a videotape. One

that would presumably show Summer alive and in captivity. Duncan experienced a sudden, intense craving for a glimpse of the woman he loved, even if only on film.

Julian Stein, thank God, was en route to Miami. A perfect excuse for Duncan to bypass the FBI director and take the videotape directly to Summer's father. He got into his sister's car and drove as fast as he could to Gordon Shepherd's house.

# *Six*

In the ten days since his arrest, Joseph Malone had managed to cope fairly well with the brutality and squalor of prison life, partly because he was now less afraid of being assassinated than he had been at any time in the past six months. His enemies had apparently realized they needed him alive in order to rake in the money, and although he still couldn't understand why they wanted him shut up in an American jail, he'd decided it was a hell of a lot better to be warehoused than dead. Of course, there was always the chance that a fellow inmate might get pissed off and murder him, but his thin body hid wiry muscles and he'd already proved to his own satisfaction that he wasn't entirely defenseless against the gang bullies. He'd learned hand-to-hand combat from a Xuaxanu warrior chief, and for the price of a cracked rib and a bloody nose, he'd been able to hold his own against the intimidation squads determined to show him who was master of the prison yard dung heap.

The constant cacophony of noise was almost harder to bear than the simmering threat of violence. Joseph yearned for the tranquillity of the rain forest, where the loudest sounds might come from a flock of macaws flying overhead, or from the slap of wooden pestles against hollow gourds as the Xuaxanu women peacefully repeated the ancient process of grinding poison-ous manioc roots into edible flour.

Worse than the casual savagery, or the sour smells, or even the noise, was his feeling of utter helplessness in the face of an intractable criminal justice system. There was so much he needed to do if lives were to be saved, and every day that he remained locked up corroded his reserves of patience.

Joseph's frustration was compounded by his lack of confidence in Pedro Goulart, the lawyer sent by Fer-nando Autunes da Pereira to spring him from jail. A man as powerful as Fernando would never keep an incompetent lawyer on his payroll, but Goulart ap-peared to be incompetence personified. How come? As far as Joseph could see, there were only two possible explanations: Fernando had betrayed him, or Pedro Goulart had betrayed Fernando. Joseph had almost no trouble picking Goulart as the traitor.

Whoever Goulart's paymasters might be, it was clear that Joseph couldn't count on his lawyer for any useful advice. Memorial Day was right around the cor-ner, but at the rate Goulart was going, they'd be cel-ebrating Memorial Day 2020 before the pretrial pa-perwork had been shuffled through the system. The government's case was entirely circumstantial, and any decent lawyer would have made the charges go away within hours, or at most a couple of days. Gou-lart had done nothing, so Joseph tried frantically to get himself another lawyer.

Prisoners awaiting trial were allowed access to a phone four times a week, but prison rules required that all calls be placed collect, and except for the original phone call made when he was arrested, Joseph had never managed to reach Fernando. Since the day of his arrest, there had been no response from the emergency contact number that he and Fernando had set up weeks before Joseph left Manaus. By Friday, he had become so desperate for efficient legal help that he'd actually called Summer, even though he'd sworn to himself that he wouldn't drag her any farther into the war zone that his life had become. Mailing the computer disk from Manaus airport had already involved her far too deeply in his problems, but she was the only person in the world he could trust with something so vital. When she didn't answer his call, he wasn't sure whether to be relieved or sorry.

His desperation had mounted steadily over the weekend, and he was waiting with finger-gnawing impatience to get his two hours of rec time—and access to the phones—when a guard came to the cell and ordered him to get spruced up and dressed in a brand-new uniform.

"You got visitors," the guard said.

"Visitors? Who?"

"Shut the fuck up and get dressed."

Joseph was more than willing to comply. The second he finished changing, the guard—a bull-necked sadist called Erickson—shoved him out of the cell. "Okay, asshole, you'll do. Get walking. Fast."

"Where are you taking me?"

"Don't ask questions." For emphasis, Erickson thwacked him across the calves with his nightstick. "Hurry up. You got important people waiting to see you."

"Who? My lawyer?" Joseph shuffled faster, chains clinking.

"You'll find out. Anyway, I told you no questions." The guard reached out and grabbed a hank of Joseph's

hair, yanking his head around until they were nose to
nose. His breath smelled of garlic and peppermint
chewing gum. "And watch what you say once you get
there, Doctor. You make sure you tell everyone you've
been treated real nice, you hear? Otherwise you're
gonna regret it. You got that?"

"Yes."

"Then don't forget it, asshole." Erickson sounded
scared, which was probably good news. Anything that
scared Erickson was a move in the right direction as
far as Joseph was concerned. His mind raced as he
stumbled along the corridors, his mood shifting from
despair to a hint of hope. The fact that he'd been issued a new uniform suggested that he was going to
meet someone important rather than being hauled off
to another interview with his jackass of a lawyer. The
fact that Erickson was scared confirmed the possibility.

They passed the turnoff that led to the area where
prisoners usually met with their lawyers, and reached
the steel barricade that separated inmates from the reception and administrative areas of the prison. When
Erickson unlocked the massive door, Joseph could no
longer squelch his optimism. Fernando must have used
the power of his enormous wealth to persuade somebody in authority to take action. Thank God! He was
going to meet with somebody competent at last.

The guard paused in front of the final blockade of
floor-to-ceiling steel bars, arranged in a grid of three
gates. He adjusted his collar and straightened the hem
of his jacket, then turned to look at Malone. "You
ready, asshole?"

"Ready for what?"

"Don't get smart with me." Erickson's response

was mechanical and lacked the usual accompanying whack with his nightstick. Tongue protruding from his mouth as he concentrated, he keyed in the code that opened the first barred gate, then repeated the process for the remaining two. He frog-marched Joseph across the entrance lobby to a closed wooden door that was guarded by two men wearing dark suits and white shirts so full of starch that you could see the sheen of crispness clear across the lobby.

Erickson puffed out his chest and stood at attention before he spoke to them. "This here is Joseph Malone, the prisoner that the director wants to speak with. Sorry to have kept you waiting, gentlemen."

The men didn't reply. One of them frisked Joseph with swift efficiency, his shirt crackling as he moved. He nodded to the other. "He's clean. No concealed weapons."

"Okay." The man straightened and dismissed Erickson with a curt nod. "Thanks, we'll take it from here."

"I should escort the prisoner into the boardroom to meet the director. Regulations, sir. A guard is to accompany prisoners at all times in unsecured areas."

"We've taken full responsibility for securing this area, so the rule doesn't apply. You can return to your duties, Erickson. I'm sure you have a lot to do."

"Yessir." The guard shot a look of intense dislike at the two men, but he seemed resigned to his exclusion.

Who the hell could be waiting in the boardroom? Joseph wondered. It had to be somebody really important to arouse this much subservience in a sadist like Erickson.

The two men opened the door they'd been guarding

and fell into step beside Joseph, one on either side of him as they escorted him into the room. The low murmur of voices around the table immediately quieted. Starched shirt number one spoke up. "This is the man you wanted to speak with, sir. Dr. Joseph Malone."

A thin, good-looking man of about fifty rose from his seat at the head of the polished conference table that dominated the room. "Dr. Malone, I'm pleased to meet you. Thank you, Krinsky. I'll take it from here." The man spoke in a low, clear voice, the aura of command sitting comfortably on his narrow shoulders.

"Yes, sir."

"You and Paglino can wait outside. I'll be ready to leave for D.C. in about thirty minutes, if you could inform the pilot."

"Yes, sir." Krinsky and Paglino didn't look much happier at being dismissed than Erickson had, but they exited promptly, without a murmur of protest. Who was this thin, middle-aged guy that he could command such unquestioning obedience? Joseph cast a covert glance at the men seated around the imposing table, searching for clues. There were five of them, all wearing formal dark suits. The only faces he recognized were those of his lawyer and the governor of the prison, who'd delivered a pep talk to prison inmates the previous Sunday.

The man at the head of the table looked at Joseph assessingly, his gaze alert but expressionless. "Dr. Malone, you may be wondering why you've been brought here."

"Yes, sir, I was wondering."

"Let me introduce myself. I'm Julian Stein, director of the Federal Bureau of Investigation, and I've come to ask you some questions. These other gentlemen are

Mr. Simon, the governor of this prison, Agent Perkins, the FBI station chief for Miami, and my personal assistant, Agent Wallace. And you know Mr. Goulart, of course, who is your lawyer and is here to insure that your legal right to counsel is not infringed.''

Holy shit! The director of the FBI! When Fernando finally got around to pulling strings, he certainly pulled some big ones. ''I'm honored to meet you, sir,'' Joseph said. ''Honored and...surprised.''

The FBI director registered no reaction to Joseph's comments. He gestured to a file on the table in front of him. ''I've read the record of your arrest,'' he said. ''Customs officials in Miami discovered fourteen hundred grams of cocaine in your suitcase, Dr. Malone. Do you have anything you'd like to tell me about this incident?''

''There's nothing I can tell you, sir, except that I was set up. I never saw that cocaine until the Customs officials opened my luggage in Miami.''

The director finally showed some emotion. He gave a chilly and sardonic smile. ''How unoriginal your defense is, Dr. Malone. I have yet to encounter a drug courier or dealer who hasn't made the same claim. It seems that the drugs in our country are all being distributed by innocent persons who have no idea how these illegal substances happened to fall into their unsuspecting hands.''

''Maybe my defense is unoriginal, but the truth often sounds like a lie. Think about it, Mr. Director. If I wanted to smuggle cocaine into the United States, why would I be stupid enough to stack it on top of my clean socks, where there's an almost hundred percent certainty that it would be found by the first Customs official who opened my bag?''

"Hubris?" the director suggested. "Many drug couriers believe they're too clever even to be suspected, let alone caught."

"I never saw that cocaine until the Customs officer found it," Joseph repeated.

"Then tell me why you believe the cocaine was in your suitcase, Dr. Malone, if it wasn't placed there by you?"

"Dozens of baggage handlers had access to my luggage between Manaus, Recife and Miami. Obviously, somebody planted that cocaine in my suitcase."

"Why?" the director asked. "Why you?"

"I don't know." Joseph hesitated before admitting at least part of the truth. "But I think it was because having me accused of smuggling drugs was the easiest way to get me locked up the minute I landed on American soil."

The man who'd been introduced as the FBI bureau chief in Miami snorted in disgust. "So now you're asking us to believe not just that you're innocent, but also that there's a bunch of people out there working a conspiracy against you. What's so important about you that somebody would go to such lengths to get you locked up in a federal prison?"

"I don't know." It was only a half lie. He knew exactly why he was important to his enemies, but after ten days of racking his brains, he still couldn't work out why he'd been set up in this precise way. The opposition obviously knew what flight he had taken out of Recife. So even if they didn't want him killed because of the vital information stored inside his head, why hadn't they snatched him from the airport and taken him prisoner where they had direct control over him? Why did they need him locked up in jail?

The hell of it was that until he knew why he'd been locked up, he couldn't begin to guess whom he could trust, and what he could risk saying.

The prison governor spoke up. "Even if we concede that you've got enemies, Dr. Malone, if these mysterious people want you out of the way, why don't they just kill you?"

It was ironic that the governor should echo the precise question Joseph had just asked himself. For a moment he debated explaining what he'd discovered in the hidden depths of the rain forest, and why his enemies needed him alive, but that was too big a gamble. Any one of these men around the table might have been bought off. Goulart almost certainly had been bought off. There wasn't even any way to be totally sure that the man questioning him was the director of the FBI. He had never met the real Julian Stein and this guy could easily be a hired look-alike. Joseph gave a mental groan. Wouldn't his enemies love it if he fell for one of the oldest tricks in the book and confided everything to a group of men in their pay?

The stakes were high enough that he had to consider every possibility.

"I don't know why they set me up," he said finally. "I don't even know who they are. I've offended a lot of people over the past few years, from industrialists to CIA agents. The Amazon seems to be one of those places that makes smart people behave like idiots. I've had a habit of pointing that out, and people don't like it when their stupidity is publicized."

Julian Stein gave him a look that was suddenly speculative. "But I'm here, Dr. Malone, not because you've made a lot of enemies, but because you seem to have acquired some very devoted friends."

*Fernando really had come through for him. Thank God.*

Julian Stein continued. "I understand that you, Dr. Malone, are the leader of an organization known as the Brazilian Justice League."

Joseph frowned, puzzled. "I was leader of the League for three years," he agreed. "But I haven't been active since 1996. In fact, the League hasn't been active—"

Before he could say anything more, Pedro Goulart was on his feet. "Mr. Director, with all due respect, my client needs to be informed why he has been brought here before he answers any further questions about his role as leader of the Brazilian Justice League."

"He has only to tell the truth—"

"And he also has a right under the Fifth Amendment to be protected from unwitting self-incrimination."

Pedro Goulart looked and sounded like an entirely different man from the sleepy, disorganized lawyer that Joseph had previously encountered. "How can I incriminate myself by discussing the Brazilian Justice League?" he asked. "When I was last actively involved with the organization, they'd done nothing illegal. And for the past two years, they've been almost completely inactive."

Goulart walked around the table and fixed his gaze on Joseph's. "You need to trust my advice on this," he said. "The director of the FBI is here to negotiate a deal with you in regard to the charges outstanding against you. I recommend that you listen to the terms of the deal before you respond to any further questions about anything. Don't speak, Dr. Malone, until you know what's at stake here.''

Joseph looked steadily at his lawyer—and saw everything he needed to know about treachery in Goulart's too-innocent brown eyes. "Why don't you want me to answer Mr. Stein's questions about the Justice League?" he asked.

"You misunderstood my advice, Dr. Malone." The lawyer's mild brown eyes glowed with fake integrity. "I cautioned you to find out what is at stake here before you speak. I warn you that if you are too frank, you may regret it later.''

An interesting example, Joseph thought wryly, of a violent threat being hidden in the language of legal caution.

"Mr. Goulart, I appreciate that you're here to protect your client's legal interests," Julian Stein interjected coldly. "However, the government has its own vital interests to pursue, and if Dr. Malone refuses to cooperate, we may not be able to offer him a deal.''

"My lawyer is right to caution me, Mr. Stein." Even if Goulart was a lowlife slug who'd sold out to the opposition, his advice was sound in this instance. "It's my freedom and my life that are at stake here. I need to know why you're asking me these questions. In fact, why are you even here? The director of the FBI doesn't make personal prison visits to settle a case as ordinary as mine. Couriers trying to sneak a kilo of cocaine into Miami are a dime a dozen.''

"I'm here, Dr. Malone, because your friends at the Brazilian Justice League have made you my business. They were unwilling to wait and see if your lawyer could win an acquittal for you. They are demanding your immediate freedom, and they have taken a hostage to pressure the authorities into agreeing to your release from prison. The League has not only given us explicit instructions as to how we are to exchange you for their hostage. They have also given us warnings that their hostage will be executed if we don't comply with their demands and release you.''

Joseph wondered if the FBI director had truly been deceived, or if he knew there wasn't a word of truth in what he'd just said. The Brazilian Justice League was so inefficiently organized that it would take the membership six months to plan a group trip to Disney World. It was absolutely laughable to consider them capable of seizing hostages as a precursor to demanding his release from prison. Quite apart from that, he barely knew the current leader of the League, and wouldn't recognize half of the twenty or so bumbling, well-meaning members. There was no reason on God's green earth for the League to know he was in jail, much less to care how long he stayed there.

Joseph rubbed his forehead, dizzy with confusion. How was he supposed to respond to such a farrago of nonsense? He returned doggedly to his previous question. ''I still don't understand why you're taking a personal interest in the case, sir. I know kidnapping is a federal crime, handled by the FBI, but the director of the bureau doesn't usually get involved with the nitty-gritty of an investigation.''

For the first time, Julian Stein visibly hesitated before replying. ''This is an unusual case,'' he said. ''There are reasons why we might be willing to comply with some of the Justice League demands. Under certain carefully defined circumstances, of course.''

Joseph felt an immediate pang of foreboding. The more he learned, the less he understood what was going on, and the less he trusted anyone in this room. But he knew one thing with absolute certainty. The Brazilian Justice League hadn't kidnapped anyone. They were more likely to break into a zoo and set the snakes free than they were to seize a human hostage and threaten murder.

Before he could decide how to respond, Pedro Goulart intervened again. "The government needs your cooperation, Joseph. That's why the director is here, to request your assistance. I've pointed out to Mr. Stein that the government's case against you is very weak, and he agrees that the evidence is circumstantial and not likely to hold up in court. As you yourself mentioned, baggage handlers at three airports had access to your suitcase and there is absolutely no evidence that you were aware of the presence of any illegal substances in your luggage."

Joseph barely refrained from asking Goulart why it had taken him ten days to work out that the prosecution didn't have a viable case. "If the government doesn't have a case that will stand up in court, then I should be free to go," he said. "Regardless of anything the Justice League may or may not have threatened."

"Mr. Goulart exaggerates the weakness of the government's case," Julian Stein said. "However, we're willing to drop the charges against you in certain circumstances. But before the government agrees to let you out of jail, we need your help to insure the safe return of the Justice League's hostage."

Goulart gave Joseph a friendly pat on the arm. "I'm sure you'll want to help the FBI," he said. "Quite apart from the fact that you're an honest, law-abiding citizen, you have a vested interest in the outcome of this kidnapping. The hostage taken by the Justice League is a young woman you know.''

Joseph felt another premonition of disaster. And a giant flash of fear. "Who is she?" he asked. "Who is the League supposed to have kidnapped?''

''If you really don't know already, it's Summer Shepherd,'' Julian Stein said.

For a moment Joseph couldn't move or breathe. Then he turned and forced Goulart to meet his gaze. ''Summer Shepherd has been taken hostage?''

''Yes.'' Goulart didn't need to elaborate.

''If you didn't understand my personal involvement before, Dr. Malone, I'm sure you understand now.'' Julian Stein sounded as pissed off as he looked. "I hardly need to tell you that the kidnapping of the daughter of the secretary of state raises many issues of national security.''

They've kidnapped Summer. Joseph's brain felt leaden, and the only coherent thought he could grasp was that Summer's life was at risk. Not from the bumbling do-gooders of the Justice League, of course, but from the same shadowy group of enemies who had masterminded his arrest in the first place.

''Joseph, I'm sure this can all be worked out to everyone's satisfaction.'' Pedro Goulart's voice was smooth as snake oil. "I'm sure that the Brazilian Justice League has no interest in hurting Ms. Shepherd. They are only interested in your release from jail and your return to them as their leader and guide. Once you agree to the terms of the exchange, I believe we can count on Ms. Shepherd's return to safety.''

A searing, white-hot flash of enlightenment melted the leaden density of Joseph's brain. Of course! Finally he understood what his arrest was all about! Jesus, he'd been slow on the uptake. Now he understood what was going on—not all of it, but enough to realize that his arrest had simply been the prelude to Summer's kidnapping. The opposition was tired of his refusal to cooperate and they wanted him to know that he was risking a lot more than his own life by his stubborn refusal to hand over the results of his research. He was being given a demonstration of just how far their tentacles reached, even here in the United States. He was being forced to acknowledge that unless he changed sides, Summer would die.

Somehow—God knows how—he managed to keep his face impassive. He turned to his smoothly treacherous lawyer, locking his manacled hands together to hide his suppressed rage. "I'm sure you're going to tell me that it would be in my best interests to agree to the proposed exchange, Mr. Goulart."

"Oh, definitely." The lawyer was all suave professionalism. "The authorities have been quite generous, partly because they realize their case against you is less than strong, partly because they desperately need your cooperation in order to get Ms. Shepherd back. You're in the driver's seat here, Joseph, and I say that in full awareness of the fact that Mr. Stein and various other government officials are listening to our conversation."

"And what are the government's terms if I agree to this exchange?" Joseph asked wearily.

"They agree the drug-smuggling charges will be dropped, and your arrest record expunged in recognition of your willingness to cooperate." The lawyer produced another smile that was all teeth and no heart. "Quite apart from the fact that this is a good deal for you, Joseph, I'm personally convinced it's the best way—perhaps the only way—to insure that Ms. Shepherd is returned swiftly and safely to her family. The Brazilian Justice League is full of political extremists, and we can't discount the possibility that they may do something foolish if we don't comply with their demands."

Goulart knew as well as he did that the Brazilian Justice League was barely a functioning organization, much less a group of political extremists. His enemies had simply expropriated the name. Joseph turned away before he lost control and threw a punch at Goulart's smugly smirking mouth. "I thought the federal government had a strict policy of not negotiating with terrorists," he said to the room at large.

Julian Stein responded. "Policies sometimes conflict. Our first obligation is always to insure the safe release of the hostage."

Joseph noticed that the director hadn't quite answered his question, but he had no reason to press the issue. From his point of view, he hoped to God the man standing in front of him was the real Julian Stein, FBI director, and that he was an incorruptible pillar of honesty. Most of all, he hoped that the FBI had some clever contingency plan up its sleeve so that they'd be able to double-cross the kidnappers and arrest all of them the minute Summer was safely released.

"Where is my exchange for Summer Shepherd supposed to take place?" he asked. "And when?"

"We are still working on the precise details of the exchange," Julian Stein said curtly. "However, time is of the essence, and if you agree to help us, you can count on being out of this prison within thirty-six hours."

"What happens if your agents find where Summer's

being held captive before the exchange can take place?'' Joseph asked. ''Do I still get released?'' If the FBI could find Summer, that might be his only hope of saving her without handing himself over to his enemies.

''That would be only fair, Mr. Director, since my client has been more than willing to cooperate with you.'' Goulart spread his hands in a gesture of appeal. He was real good at faking concern, Joseph thought bitterly.

''On the contrary, I'm quite sure he hasn't told us even a fraction of what he knows,'' Julian Stein said. ''That being so, if the FBI finds Ms. Shepherd before the exchange occurs, the charges against Dr. Malone will be dropped only if I believe he is genuinely cooperating with us.''

''Mr. Director, I protest. Surely you can see that my client is as much an innocent victim as Ms. Shepherd—''

''That's entirely possible,'' Julian Stein said dryly. ''Since I doubt very much that there are any innocent victims in this situation.''

He rose to his feet, handing a slim file of papers to his silent assistant. ''Add these to the official record of this meeting, Wallace, and notify the pilot that I'm on my way. Gentlemen, if you'll all excuse me, I need to get back to Washington as quickly as possible.''

The prison governor stood up, looking none too happy. ''Just a moment more of your time, Mr. Director. I need to know the exact procedure to follow in releasing Dr. Malone from custody. We sure don't want any screwups on this one.''

''Agent Wallace will be in touch with you, Governor, regarding the final details. And don't worry. It'll be clear to everyone that the responsibility for Joseph Malone's release is entirely mine. Nobody's going to find themselves hung out to dry while the heavyweights back in Washington run for cover. And in that context, I remind you that our conversations today are classified as top secret. Those of you in government service understand what that means. Mr. Goulart, you understand that any breach of the secrecy agreement you signed—however small—is an indictable offense? Dr. Malone, you understand that before you are returned to your cell, you will also be required to sign such an agreement?''

"I understand, Mr. Director, and so does my client."

"Good." Stein walked swiftly around the table toward the door, stopping only inches away from Joseph. "I don't like doing deals with criminals, Malone, so when you're reunited with your friends in the Justice League, give them a message from me. Tell them I'll find them. And when I do, I'll put them away for life. You, too, if I find you had any prior knowledge that this kidnapping was going to take place."

Joseph hoped like hell that the FBI director would be able to make good on his threats. Unfortunately, he doubted it. As for his own fate, the threat of more jail time didn't worry him in the least.

He expected to be dead long before anyone involved in the kidnapping of Summer Shepherd was found and brought to justice. He'd just about given up on saving his own skin, much less relieving the world's suffering. Right now, about the best he could hope for was that by willingly surrendering himself to his enemies, he would prevent Summer's execution.

It was far from a sure bet.

# *Seven*

The silence combined with the darkness made it impossible for Summer to keep track of time. She had no idea whether it was day or night, much less how many days and nights had passed since she was kidnapped. Every so often, a vague thought would flit across her mind that she ought to feel frightened, but true fear had vanished along with her sense of time. Disconnected from the most basic forms of human awareness, she had lost the capacity to feel emotion as well as her capacity to think logically. Her world had narrowed to a purgatory of pain and thirst, interrupted by periods of restless sleep, punctuated by nightmares.

In her state of suspended animation, it seemed as if she'd been a prisoner forever. Her walk across the university campus on Sunday morning had long since taken on the misty glow of an ancient memory. The videotaping session seemed to have taken place months ago, although she realized in her brief periods of lucidity that she wouldn't be alive if more than a few days had passed since her last drink of water.

When the silent hands came for her again, releasing her from the tether and hauling her to her feet, she was too emotionally battered to offer even token resistance. The tape around her ankles was cut apart and

she instinctively stepped forward, but after a single
step her legs buckled at the knees and she crumpled
onto the floor.

Her captors responded to her collapse with their
usual mute indifference, pulling her back onto her feet
and dragging her bodily when it became apparent that
she was too disoriented to walk. She didn't try to judge
how far they took her because she was too numb to
care.

She finally heard a jumble of sounds, including the
soft whir of machinery. Earlier in her captivity the
sounds would have been incredibly welcome, but now
they made little impact. Although the act of walking
had marginally revived her, she could only focus in
short bursts, and the whoosh of doors sliding open
barely registered until her stomach swooped, making
her retch. Then she realized they were in an elevator,
traveling rapidly downward.

*Elevator.* The word floated around in her brain for
a few seconds more until she grasped hold of the idea
that if she was in an elevator, she was almost certainly
being moved to a different location. That realization
was sufficient to jolt her into a temporary state of alertness. With supreme effort, she brushed aside her
lethargy and forced herself to concentrate. When she
was rescued—if she was ever rescued—she wanted to
be damn sure she could give the FBI every scrap of
information that might put the bastards who had held
her captive behind bars.

The whooshing noise came again. That must mean
the elevator doors had opened. She'd never realized
how difficult it was to identify sounds when you
couldn't see. Hands grabbed her waist and elbows,
leading her out of the elevator. The floor felt hard

beneath her feet, no longer cushioned by the foam mats of her prison. And it felt warmer down here without air-conditioning, and very humid. Maybe she'd been taken to a basement?

Summer heard a car door open, and the odor of engine oil and gasoline seeped through the hood covering her head. This wasn't just a regular basement, then, but most likely a parking garage. Which tended to confirm her suspicion that she'd been imprisoned in an apartment building.

Great detective work, she told herself with woozy self-mockery. The fact that she might have been held captive in an apartment complex narrowed the search for her place of imprisonment to around twenty million buildings in the continental United States, give or take the odd million. There was a clue the FBI could really run with.

Footsteps clicked across the concrete floor, and she sensed a heightened tension in the people gathered around her, which probably meant the person whose footsteps she'd heard wasn't an ally of the kidnappers. Summer tried to scream for help, but a hand was clamped over her mouth and a car engine was simultaneously turned on, drowning the little grunting sounds she was able to make. Hands seized her—how she loathed the faceless intimacy of those groping hands!—and she was tossed into a cramped space. The trunk of a car? Oh, God, she hoped not. After so much dark and silence, she'd developed a horror of enclosed spaces.

Blindfolded, hands tied, and surrounded by her captors, she could manage no meaningful way to resist. She let her body go limp, feigning unconsciousness as she heard vehicle doors being slammed shut all around

her. It couldn't hurt to fool the kidnappers into thinking she was even more weak and helpless than she
actually was, Summer decided. At the very least, it
might ward off another injection of whatever drug they
were using to keep her tranquilized.

The vehicle moved forward, slowly at first, then
much more rapidly, before swinging into a sharp turn
and presumably heading out of the parking garage.
Because she couldn't see where they were going, Summer didn't know when to brace herself, and her body
rolled around before being brought to an abrupt stop
by a solid object that, like her previous prison area,
felt as if it had been cushioned with heavy-duty foam
floor pads.

The space confining her was too big for the trunk
of a car, Summer decided, fighting against the increasing fuzziness of her thoughts. Maybe she was lying in
the bed of a truck? No, not possible. She wasn't getting any sensation of fresh air blowing over her body,
and if she'd been covered by a tarp, she'd have felt
the weight of it. So where was she? A small bus, possibly, but more likely in the back of some type of van.

With an effort of will that drained her physical resources to their limits, she managed to sit up and fum-
ble around her new prison, defining its boundaries. She
could sense the presence of other humans in the same
general space. In fact, if she kept very still and listened
hard, she could hear the rustle of their movements.
Once, she even heard somebody cough. She concluded
that she was most likely in the rear cargo area of a
minivan, sitting on a giant pad that had been arranged
as a cushion to protect her body from bumps, cuts and
bruises.

The padding suggested that her kidnappers wanted

to prevent her sustaining a serious injury, and yet they were quite willing to inflict pain and mental suffering by keeping her drugged, deprived of food and almost desperate for water. Maybe her addled brain was missing something, but it struck Summer as odd that they should demonstrate such contradictory attitudes. Unless it was simply that they wanted her alive to ransom, but didn't care how much discomfort she endured in the meantime? That was definitely possible.

The van stopped briefly—perhaps for a traffic light—then zoomed forward again. Summer could hear the constant hum of other traffic, which meant that they were traveling along a fairly busy road. Another really useful deduction, she congratulated herself. Now she'd narrowed the search for her former prison from twenty million apartment buildings nationwide, to the approximately nineteen million apartment buildings with nearby access to a busy road.

God, she was thirsty. It was hard to concentrate on anything except how thirsty she was. Summer fantasized about glasses of ice water—large glasses, elephant-size buckets of water—then wished, passionately, that she hadn't allowed herself to think about drinking. Her empty stomach was so busy roiling with nausea that she didn't feel hungry, but her thirst had long since passed through the stage of uncomfortable and progressed to unbearable. Except that it wasn't unbearable, because here she was, enduring it.

Better not to waste her limited energy waxing philosophical. Activity, that's what she needed to take her mind off things. Summer slid onto her back and hunched her knees upward, thrusting her bound wrists into the base of her spine and trying to work some coordination into her flaccid muscles. She hurt everywhere, inside and out, but her arm sockets caused the most pain. Her shoulders felt permanently wrenched because her hands had been tied behind her back for so long and her upper body muscles screamed in loud protest when she forced herself to flex them.

After a while, she was afraid she'd throw up if she continued exercising and she lay still, waiting for her stomach to stop heaving, her eyes staring into the black void behind the hood. A fierce, burning anger gradually took the place of lethargy and self-pity. Dammit, why wasn't she doing a damn thing to make life difficult for her kidnappers? It was all very well to make a conscious decision to cooperate with the kidnappers in hope that she would stay alive long enough for the FBI to find her, but that plan didn't seem to be working. And if humble subservience to your own torture was what it took to stay alive, then maybe it was too high a price to pay, anyway. Time to switch to plan B, she decided.

"I want something to drink," she said belligerently. Or that was what she tried to say. Her throat was so parched that she knew she hadn't managed to articulate a single intelligible word. Of course, the kidnappers totally ignored her, even if they'd heard her, which was just what she should have expected.

Their willful silence made her even more angry. It was pathetic that she had allowed herself to become so weak that she couldn't even shout and annoy her captors. She hauled herself into a sitting position and tried to visualize the rear cargo compartment of a Dodge Caravan, which was the only minivan she'd ever traveled in. The solid objects on either side of her to the left and right must be the rear door and the back bench seat. The big bumps at her head and feet must be the housing for the rear wheels. She vaguely remembered that the rear bench seat in a Dodge Caravan was removable, and that there had been various levers and latches to make this removal possible. Presumably other minivans had a similar configuration. Which would explain why the kidnappers had padded the rear of the van so thoroughly. They didn't want her to gouge out an eye, or some other body part, on a protruding seat latch.

Her thoughts wandered away into a surrealistic daydream of dancing eyeballs impaled on hooks, and it took her a while to bring herself back and reassemble the reality of her situation. What had she been doing when her mind wandered off into la-la land? Oh, yes—she'd been trying to find a protruding seat latch. Summer fumbled around with her bound hands, searching for the latch, and gave a triumphant squeak when she found it. Now what? Closing her eyes to shut out the darkness, listening to the hum of traffic, she tried to remember why she'd wanted to find the latch in the first place.

Then it came to her. She wanted to use it as a hook. The hood was simply a square of black cloth, draped over her head and fastened around her neck with athletic tape. The tape was wound securely, but not so tight that it risked choking her. If her hands had been untied, or even if they'd been tied in front of her, she'd have been able to pull the blindfold off without difficulty. However, since her hands were tied behind her, removing it was impossible. But it should be fairly easy to hook the seat latch under the folds at the nape of her neck and jerk until the tape broke, at which point she would be able to pull the hood off—and see exactly where she was.

Summer squirmed and wriggled until she had the seat lever hooked under the hood. She jerked her head sideways, winced when she yanked at a tangled hank of hair, then gritted her teeth and repeated the procedure until, as she'd expected, the tape finally snapped and the blindfold was left hanging loosely over her head. Feeling triumphant, she shook her head until it tumbled into her lap.

She could see again! God, the world looked wonderful even though it was night. She'd never realized that a dark interstate highway could be so magnificently beautiful. She drank in the flash of passing cars, the road signs, the exit ramp leading to a gas station and a twenty-four-hour diner. A sign gleamed in the headlights of the van. Savannah, 10 Miles.

They were going south on Interstate 95, heading for Savannah, Georgia. Summer drew in a sharp breath and clamped her lips together to prevent herself crying out with relief. Her whole world took on sharper definition now that she knew where she was.

Having brought herself out of the land of nightmares and back into the real world, she turned her attention from the road to the vehicle she was traveling in. It was a minivan, as she'd suspected, and the gray interior was configured more or less as she'd remembered from the trip in her friend's Dodge Caravan. There were three rows of seating, with four men occupying the first two rows. Thank goodness the rear bench seat was empty, or they would have noticed long ago that she was not only conscious, but actively working to remove her blindfold. The driver and the man in the front seat were awake, the other two were slumped in their seats, dozing. None of the men seemed to be carrying a gun, but with four of them and one of her, they didn't need to. Realistically, her chances of escape rated right around zero.

In the darkness, it was impossible to make out the individual features of her kidnappers, except for the man sitting in the front passenger seat, whose profile was illuminated by the headlights of the oncoming traffic. She studied him intently until he suddenly turned to look toward the back of the car, as if alerted by some sixth sense to her wakefulness.

Summer ducked with lightning speed as it dawned on her that in removing the hood she'd done something incredibly dangerous. She was damned lucky the two men in the second row of seats were no more than half-awake. If the kidnappers ever realized that she'd glimpsed their faces, she'd never survive this car ride alive, much less be released to give a description of them to the FBI.

When the car didn't stop and nobody came to check on her, she slowly inched upright again, determined to take another look at her captors. Despite the risk, she stared long and hard at the man whose face she could see most clearly, imprinting his broad forehead, snub nose and full-lipped mouth on her mind's eye. Then, with extreme care, she scrunched down below the level of the rear seat, out of the kidnappers' range of vision.

She was mentally congratulating herself when a frightening new problem presented itself. How in the world was she going to get her head back under the hood? With her bound hands, it would be a lot more difficult to put on than it had been to take it off. The best solution she could come up with was to nudge the hood—now not much more than a shapeless piece of cloth—to a position on the padded floor of the van that would be close to her head when she was lying down and hope that she'd be able to wriggle into it.

She wasted at least half an hour and exhausted her diminished reserves of energy before she gave up and acknowledged that her head was never going to be inserted back into the hood that way. She tried to think of some other method of getting the blindfold on, but her problem-solving skills were hampered by the renewed waves of dizziness threatening to overtake her. She was drifting toward another bout of unconsciousness when she was brought abruptly to full alertness as the van shifted direction and her shoulder bumped painfully against the steel struts that supported the rear seat.

Summer realized that the minivan was slowing as it followed a curved exit off the highway, and suddenly the kidnappers began to talk among themselves. She was shocked to realize that they were speaking Portuguese. She knew just enough of the language to recognize the odd word, but not enough to have a clue what the men were saying. She struggled to readjust her ideas about who her captors might be. She'd fallen into the trap of stereotyping, and had assumed they were Islamic fundamentalists with a fierce hatred of American policies in the Middle East. It was disconcerting to discover they were nothing of the kind. Why would people from Portugal or Brazil want to kidnap her, for heaven's sake? She wasn't a political junkie, to put it mildly, but off the top of her head she couldn't think of any radical Portuguese or Brazilian groups that were so strongly opposed to U.S. government policies that they'd kidnap and imprison the daughter of the secretary of state to get their message across.

Still, right now, what motivated these people was a

hell of a lot less important than getting the blindfold back on and saving her skin. Portuguese, Brazilian or aliens from Mars, it hardly mattered. She was going to be in really deep trouble if they stopped the van to check on her and realized that she'd seen them. Desperation finally gave rise to inspiration. Summer grabbed the hood with her teeth, hung it back on the seat latch and wriggled herself into position beneath the opening. She had the blindfold over her eyes and nose but not her mouth when the car stopped—and her heart right along with it.

In seconds, the kidnappers would surely be checking up on her. Impelled by sheer survival instinct, Summer gave up on her attempts to push the hood over her chin. She lay down and rolled onto her side, facing inward, her head wedged right up against the steel bars that kept the back seat locked into position. When they opened the rear hatch, the kidnappers would be presented with a view of her back, her bound hands and a blindfold that covered the top three quarters of her head. With a bit of good luck, they would assume that the movement of the car while she was asleep had jolted her and somehow caused the tape on the hood to snap.

The front doors of the car opened and she heard the men get out, gravel crunching beneath their feet. Not moving, willing her bound hands to lie limply behind her, she waited while the latch on the cargo door was sprung.

Please, God, let them believe that I'm asleep. Or better yet, unconscious.

One of the kidnappers reached into the cargo hold and rolled her onto her back. The hood moved as she rolled but, by a miracle, remained in place over most

of her face. Of course, the man examining her noticed
right away that the athletic tape had been broken. He
gave a sharp exclamation and jerked her upright, pulling her out of the van.

Summer shivered, her full capacity to feel fear returning in a thundering cascade of terror. She couldn't
give them time to wonder how the hood had come
loose or whether she'd seen their faces, she thought
frantically. If they started to question her, she was lost.
She stiffened and jerked away from the kidnapper's
prying hands as if just returning to full consciousness.

"I want a drink," she croaked. Seized by inspiration, she pretended to faint, crumpling right where she
stood to make her collapse appear authentic. Fortunately, she encountered the support of a human body
before she hit the ground. After a few seconds, she
stirred in the kidnapper's arms, feigning revival. "I
need water. I'm dying..."

Of thirst, she'd been going to say until it occurred
to her that a little melodrama might be her best hope
of avoiding disastrous questions and getting a drink.
She stopped in midsentence. Let them fret and wonder
if their bargaining chip was going to die on them.

The kidnappers exchanged several sharp, incomprehensible sentences. Their policy of silence seemed to
have been abandoned, which meant that wherever
they'd stopped the van there was no one around to
overhear them or to ask awkward questions about what
four men were doing escorting a woman with hands
tied behind her back and wearing a black hood over
her head.

The discussion among the kidnappers ended
abruptly. Footsteps crunched in the gravel, a car door
was opened and shut. Then hands grasped her by the

shoulders. "I need to drink," she mumbled, only half feigning desperation. "Please…"

Nobody replied. So what else had she expected? Feeling forlorn, she submitted numbly as the blindfold was gathered around her neck and taped into place far more firmly than before. Summer swayed, this time genuinely on the verge of fainting. Maybe she'd got it all wrong and her captors didn't care if she died. Why else were they so brutally depriving her of water?

She was sunk so far in despair that it took her a second or two to register that one of the kidnappers was speaking to her. "If you want to drink, hold completely still while we make an opening in the mask near your mouth. Nod if you've understood what I'm saying. We don't want to cut your face."

Summer was too thrilled at the possibility of getting a drink to wonder at this further evidence of the kidnappers' concern to avoid her injury. She nodded eagerly, holding herself still while one of her captors cut a slit in the hood with a razor-sharp knife blade. A gloved hand reached out, fumbling before getting a straw inserted into her mouth through the small opening in the cloth.

She sucked avidly, terrified that they'd snatch the cup away after a couple of sips. She gulped the liquid so fast that it was a few seconds before she discovered that she was drinking not just water, but apple juice. Summer was sure that never, in the entire history of the universe, had lukewarm juice tasted so wonderful. She kept expecting the supply to run out, or the straw to be yanked away, but the kidnappers had obviously decided that she was in serious danger of dehydration and they let her drink her fill before she was bundled back into the van, replete to the point that she could almost feel the juice circulating through her parched body, revitalizing her.

The driving resumed within seconds of her return to the van, and since she didn't dare remove the blindfold again, she had no idea where they were headed. If they continued straight south from Savannah, they'd eventually reach Florida. Was that their destination? Miami would be a good city to hide her in from the kidnappers' point of view. Perhaps they were planning to stash her on a houseboat, hidden like Andrew Cunanan. Or maybe they were planning to smuggle her across the narrow stretch of ocean that separated mainland Florida from the island of Cuba. Maybe the kidnappers were Cuban expatriates, not Portuguese or Brazilian citizens. The language she heard them speaking might have been Spanish, not Portuguese. God knew, in her current ditzy state of mind, she could easily confuse the two, which were very similar to a person with a tin ear for languages, which she definitely had.

Cuban kidnappers made much more sense than Brazilian ones. The daughter of the secretary of state would surely be a useful bargaining chip for one of those crazy Cuban exile groups that had been trying for years and years to persuade the American government to send an invading army into Cuba, or at the very least to dispatch CIA operatives to assassinate Fidel Castro.

On the other hand, she had no logical grounds for assuming the van was headed toward Miami. She wasn't even sure they were still driving south. For all she knew, they could have turned back on themselves and be traveling a circuitous route north to Canada. The harsh truth was that she'd expended a lot of effort and energy to get rid of her blindfold, but her struggles didn't amount to diddly-squat in terms of useful information.

Summer realized she was crying, not from fear but from sheer, gut-churning frustration. Hostages were supposed to come up with brilliant schemes to rescue themselves. They weren't supposed to lie in the back of a minivan, cravenly waiting for "somebody" to rescue them. Unfortunately, however hard she tried to come up with an escape plan of her own, her brain remained stubbornly blank, empty of even a whiff of creative plotting. She was a real wimp, Summer concluded gloomily, and a self-pitying wimp to boot.

The euphoria induced by the drink of apple juice dissipated, leaving Summer no more than semiconscious. After what seemed like several hours, the van slowed to a bumpy stop and she was abruptly jolted back to full alert. She registered belatedly that they hadn't been driving on a smooth highway for some time. The noise of traffic was incredibly loud, and when the minivan doors were opened, gusts of sound swept toward her in deafening waves.

It wasn't the roar of regular road traffic she was hearing, Summer realized groggily, but the whirring rotor blades of a helicopter. Her spirits rose. A helicopter seemed like a very promising sign. She hoped to God the chopper was loaded with FBI agents swarming to her rescue, and that she was soon going to have the supreme pleasure of watching her kidnappers get carted off to jail, preferably en route to the gas chamber. After the events of the past few days, Summer was ready to reconsider her lifelong opposition to the death penalty.

The hatch door opened and a blast of warm, humid

air rushed into the air-conditioned coolness of the van. This time her blindfold was pulled off at the same time as hands reached for her, and as soon as she was on her feet, a knife sliced through the duct tape around her wrists. Summer breathed a relieved sigh. This had to be the FBI. Thank God, they'd found her before she could be carted off to Cuba or wherever. Smiling and blinking against the early-morning sun, she turned to greet her rescuer.

"Put this on," a voice yelled in her ear.

Shielding her eyes from the light, Summer looked up and found herself eyeball to eyeball with Richard Nixon, who was holding out an orange jacket made of heavy-duty reinforced nylon. Shocked by the surreal sight of a dead president handing her a life jacket, she blinked and instinctively stepped backward, only to find her passage blocked by John F. Kennedy. Her mind froze in rejection of what she was seeing.

When President Ronald Reagan stepped forward from behind a clump of bushes and began shoving her arms into the sleeveless orange jacket, her mind jolted back into action. Whoever these people were, they sure as hell weren't an FBI rescue team. Belatedly, she struggled to get away but didn't manage to do much beyond landing a glancing punch on Reagan's jaw.

When her fist brushed against Reagan's face, she felt the latex covering his chin and finally understood that she wasn't having visions of dead presidents, she was seeing criminals wearing highly realistic masks to disguise their appearance. Reagan, completely un-scathed by her punch, pushed her against the side of the minivan and finished lacing up the jacket without even bothering to rebuke her. As he started to march her toward the helicopter she could see Gerry Ford, Harry Truman and Jimmy Carter unloading submachine guns from the helicopter and stashing them into a Humvee. Her kidnappers, she decided, had a very sick sense of humor.

"Duck," Reagan ordered her as they approached the chopper, which was marked with the insignia of Medivac, and bore the logo of Mercy Memorial Hospital, in Lakeland, Florida. Summer didn't even try to understand why her kidnappers were flying a medical rescue helicopter. Reagan put his hand on top of her head and pushed to make sure she got the message that she needed to stay low. "Hurry."

"Where are you taking me?" The question was sheer wasted breath, drowned in the roar of the whirring chopper blades.

President Ford was waiting inside the helicopter to pull her in. President Eisenhower was at the controls, and he lifted off the moment she and Reagan were seated, leaving Truman, Kennedy, Carter and Nixon on the ground, along with the Humvee and the minivan that had been used for the journey south. Reagan fastened his seat belt and gestured for her to do the same, indicating the headphones draped over the arm of her seat. Summer put them on because there seemed nothing to gain by refusing, except a considerable chance that she'd go deaf.

Reagan's voice rumbled in her ears. "Welcome aboard, Ms. Shepherd. Lean back and relax in comfort. We have a twenty-minute flight to our destination."

"Where are we going?" She couldn't help asking the question again, even though she expected to be ignored.

Surprisingly, Reagan chose to respond. "We're going to Mason Airport,'' he said. "It's an abandoned airstrip, dating back fifty years, located twenty-five miles northeast of Orlando, Florida.''

"Why are we going there?''

"You'll find out,'' Reagan said.

Summer was tired of cryptic answers, tired of being a prisoner, tired of feeling hungry, sick and in pain, but there was nothing she could do to force Reagan to respond more intelligibly. In fact, there was nothing she could do to effect any change in her situation. She'd been way too arrogant in the past, she acknowledged ruefully. In future, if she ever regained her freedom, she'd be a lot more tolerant of people who claimed to be helpless victims of their circumstances.

Right now, the only thing she could do that might improve her situation was to work on restoring some of her physical strength. She leaned back in the seat, consciously forcing herself to relax. Massaging her wrists and flexing her ankles, she wondered how far toward recuperation she could bring her abused body in the space of twenty minutes. She had to pin any faint hope of escape on whatever was going to happen at Mason Airport, and she was determined that if any chance came to flee, she'd find the strength to force her legs to run as hard and fast as necessary to carry her to freedom.

The three men in the helicopter ignored her armchair aerobics, which suited Summer just fine. Even though their presidential masks remained fixed in permanent grins, the tension that overtook them was palpable as they flew over the outskirts of a city. The houses and streets down below must be the outer suburbs of Orlando, Summer concluded, at least if Reagan had been truthful about where they were going.

"Mason Field is at one o'clock," the pilot said, finally speaking loudly enough for her to hear. He sounded American, with no hint of a foreign accent, the first of her kidnappers who hadn't been able to cut her out of the information loop by speaking Portuguese. "I've scanned the area, and I can't detect any visible military or police presence."

Gerald Ford grunted. "The FBI is too smart to put cops right there at the airport where we can see them. But you can bet they have plenty of backup troops they can call on. Mark my words, they'll have police blocks on every road within minutes of our arrival."

"Then it's lucky our immediate plans don't call for road travel, isn't it?" Reagan unbuckled his seat belt and came over to Summer. "Well, here we are, Ms. Shepherd, and right on schedule. How fortunate that the flying weather is so good today."

"What are you going to do here?"

Reagan spread his hands, as if the answer to her question was obvious. "We are going to pick up our ransom and you are going to return to your friends and family."

"You're letting me go?" Summer didn't even try to hide her amazement.

"Yes, we are letting you go. We are generous people, are we not?"

Summer tried to absorb the stunning fact that the moment of her release had come, and that she was not only alive, but basically unharmed and in possession of all ten fingers and toes. "Does that mean my father was able to meet your ransom terms?"

"He tells us that he has done so. For your sake, Ms. Shepherd, let us hope that he speaks the truth. Lean forward, please. I need to attach this safety harness to your life jacket.''

Summer had never flown in a helicopter, but she'd seen plenty of news clips and movies with people getting in and out of helicopters. Nobody on TV or in the movies had ever needed a safety harness and a life jacket. ''Why do I need a safety harness?'' she asked, seized by sudden foreboding.

''You'll find out.'' Reagan attached a giant steel locking clip to the webbing of her jacket. The clip was, in turn, attached to a thin cable that was wound around a winch welded to the central floor area of the chopper cabin. Summer's foreboding gave way to a horrifying flash of comprehension.

They weren't going to land. They were going to suspend her hundreds of feet above the ground on a cord, hooked to her life vest, and winch her down to the ground.

If she didn't die because the cable snapped, she'd almost certainly die of a terror-induced heart attack. She gulped, hoping Reagan couldn't see that she was shaking. ''Why don't you just land the helicopter and let me walk away?''

''Because we are kidnappers and we can reasonably assume that the American government intends to capture us if they can.'' Reagan's smiling mask contrasted oddly with the sneering contempt of his voice. ''We, on the other hand, intend to get out of here alive and unharmed, with the prize we came to claim. And you, Ms. Shepherd, are both our bargaining chip and our passport to safety.''

Neither of those roles sounded very appealing, but Summer didn't waste her energy protesting. She needed all of that for indulging in a full-fledged attack of panic. As fun activities went, hanging from a helicopter on the end of a thin cable ranked right up there with having red-hot shards of metal pushed under her fingernails.

She made the mistake of looking down and saw a weed-strewn runway leading to a ramshackle hangar. The ground looked very far away. A Humvee waited on one side of the tarmac. As she watched, another Humvee approached from the opposite side of the runway. Three men got out of the first vehicle, one of them wearing a bright orange jail uniform. Four men got out of the second vehicle, all of them armed.

The two sets of men lined up on opposite sides of the tarmac, weapons aimed at each other. It seemed safe to assume that one Humvee had disgorged allies of the kidnappers, and the other Humvee had disgorged government agents who had come to ransom her. But who was the man in the prison uniform? Maybe a political prisoner who was being swapped for her. Although "political prisoner" was likely to be a euphemism for political terrorist, since his cronies were willing to resort to kidnapping and threats of murder in order to get him released.

Gerald Ford twisted in his seat, then adjusted a pair of binoculars and focused them on the man in the orange jail uniform. He studied the prisoner and the other men on the ground for several moments before saying something in Portuguese and handing the binoculars to Reagan.

Reagan took the binoculars and studied the man in jail uniform for at least a minute. *"Concordo,"* he said. *"Com certeza, e Malone."* He handed the binoculars back to Ford.

Summer finally understood what was being said and

silently translated the two simple sentences. "I agree," Reagan had said. "It's Malone for sure."

Malone? The kidnappers couldn't possibly be talking about Joseph Malone, could they? No, it was ridiculous—impossible—to imagine Joe being in jail. Almost as ridiculous as imagining him being involved in her kidnapping. The fact that Joe had been living in Brazil and that her kidnappers were speaking Portuguese made for a weird coincidence, but nothing more.

Summer squinted toward the ground, trying to get a better view of the man in the orange jumpsuit. She was too far away to identify his features, but he had reddish brown hair like Joe, and his height and wiry build were about right. Still, she refused to believe it was Joe down there, dressed in a prison uniform. If it was Joe, the final remnants of her faith in a rational world would vanish.

And it simply couldn't be Duncan Ryder standing next to Joe with a submachine gun nestled in the crook of his arm. If the sight of Joe Malone and Duncan Ryder standing shoulder to shoulder on a deserted airfield in rural Florida boggled her mind, then the sight of Duncan Ryder holding a submachine gun pushed her sanity to its uttermost edge—and beyond. There were limits to how far she could stretch her imagination before deciding that her mind had flown the coop and she was in the midst of a horrible, drug-induced nightmare.

The pilot spoke rapidly into his microphone, issuing what sounded like a series of terse instructions to his cronies on the ground. He spoke in English again, but she guessed he must be using a prearranged code, since she could make no sense of what he was saying.

Ford and Reagan, on the other hand, seemed to understand him perfectly. They exchanged glances and nodded, as if the pilot's instructions were some sort of signal.

"Okay, Ms. Shepherd, time to go flying," Ford said, getting to his feet.

"Here we go, Ms. Shepherd. Enjoy the ride." Reagan grabbed her headphones and threw them into the rear of the chopper. Without giving her time to react in any way, he and President Ford lifted her bodily out of her seat and thrust her out of the door, holding her suspended but immobile for a couple of minutes while the helicopter stabilized. Then he released the cable.

Sailing through space, Summer shut her eyes, muttered a prayer and accepted that she was going to die. Whatever elaborate ransom scheme had been worked out wouldn't matter, because by the time somebody removed her from this aerial meathook, she'd be deader than a slab of cooked bacon.

After an eternity of terror, the cord—her lifeline—tautened and held. Suspended twenty feet above the ground, swaying in the early-morning breeze, Summer realized to her total astonishment that she was still alive. Drawing in a shaky lungful of air, she promised herself that if by any amazing and totally unforeseen chance she actually survived this kidnapping, she was never going to waste another second of her life sweating the small stuff. And, in comparison to hanging from a helicopter, with two rival sets of gunmen below you on the tarmac, everything was small stuff.

Glancing down, she saw the man in the orange prison suit start to walk forward, his progress impeded by the steel leg shackles he was wearing. Her eyesight was significantly impaired by terror, but at a distance of twenty feet, there was almost no room left for doubt about the man's identity. The prisoner being ransomed was Joseph Malone—and the man standing guard with a submachine gun was indeed Duncan Ryder.

She tried to scream a warning—there was no way Joe could be an ally of the bastards who'd kidnapped her—but he didn't look up. Oh, God, what should she do? Much as she wanted to be released, she didn't want to win her freedom at the expense of handing Joe over to her kidnappers.

She screamed his name again, but she was far enough from the ground that there was absolutely nothing she could do to stop him walking across the no-man's-land of empty tarmac. She watched helplessly as Joe halted in the middle of the tarmac while somebody in the helicopter winched her closer and closer to the ground.

When her feet were just about level with the top of Joe's head, he looked up at her and said something.

"I can't hear you," she said desperately.

"Go to…"

His words were swallowed up in the roar of chopper blades. Before he could speak again, two masked gunmen grabbed him by the arms and dragged him toward the Humvee that waited with its engine revving. Simultaneously, Duncan Ryder sprinted toward her, but as he reached out to grasp her ankles, she was jerked rapidly upward and the helicopter swung away toward the east. As they flew, she could feel herself being drawn up into the plane as the cable was winched back to a shorter and shorter length. On the ground, she could see Joe and the four gunmen piling into the Humvee, which took off in a hail of submachine gunfire from Duncan and his partner, before disappearing into the same area of tropical swamp from which it had appeared.

Below her, she heard voices shouting and the stampede of running feet as the helicopter flew higher, carrying her away to captivity. Despite the rage Duncan and the other government agent must be feeling at the duplicity of her captors, not a single shot was fired at the helicopter, presumably because they couldn't bring it down without killing her right along with the kidnappers. Reagan had called her their passport to freedom, and he'd been right about that, Summer reflected bitterly. Obviously, the kidnappers had never planned to set her free. They were going to haul her back on board the helicopter and she would be a prisoner once again. Until she became too much of a nuisance to keep hidden and they decided to simplify their lives by killing her, which would be the one sure way to guarantee that she could never testify against them.

For some reason, Reagan and Ford didn't haul her all the way back inside the plane. Instead they left her dangling less than two feet below the belly of the aircraft. The helicopter was flying about a hundred feet up in the air so that even if Summer could have unhooked herself from the safety latch—an impossibility—she would simply have fallen to her death. She wondered how long the kidnappers would keep her dangling in space, and if this was a necessary part of their escape plan or simply a new form of tormenting her.

But she soon discovered that torture wasn't the kidnappers' goal. When the helicopter cleared the lake and swamp that bordered the eastern boundary of the airport, the pilot made a sudden sharp turn and began a rapid descent toward the ground. Summer's feet were touching solid earth before she fully grasped what was happening. She just had time to cover her head with her hands and throw herself face forward into a stretch of velvet-smooth grass before the cable was cut loose from the winch and the two-foot remnant landed across her back with a stinging lash.

As soon as she was cut free, the helicopter quickly rose high in the sky, circled once, then disappeared over the horizon, the roar of its engines and rotor blades fading, leaving behind the quiet of a peaceful morning.

Summer rolled over onto her back and stared at the empty sky. After several stunned minutes of blank, unmoving silence, she sat up, flung her arms wide and laughed out loud from sheer, incredulous relief. She was battered, bruised, exhausted, dirty, hungry and freaked out. She was also free.

And sitting, she realized, in the middle of the putting green on the thirteenth hole of a golf course.

# *Eight*

More than an hour had already passed since the failure of their attempt to ransom Summer, and tension at the command post in the U.S. Marshal's Orlando office was rising rapidly. Tempers hovered somewhere between barely controlled and outright explosive, with the cramped space of their makeshift quarters adding to the general level of frustration.

Having completed the grim task of calling Gordon Shepherd to inform him that Summer not only remained in the hands of the Justice League, but that the government no longer had Joseph Malone in custody, Duncan was left with nothing more useful to do than curse, pace, sweat and then curse some more. He knew that he appeared calmer than anyone else in the overheated room, but in reality, he was close to losing it. His brain had long since zoomed into overdrive and his body thrummed with the need for action—preferably the chance to beat the crap out of Joseph Malone or one of his cronies.

Duncan poured himself yet another mug of black coffee and ignored the acid churning in his stomach as he slugged it down. He listened as Wes Perkins, the FBI station chief from Miami and designated commander of Operation Rescue, tried to explain to Julian Stein, back in Washington, precisely why and how

Summer had eluded them. Wes was obviously being given a hard time by the director and was hanging on to the remnants of his temper with visible difficulty. In retrospect, blame was easy to assign, and there sure was plenty to spread around.

Things weren't going any better for Rodney Hubbard, the U.S. marshal who had escorted Joseph Malone to Mason Field. Hubbard was becoming increasingly crabby as negative reports poured in from the deputies and other law enforcement officials who were manning road blocks and checkpoints on the roads around Mason. As for the hastily assembled aerial surveillance team, it was having no better luck than the officers working the road blocks, which wasn't surprising given the acres of dense foliage where the Humvee could potentially be hidden.

In Duncan's opinion, all this activity was pissing into the wind. Common sense suggested that Malone and his pals would have ditched the Humvee within minutes of leaving Mason Field. By now, the kidnappers had split up and were most likely disguised as harmless tourists, driving inconspicuous family sedans, heading undetected toward Miami, Orlando or Tampa. It was surely no coincidence that the Justice League had chosen a ransom location that was close to three major international airports with flights leaving hourly for all major foreign cities.

At this point, there was only one question that really interested Duncan. Was Summer going willingly with Malone or was she being coerced? As far as Hubbard and Perkins were concerned, the answer to that question was a no-brainer. The only reason Summer hadn't been released was because she didn't want to be. Duncan saw the logic of their opinions, but he couldn't bring the picture of Summer as criminal extortionist into focus. Maybe years of unrequited love had fried his brain, but he refused to believe that Summer was capable of plotting her own kidnapping.

When his cell phone rang, he jumped to answer it, glad of almost any relief from his paralyzing sense of uselessness. "Yes, this is Duncan Ryder."

Gordon Shepherd spoke tersely. "Duncan, I just had a call from Summer."

The vice squeezing Duncan's gut eased fractionally. "Thank God! Are you sure it was Summer? How did she sound?"

"A little hoarse and very tired, but otherwise okay. And yes, I'm sure it was Summer. She repeated an anecdote from her childhood that nobody could know except the two of us."

Duncan waved his hand to quiet the swell of voices all around him. "What are the new ransom terms? Any chance we can comply?"

"There are no new terms for us to meet." Gordon sounded subdued. "Apparently, she's already been set free."

"She's free? Gordon, that must be a hoax—"

"No, she insisted she wasn't under any sort of duress when she called, and she gave me a number to call back so that I could confirm her location."

"*What?*" Duncan could hear the incredulity in his own voice reverberate through a room that was suddenly silent. "Then where is she?"

"She was calling from the Royal Palms Country Club in Cocoa Beach. Apparently, the kidnappers set her free on the thirteenth green of the golf course—"

"They left her on a golf course?" Duncan was too stunned to do anything more than parrot Gordon's words. "How did they do that without getting caught?"

"According to Summer, they brought the helicopter down low, cut her loose as soon as she had her feet firmly on the grass, then flew away again."

The Justice League, no fools, had worked out that they had a lot less chance of being captured if they set Summer free miles away from Mason Field—which they must have realized was loaded with commandos. The helicopter would certainly have been fired on if Summer had ever been cut loose from that damned cable. Duncan rubbed his forehead in frustration, then felt his mouth stretch into a slow, wide grin. "Well, she's free and I guess that's all that matters right now. This is fantastic news, Gordon. Did the kidnappers treat her okay? Has she been checked out by a doctor?"

"She insisted she doesn't need medical help and I didn't attempt to change her mind. I don't need to tell you that we're in a very delicate situation here, and the fewer people involved the better. I've warned Summer that it's imperative no word of her kidnapping should leak to the media."

Duncan frowned. "Isn't it already too late for secrecy, sir? A lot of people at the golf club must be aware of her story and we can't stop them talking to journalists."

"I hope it's not too late. Summer indicated that she hadn't spoken to anyone when she contacted me, except to request the use of a phone from the general manager."

"So how did she explain turning up on the thirteenth green of a private golf club without mentioning that she was kidnapped? Besides, somebody must have noticed the helicopter landing on the putting green!''

"Apparently nobody saw her arrival. It was very early, remember, and the course doesn't open for play until eight. A landscape crew found her wandering on one of the cart routes and escorted her back to the club, but none of them spoke English, so she didn't have to explain herself to them. Then, somehow, she persuaded the club manager not to call either the police or the paramedics.''

"That's a miracle in itself.''

"One we should take advantage of. Naturally, I warned her to say absolutely nothing more until you arrive. We have to keep this under wraps, Duncan, for Summer's sake as much as anyone's. Publicity would be a disaster for her and a real threat to national security. The last thing we want is for every kook and weirdo in the world to start thinking how easy it is to pressure the government by kidnapping relatives of cabinet officials.''

"I realize the importance of keeping the media away from Summer—''

"It's not just important, it's absolutely essential.'' Gordon's voice rose anxiously. He cleared his throat, struggling for control. "I'm counting on you, Duncan, to keep this whole unfortunate incident under wraps.''

"Yes, sir. I understand.'' Duncan keyed in the commands to change the map displayed on his laptop computer from the Orlando area to Cocoa Beach. He turned to maximum magnification and spotted the Royal Palms Country Club almost at once. "Okay, I've found the golf club. It's located close to the highway, so it shouldn't take more than an hour to make the drive from here. If there's nothing else you need to tell me, I'll get started right away—''.

"I do have one more thing.'' Gordon not only sounded worried and exhausted, he also sounded depressed. "I don't want to say too much at this point, but Julian Stein is very hostile, and he's threatening to press conspiracy charges against Summer. Get her back to Washington as soon as you can, will you?''

"Yes, of course. We'll take a couple of hours to get back to MacDill Air Force Base—''

"No, don't bother with driving back to Tampa. Go directly to Patrick Air Force Base in Cocoa Beach. I'll arrange transportation from there. I've already cleared a landing for you at Andrews. I'll expect to meet you both there in less than four hours. And Duncan—''

"Yes?''

"Tell everyone that Summer is in no condition to answer questions. Everyone specifically includes Wesley Perkins. He'll undoubtedly insist on flying back with you from Cocoa Beach, but don't let him question Summer. We don't want to provide him with ammunition he can pass on to the director.''

"I understand.'' All too well, Duncan thought grimly. Gordon, along with everyone else, was obviously wondering whether his daughter had been a victim or a conspirator. "I'm on my way to the Royal Palms Country Club right now, and I'll call you again as soon as I've seen Summer. Don't worry, Gordon. I'll take care of everything.''

As expected, Wes Perkins and Rodney Hubbard both insisted on going with him to retrieve Summer. Duncan didn't protest. As chief marshal and head of the regional FBI office, they had every right to accompany him, and he would only arouse their suspicions if he tried too obviously to keep them away from Summer. Besides, if they were safely under his nose it would be easier to limit the amount of trouble they could cause. Whatever Summer's role in the kidnapping might turn out to have been, he intended to persuade both men that it wasn't in anyone's interest to let word of the incident leak out to the media. The Brazilian Justice League had won every round of this fight, and there was no beneficial spin that could be put on the unpalatable facts.

Wes elected to drive them in his official car. They drove right at the speed limit, without holdups, until they were stopped at a police checkpoint, fifteen miles east of Orlando. Perkins showed his FBI identification, and they were waved on by a harassed-looking state trooper.

"All we're doin' with those road blocks is wasting the taxpayers' money," Hubbard grouched as they accelerated away from the stop. He'd been a sheriff for twenty years before his appointment as U.S. marshal for southern Florida, and he spoke with a strong Southern accent. "Those sons of bitches aren't drivin' that fancy Humvee around Florida anymore. No, sir, they're in a jet plane, fixin' to land in some Brazilian jungle by now."

"I agree," Duncan said. "The fact that the kidnappers have let Summer go suggests that the only thing they were interested in was getting Malone out of jail and then hightailing it back to Brazil."

Hubbard grunted. "If Malone was all they wanted, they didn't need to kidnap the secretary of state's daughter to achieve their goal—"

"What if they didn't really kidnap her?" Perkins

interjected. "What if she organized this from the beginning as a way to free Malone?"

"She didn't need to fake a kidnapping for that," Duncan pointed out quickly. "They could have provided Malone with a competent lawyer and he'd have been sprung from jail within a few hours."

"Then what's your explanation for why they kidnapped Summer?" Hubbard asked.

Perkins gave a sour smile. "If I knew that, I'd be everybody's golden boy. But I do know that the people behind this operation aren't your typical criminals, and they for sure aren't your typical terrorist fruitcakes. They're smart and competent, so if they kidnapped Summer Shepherd, they had a good reason for it. And they had an equally good reason for setting her free."

Duncan couldn't have agreed more. He stared at a passing strip mall without seeing it. "The kidnappers aren't just smart, they've got money, too. There were four fully armed professional fighting men on the ground at Mason Field and another three in the chopper. We've already determined that the helicopter wasn't stolen, nor was the Humvee. So apparently the Justice League—whoever the hell that really is—can afford to pay enough to buy the services of seven professional mercenaries, plus a helicopter that they painted with the Medivac logo and equipped with a rescue winch, plus they owned a Humvee that they've most likely abandoned. We have to be looking at half a million bucks in upfront expenses."

"I'm still not convinced the Humvee wasn't stolen," Perkins said. "And the men could be unpaid volunteers, true believers in the cause—"

"Which is what? What the hell is their damn cause?" Duncan demanded.

"Seems to me, that question is where this conversation got started." Hubbard hunched forward in his seat, frowning. "You know what's real odd?"

"Everything about this damn kidnapping is odd," Perkins muttered.

"Yeah, but this is something about Joseph Malone. I've escorted more prisoners than I can count, and I'm willin' to swear that Malone wasn't all that happy at bein' delivered to his so-called pals in the Justice League."

Duncan felt a stab of surprised agreement. He'd noticed himself that Malone had barely spoken during the drive from Miami to Mason Field, and his attitude had been one of brooding resignation rather than sullen defiance or cocky triumph. He shifted restlessly on the hot car seat, sure this insight was important, but when Perkins spoke again, his train of thought broke and couldn't be re-formed. "If Malone wasn't willing to be ransomed for Summer Shepherd, then all he had to do was say no."

"Mebbe." Hubbard reached inside the buttons of his shirt and scratched his chest. "Except it's not that easy sayin' no to the director of the FBI and the governor of the prison, not when you're wearin' an orange jumpsuit and you've got your hands tied to your feet with steel chains."

Perkins swung out to overtake a senior citizen in a Porsche, who was puttering down the highway at a roluctant forty miles an hour. "An illiterate immigrant might have been intimidated by so many high-powered government officials, but Malone is smart, educated and a U.S. citizen. He must have realized the government wasn't going to torture him or take away any of his legal rights if he refused to cooperate. We were in his power, not the other way around."

"I'm not claimin' it makes sense," Hubbard said. "I'm just tellin' you that Malone wasn't happy at bein' taken to meet up with his pals. He was... resigned. Willing to go along with me because he didn't see any alternative."

That was it, Duncan realized, tuning out Perkins's reply. That was the insight he'd been trying to grab hold of earlier. Joseph Malone agreed to surrender himself to the Brazilian Justice League because he wanted to secure Summer's release, and not because he was one of their cronies. Jesus, he must be tired if it was taking him this long to understand something so simple. Either that, or he'd been more infected than he wanted to admit with the fear that Summer had been a party to her own kidnapping.

He tuned in to the exchange between the other two men just as Hubbard spoke again. "All I know is that Malone seemed a real unhappy man when he was in my custody. And that doesn't fit with the bureau's theory that this kidnapping was a put-up job, with him and Summer Shepherd in it together. In my opinion, we've got two victims here, not two conspirators."

The disagreement between Hubbard and Perkins gave Duncan the opportunity he needed, and he seized it. "Seems to me we're not going to resolve what Malone's motives were in agreeing to be ransomed until we have a few more facts to go on. So I guess we'd all be smart to keep this episode under wraps until the brass in Washington have had a chance to debrief Summer. It's real easy to make a horse's ass of yourself when you're punting blind."

"You'll get no arguments from me on that," Perkins said.

"Me, neither." Hubbard gave his chin a meditative scratch. "Okay, we want to keep the media out of this. Next problem. How are we goin' to get Summer away from this golf club without a bunch of journalists yappin' at our heels?"

"It may be easier than you expect," Duncan said. "With any luck, nobody at the club realizes that anything important has happened...."

"I wouldn't count on luck," Perkins said. "We seem to be running real low on that right now. If Shepherd has already told anyone that she was kidnapped, we're screwed. We'll be seeing ourselves all over the evening news, bundling her into the car with a voice-over commenting that law enforcement fucked up and the kidnappers got away."

"Maybe not," Duncan said, with a mental apology to Summer. "Provided the media hasn't already arrived in force, I have an idea how we might be able to persuade the people at the club to keep quiet."

The guard at the Royal Palms entrance gate was not impressed by Wes Perkins's FBI identification and insisted on calling the general manager before their car was allowed to proceed into the manicured grounds of the country club. By the time they arrived at the main clubhouse entrance—which sported columns slightly larger than the Parthenon's and a door guarded by life-size stone lions—the general manager was already waiting for them under the portico. All good signs, Duncan decided. With this much money combined with this much bad taste, there had to be a substantial chance that the club was even more anxious to avoid publicity than he was.

The general manager stepped forward as the parking valet drove their Taurus toward a shrub-screened parking lot filled with Mercedes, Lexus sedans and boat-size Lincoln Town cars. "Gentlemen, I'm Alan Fitzgerald, the general manager of Royal Palms. How can I help you this morning?"

"We've come to provide an escort home for Ms. Summer Shepherd." Wes Perkins stepped forward, holding out his badge.

"Yes, I've been expecting you, Mr. Perkins. Her father called to tell me you would be coming. If you'll follow me, gentlemen, my office is along this corridor. Ms. Shepherd is waiting with my secretary."

"We appreciate the courtesy you've shown her," Perkins said.

"To be frank, when Ms. Shepherd was first brought in, I though she was a homeless person, but I've learned in this job never to judge people by their appearance. For every millionaire who drives a Jaguar and wears monogrammed silk shirts, there's another who drives a Jeep and wears jeans."

"In the circumstances, it was good of you to take her in," Duncan said smoothly.

"Well, she explained right away that she was the daughter of the secretary of state and that kidnappers had been holding her hostage, and she needed to call her father to let him know that she was safe."

Oh, shit, Duncan thought. Perkins and Hubbard both looked at him expectantly. Realizing that there was no way to avoid it, he sent Summer another silent apology and cozied up to the manager. He spoke in a low, confiding voice that he hoped didn't sound too patently insincere. "Mr. Fitzgerald, we're going to have to count on you to help us out here. Since you're the general manager of a club that obviously has a lot of wealthy and important members, I'm sure you have a great deal of experience in being...discreet."

"Of course. I wouldn't survive in this job otherwise."

"Then we're going to entrust you with one more secret and ask that you handle it with your customary excellent discretion."

"I'll do my best."

"Thank you. We appreciate your cooperation." Duncan felt as unctuous as a salesman in a sleazy funeral parlor. "The truth is, Mr. Fitzgerald, that Summer Shepherd is a sweet young lady—but unfortunately she's also a very sick young lady. She suffers from mental health problems, and to be blunt, she can't always distinguish between events that are taking place only inside her head and events that are taking place in the real world."

"I see. What are you trying to tell me? Are you suggesting that she really wasn't kidnapped at all?"

"Well, we haven't spoken to her since she disappeared, so it's possible that she was kidnapped, I guess." Duncan gave a smile that suggested the exact opposite. "But let's just say the last time Summer had one of these periods of mental confusion, she swore she was abducted by a group of white slavers who planned to sell her to an Arab prince for his harem. Actually, she'd spent the night at a bus station."

"She didn't seem mentally disturbed," the manager said.

"That's the problem," Hubbard interjected. "The

nuttier she gets, the more she manages to convince people she's tellin' the truth.''

"Because she believes it herself,'' Duncan added quickly.

"Then I'm sorry for her, and for her father,'' the manager said. "My cousin suffers from schizophrenia, and when he's on his meds, he does just fine. Holds down a job, lives quietly at home with his mother and sings in the church choir. But on a couple of occasions he decided he was cured and stopped taking the medication. You've never seen anyone get so whacked out so fast. He ended up on the streets both times.''

"That's just like Ms. Shepherd,'' Duncan said. "If she takes her medications and stays quietly at home, she does just fine. But every so often she rebels and then—to be honest with you—all hell breaks loose. She takes off, we're chasing all over the country looking for her, and when we find her, she always invents some wild story to explain her absence.''

"Poor lady. It must be terrible to go through life imagining half the people you meet are your enemies.'' The manager stopped in front of a dark oak door. "This is my secretary's office. Ms. Shepherd is waiting for you there.''

"Just one more thing before we go in, Mr. Fitzgerald.'' Wes Perkins spoke with a hearty sincerity that radiated subterfuge. He stepped in front of the door, tension in every line and angle of his body. "Since you understand the problems of mental illness in the family so well, can we count on you not to spread gossip about the crazy stories you heard from Mr. Shepherd's daughter? I'm sure you can understand how harmful it would be to our national security if rumors started to circulate that the secretary of state's daughter had been kidnapped. We're especially anxious that journalists shouldn't hear any rumors about this supposed incident."

Oh, Christ, Duncan thought. Wes, you've just blown it.

The manager was no fool, and he sent a distinctly speculative glance first toward Perkins and then toward Duncan. In the end, whatever his private thoughts, he apparently decided to go along with their story. "Ms. Shepherd only spoke about being kidnapped to me and to my secretary. I can promise you that nobody will hear about the kidnapping from either of us."

Duncan shook the manager's hand. "Thank you," he said fervently. "We really appreciate your cooperation. I'm sure you realize how important your discretion is."

The manager nodded in acknowledgment. "My office is right next door to this one. Please let me know when you're leaving. For security purposes, all nonmembers have to be escorted to the parking lot." He opened the door. "Go ahead, gentlemen. I'm sure Ms. Shepherd will be relieved to see you."

Duncan followed the other two men into the small office. Summer was standing by the window, chatting to an elderly woman as they looked out onto a sweeping vista of golf fairway and blooming hibiscus bushes. She turned around as they came into the room, and for a split second, she didn't move. Then her face broke into a radiant smile and she ran toward him.

"Duncan!" She threw herself into his arms and rested her head against his chest, laughing. "In my wildest dreams, I never imagined I could be so ecstatically happy to see you."

He'd never imagined it in his wildest dreams, either. "Summer, you look wonderful. Thank God you're safe." He put his arms around her and held her close, patting her back soothingly—like a goddamn eunuch. He wondered how she would react if she knew that what he really wanted to do was kiss her senseless. And then run fast to the nearest bed.

She'd greeted him so cheerfully that if he hadn't been holding her, he'd never have realized that she wasn't anywhere near as composed as she appeared. She was trembling, and her hands were balled into tight fists against his chest. He covered her hands with his and murmured calming platitudes until she got a grip on herself. It was a long time before the trembling stopped, but as soon as it did, she straightened and stepped away from him, her cheeks flushed but her manner once again cool and self-possessed, the Summer he was accustomed to.

The secretary spoke briefly to each of them, then said goodbye to Summer and tactfully left the room. As soon as she'd gone, Duncan took Summer's hands, despite her momentary resistance, and led her across the room to the window. Highlighted in the brightness of the midday sun, her face looked thinner than he remembered, although it was only four days since he'd seen her. Hard to believe that the last time they'd been together, they'd been dancing in the formal splendor of the Benjamin Franklin State Dining Room.

"Did they hurt you?" he asked, brushing his thumbs lightly across the reddened skin of her wrists, which were chafed but not rubbed into open wounds. He worked hard to make the question sound impersonal. No need to let Perkins and Hubbard know that his bones and brain both turned to boiled oatmeal every time Summer looked at him.

She shook her head. "It wasn't too bad. I'm okay now that I've had a shower and some breakfast. The kidnappers kept me tied up, so my muscles are sore and I have a few bruises. But they didn't beat me or anything."

Normally she was so good at masking her feelings that he had no idea when she was lying, but this time, he knew she was. The bastards had hurt her, mentally if not physically. Duncan fought an almost over-whelming urge to take her into his arms and promise that he was going to find the kidnappers and person-ally make them regret every bruise, every drop of mental pain they'd inflicted.

"We need to get you back to Washington," he said. "Your father is really anxious to see you, and there are a lot of people waiting to talk to you."

She pulled a face. "Reporters or law enforcement?"

"Only law enforcement people, no reporters. So far, we've managed to keep the fact that you've been kid-napped a secret."

She looked up at him, her eyes widening. "How did you manage that?"

Wes Perkins intervened before Duncan could an-swer. "We'll explain more once we have you safely on a plane back to Washington," he said. He held out his hand. "By the way, I'm Wesley Perkins, station chief for the FBI office in Miami, and this is Rodney Hubbard, the United States marshal for the southern Florida region, also working out of Miami."

She gave both men a tentative smile. "Hi. I'm glad to meet you."

The men shook hands with her. "You're lookin' real good, Ms. Shepherd," Hubbard said.

"Thanks, I feel okay, all things considered."

"There's a doctor on the plane waiting to check you out," Perkins said. "Duncan, find Mr. Fitzgerald or his secretary and let them know we're ready to leave, will you?" The FBI agent made it plain that he was taking charge now that the preliminaries were over. "Ms. Shepherd, we have a plane that's been waiting on standby to take us back to Washington since 0600 hours this morning. If you're ready, we should leave. We have to get you debriefed as soon as possible."

"Yes, of course," Summer said. "I'm ready."

"Then let's get out of here. We have a bunch of kidnappers to catch."

# *Nine*

Summer pummeled her pillow into a fresh shape and flopped onto her stomach. Seconds later, she rolled onto her side, poking her feet outside the blanket and wriggling her toes and ankles just to remind herself that she was free to do so. The ritual completed for the fourth or fifth time since she got into bed, she closed her eyes and willed herself to fall asleep.

An hour later, she admitted defeat. Every time sleep started to take her, she felt as if she were being smothered by dark shadows that crept out of the corners of the room and pinned her to the bed. The doctors had warned her that nightmares would probably haunt her for a few weeks. Right now, she'd be willing to take the nightmares if she could only manage to fall asleep.

Sitting up, she kicked the covers aside and turned on the bedside lamp. Light flooded the guest bedroom of her father's house, instantly dispelling the shadows. Unfortunately, the shadows in her mind weren't vanquished so easily. They lingered, enveloping her in frightening memories of silence, darkness and pain.

Summer wrapped her arms around her knees, then scowled at the cowering image reflected in the antique pier glass mirror placed kitty-corner to the foot of the bed. Enough of this, already. Her mother had always maintained that a cup of hot herbal tea could cure every ailment that didn't require major surgery. This seemed like the perfect moment to give Mom's advice a try. Any alternative to huddling in the bed, wondering how long it would take before she stopped shaking, had to be an improvement. Shoving her feet into a pair of cream satin slippers, thoughtfully provided by Olivia, she pulled on an equally tasteful silk robe, also courtesy of Olivia and five times as elegant as anything she owned, before going down to the kitchen.

Given the way her life had been going recently, she shouldn't have been surprised to discover Duncan sitting at the table, files and papers spread out all around him. He was wearing jeans, his shirt was unbuttoned to the waist, and his jaw was stubbled with dark beard. She felt a spurt of hot emotion, and decided it was resentment. It was four o'clock in the morning, for heaven's sake! Didn't the guy ever stop working?

"Summer." He stood up, but he didn't ask how she was or if she was having trouble sleeping, or any of the trite questions that would have helped to get the conversational ball rolling. He didn't button his shirt, either. Just said her name and then watched her with that courteous, controlled expression she found so intimidating. And...frustrating.

Tightening the belt of her robe, she walked over to the sink and opened cupboards in search of a kettle. "I came down to make some tea," she said. She meant to sound casually courteous. Instead, she sounded childish and belligerent, as if she expected him to refuse permission and send her back upstairs to bed.

"There's a tap that delivers instant boiling water," he said. "There, on the right-hand side of the sink."

"Oh, yes. Thanks." He would know his way around

the kitchen, of course. She had set foot inside this house only twice before, but Duncan was a frequent visitor. Not only was he Olivia's favorite relative, he was her father's golden boy, the handsome, ambitious son he'd always wanted and never had. The man her father wanted her to marry. Yeah, right.

Summer pulled open various cupboard doors, searching for a cup. Duncan walked over to a cupboard near the fridge and produced a fancy Dresden china mug and a canister of tea bags. She glared at him.

"What flavor do you prefer?" he asked, tipping tea bags over the counter and ignoring her scowls. "There's regular and assorted herb flavors. Lemon zinger...spearmint...peach. The apple cinnamon seems to be all gone."

"Peach would be nice." She took the mug and the tea bag, carefully avoiding touching him. If he felt her shaking, he would recognize her for the coward she was and despise her for coming apart at the seams. She'd already sobbed all over his shirt once in the past twenty-four hours, and she didn't intend to break down in front of him again. He had shown a slightly more human face at the state dinner on Friday night, but he was still way too close to perfect for her to relax in his company.

Pouring steaming water onto her tea bag, she brooded over the certainty that if Duncan had been kidnapped by Brazilian terrorists, he wouldn't have submitted meekly as she had. With his fluent command of Portuguese, he'd have understood everything the kidnappers said and been able to give the FBI a complete rundown on their aims and agenda the second he was rescued. Always assuming, of course, that

he hadn't gnawed through the tape on his wrists, ka-
rate-chopped his guards into unconsciousness and escaped under his own steam before a rescue team could
reach him. Which is what Julian Stein seemed to think
she should have done to prove that she hadn't been
cooperating with her kidnappers.

To hell with Julian Stein and his midget brain, over-
flowing with suspicions. Summer drew in a steadying
breath and discarded the tea bag, aiming a superpolite
smile at Duncan. "Are you going to have something,
too?"

"Maybe another beer." Duncan opened the fridge
and helped himself to a bottle of Heineken, pushing
the cap off with his thumbs. Very macho, Summer
thought acidly. But she found herself watching as he
slugged down a third of the bottle in a single swallow.
She didn't turn away quickly enough when he stopped
drinking, and he caught her looking at him. His gaze
held hers for a tense second or two. Then he put the
bottle down on the table with a thud and started to
gather up the papers he'd been working on, shoving
them into a leather briefcase.

"What's the problem?" he asked, his back toward
her. "Why the sudden need for tea?"

"Insomnia," she said curtly.

"Didn't the doctor give you anything to help you
sleep?"

"He offered, but I refused. I think I've got enough
drugs sloshing around in my system right now. I'd like
to give my body a rest."

He closed his briefcase with a snap and scrambled
the numbers on the lock. "You mentioned during the
flight back to Washington that the kidnappers had kept
you shot full of tranquilizers."

"Yes, they did." The air-conditioned kitchen suddenly felt very cold and she cradled the mug of tea with her hands, glad of the warmth. "They didn't give me any food, and almost nothing to drink for the entire three days, but they were generous with their supply of drugs."

Duncan swung around, his gaze flinty. "We'll find them, Summer. They won't get away with what they did to you, that's a promise."

"Won't they?" She couldn't help sounding bitter. "How hard will anyone be looking? And will they look in the right places?"

"Julian Stein is a fine investigator, and he has some brilliant agents working for him—"

"Julian Stein thinks I orchestrated my own kidnapping. That I have some kooky agenda about freeing Joe to publicize the destruction of the Brazilian rain forest."

Duncan took another long slug of beer before he replied. "Yes, he does, but he's a professional and he'll do his job."

She couldn't help asking the question. "What about you, Duncan? Do you agree with the director? Do you think I arranged to be kidnapped so that I could pressure the government into releasing Joe Malone from prison?"

"No."

"It's what my father believes," she said, then cursed herself for revealing the problem that had been the root cause of her insomnia. Not the fact that the FDI director believed she was a criminal, but that her father suspected she might be, too.

"Gordon doesn't really believe that," Duncan said quietly. "Although it might be what he fears."

"He should know me better than that."

"Yes, he should, but cut him some slack. He's being torn in two directions, and he's falling over backward not to let his personal feelings get in the way of his obligations as secretary of state."

All her life it seemed that her father had been campaigning for some public office or other, and all her life she'd been listening to people telling her she had to understand what an important man he was, and how his public duties had to take precedence over her needs "just this once." Except that by the time she entered her teens, she'd realized that "just this once" meant "always," and that every time there was a conflict, she was going to lose out.

Summer felt a flash of anger that she was too tired to conceal. She'd undergone three days of sheer hell, and instead of sympathy, her return had been greeted with universal suspicion. "Why don't you tell my father to cut *me* some slack and trust in my integrity? The fact that we have different political views doesn't mean that I would ever do anything to compromise his position or hurt my country."

"I have told him that," Duncan said.

"Always the perfect diplomat," she said, still angry because that was the least painful emotion to feel.

"Not always," he said coolly. "And in this case, hardly at all."

For some reason, it was deeply satisfying to transfer her hurt away from her father and translate it into anger against Duncan. "You're always so damn controlled. Doesn't it ever get lonely up there on your pedestal, looking down on the mess the rest of us are making of our lives?"

"If you think I'm in control when I'm around you, then you're not very perceptive."

Summer was startled by the sudden edge to his voice, even more startled that she found it gratifying to know she'd rattled him. What she'd wanted for a very long time, she realized, was to see Duncan when he wasn't master of himself and the situation.

She put down her half-empty mug of tea and sent him a challenging stare. "What is it about me that annoys you so much, Duncan?"

"There's nothing about you that annoys me," he said flatly.

"Hah! Try that one more time—only this time, look at me when you say it."

He turned his head in a jerky motion and met her gaze, his dark brown eyes opaque. "There's nothing about you that annoys me, Summer."

"I could almost see you gritting your teeth when you said that."

"You misinterpreted my reaction, which is something you do quite often. You don't annoy me. You drive me crazy."

Summer gave a short laugh. "If this is how you act when you're being driven crazy, I'd hate to spend time with you when you're feeling bored. Would I know that you were awake?"

He was still looking at her, but there wasn't an ounce of expression in his face. "Do you want to tell me what game we're playing here, Summer? Maybe I'd like to join in if I knew the rules."

"I'm not playing games." Her voice shook. "I want to see if you can feel any normal human emotions, that's all."

"Where you're concerned, I feel plenty of emotion. Way too much, in fact."

Her stomach gave a little jump. She tilted her head and looked at him with self-protective mockery. "And which emotion would that be, Duncan? Spell it out for me, since I lack your diplomatic training and I can't seem to interpret the subtle nuances of a quirked eyebrow."

Emotion, hot and primitive, flashed in his eyes. He didn't reply with words, just reached out, pulled her into his arms and slammed his mouth against hers. For a timeless moment, Summer froze in shock. Then desire exploded deep inside her, rushing through her veins at breakneck speed. She opened her mouth to his kiss, feeling instantly aroused when his tongue thrust fiercely against hers.

She had wanted to know what Duncan would be like when he lost control. Now she knew. He was aggressive, passionate, demanding—and the most exciting man that she had ever kissed. Her body was on fire, her mind a seething turmoil that obliterated logic, but instinct told her that she had pushed him over the brink. Through a maze of sensations, one coherent thought emerged. Thank God, she'd finally done it.

His mouth fit perfectly over hers: So perfectly she wondered why it had taken her this long to understand that Duncan was the embodiment of her most compelling secret fantasies. His hands tangled in her hair, forcing her head back so that he could rain kisses down the length of her throat, but she didn't feel overpowered for the simple reason that she was eager to surrender. She shivered with pleasure when he pushed her robe from her shoulders and fastened his mouth on her breast. On fire with the need to touch him, her hands streaked over his naked chest and down toward the waistband of his jeans. She had been wanting this for a long time, she acknowledged, and it was every bit as exhilarating as her subconscious had dreamed of.

If they had been anywhere other than Olivia's home, she would have gone to bed with him in a heartbeat and worried about the consequences later. But the realization that they were in her stepmother's kitchen, and that a Secret Service agent was patrolling the house, finally penetrated the hot haze of her desire. Gasping for air, searching for the murky dregs of her common sense, she broke off their kiss and pulled herself out of his arms.

Duncan murmured a hoarse protest and reached for her again, but when she continued to resist, he stepped back and stood propped against the doorjamb, fists clenched at his sides, breathing hard. He didn't speak or look at her, and his profile was forbidding, but this time she wasn't deceived. Duncan wanted her, and he was having a hard time not taking what he wanted. His self-control teetered on a knife edge.

It would have been easy just to go to him and let the inevitable happen, but Summer fought the temptation, despite the fact that her body throbbed with unfulfilled needs. Until now, she'd always thought of herself as a woman who was difficult to arouse. She wondered why Duncan, of all the men in the world, should be the one who had unleashed such a storm of pent-up desire.

She waited for a full minute before she spoke, in the hope that her voice might sound halfway normal. "I'm sorry, Duncan, that was my fault. I deliberately set out to provoke you."

He gave a tight smile. "I didn't need much provocation. I've been looking for an excuse to take you to bed since the first day we met."

Astonishment conquered her other feelings. "You can't be serious!" She gave an uncertain laugh. "My God, you are serious."

"Don't sound so horrified." Duncan picked up his empty beer bottle and pitched it into the trash. "Fortunately, I have lots of experience in faking total indifference to your charms. So there's no need to run away on my account. I've refrained from jumping your bones for the last ten years. I guess I can hold out for the rest of the night."

Even if he was telling the truth, in the grand scheme of things it was probably less amazing that Duncan had lusted after her for ten years than that she had been kidnapped by terrorists, suspended from a helicopter a hundred feet above the earth and survived to tell the tale. But it was a close run thing, Summer decided. Damned close.

She made an embarrassed gesture, oddly defenseless now that Duncan couldn't be pushed back into the safe mental box where she had kept him stowed and labeled for the past decade. "I want you to know, I didn't stop just now because..." She floundered to a halt, drew in a shaky breath and tried again. "I remembered there's at least one Secret Service agent on duty inside the house. I didn't think it would be a good idea if he walked in to fix himself a pot of coffee and found us rolling around naked on the kitchen floor."

Duncan smiled again, this time with genuine amusement. "Not on the floor, Summer. I'm a class act. It would have been the table at least."

She laughed, then fell silent when a vivid image of

their naked bodies spread-eagled across the kitchen table flashed through her mind. She hadn't realized Duncan was reading her thoughts so accurately until he crossed to her side and cradled his hand against her cheek. "Later," he said softly. "Another time and another place, but we'll get there, Summer."

Tiny pinpricks of flame danced over her skin, his touch sufficient to reignite the desire she'd only just brought under control. Until tonight, she would have told him not to make arrogant assumptions, but now it seemed pointless to deny something that they both knew was true. She'd discovered that she quite badly wanted to have Duncan Ryder make love to her, so she moved to a safe distance before saying his name. "Duncan..."

"Yes?"

"Let's not wait another ten years before we try this again, okay?"

He sent her a look that made her toes curl. "Trust me, I'll call you as soon as you get back to New York. You can count on it."

She turned away, afraid that if she continued to look at him she'd consign worries about Olivia and the Secret Service agent to the scrap heap and start ripping off Duncan's clothes. Or her own. Or both. She emptied the dregs of her tea into the sink and determinedly changed the direction of their conversation. "I have to thank you for putting up with me yesterday on the plane ride back to Washington. I know I was a royal pain in the ass."

"Yeah, you sure were." Laughter warmed Duncan's voice. "On the whole, though, it was a hell of a relief to know that you hadn't been tortured into unnatural meekness."

She rinsed the mug out, stuck it on the draining board, then turned around to glare at him. "You were supposed to lie and say I was delightful company."

He looped his arm casually around her waist. "I don't lie," he said. "Not to you."

It felt good, too good, to have him holding her again, so she leaned away, just a little, and spoke with determined brightness. "Good grief, is that clock right? I can't believe it's five o'clock already. I guess it's too late to go back to bed."

"It is for me, since I have to be in the office by seven-thirty. What are your plans for the day?"

"Bram Cooper hasn't finished asking me questions yet, so I'm scheduled back at CIA headquarters for another debriefing session. I saw one of the kidnappers quite clearly, so the FBI has rounded up a bunch of mug shots they want me to look through." She yawned. "They're sending a limo for me at eight o'clock."

"Is your father going with you again?"

"Yes. Although he has meetings this afternoon with the Czech foreign minister, so he won't be there after lunch." She yawned again. "Wouldn't you know that now it's too late to do anything about it, I'm starting to feel sleepy."

"I'll brew us a pot of coffee. That might help to wake you up. And I saw a box of muffins in the fridge, if that sounds like an appealing breakfast."

"Sounds great. Now that you mention food, I realize I'm hungry."

Duncan made coffee while she carried a selection of oversize muffins to the table and found plates and paper napkins. When the coffee was brewed, they sat on opposite sides of the table, drinking, eating and chatting about nothing in particular as they watched the morning sun gradually light up the kitchen.

"Why do you think the kidnappers selected you as the person to pick up their ransom note?" Summer interjected the question out of nowhere into the midst of a discussion about European breakfast foods. It was only then that she realized how close to the forefront of her mind the horrific events of the past few days remained, and how much she resented the way Julian Stein and Bram Cooper were keeping her in the dark about the details of her own kidnapping. "Wouldn't it have been more logical for the Justice League to deal directly with my father?"

"More logical, maybe, but also a lot more dangerous." Duncan accepted her sudden change of topic without comment.

"More dangerous for the Justice League, you mean."

"Yes. Your father has instant access to a direct emergency hot line here at home as well as in his office, so by calling him directly the kidnappers would have faced a much greater risk of having their call monitored and traced."

"Since they chose you, the Justice League must have known enough about our family to be confident you would be able and willing to pass their message on to my father. Do you think that's significant?"

Duncan shook his head. "It's no secret that Olivia's my sister, and that I'm on friendly terms with your father, so the fact the kidnappers used me to get to Gordon doesn't prove they had unique insider knowledge. But I guess it's one more piece of evidence that this operation was planned by people who knew exactly how to push all the right buttons to produce the results they wanted.''

"Which were what?" Summer asked. "None of the theories I heard yesterday made much sense.''

"I wish I could give you a brilliant explanation of what the Justice League is really up to, but I can't. I can only tell you that I'm sure this kidnapping was arranged with a very specific purpose in mind. And that's a conclusion based on the efficiency of their operation, not on any idea of what it is they're trying to achieve.''

Summer gave up on grand theory and returned to more minor mysteries. She had a long list of puzzles that had been dismissed or ignored by her interrogators at the CIA and the FBI. "Why did the people in charge agree to let you be one of only two government officials assigned to escort Joe Malone to the ransom site? I'd have expected Julian Stein to order up an entire squad of Special Forces to confront the kidnappers.''

"He couldn't do that. The Justice League stipulated an armed guard for Malone of no more than two law enforcement officials. If they'd seen any sign of combat troops or police SWAT teams, then the deal would have been off and you wouldn't have been released.''

"But that doesn't explain why you were one of the two. You're a diplomat. You've got nothing to do with law enforcement.''

"No, but I know you personally, which was the most important consideration. You would recognize me and I would recognize you, which cut down on the chance of fatal accidents.''

"Why didn't my father come?"

"He had to stay here in Washington.''

"Why? Because lunch with some ambassador was more important than finding out if his daughter was alive or dead?" Damn, Summer thought. She'd done it again. Revealed to Duncan how hurt she'd been by her father's absence at the rescue scene.

Duncan, who knew her much too well, didn't make the mistake of offering explicit sympathy. "Your father wanted to go to Florida," he said. "But he knew it wasn't the wise thing to do. If he'd canceled his scheduled meetings, we'd never have been able to keep news of your kidnapping from leaking to the media, and that was something we wanted to avoid at all costs. Your abduction was a nightmare come true for the FBI, and Julian Stein is determined to prevent a rash of copycat abductions, with terrorist organizations snatching family members of cabinet officials and holding the government to ransom for dozens of insane causes."

"I guess I can sympathize with Stein on that particular point."

"Absolutely. So with your father out of the picture, that left me as the only other person already involved in the investigation who knew you well enough to make a positive identification."

"I see. Thanks for explaining." It was a huge relief to know that it had been national security concerns, not indifference, that had kept her father away. "Still, I'm surprised the government agreed to such unequal terms for the exchange. With only two armed men on your side, you had no hope of arresting the kidnappers. You're lucky they didn't kill you." Her stomach swooped at the thought.

"We equalized the odds as best we could. We wore full-body armor—"

"Oh, great. That only left your head exposed." Sarcasm helped to take the sharp edge off her fear.

"If they'd started shooting, we would have returned fire." Duncan gave a sudden grin. "Besides, we had a fully armed SWAT team hidden inside the hangar and we had state troopers on standby to mount instant road blocks. The only thing we couldn't risk was putting armed personnel out in the open and scaring the kidnappers off. Our number-one priority was to get you back alive. You were much too valuable a weapon to leave in the hands of terrorists."

"Despite all the government's precautions, though, the Justice League managed to deliver me entirely on their terms and get off scot-free themselves. They'd planned very well, hadn't they?"

"Too damn well."

"I guess nobody considered the possibility that they'd use a helicopter."

"Since they'd designated a disused airfield as the ransom site, we half expected them to use a plane. But not a helicopter, which could have landed anywhere. In a sense, they double-bluffed us and we fell for it."

"Didn't the FBI monitor the airspace around Mason? Or was that impossible because of the need for secrecy?"

"There were secrecy concerns, of course, but Florida is full of military bases and we thought we had the airspace over Mason sewn up tight. Then an emergency medical helicopter pilot radioed in that he had a sick newborn baby on board, being transferred to Lakeland Community Hospital. The chopper carried all the correct identifying insignia, and the pilot used appropriate codes and signals, so there was no reason to suspect him of being anything other than what he claimed. Although, even if we'd suspected him, I'm not sure what we could have done. With you on board, the kidnappers had us by the balls. If we'd threatened to blow the chopper out of the air, they wouldn't have believed our threats.''

"Did you know that the FBI has traced the pilot of the helicopter already? That was one piece of information Mr. Stein did give me.''

Duncan's head snapped up. "He's been arrested, you mean?"

"No, but the FBI knows who he was. Apparently one of the Medivac pilots didn't show up for his night shift on Monday, and when local police finally checked his apartment yesterday afternoon, it had been cleaned out. The FBI got a set of the missing pilot's prints and ran them through the bureau's database. It turns out he was not only using an alias, he also had served time in federal prison for arms smuggling under his real name, which was Lawrence Nubchek, or something similar.''

"At least that explains one small part of the mystery,'' Duncan said. "I guess we can safely assume ol' Larry is sitting on a tropical beach, sipping rum punch and planning how to spend his payoff money.''

"Nubchek had been working for Medivac for almost three months," Summer said. "Was he a plant, waiting for orders, do you think? Or did the Justice League manage to find the one helicopter pilot in the state of Florida willing to be bribed?''

"Miami's a major center for illegal drug distribution. Unfortunately, I'm guessing that Larry Nubchek was one of any number of pilots who hang out in Florida and are willing to fly anything anywhere for the right price.''

"Still, it makes you wonder how long the Justice League had been planning to kidnap me." Summer scooped crumbs of blueberry muffin from one side of her plate to the other. "My father mentioned that Joe had been in jail for less than two weeks. Do you really think the kidnappers could have organized such a complex operation in such a short time?"

"Not unless they had access to almost unimaginable amounts of money and expertise."

"Then they definitely aren't friends of Joe's," Summer said wryly. "Joe has less interest in money and material possessions than anyone I've ever met. He's got patents on a profitable drug and a fungicide that's used in agriculture, but he spends all his income on new research projects, so he's always broke."

Duncan didn't reply, and Summer leaned forward across the table. "What is it? What did I just say?"

"Joseph Malone isn't broke," Duncan said. "Far from it. His mother comes from one of the wealthiest families in Brazil, and Malone has access to a sizable trust fund."

"You must be wrong—"

"No, the information about his family background came from a CIA briefing when you were kidnapped."

Summer stared blankly at Duncan. Why hadn't she known that about the man she considered her best friend? It wasn't as if she'd met Joe for the first time a few weeks ago. On the contrary. She'd met him when she was an eighteen-year-old undergraduate and he was a twenty-five-year-old doctoral candidate at Stanford University. They'd been friends for almost twelve years. He'd comforted her when her mother had died, celebrated with her when she received her doctoral degree, slept on her apartment sofa whenever he was in town. In fact, they'd been best friends for so long she'd even convinced herself that maybe she could fall in love with him if they started a sexual relationship. Hence the disastrous experiment in Brazil last fall.

But despite their long history of friendship, she had never known about Joe's trust fund, or the fact that his mother came from a wealthy family. Because she hadn't wanted to know about his parents or his background, she realized. She wanted Joe to come from a regular middle-class family and share her own indifference to wealth, so she'd ignored every clue that the real Joe Malone might be a more complex person than her limited image of him allowed.

It was disconcerting to realize that her willful ignorance about Joe's background bore a striking resemblance to her attitude toward Duncan. She had formed superficial impressions of both men, and she'd clung to those impressions until forced to change them. She wondered what it was that made her so reluctant to probe beneath the facades people presented to the world. She had an uncomfortable suspicion that it was something to do with her acute need to protect her own vulnerabilities from outside scrutiny. That, and an unwillingness to open herself up to the potential hurt that came from trusting people enough to accept them on their own terms.

"It's embarrassing to admit that I didn't know Joe had access to family money," she said. "But my comment about him is still true in its essentials. Trust fund or not, Joe doesn't care about money. That's why he's not wealthy, even though he's patented two successful drugs already. And as for working with a group of political terrorists, it's flat-out nuts to believe that Joe is capable of any such thing. He's the gentlest, most humane man I've ever met.''

"Even gentle and humane people can become embittered," Duncan said.

"I realize that." She flicked her hair impatiently out of her eyes. "But I spent over two weeks with Joe last fall, and he certainly wasn't embittered then. He was still as passionate and good-humored as ever—about his research work, and about helping the peasants who are trying to scrape together a living in Amazonia."

"Passion can sometimes be a half step away from violence."

"Not in Joe's case." She might have had a truncated view of Joe's personality, but there were certain rock-solid fundamentals she would never doubt. "Trust me, Duncan. I know Joseph Malone, and he would never be involved in a scheme that involved kidnapping, or threats of death and brutality. Which is why I have this horrible fear that right now, Joe is just as much a prisoner of the so-called Justice League as I was this time yesterday."

"Have you expressed that view to Julian Stein?"

She sighed. "Yes, and to Bram Cooper, for all the good it did. They pointed out that there are plenty of environmental fanatics who wouldn't chop down a tree, but they'd have no qualms about blowing up a school bus to publicize their message. I told them that Joe was light-years away from being an environmental activist, and that we often disagreed about environmental issues. In fact, Joe is much more willing than I am to accept that the rain forest has to be developed. He just wants it to be developed responsibly, in a way that's scientifically rational." Summer pushed aside her coffee mug with a frustrated gesture. "Maybe I didn't know as much about Joe Malone's finances as I should have, but I know for sure that he would never ally himself with any group that was using violence to pursue its aims.''

"Drug trafficking is a pretty violent occupation," Duncan remarked. "And Malone was caught with more than a kilo of cocaine in his luggage."

Summer exhaled impatiently. "You don't believe Joe smuggled coke, do you? Of course he didn't. He was set up."

"Maybe. But if that's true, who set him up? And why?"

"I don't know." She pressed her hands to her forehead, trying to massage away the start of a pounding headache. "All I know is that I'm free and Joe is a prisoner. And I'm mortally afraid that the only reason he gave himself up to the Justice League is so that they would let me go."

"That isn't likely," Duncan said, taking her hands and rubbing his thumbs soothingly across her knuckles. "Think about it, Summer. If you follow the thread of what you're suggesting back to its beginning, you're faced with the absurd premise that the Justice League arranged for Joseph Malone to be arrested on false smuggling charges, and then orchestrated your kidnapping just to get their hands on him."

"It's possible. More possible than that Joe smuggled coke or plotted a murder."

"Possible—but crazy. Why would they dream up such a complicated plan to achieve something so simple? Why wouldn't they just kidnap Malone directly and save themselves a hell of a lot of hassle? These are not stupid people. If they had the resources to get Malone arrested on false smuggling charges the minute he landed at Miami Airport, then they for sure had the resources to kidnap him from there.''

Duncan's questions were all valid and logical. Summer shrugged helplessly. ''I don't have any answers,'' she said. ''Right now, my mind feels like a hollow ball, stuffed with lead pellets.''

''Then don't try to think anymore.''

She stared at his hands, wrapped around hers, and realized that his touch not only had the power to arouse her, it had the power to comfort her, too. She didn't want to find Duncan comforting. Contemplating great sex with him was one thing. Allowing herself to depend on him was something else again. Alarmed, she tugged away from his grasp and carried her plate and mug over to the sink. ''Nothing makes sense,'' she said. ''If I try to close one end of the puzzle, the other end simply bursts open in protest.''

He came and stood behind her, putting his arms loosely around her waist. ''You're not responsible for solving this puzzle, Summer. That's up to the FBI. You were the victim, nothing more and nothing less. You don't have any obligation to find out why the Justice League did what they did.''

''I wish that were true, but right now, I'm not only the victim, I'm also the FBI's favorite suspect.''

''Stein is too smart to chase after the wrong suspect for long,'' Duncan said. ''He'll soon get on track.''

She turned within the circle of his arms, telling herself that feeling secure wasn't the same thing as feeling dependent. ''I wish I shared your optimism.''

''You've had a rough few days, Summer. You'll feel better after a good night's sleep.'' He tucked a loose strand of her hair behind her ear and gave her a reassuring squeeze.

"I guess so." She was looking up at him, and so she saw the exact moment that his friendly reassurance changed to something quite different.

His eyes narrowed, glinted. "Summer, don't look at me like that."

She should have turned away. Instead she leaned closer. "How am I looking at you?" she asked, knowing the answer.

He bent toward her. "As if you want me to do this."

She closed her eyes and cast caution to the far winds. His mouth lowered, touched hers. The same incredible rushing sensation that she'd felt before instantly swept over her.

"Good morning!" Olivia's voice reverberated through the kitchen, rich with false cheer. "Summer, my dear, you must be feeling much better than any of us could have hoped. How nice to see you up and about so early."

Duncan muttered an expletive. Summer contemplated murder. Keeping his arm around Summer's waist, Duncan turned to face his sister. "Hello, Olivia. I didn't know you were such an early riser."

"Usually I'm not. But I have a meeting at the White House this morning with the First Lady. We're working together on the wording of a letter to accompany a gift from the Red Cross to the war orphans in Africa." Olivia seemed oblivious to the fact that she'd interrupted her favorite brother in the act of exchanging a passionate kiss with her despised stepdaughter. She smiled brightly at them both.

"I'm sure the orphans will be thrilled," Summer said. "Duncan, I expect you'd like to have a few moments to catch up with your sister, so I'll go upstairs and get showered. I don't want to keep my father or the FBI director waiting.''

"I'll talk to Duncan later," Olivia said. "I'll come upstairs with you, Summer. We need to look through my closet and see if we can find you something to wear. Although, of course, you're a larger size than I am, aren't you?''

"Only in the bust," Duncan said blandly.

Olivia flashed an outraged glance not at her brother, but at Summer, who smiled with sugary sweetness. "Thanks for the kind thought," she said to her stepmother. "But Mr. Stein already provided me with everything I need for today in the way of clothing.''

"At least let me find you a scarf or a necklace," Olivia said, linking her arm through Summer's and heading determinedly for the stairs. "After three days of being tied up, you need something pretty and frivolous to cheer you up. And knowing Julian Stein, I'm sure any outfit he found for you will be the next best thing to a military uniform.''

Summer wondered if she needed to add Olivia to the lengthening list of people whose characters she had willfully misunderstood for the past decade. She soon found out that she didn't. The moment they arrived upstairs, Olivia rounded on her, cheeks flaming. "Stay away from my brother!" she ordered, her voice vibrating with suppressed anger. "He has a brilliant future ahead of him and you're not going to mess that up. He's already made one disastrous marriage, and I won't stand by and watch him make another.''

"Then don't look," Summer said, and turned to walk into the guest room.

"Not so fast!" Olivia grabbed her arm. "Sex may get you into bed with Duncan, but it's not going to get you out of the bedroom and into the rest of his life. My brother is smart enough to know that when he marries again, he needs a woman who shares his dedication to public service.''

''If that's true, then you can't possibly suppose that he's in any danger of marrying me. What are you so worried about, Olivia? Did you pick Duncan a wife and he hasn't signed on the dotted line like he was supposed to?''

Olivia's nostrils flared. ''Duncan realizes very well that any woman I introduce him to will be exactly the sort of wife he needs.''

''Needs? Or wants? I'm willing to bet big bucks that Duncan isn't looking for the sort of Stepford wife you keep finding for him.'' Summer gave a cheerful smile, gratified that Olivia seemed to have lost the power to intimidate her. ''You shouldn't glare at me like that, stepmommy dearest. It's giving you wrinkles.''

She shook Olivia's hand from her arm and closed the guest room door, basking in the satisfying knowledge that, for once, she had not only enjoyed the last word, she had left her stepmother speechless.

# Ten

It was a strange experience to walk into her apartment after an absence of less than a week and discover that her home of the last two years looked totally unfamiliar. Perhaps it was the iron grilles newly installed over her windows, or the dead bolt that she'd just locked behind the departing Secret Service agent. Whatever it was, the place she had lived in for two years felt alien, and Summer hated the sensation of being under siege, protecting herself against an enemy who was not only nameless and almost faceless, but whose motives were incomprehensible.

She wandered from the cramped kitchen to the bedroom, to the minuscule bathroom and back to the living room, noticing subtle changes made by the FBI investigators when they'd searched the apartment. She moved her pile of books waiting to be read back from the left-hand side of her bed to the right, threw away her old toothbrush, adjusted the angle of her favorite photograph of her mother and emptied a carton of sour milk into the kitchen sink.

Too restless to settle, she ended up in her living room, standing in front of the marble fireplace, a relic that had survived from the building's days of glory at the turn of the century. She'd probably burn the place down if she ever tried to light a fire in the antique grate, but she loved the mantel's ornate carvings, and the air of incongruous opulence it imparted to a living room that was barely large enough to hold a sofa, a coffee table and a desk crammed up against the wall.

Summer wound up the seventy-year-old chiming clock that had been her mother's and her grandmother's, relaxing slightly as she listened to the familiar ticking. After the silence she'd endured during her captivity, the sounds of everyday life had become very important to her. At that moment, a police siren howled in the distance, fighting to be heard over the wail of some other emergency vehicle. She smiled ruefully. Okay, so not all noise was beautiful, but it might be a while before she started to complain again about the constant blare of New York's traffic.

Energized by the comforting noise, she microwaved a package of frozen lasagna, improving the taste by washing it down with a half bottle of Beaujolais nouveau and Beethoven's ninth playing full blast on the stereo. She'd been saving the wine for a special occasion and she figured tonight qualified. Against the odds, she was alive. But even through the mild buzz of red wine, the apartment still felt alien, as if it belonged to someone else. In a way, it did. There was an impassable divide between the person she had been before the kidnapping and the woman she was now.

Still, she was home and safe and it was time to get on with her life again. The FBI and the CIA had sworn her to secrecy, threatening prosecution if she breathed a word about her kidnapping to anyone, so it wasn't as if she could get rid of her angst by calling her friends and talking about the events of the past few days. Of course, she could always call Duncan and talk to him....

Sure she could, if she wanted to lay herself wide open to rejection. Or the even more confusing possibility that he wouldn't reject her at all, which would leave her forced to deal with the fact that right now, of all the people she knew, the one she most wanted to be with was Duncan Ryder. Summer resolutely pushed aside images of Duncan and washed up her dinner things. Then, beset by the need to renew links with her own home, she retrieved cleaning supplies from under the kitchen sink and began to dust, polish and generally tidy up clutter. She found Sunday's edition of the *New York Times* sitting where she'd left it, unread, and paused to leaf through the pages of the main news section before tossing it in the trash.

A headline and a picture on the center of page three caught her eye, and she spread the paper out on the kitchen counter to look more closely. The headline read Brazilian Industrialist Found Murdered. The picture was of a man she recognized: Fernando Autunes da Pereira, the guy who'd been traveling on the train from Washington to New York with her stepmother. It seemed a couple of lifetimes ago, but actually that train journey had been only last Saturday, hours before this edition of the paper must have gone to press. And it seemed that while she'd been getting herself kidnapped, Senhor da Pereira had been getting himself killed. Life was full of coincidences, but this one was surprising enough to catch her attention. Propping the paper against the toaster, Summer skimmed the introductory paragraph to the story.

Late on Saturday night, Fernando Autunes da Pereira, chairman of Industria Agricola do Norte, the largest family-owned conglomerate in South

America, was found dead in a suite at the Carlyle, one of Manhattan's most famous hotels, located at 35 East Seventy-sixth Street, at Madison Avenue. Shortly after 9:30 p.m., Senhor da Pereira ordered dinner for two from room service. At two minutes after ten the waiter delivering his order was unable to obtain any response to his repeated knocking. When a call from room service likewise failed to produce a response, the duty manager was summoned to unlock the door. Senhor da Pereira was lying fully clothed on the sofa, with multiple bullet wounds to his head.

Beyond confirming that the death was being treated as a murder case, the police were making no official statements, pending initial results of the autopsy.

Senhor da Pereira was fifty-one years old and the patriarch of one of Brazil's most prominent families. He left his wife of twenty-seven years, Anna Xavier Salazar, and four daughters.

Summer realized her hands were shaking. She carried the paper back into the living room and sat down on the sofa to read the rest of the article, which was basically an obituary. Fernando Autunes da Pereira had been chairman and general manager of Industria Agricola do Norte, one of Brazil's largest and most successful companies, with interests in mining, agriculture and pharmaceuticals. Fernando had been among the richest and most influential men in Brazil, and his death was likely to precipitate a scramble for power, both corporate and personal, among his potential successors. He had inherited modest land and mining operations from his grandfather and had parlayed

them into a family company that today was a hundred
times larger than the one he'd inherited. He wasn't
quite a billionaire, but the success of Industria Agricola do Norte had provided him not only with a life-
style that reached fantasy levels of luxury, but also
with the economic power base to wield enormous influence on Brazilian politics. In an era when politics
and economics often seemed interchangeable terms,
Senhor da Pereira only needed to voice a wish and the
Brazilian government was forced to listen.

In recent years, according to the article, Senhor da
Pereira had invested heavily in development projects
in Amazonia, and ten years ago had been one of the
main targets of the international environmentalist
movement. In the last three years, however, evidence
began to surface that Senhor da Pereira had undergone
a change of heart, and he had recently positioned himself as a leading advocate of more responsible development of Brazil's vast Amazon territory. He had
bought TV time and used dramatic film footage of the
out-of-control forest fires burning in Malaysia as an
effective propaganda tool to whip up Brazilian public
opinion against slash-and-burn land-clearing techniques in Amazonia. In the process, he had aroused
vociferous opposition from fellow industrialists, who
felt that his vast wealth permitted him to adhere to
standards that posed severe economic penalties on the
average developer. In recent months, his rivals, who
usually couldn't agree about anything, had united in
their determination to prevent the passage of legislation sponsored by Senhor da Pereira's allies in the Brazilian congress. This legislation would have permanently prevented commercial exploitation of vast tracts

of pristine Amazon rain forest that had been deemed especially sensitive from an ecological perspective.

In his native Brazil, Senhor da Pereira lived in a fortress, protected by every electronic security device known to humankind, plus a small army of highly trained bodyguards. Even in the States, he rarely traveled without an escort of bodyguards, but on this occasion it seemed he had broken with his usual custom. A spokesperson for the hotel insisted that Senhor da Pereira had been alone when he checked in, and there was no advance guard waiting for him in his suite.

He had been shot in the head at point-blank range, but Sergeant Callahan, a detective assigned to the case, indicated that this did not indicate that he had known his killer. "In a hotel situation, people get careless and let anyone into their room who says they're a maid or a maintenance person," he explained. "This is true even for people who have good reasons to be cautious. Mr. Pereira was expecting a room service delivery, and he might have let in anyone pushing a dinner trolley who claimed to be a waiter."

There were currently no specific theories about the motive for the murder, at least officially, but as with any rich and powerful industrialist, Senhor da Pereira had acquired plenty of enemies, quite apart from his recent disagreements with fellow developers in Amazonia. It seemed likely that there would eventually be no shortage of suspects. In the meantime, Sergeant Callahan admitted that he was eager to interview the person with whom Senhor da Pereira had planned to share dinner. So far, there was no evidence to suggest who this putative dinner companion might have been. Sergeant Callahan hoped the person involved would come forward and help advance the investigation.

It wasn't until the second time that she read the article that Summer realized why she found the story of Fernando da Pereira's death so riveting. It was because Olivia must surely have been one of the last friends—perhaps the last—to whom Fernando had ever spoken. In fact, it seemed reasonable to speculate that Olivia had been the "dinner companion" the police were anxious to interview. And it was a no-brainer to conclude that her stepmother was never going to volunteer that information or submit to an interview by any of New York's finest.

No longer in the mood for the classics, Summer changed the CD of Beethoven's ninth to the soundtrack of *Rent*.

She couldn't entirely blame her stepmother for not identifying herself to the police as Fernando's intended dinner companion. Law enforcement agencies leaked information to the press whenever it suited them to do so, and quite often their internal security was so bad that they even leaked juicy tidbits when it would have been to their advantage to keep quiet. The fact that Olivia might have been having an affair with Fernando would make for great media gossip, and would surely get sold to a sleazy tabloid by some police clerk looking to make a few extra bucks. Since Olivia probably reasoned that she couldn't provide any really useful clues as to who had murdered Fernando, there would be no point in embarrassing herself by coming forward and telling the world that she'd been with Fernando right before he died. Certainly it wouldn't help her father's career—or his personal happiness—if Summer blundered into the middle of this sticky situation by informing the police that her stepmother and Fernando had traveled from Washington, D.C., to New York on the same train and looked as if they'd been planning a sexual assignation. For her father's sake, if for no other reason, Summer decided she had better keep quiet about what she had seen.

She stuffed the newspaper into the trash, then stared at it for a few seconds before pulling it out again. Okay, so she was having a hard time leaving this story alone. How likely was it that Olivia had actually been Fernando's intended dinner date? The train she had taken with them from Washington to New York had been scheduled to arrive in Penn Station at eight-forty. It had actually arrived about ten minutes late. That meant Fernando and Olivia would have been getting off the train shortly before nine. Everything about their behavior during the journey suggested that the two of them had been embarking on some sort of tryst, so it was only logical to assume Olivia had traveled uptown with Fernando to the Carlyle.

Most likely they hadn't wanted to arouse suspicion by arriving at the hotel together, so they probably took separate cabs, rather than sharing a limo. The journey must have taken each of them at least fifteen minutes, possibly a lot longer. As far as Summer could remember, the traffic hadn't been terrible, but Manhattan was Manhattan, and on a Saturday night, in drizzling rain, it must have been at least nine-fifteen by the time Fernando checked into the hotel. Super-rich industrialists staying in a large suite presumably got swept up to their accommodations at high speed, with an entourage of bellhops and assistant managers. Still, if Fernando was calling down to order room service dinner for two at nine-thirty, where was Olivia when he made the call? Still checking in? Already in his suite?

Summer mentally shook her head. Hard as it was to

visualize her stepmother engaged in an extramarital affair, it was flat-out impossible to imagine her sharing Fernando's suite for the entire night, leaving herself nowhere to receive phone calls from her husband. So that meant her stepmother would have booked herself a separate room at the hotel. Under her own name? Definitely, Summer decided. Olivia shopped in New York all the time and the Carlyle was her favorite hotel. In fact, using a false name would only rouse people's suspicions. But if she checked in openly, telling her husband in advance, nobody would ever think to question why she was there at the same time as Fernando da Pereira. Nobody would assume there was any connection between the two of them, even if they checked in within minutes of each other.

So Olivia had checked into the hotel either shortly before or shortly after Fernando and had been freshening up in her own room—more likely, her own suite—while Fernando called room service and ordered dinner for the two of them. Summer frowned. Was she leaping to conclusions? It was perfectly possible that Fernando had been ordering dinner for a third party, not for Olivia at all. And yet…they had seemed so intimate on the train and the timing was so tight, it was hard to avoid coming back to the conclusion that her stepmother was the person Fernando planned to share his meal with.

Summer got to her feet and paced, gripped by so much tension that she felt as if she were wired. Her scenario couldn't possibly be true, she decided, crunching on an ice cube left from her drink. It was taking a wild leap into uncharted territory to assume that Olivia had been planning to dine with Fernando in his suite just because they'd traveled on a train together earlier in the evening. Her stepmother was a calculating woman. If she had decided to throw caution to the winds and embark on an affair with Fernando, she would have been twice as circumspect as usual. She would never have burned her boats by openly traveling on the train with him. Undoubtedly Summer had misinterpreted all the hints and body language. Olivia and Fernando were simply friends and their presence on the train together was entirely innocent. She had spent the past half hour building a huge edifice of suspicion on a foundation way too flimsy to support it.

Summer realized she had the lid off the trash and that she was still staring at Fernando's picture. Dammit, Olivia had been flirting with Fernando. Maybe traveling by train from Washington to New York had actually offered the two of them a better chance of escaping scrutiny than taking a limo. Whether they used Olivia's chauffeur or Fernando's, the fact that they had traveled together would be known to their staff. Whereas a train, with luck, would be completely anonymous.

Summer paced, trying to make up her mind if she ought to confront her stepmother. Another thought occurred to her. When Duncan had called her father to report the news that she'd been abducted by a group of terrorists, she'd been told Olivia had answered the phone. Which meant that her stepmother had been back in Washington, D.C., before noon last Sunday, a mere fourteen hours after Fernando was killed. How would Olivia have explained such an abrupt return to her husband? If she'd been having an affair with Fernando, wouldn't she have felt obligated to remain in

New York and do some shopping so as to appear un-affected by his death?

With an impatient shake of her head, Summer shoved the paper deeper into the bin and closed the lid. Enough of this. There was a stack of mail waiting for her to deal with, and she'd better get on with it instead of brooding about what Olivia had and hadn't done the night Fernando was murdered. Since Fernando was dead, even if her stepmother had been involved with him, the affair was now over. Better, much better, not to go poking around and opening up a scandal that could only hurt her father. Summer grimaced. Jeez, she couldn't believe she was protecting her stepmother! She must be suffering from a sudden attack of maturity.

Smiling ruefully, Summer crossed to her desk and took the envelope from the top of her stack of mail. A bill, naturally. She slit the envelope, but that was as far as she got before she put it down and reached for her Rolodex to find Rita Marcil's phone number. Dialing, she made a bargain with herself. She'd hang up if she got the answering machine. If Rita wasn't home, she'd take it as a sign that she was obsessing about nothing.

Rita picked up the phone on the first ring. "Hello."

So much for signs, Summer thought. "Hi, Rita, this is Summer. Are you busy? Or is this a good moment to talk?"

"It's a great moment. I dumped Mark Scofield last week, and I'm so bored and pissed off with life that I was watching *I Love Lucy* reruns. What's up? Discovered any new ozone holes since last week?"

"You of all people should know that there aren't any holes in the ozone, only areas where it's thinned—'' Summer did a double take. ''Wait! Back up a minute here. You dumped Mark Scofield? Marvelous Mark with the great pecs and cute dimples?''

''That's the one.''

''But why?''

''He's a neurotic jerk and I'm a neurotic idiot and we decided our neuroses didn't match. End of story.'' Rita drew in an audible breath. ''Don't get me started on the subject of men. Especially New York men. You're smart to stick to dating guys who are too busy saving the planet to notice that you're the one calling all the shots in the relationship.''

That wasn't what she did, Summer protested silently. Was it? ''I don't call all the shots,'' she said. ''I just don't want to hop in the sack on the first date. I like to be good friends with a man before I have sex with him.''

''Hello, little Ms. Sunshine. Haven't you noticed by now that if you're good friends with a guy, it's because there's zero sexual attraction between the two of you?''

''That's such a retro attitude,'' Summer said indignantly. ''Men and women can be friends.''

''Sure they can. But don't expect your good friends to turn into great lovers.''

''It happens,'' Summer protested. ''I'm sure it does.''

''Do you moonlight as the scriptwriter for 'Ally McBeal'?''

''True love isn't just a sitcom fantasy, you know. There are a few of us left out here in the real world who still believe men and women can live together happily ever after.''

''I guess.'' Rita sighed. ''Ignore me, okay? My

mood is hovering right between homicidal and suicidal, with occasional upswings into mere depression. What did you call me about? I know it wasn't to talk about Mark. The jerk.''

''I wanted some insider information if you can get it for me. About a man who was murdered this past weekend at the Carlyle, here in New York. He was shot through the head, right in his hotel room.''

''Ouch! What was his name?''

''Fernando Autunes da Pereira. He's from Brazil, owns land the size of a small European country and has enough money to sit nose to nose with Donald Trump and play Monopoly with real money. This was an important, powerful guy, Rita.''

''He sure sounds it. Why are you so interested in him?''

''Well, his corporation owns vast tracts of rain forest in Amazonia for starters.''

''What do you want to know about his murder, specifically?''

''Everything. Maybe the case is closed and they've already arrested someone. I've been...out of touch... for the last few days, so I don't know what's happened since Sunday. Could you find out which reporter is covering the story? Fernando was rich and powerful enough that I'm assuming the *Times* has somebody following up on this. I'm sure the Brazilian embassy and the consulate will be pressuring the State Department for answers, and since the mayor keeps telling everyone how safe New York City is these days, I bet there's a lot of local pressure on the police to find the guy who pulled the trigger.''

''I'll have the name of the reporter who's working

on the case first thing tomorrow morning. Since tomorrow's Saturday, are you going to be home?"

"No, I'll be in the office. Like I said, I've
been...away...for a few days and I have a lot to catch
up on."

"Do you want to be called at work?"

"Yes, please. If the reporter says he's too busy, tell
him I may have some exclusive information for him."

"Do you?"

"I'm not sure. Possibly." She hoped to God she'd
be able to think of something to tell the reporter that
didn't involve either her stepmother or a breach of the
Official Secrets Act.

"Spell the dead man's name for me," Rita asked.

Summer complied. "Thanks, Rita. Any time I can
return the favor, let me know."

"You're welcome, although I notice you've
avoided explaining precisely why you're so interested
in the case. Did you know da Pereira personally?"

"Only slightly, in a roundabout sort of way. He was
a guest at the dinner we both went to at the State
Department last Friday. I guess you didn't meet him?"

"No, or I would remember the name. But the fact
that he owns land in Amazonia and you met him at a
state dinner can't be the only reasons you're interested
in his murder. What gives, kiddo?"

It was difficult to answer Rita's questions without
either lying or getting dragged into revealing forbidden information about her kidnapping. In the end, she
had no choice but to lie. "There's something going on
with a friend of mine," Summer said finally. "She
and Fernando had a business deal set up, something
to do with property investments in São Paulo. The
money involved was peanuts to him, but it's a big deal

for her and she's anxious to find out what's going on. She's afraid the deal's going to fall through now Fernando is out of the picture.''

If Rita hadn't been so preoccupied with thoughts of Mark, she'd have realized that a friend's property deal was no reason for Summer to be checking on the details of Fernando's murder. As it was, she let the inconsistencies slip by. ''Well, I don't want to rain on your friend's deal, but I hope she had the details of their agreement in writing.''

''I think that's part of the problem. They met socially, and this was one of those handshake kind of things—''

''A fatal mistake to shake hands with a man,'' Rita said. ''That's how my relationship with Mark Scofield started. He was supposed to provide great pictures for a travel book and I was going to do the text. If I'd listened to my head instead of my hormones, I'd have known by our second date that he was simply a vacant mind fronted by a cute smile, with zero talent to back up the great physique.''

''But it was a truly spectacular body,'' Summer pointed out. ''Not to mention a really cute smile.''

''Don't remind me. I've spent the past twenty-four hours sublimating my lust in chocolate truffles, and my hips have the extra inches to prove it.''

Summer laughed. ''Get the reporter who's covering Fernando's murder to call me by midday tomorrow and I'll personally pay for you to get the extra inches pounded out of your thighs at the massage parlor of your choice.''

''That's a deal. By the way, how's that gorgeous hunk of manhood you had dinner with on Friday night? He's not the loves-puppies-and-trees sort of guy you usually hang out with.''

Summer tried to sound casual. "Do you mean Duncan Ryder?''

"I sure do. Now there's a man who has a brain and a cute smile. Not to mention a body worth panting over.''

"He's also my stepmother's brother,'' Summer said dryly. "Whenever I find myself getting too entranced by his flashing brown eyes and broad shoulders, I remind myself that he and Olivia share at least two-thirds of their genes. You've no idea how quickly that dampens my enthusiasm.''

"Honey, we share ninety-nine percent of our DNA with chimpanzees. It's the one percent difference that matters. In fact, my hormones are perking up just thinking about Duncan Ryder. He's supposed to be taking me to dinner next month when I'm back in Washington. I might even haul out the NordicTrack and build thirty minutes of sweat equity in his honor.''

"Feel free. But if you decide to go to bed with him, be warned. His average relationship lasts about three weeks. And I plan to be callously unavailable when you call and expect me to sympathize.''

"Okay, I hear you. But three weeks of sex with Duncan Ryder might be worth it.''

So help her, Summer thought, but since that incredible kiss, she'd almost decided the same thing. Which made you wonder if the genetic differential from chimpanzees had actually added many IQ points to the human brain. She and Rita talked for a few minutes more, mostly about Mark Scofield's newly discovered imperfections, before they hung up.

Summer went back to her mail and dutifully wrote

a check for the phone company, and another one to MasterCard before pushing the remaining stack of mail aside and gazing blankly at the fat plaster cupid who adorned the corner of her mantel. He stared back at her with smug self-satisfaction, as if he knew exactly what she was thinking. Finally she stuck her tongue out at the cupid and went in search of her purse and the card Duncan Ryder had given her with his phone number written on it. She dialed the number and felt her mouth relax into a soft, goofy smile when he answered on the second ring.

"This is Summer." She was annoyed about the goofy smile, so she spoke curtly.

"I was about to pick up the phone and call you." Duncan's voice was warm and slightly husky. She'd never noticed that undercurrent of huskiness in his voice until last week. "How was your trip home?"

"Just yummy. Secret Service agents are always a barrel of laughs."

"I wanted to drive you back to New York, but your father insisted on a Secret Service escort and I could understand why he needed the security of knowing that you were being guarded by professionals."

"I wasn't complaining. Not much, anyway. I realize Secret Service agents are trained to keep people alive, not entertained."

"This will be the first night you're sleeping alone since the kidnapping. Are you okay with that?"

"I'm fine." Summer cast a glance around her apartment and discovered that it looked less alien than it had an hour earlier. "I have a lot of work to catch up on before Monday, which is good because it keeps my mind off the kidnapping. But if I get an attack of nighttime terrors, I promise you'll be the first to know."

"Good. Call anytime, Summer. Don't try to be a heroine and tough this out alone."

"Don't worry. I don't do heroics. I have a lifetime history of supreme cowardice."

Duncan laughed, as if she had been making a joke instead of telling the simple truth. "I'm going to be in Manhattan on Monday for a session at the United Nations," he said. "If you're free that evening, would you have dinner with me? I've found a restaurant on the Lower East Side where the owner is Mexican and his cooks are all Russian immigrants. It makes for an interesting meal."

Duncan wanted to have dinner with her. Summer realized her sappy grin had expanded into a dreamy, self-satisfied smile. She sat up straight and glared at the smug cupid, her refusal automatic. "I'm sorry. Monday night isn't good for me—"

"Then how about Sunday? I'll come into Manhattan a day early. Say yes, Summer."

The sappy grin returned, and this time she didn't have the willpower to banish it. What the heck, it would be churlish to refuse him twice. "All right, thank you. Sunday would be great."

"I'll pick you up at five. We could take in a movie before we eat. If you're free that early."

"I'm free, and I'd love to go to the movies." Obviously, she was not only free, she was also nuts. This was Duncan-Ryder-Olivia's-brother she was agreeing to meet. She spoke brusquely into the phone. "Do you have my address?"

"Yes, I have it."

"Then I'll look forward to seeing you on Sunday."

On the point of saying goodbye, Summer remembered belatedly that she'd called originally to ask for some practical help. "Duncan, wait! Don't hang up."

"I'm here."

"I called to ask a favor. I was hoping that you might be able to track down some background information for me about Joe Malone's family—"

"You don't have to call in any special favors for that. Luckily for you, the head of the CIA, the FBI director and the entire cabinet of the United States government wants to know more about Malone's background. Ask them."

Summer gritted her teeth. This sounded more like the patronizing Duncan she was used to dealing with. "You know as well as I do that the government is convinced Joe wanted to disappear and that I helped him achieve his goal. I think they're wrong about Joe, and I know they're wrong about me. But the net result is that nobody in the FBI is going to give me yesterday's weather forecast, much less reveal confidential background information about Joe's family."

"Whatever the FBI suspects about your motives, that doesn't change the fact that your best hope of vindication is to be totally upfront with them. They'll come around when the evidence shows that they were wrong."

"Sure they will—"

"Yes, they will. I'm not saying this as a government flunky, I'm saying it as your friend. If you have any line of investigation you think it would be worthwhile to follow, you should tell the FBI. Or your father. Between them, they can call on resources no private citizen can begin to match—"

"I understand all that, and I'm not holding back

anything relevant from the FBI. At least I'm not sure
if it's relevant. Maybe you can help me decide that.
All I need to know is whether Joe Malone's mother
was related to a very important Brazilian industrialist
called Fernando Autunes da Pereira. Joe's mother is
dead now, and I know her maiden name was Ribeiro.
But when I was in Brazil, I met some of Joe's cousins,
and I remember they were called da Pereira. The name
didn't mean a thing to me at the time, and I'm not
even sure why I remember it now, except that Joe
explained there were da Pereira family members all
over Brazil and he could never get away from them.
He was joking and yet not joking, if you know what
I mean? Even at the time, it struck me that his relationship with the da Pereira side of his family sounded
a bit rocky.''

"You realize, of course, that there must be hundreds
of thousands of people with the same name? The fact
that Fernando and some of Joe's cousins are both
called da Pereira doesn't mean that Malone is related
to Fernando.''

"Of course it doesn't. And that's why I need to find
out for sure. Fernando da Pereira was such a prominent man in Brazil, and they're so hung up on family
down there, I thought you could probably find out if
he and Joe were related with a couple of phone calls.''

There was such sudden and complete silence on the
other end of the phone that Summer thought they
might have been cut off. "Duncan, are you still
there?''

"I'm still here,'' he said slowly. "I was thinking
about what you just said. I had meetings with Fernando da Pereira a couple of weeks ago. He was an
impressive man, part old-style South American feudal

baron and part twenty-first-century internationalist. Do you know that he's dead?"

"Yes, I just read the account of his murder in Sunday's *New York Times*. He was killed on Saturday night, a few hours before I was kidnapped."

"Are you suggesting there's a connection between da Pereira's murder and Malone's disappearance? That your kidnapping is somehow tied in to da Pereira's death?"

It seemed absurd expressed in those terms, and yet Duncan had made the same instant, intuitive leap that she had. Summer drew in a shaky breath. "Tell me if you think I'm crazy, but if it turns out that Joe Malone and Fernando are relatives, doesn't it strike you as a strange coincidence that the Justice League decided to kidnap me and ransom Joe the precise same weekend that Fernando was getting himself murdered?"

"For sure it's an odd coincidence," Duncan said slowly. "But the fact that they might be distant cousins is too frail a link to be truly meaningful. The da Pereira family is big. Even if Malone turns out to be a member of the family, he's one of dozens of miscellaneous cousins."

"It's not just that they might be cousins. The *Times* mentioned that Fernando had recently changed his attitude toward the development of Amazonia. According to the paper, he was trying to get legislation through the Brazilian congress that would set aside huge tracts of land as permanent wilderness. Since preservation of the rain forest has been one of Joe's obsessions for at least a decade, I wondered if maybe Joe had managed to make a convert out of Fernando."

"Which makes you suspect that Fernando might have been killed by people who had commercial interests that were threatened by Fernando's sudden conversion?"

"It's possible, isn't it?"

"It's possible," Duncan agreed. "Amazonia is one of the world's last frontiers, a place where multimillion-dollar fortunes can still be made and lost with astonishing speed. Opposition to his views on how to develop the region might easily explain Fernando's death. But it doesn't shed any light on what happened to Malone. If hard-line developers wanted to get rid of Malone, they didn't need any fancy schemes. They could have put the word out in Manaus. For a hundred bucks, they'd have had people lining up to take on the job of murdering him."

"It's not that simple," Summer protested. "Maybe they didn't want Joe dead. Perhaps they arranged to have him kidnapped because it was essential to take him alive."

"Let's suppose you're right and Fernando's enemies are Joe's enemies, and they want to take Joe alive at the same time as they kill Fernando. Why wait until he's in jail in the States before they go after him? For two hundred bucks and a plane ticket to Rio, there are plenty of men in Amazonia who would have kidnapped Joe and served him up on a silver platter with an apple in his mouth."

"And you've just summed up all the reasons why I didn't want to make a big deal of this with Julian Stein." Summer didn't feel as relieved as she should have that Duncan seemed convinced that there was no real connection between Fernando's murder and Joe's disappearance. She hesitated for no more than a split second before deciding that she couldn't confide her real dilemma about the murder to Duncan, since it

involved his sister's possibly adulterous relationship
with Fernando. Still, one step at a time. Despite every
logical argument, she wanted to know if there was a
family connection between Joe and Fernando.

"Duncan, just to set my mind at rest, I really would
like you to find out if Joe and Fernando are related. If
they're not, then we don't have to consider even the
remote chance that there's some sort of link between
Joe's disappearance and Fernando's death. If they turn
out to be cousins…well, then I'd feel a lot more comfortable about going to Julian Stein and suggesting that
the FBI should look into the timing of Fernando's
murder."

"I agree it would be good to have a definitive answer. I'll see what I can find out, and I'll call if I get
anything interesting."

"Thanks, Duncan. I appreciate your help."

"You're welcome," he said. "See you Sunday.
Five o'clock."

Summer hung up the phone and wrinkled her nose
at the remaining pile of mail. She rooted through the
circulars and professional journals until she came
across a small square package that obviously held a
CD. She reached for her letter opener, trying to remember if she'd ordered any music recently. Slipping
the knife under the sealed tape, she noticed that the
return address suggested the disk came from Sony, but
the postage stamps were Brazilian, and there was a
customs declaration form that was also Brazilian—

Summer's stomach swooped and she slit open the
package with hands that had suddenly started to shake.
Inside was the typical clear plastic case, protecting a
shiny, unlabeled CD. A sheet of white notepaper had
been pushed between the CD and the case. It bore a

pen-and-ink sketch of a drunken-looking frog aiming his tongue at a large, cross-eyed fly. There was no written message, but the drawing was unmistakably Joe's. He had a real talent for sketching, and he'd signed every note he'd ever written her with a drawing of a frog.

So tense that she could hardly breathe, Summer turned on her computer and slipped the disk into the CD-ROM drive. The screen flickered and finally settled on its message.

Enter password.

# *Eleven*

**W**ithin the first twenty-four hours of Joe's arrival at the da Pereira estate outside Manaus, Alonzo Salazar da Pereira had greeted him personally. A terrible mistake, Joe reflected, if his captors wanted him to believe that they planned to let him live. He would have preferred masked faces and a serious attempt to conceal the whereabouts of his prison. At least that would have meant there was a chance his captors expected him to remain alive long enough to identify them to the authorities.

While waiting for the moment when they would feel free to kill him, Alonzo's henchmen treated Joe with all the courtesy of an honored guest. The suite of rooms set aside for his use, though locked and barred, was equipped with an assortment of journals in both English and Portuguese, a whirlpool, a bed large enough to host a modest orgy and a state-of-the-art computer, minus its modem, of course. The built-in bar contained a small fridge stocked with fresh fruit and soft drinks. There was even a TV that worked off a satellite and received programs from all over South America.

For two days Alonzo's people left him entirely alone, except to bring him gourmet meals. He was apparently destined to die well-fed. Once he'd explored every inch of his prison and confirmed that there was no way to make contact with the outside world, and no possibility of escape, Joe occupied himself alternately worrying about Summer and trying to work out what the hell had happened to Fernando. Clearly Fernando didn't realize that Alonzo, their mutual cousin, had sold out to the opposition. If Fernando had known about Joe's kidnapping, he would have intervened to prevent it. Which meant—however you massaged the facts—that Fernando was out of commission and Joe was already up to his ass in crocodiles. Worse, the piranhas would soon be moving in to attack whatever pathetic shreds of flesh the crocodiles left behind.

Joe expected to be left to languish for several days as part of the softening-up process, but obviously his captors were impatient for results, and on the third morning of his captivity, Alonzo da Pereira returned. He entered the room alone, carrying a slim briefcase that he set on the coffee table.

"Joe, my friend, how are you doing today?" He spoke in Portuguese, and clapped his arm around Joe's shoulders, the epitome of goodwill and joviality.

With pointed disdain, Joe removed himself from Alonzo's embrace. He walked across the room, keeping his back turned, and stared silently out of the barred window. He figured that since death was inevitable, he had no reason to play the death scene according to Alonzo's game plan.

"Joe, I'm disappointed in you." Alonzo managed to sound genuinely hurt. "Como, old friend, accept that there is nothing to be gained by sulking. Let us be reasonable and discuss the issues between us like sensible adults."

Anyone listening would think that Alonzo was the soul of sweet reason and Joe a surly grouch. Joe remained silent, the only defense he had, and a pretty pathetic one. He crossed his arms over his chest and watched the armed guards patrol the walled boundaries of the estate. They wore black uniforms that made them look like extras in a Bruce Willis *Die Hard* movie. Their uniforms also made them highly visible targets against the brilliant bird of paradise plants and cattleya orchids that grew in abundance in this section of the garden. But then, the guards were more for show than for function, since nobody was likely to mount an attack on Alonzo da Pereira's estate, not in Manaus, where the family company owned half the real estate and probably ninety percent of law enforcement personnel.

Alonzo sighed. "Joe, you are a stubborn man. Why are you ignoring me? Have you been badly treated? No, of course you have not. All I have done is rescue you from an American jail. Is that a crime? Can you not accept that we share the same ultimate goal?"

Joe didn't speak.

Alonzo clicked his tongue angrily. "Every day that passes is a day when people die needlessly. If you will only share the details of your discovery with me, then we can work together to see that your goals are achieved."

Joe finally turned around. "What discovery?" he asked blandly.

Alonzo's smiles disappeared, along with his elegant speech. "Don't fuck with me, Joe, or I'll fuck you right back. We both know what you've discovered. I've seen the material you sent Fernando."

Joe's palms started to sweat. There was no way Fernando would voluntarily have shown those documents to anyone, not even if he still trusted Alonzo as a completely loyal second-in-command. Joe looked at Alonzo, trying to read the truth of what the man knew, but it was hopeless. Alonzo was a world-class liar and Joe an absolute novice at the game of deception.

A gleam of scornful amusement glittered in Alonzo's eyes. The bastard actually enjoyed deceiving people, and didn't give a damn that Joe knew he was being lied to. Alonzo sat down and propped his feet on the antique brazilwood coffee table. His refined manners returned. "Come, Joe, let us stop skirting around the truth. We are not enemies, or at least we don't need to be. We both wish to provide the people of the world with a great benefit—"

Joe's temper snapped and with it his resolve not to speak. "Don't pretend that we have interests in common. We have nothing in common—"

"Sure we do, Joe. We are blood relatives, after all."

"Barely, thank God. Besides, all we share is a few ancestors, nothing else. Your goal is to make money. Mine is to save lives—"

"Right. You are the soul of nobility, and I am scum. Spare me the lecture." Alonzo yawned, then leaned closer, beaming with sincerity. "Believe me, Joe, I am as anxious to save lives as you are. Absolutely. It is merely that as a businessman, I recognize that the quickest, easiest and most efficient way to insure the success of any new product is to show investors how they can make money."

Joe moved out of range before Alonzo could administer another of his poisonous hugs. "Why am I having this conversation with you? Where is Fernando? He and I have already reached an agreement that satisfies both of us. We've negotiated a schedule for building the production plant and signed a contract binding us to an equitable split of the profits.''

Alonzo stood up, his pretense of languor vanishing. "It is true that you and Fernando had reached an agreement that satisfied the two of you. Unfortunately, it did not satisfy my associates. In fact, I would go so far as to say it royally pissed off several prominent members of our extended family.''

Alonzo was radiating a barely concealed glee, the first genuine emotion that Joe had sensed in him. Not good news, Joe thought, his stomach dropping. Alonzo was a bootlicker, and he would only defy Fernando if he had gotten some really heavy-duty allies lined up to cover his ass.

"We both know that our cousin doesn't run Industria Agricola do Norte as a democracy,'' Joe said, testing the waters. "Fernando makes the decisions and the rest of you see to it that his decisions are carried out. All the executive power is concentrated in Fernando's hands. So even if you and your gang of allies disagree with Fernando, there's nothing you can do about it.''

"You are only half right, Joe. The company is organized so that power is concentrated in the hands of the corporate president, whoever that might be. As of last week, I am the president of Industria Agricola do Norte.''

Joe's lungs constricted and his body froze into absolute stillness, although he could feel sweat trickling down his spine. There was only one way that control of the company could have passed out of Fernando's hands. He looked up and saw the triumph glittering in Alonzo's eyes and understood what that meant. He sucked in a gulp of air, trying to stay calm and refusing to reveal the depths of his despair. He managed to meet Alonzo's jubilant gaze with a look of cool calculation. "You murdered Fernando," he said flatly.

"How could you imagine me capable of such a dastardly deed?" Alonzo was openly mocking. "Alas, my poor cousin was killed in New York City, late last Saturday night. Here in Brazil, we complain all the time about the threat that thieves and beggars pose to personal safety, and yet it seems that in the United States, the richest country in the world, people are no more secure than we are here."

Joe ignored the rhetoric and concentrated on the fundamental truth that Fernando had been murdered. He thought he'd been resigned for months to the probability of his own death. Now he realized just how much he'd been counting on Fernando's power and cunning to keep him alive. He felt a surge of intense, bitter regret and understood for the first time just how much he loved the simple fact of being alive.

"How did you manage to kill him?" he asked Alonzo, partly playing for time, but mostly out of genuine regret. "Fernando was too smart to make himself an easy target."

"My poor cousin was foolish enough to fall in love. A terrible mistake for a man of his age, wouldn't you agree?"

"What do you mean?"

Alonzo's voice thickened with contempt. "I mean Fernando was thinking with his dick instead of his brain and he opened a hotel door that he'd have been a lot smarter to keep closed."

"You killed him in a hotel in New York?"

"My dear Joe, I did no such thing. Of course not. However, it is regrettably true that Fernando was shot in his hotel room in Manhattan. Sadly, no trace of his murderer has yet been found. I imagine a tip-off will alter that situation shortly, and the police will be able to make an arrest. Case closed. The mayor will be so pleased that his crime-solving statistics are holding up."

Joe walked into the bathroom and slammed the door, but there was no bolt on the door and Alonzo simply crashed it open and pushed him back against the counter. "I'm a busy man and I'm tired of waiting for you to agree to cooperate. No more screwing around, Joe. Now that we both know Fernando is dead, perhaps you would like to resume our discussion in a more accommodating frame of mind? For example, would you care to tell me where I can find samples of this precious wonder drug you have concocted? And also a listing of the trials you have presumably conducted that document its effectiveness. That would be an agreeable starting point for our negotiations, I believe."

"Go to hell."

"No, Joe, that is where you will go unless you cooperate with me. You know, I truly do not understand your reluctance to cooperate with me. I am more than ready to cut you in on the profits of this deal. I must say, it's hard for me to grasp exactly what your hangup is."

"Let me spell it out for you. I don't like dealing with murderers. There, that's my hang-up."

"You're a hypocrite, Joe. You were quite happy to deal with Fernando, who had dozens of his rivals killed in the first few years of his business career. His sudden turn onto the path of virtue didn't happen until he'd eliminated all serious opposition."

Was that true? Joe wondered. Probably not. Fernando had always been ruthless, but he'd also possessed a core of integrity that would have prevented his murdering to achieve his goals. Besides, whatever ethical shortcuts Fernando had taken in the past, he'd genuinely come to regret his earlier crimes. His determination to get Joe's wonder drug to market at the lowest possible cost had been one of the ways he hoped to make amends for past sins. Joe had a fleeting thought that, bad as it was to know that Fernando was dead, it was almost consoling to realize that his respect for his cousin hadn't been misplaced. Obviously, Fernando's promises of minimizing profits and maximizing benefits for the world's poor had been entirely sincere. Otherwise he would never have been murdered.

"At least I can die with a clear conscience," Joe said. "Which is more than I could do if I sold out to you."

"Sit down, Joe." Alonzo dragged him out of the bathroom, pushed him into a chair and sat down on the opposite side of the coffee table. "Let's get the facts straight here. Sure, you can die a martyr if that's what turns you on. But if you die today, your knowledge will die with you. What will that achieve?"

"You'll lose," Joe said. "That's worth a lot in my book."

A vein throbbed in Alonzo's temple, and his face turned red and then white as he fought for control. "Okay, it's true that if I kill you, I'll lose out, big time, and you consider that a major benefit. On the other hand, you will be dead. And that means your drug will never make it to market, and you will never have the satisfaction of seeing it work its healing miracles. Seems like a lousy trade-off to me."

"My drug won't work any miracles if you're in charge. Nobody except a few wealthy people will be able to afford to buy it."

"Not so. The marketing of this AIDS drug will be a straightforward commercial decision on my part, and you can be sure that I will find a price point for the drug that maximizes its potential. I am not so stupid that I can't grasp the simple fact that a million sales at twenty bucks a pop will bring me more money than a thousand sales at a thousand dollars each. You see, Joe, you have everything to gain and nothing at all to lose by cooperating with me."

Joe smiled bitterly. "I'm not a total fool. I know that what you're saying is just window-dressing to tempt me into trusting you. As soon as you have all the information you need, you'll kill me."

"You are wrong. I am a businessman, not a thug, and I have no interest in killing you. On the contrary. I look forward to establishing a long-term partnership between the two of us. I hope you spend many productive years making friends with primitive tribes in the rain forest and talking to their medicine men. You're a brilliant biochemist. Who knows what other goodies you may discover for me to exploit?"

God help him, but Joe realized he was actually tempted. If he didn't cooperate, he would die. He had no illusions about that. Would it be so bad to save his own life, and the lives of hundreds of thousands of people around the world, by agreeing to cooperate? Of course, there was a good chance he would cooperate and Alonzo would kill him despite all his promises to the contrary. But, from the point of view of millions of people around the world who were sick with AIDS, his death was a relatively small price to pay for getting the drug to market. And he could count on Alonzo da Pereira doing that one way or another. There was too much profit potential to even consider otherwise.

Alonzo leaned forward. "I see that you are beginning to understand that I am not a monster, Joe. And just to encourage you to view my proposals favorably, I have a videotape I would like to show you."

"A videotape?"

"Yes. Of an old friend of yours. Summer Shepherd."

"What have you done with Summer?" Joe grabbed Alonzo's arm. "My God, if you've harmed her, I swear you can kill me before I'll give you so much as a used Kleenex."

"There's no need for melodrama." Alonzo opened the briefcase he'd brought with him and extracted a standard videotape, which seemed to be the only thing inside the case. He slipped it into the VCR and pressed the play button. "I certainly wouldn't dream of killing you and losing all that valuable information you are holding in your head."

A blurred close-up of Summer filled the TV screen. Despite the less-than-perfect focus, Joe could see that she looked pale and tired, but as breathtakingly beautiful as ever. A lump formed in his throat. If he could ever have felt sexual desire for a woman, Summer would have been the one. Last fall, for a couple of weeks, he'd even allowed himself to indulge the fantasy of marriage and family life. He would have loved to see the kids he and Summer would make together. Their disastrous night together had simply proved that it took more than deep affection and a villa overlooking a moonlit beach to make for adequate sex between a man and a woman.

The camera followed her as she got into a limo, escorted by two men who were obviously Secret Service.

"When was this taken?" Joe asked through clenched teeth.

"On Wednesday, in Washington. And now you see her coming home to her father's house again. The FBI questioned her all day. They really are very suspicious of her, you know. They can't help thinking that she is such a good friend of yours that she must have staged her own kidnapping in order to achieve your release from jail."

With superhuman difficulty, Joe managed not to display any of the myriad emotions he was feeling. He watched Summer go into her father's town house, followed by the inevitable Secret Service escort. "Why are you showing me this?" he asked as the screen showed a much clearer shot of Summer getting out of the limo again, this time at the entrance to her apartment in New York.

"Summer no longer has the Secret Service to guard her," Alonzo said. "As you can see, she is back in Manhattan now, and I understand she plans to return to work on Monday morning. We kidnapped her once with no difficulty at all. This little video is to remind you that we can take her again, at any time. And from our point of view, the lovely Ms. Shepherd is eminently disposable."

"What would you achieve if you killed her?"

"For a start, we could be sure that she would ask no more annoying questions. We are monitoring her phone conversations and not much liking some of what we are hearing."

"If you harm Summer, you can roast in hell before

I'll give you the time of day, let alone access to my formula.''

"Big words, Joe, covering empty threats. If you persist in your refusal to cooperate, we shall bring your friend down here to Brazil and torture her until you agree to give us the information we require. I believe we would both of us find that a...distasteful...method of procuring your cooperation. We both know, however, that it would be supremely effective.''

Joe walked back to the window and stared out at the flowers, afraid of what he might do or say if he actually had to look at Alonzo da Pereira. He felt sick with guilt for having implicated Summer by sending her the CD-ROM, and terrified even to contemplate what Alonzo and his thugs might do to her if they realized that Summer wasn't just the person he loved most in the world. She was also the one person, now that Fernando was dead, who might be able to get the information about his AIDS drug to the appropriate authorities.

The burning question at this moment was how to keep Alonzo and his gang running hard and fast down the wrong track. They shouldn't have left him in jail for two whole weeks, Joe reflected. And they for sure shouldn't have left him alone and comfortable in this room. He'd had more than enough time to plan ahead. Of course, whether or not his plans would be adequate to keep him alive was debatable. But he was fairly confident that he could arrange for Alonzo da Pereira to be distracted long enough for Summer to discover just what was at stake.

Joe finally turned around again. He spoke in a low voice, managing to keep a shaky hold over his rage. "All right," he said. "I don't seem to be left with any real choice. I'll give you the formula, but first you have to take me back to the States.''

Alonzo laughed. ''Good try, Joe.''

''There is only one place in the world in which there are samples of the drug available for you to access, and that's in Washington, D.C.''

Alonzo frowned. ''That's not possible. You haven't been to Washington in months—''

''Fernando took the samples with him on his last trip to the States. He hid the samples in a safety-deposit box. I have the formula in my head, and the only samples of the drug are hidden somewhere you could never find or access on your own. Now think again about whether or not you're willing to take me back to Washington.''

Alonzo scowled. ''We shall fly in my private plane. You will be sedated for the final part of the journey, and I shall carry documentation that shows you are my cousin—''

''I am your cousin,'' Joe said with mild irony.

Alonzo totally ignored the interruption. ''We will inform the authorities that you have a rare disease and that you are being flown to the States for medical treatment. Since you will be unconscious, you will have no opportunity to speak to anyone.''

''Why are you telling me this, Alonzo?''

''I'm warning you not to fuck with me. There will be no chance for you to escape, so if this insistence on returning to Washington is a vain attempt on your part to avoid the inevitable, be warned.''

''I'm a man of reason, cousin Alonzo. I don't fight losing battles, and this one is clearly lost. Tell me precisely what financial terms you were planning to offer me. Since I've decided to sell out, I want to know how much money is in it for me."

"A million dollars up front, and a five percent royalty."

"I want ten percent."

"How about splitting the difference? Seven and a half."

"No. I want ten."

Alonzo gritted his teeth. "Ten. It is agreed."

"Then let's get going. You're wasting time and money by keeping me here."

Alonzo wasn't that easy to fool. "If by any chance you are sincere, which I seriously doubt, I'm delighted that you have decided to be sensible. If you are still hoping against hope that you can escape—well, eventually you will realize that you have no choice other than to cooperate."

Joe walked over to the VCR and switched it off, blacking out the disturbing image of Summer smiling into the hidden camera. "There's nothing like a few weeks of being locked up to give a man a different perspective on his life. I guess I'm finally seeing things your way, Alonzo. If Fernando couldn't defeat you, then I know for sure that I can't."

"Idealists usually don't surrender their dreams so easily."

"I'm a scientist, not a dreamer. I'm not ready to die, and in the last resort, I guess my new drug is like everything else in the world. My discovery isn't about saving lives, it's all about money. And I've just decided to grab my share."

Alonzo gave a satisfied smile. "Now you're talking sense, Joe. I knew you would, sooner or later. In the end, everything always comes down to money."

# *Twelve*

Enter password.

Summer had been staring at the same infuriating
message for more than an hour. She had typed in at
least fifty names, words and number combinations. So
far, she had achieved nothing except a flickering
screen and the exasperating message that her choice
of password was incorrect.

Too frustrated to stay at her desk, she got up and
wandered through the apartment, trying to put herself
inside Joe's mind. He'd mailed the disk to her, so the
logical conclusion was that he wanted her to have access to it. But, since he'd gone to the trouble to encode
it, presumably he wouldn't have wanted the password
to be something too obvious, like her name, or his
birthday. So Joe probably chose a password only she
would guess—something associated with their shared
past. But what, for heaven's sake? She'd already been
through the names of their Stanford University friends.
She'd tried Stanford because that was where they'd
met. She'd tried frog and prince and princess because
they'd spent an entire summer collecting frog jokes
and E-mailing them to each other three or four years
ago. She'd tried Shakespeare, Romeo and Juliet, because the first time they'd gone out together they'd
seen a comically terrible student production of the

play. She'd even tried typing in Pereira to see if that might be the magic key that opened the disk. No luck.

The trouble was, she and Joe had so many memories to draw on that it was hard to know how to narrow the range of possibilities. Summer sat on her bed and stared at the window blinds in search of inspiration. Maybe she was reaching too far back into their shared past. She and Joe had been best friends for more than a decade, so he might have decided to go with some recent event, rather than expecting her to review years and years of friendship and hit on the correct password. The most recent time they had been together was last fall, and her memories of their tour of Brazil were crystal clear, from the brash excitement of Rio de Janeiro's nightlife to the primitive splendor of the rain forest.

In fact, some of her memories from that extended trip were not only vivid, they were acutely painful. Summer shook her head, wincing as she recalled the debacle of the night when she and Joe had broken the twelve-year pattern of their friendship and gone to bed together. It had been a disastrous-enough experiment for the details to be burned into Summer's consciousness and, she suspected, into Joe's as well.

Looking back, she could see exactly how they'd walked themselves into the trap of trying to change from friends into lovers. They both wanted to marry and have children, they had both recently ended relationships that hadn't worked out. Add to their basic situation the fact that they had been staying at one of Rio's loveliest hotels, sharing a room as they had many times in the past, and the perfect opportunity was added to means and motive.

They'd finished a bottle of wine at dinner, then gone

upstairs to their room, laughing and joking, at peace with themselves and the world. Then they'd wandered out onto the balcony, a little bit drunk on the wine and totally intoxicated with the beauty of the tropical night. Summer had been entranced with the fairy-tale view over the beach and the flickering lights from the *favelas* that dotted the hillsides. Faintly, beneath the roar of traffic, she'd convinced herself that she could hear the crash of waves breaking on Copacabana Beach, one of the most famous stretches of sand and sea in the world.

It had seemed entirely natural to share her happiness at the wonder of the moment. She had turned toward Joe and immediately sensed unusual tension in him. Good grief, she'd thought. He wants to kiss me! Too surprised to react, she simply stood and looked at him. Questioningly, he reached out and put his arms around her. Equally hesitant, she leaned toward him and tilted her head back, waiting for his kiss. He bent his head and slowly, gently, pressed his mouth to hers. The ensuing kiss had been pleasant, if not earth-shattering.

Everything that followed had been a disaster, ending with the heart-rending moment when Joe had finally acknowledged—to himself as much as to her—that he was gay.

Summer got up and paced from the bedroom back to the kitchen. Memorable as the events of that night had been, surely Joe wouldn't choose to remind her of something that must rank right up among their most devastating shared experiences? And yet, Joe must also know that she would never forget how splendidly the night had started—the magic moment when they had stood hand in hand on the balcony, looking down at Copacabana Beach. The perfect moment that had preceded the debacle.

Returning to the computer, she scowled at the cursor, which blinked at her with mindless patience, waiting for her to enter some text. She typed in Copacabana before she could change her mind, squirming with discomfort at the images summoned up merely by seeing the word in print.

Like magic, the screen went blank and reformed with a brilliant, sharp-edged photo of an unfamiliar flower. It looked like some sort of orchid, with delicate blue-tinged white petals, shading at the tips into a deep purple color. The plant wasn't identified, and there was no text to explain why Joe had sent her a picture of a flower, much less why he had felt the need to encode the disk that carried it.

Summer clicked to move onto the next screen. Another picture appeared, equally clear and equally incomprehensible. It showed a gathering of tribal people, presumably Indians, in the Brazilian rain forest. The men, naked except for woven bark loincloths, were gathered around a cooking pot set on an open fire that was built directly outside the entrance to a communal thatched hut. The tribal women, wearing heavy shell necklaces, clustered together inside the hut. The separation of the sexes, and the fact that the men were in charge of the cooking, probably indicated that this was a ceremonial ritual rather than the preparation of a regular meal. A giant gourd held by one of the old men seemed to be filled with the purple-tipped blossoms, which at least suggested a reason why Joe had sent her a picture of the orchid. Perhaps he wanted her to be able to identify the precise flower being added to whatever was being brewed in the ceremonial pot?

Summer enlarged various areas of the photo. Nothing especially noteworthy caught her attention. The chief wore an elaborate necklace of parrot feathers, and in close-up she could see that one of the younger men wore a watch. Since the building of the Trans-Amazon Highway, such odd juxtapositions of ancient ritual and modern technology weren't uncommon. Joe had told her that restless young men often left their tribal homes to travel to the outposts of civilization along the Amazon River. By some mysterious alchemy, tribes seemed to hear rumors of encroaching civilization even before government officials registered the existence of a tribe and the location of its villages. Unfortunately, these adventurous travelers often returned to their tribes bringing back the diseases of civilization along with their Nikes and their wristwatches. Without the protection of previous exposure, Joe had found repeated evidence of tribes that had been decimated by flu, or measles, or one of the sexually transmitted diseases that were rampant in Manaus.

Summer chewed on the end of a ballpoint pen and tried to work out why in the world Joe would bother to password-protect two photos dealing with such harmless subjects as jungle orchids and tribal ceremonies. If these were plants and a tribe previously unknown to the Western world, why didn't he say so?

She clicked to the next screen. No more mysterious photos, thank goodness. This time she was looking at a color chart, with areas shaded in six different hues of green through yellow to brown. To her relief, she didn't have to guess what the chart was meant to represent, since it was headed A Quarter Century Of Rain Forest Destruction In The Amazon River Basin, 1973-

1998, and a key indicated precisely what degree of forest degradation each color represented.

A copyright symbol at the foot of each page noted that the chart had been prepared by the Save The Rain Forest Fund. An address on the Upper West Side of Manhattan appeared in tiny print beneath the copyright notice.

Twenty-five pages of charts followed, each one dated for a separate year, and each one showing expanding areas of yellow and decreasing areas of dark green. By the late 1980s, the yellow on the charts had turned to specks of brown in some areas, indicating totally barren land. In the 1994-95 burning season, the worst year on record, more than eleven thousand square miles of rain forest had disappeared. That meant an area larger than the state of New Jersey had turned from pristine natural habitat into desolate mining and agricultural wasteland, taking with it a significant percentage of the world's supply of fresh water.

No surprises here, Summer thought, flicking from screen to screen and back again. Horrifying as the figures were, it was scarcely news that vast swaths of rain forest were burned or destroyed in the name of progress. She moved her cursor in an idle circular motion, frowning when it chanced to highlight the copyright message at the foot of one of the charts. She had never heard of a group called Save The Rain Forest Fund, and she thought that she knew all the reputable groups working in the area of rain forest preservation. She pulled the phone directory from its hiding place under a pile of books and folders and searched for an entry for Save The Rain Forest Fund. She found nothing. Another small mystery to add to the bigger one of why Joe had sent her this disk.

She flicked through the charts again, which only increased her confusion. Hard as it was to imagine why Joe would be sending her pictures of rain forest flowers and tribal ceremonies, it was even more difficult to imagine why he would feel the need to mail her statistical charts documenting rain forest destruction. Joe knew she was informed about the problem of rain forest loss in a general way, and if she'd wanted specific details, her position at the university would have given her access to all the information contained in these charts, plus research papers galore and hundreds of photos taken by U.S. satellites during the last decade. In fact, many of the satellite pictures were available for downloading from the Internet, and they gave a dramatic visual account of the loss of tropical vegetation in Amazonia. She seemed to recall that several conservation organizations had blown up the government satellite photos into posters and used them as fund-raisers. In view of the public availability of the information contained in these charts, why in the world had Joe bothered to send her the disk? Even if she concluded that the timing of the disk's arrival was sheer coincidence and had nothing to do with Joe's disappearance, there must be a reason why he had chosen to send her something that seemed so meaningless—and then encode the disk.

Hoping for a message that explained everything, Summer clicked onto the final page of the document, which turned out to be a letter from Joe to a company called Varsity Printing and Copying. She read the letter, progressing from confused to totally bewildered as she did so.

Joe instructed the printers to prepare color transparencies of the charts contained in the disk accompanying his letter. Joe wrote that the slides would be called for by his assistant, and asked the printers to bill the work to his account. He left space for his signature and added his full title—Dr. Joseph Malone, Honorary Professor, Department of Biochemistry, University of Brasilia, and Consultant, Department of Biochemistry, New York University.

The letter was undated, unless Joe had added a date by hand on the hard copy, and the only other piece of information was the address of the printing company, which was in Manhattan, all the way downtown near New York University.

However hard she tried, Summer could find no significance to the fact that Joe had wanted color transparencies made of his charts. Presumably he'd planned to make a presentation at some New York institution and hadn't wanted to carry bulky transparencies in his luggage all the way from Brazil. Despite rereading the letter so many times that the words blurred in front of her eyes, Summer couldn't squeeze any secret meaning out of the simple text.

Other than confirmation of Joe's academic credentials, there seemed to be no personal information in the letter at all. As far as she could tell, the job titles he cited weren't some sort of obscure code. She knew he'd been given an honorary appointment at a Brazilian university in order to facilitate his travels within Amazonia. She also remembered that he'd been kept on staff at New York University when he'd left for Brazil three years ago, although she couldn't remember his exact job title since Joe didn't discuss his academic honors very often.

Giving up on the letter as a source of enlightenment, Summer went back to the beginning of the file and reread every page, searching for some hidden message. She found nothing, and eventually concluded that Joe must have intended to call her and explain what the disk was all about as soon as he arrived in the States. Instead, he'd been arrested, rushed off to jail, and the disk had probably slipped his mind in the crush of other, far more important concerns. Instead of being a vitally important explanation of why he'd been kidnapped, the disk was, to all intents and purposes, a red herring.

Summer took the disk out of her computer and slipped it into her drawer, stretching to ease the kinks in her shoulders as she waited for the computer to shut down. Much as she wanted to solve the mystery of why she and Joe had been kidnapped by the Justice League, she didn't think this disk was going to provide any answers. Yawning, she decided that at least her efforts to decode Joe's charts had provided one useful service. After several nights of insomnia, she was now drowsy enough that there seemed a definite possibility that she would fall asleep within minutes of her head touching her pillow.

Summer came awake with a start, instantly alert and fully aware of her surroundings. Of course, she thought. How could I have been so thick-witted? Joe's letter instructed Varsity Printing to produce transparencies of the documents contained on the enclosed disk.

Since she had been reading a computer version of the letter, not the hard copy, there was no reason to conclude that the documents Joe had sent the printing company were the same ones that appeared on the disk he'd sent her. If Joe had been worried about the disk falling into hostile hands, he might have set it up so that it would seem to contain unimportant academic trivia. In reality, the printer's address on the letter was probably the only meaningful piece of information on the entire disk. Obviously, Joe intended for her to go to the printers. That's why the letter had mentioned his "assistant" who would collect the transparencies.

She glanced at her bedside clock. It was 6:00 a.m. She sincerely hoped that Varsity Printing opened on a Saturday morning. If she had to wait until Monday, she might explode with frustration. She went to her desk in pursuit of the phone book, on the off chance that a phone call to the printers would produce a recorded message that gave their hours of business.

She achieved much more than she'd hoped for. Varsity Printing, like Kinkos, turned out to be open twenty-four hours a day, seven days a week, presumably to accommodate the New York University students who needed term papers and overdue dissertations copied in the wee hours of the morning.

Summer dressed hurriedly, then took the subway downtown, arriving at the print shop before eight. A young woman wearing copious amounts of purple eyeliner and black lipstick was busy restacking shelves with multicolored copy paper when Summer came into the store, but she broke off at once and asked how she could help. Her name tag said that her name was Morticia, which Summer hoped was a joke.

"I've come to pick up Dr. Joseph Malone's color transparencies," Summer said. She'd printed out a copy of Joe's letter so that she would have something to validate her claim to his property and she dropped the letter on the counter, trying to look bored. Most people's pulses presumably weren't racing in anticipation when they came to pick up color transparencies.

Morticia didn't bother to read the letter. "Malone, did you say? Joseph Malone?"

"Yes." Summer clamped her lips shut and resisted the urge to launch into a long-winded justification of her right to take possession of Joe's transparencies.

Morticia finished her search of one drawer, obviously without finding what she was looking for. She came back to the counter and glanced at the letter. "Oh, he's Professor Malone," she said.

"Yes. Does that make a difference?"

"Of course." Morticia sounded scornful, as if even a complete moron should have realized that professors' projects were filed in a separate place from the work done for lesser mortals. This time her search was successful. She came back with a box and put it on the counter.

"Check that everything's there," she said, tearing off the bill that was taped to the lid. "It's already paid for. There're supposed to be two sets of twenty-five transparencies each."

"Two sets?"

"Yes. Should there be more?"

"No," Summer said quickly. "Two sets, fifty transparencies in all. That's it. Let me just check this is the right stuff." Heart thumping in double-quick time, she opened the box and held the first eight-by-eleven transparency up to the light. Her excitement dissipated as soon as she saw a familiar chart, with a familiar heading. A Quarter Century Of Rain Forest Destruction In The Amazon River Basin, 1973-1998. The subheading indicated that this particular chart was for the year 1973.

Damn! Summer's hopes plummeted. Her early-morning inspiration hadn't been so brilliant after all, she thought disconsolately. Barely able to conceal her disappointment from Morticia, she rifled through the remaining transparencies and swiftly concluded that the top twenty-five were duplicates of the material she already had at home. As for the remaining twenty-five sheets, a quick glance confirmed that they were either pictures of tropical plants, or close-ups of various sorts of tree bark, including a couple of the same purple-tinged orchid Joe had included on the disk he sent her. Not surprising subjects, she supposed, since Joe had spent the past three years painstakingly cataloguing the plants and the herbal medicines used by tribal medicine men in the Amazon rain forest.

These might well be photos of plants and trees that he believed had potential medical and pharmaceutical uses, and it was frustrating to think that the cure for some horrible disease might lurk hidden within these pretty pictures. It was logical to conclude that the purple-tinged orchid was especially important. But important for what? Unfortunately, without some accompanying text, the slides were virtually useless. They certainly didn't help to explain why the Justice League had kidnapped her and whisked Joe away to some unknown destination.

With a brief word of thanks to Morticia, Summer pushed the box of transparencies into her satchel and trudged back to the subway station. While she'd been chasing will-o'-the-wisps, she hoped she hadn't missed a phone call from whichever reporter was covering Fernando da Pereira's death for the *New York Times*. The way her luck was running recently, she wouldn't bet on it, though.

She was more pessimistic than she needed to be. Just as she unlocked the door of her office, the phone started to ring. Sprinting across the room, she grabbed the receiver. "Hello, this is Summer Shepherd."

"This is Bill Ogilvie of the *New York Times*. Rita Marcil told me to give you a call. She said you might have something for me on the da Pereira murder. Something about a friend of yours who was involved in a business deal with Pereira."

She should have known that Rita would explain the situation that way—as information Summer had to give, rather than information she needed to get. "It's possible I might have a couple of leads for you to follow," she acknowledged. "But I was also hoping you could fill me in on what's happened to the investigation over the past week. I was in the hospital for a couple of days having my appendix taken out—"

"I'm sorry. I hope you're feeling okay now?"

"I'm fine, thanks. These days they use laser beams to cut you open and you hardly feel a thing." She felt guilty garnering false sympathy, but the FBI had insisted she explain her unexpected absence from New York and from her job by claiming a medical emergency. "Anyway, I'm out of the loop as far as news stories go, and I wondered if you could fill me in on the current status of the Pereira investigation."

"Could you tell me first why you're so interested? Rita said something about a friend who was involved in a business deal...."

"Yes, that's right. Senhor da Pereira was a good friend to a very good friend of mine. I promised I'd find out what I could."

"This friend of yours—"

"Is out of the country. But she's very upset by Fernando's death, and she's hoping to hear that the police have made an arrest."

"Was she having an affair with him?" Bill Ogilvie asked.

Summer had been prepared for that one. "You can't possibly expect me to answer that question—"

"Sure I can. The police believe Pereira was planning to have dinner in his suite with a woman. They've no idea who that woman was. Or so they claim. Do you have any suggestions as to her identity, Ms. Shepherd?"

"None at all," Summer said, reminding herself that if she gave in to temptation and mentioned her stepmother's involvement with Fernando, she was going to create a scandal that would most likely engulf her father. Sexual scandals seemed to be a surefire way of garnering headlines. "But I know it couldn't have been my friend because she's been in Europe for the past three weeks." She transferred the phone receiver from one sweaty palm to the other, slightly appalled at how easily she managed to lie.

"Having her appendix taken out?" Bill Ogilvie suggested.

"No!" Summer realized she might not be quite as smooth a liar as she'd thought. "Good grief, if you're suggesting that I was Fernando's mistress, you're way off base! I only met the man for the first time the Friday before he was killed. We exchanged three sentences—maybe four—at a state banquet given in honor of the Brazilian foreign minister. And then I never saw him again until—" She stopped abruptly, realizing she'd just explained herself into a major blooper.

"Until when?" Bill Ogilvie asked.

"Until we happened to travel on the same train from Washington, D.C., to New York," Summer said.

"And, before you ask, I didn't speak a word to Senhor da Pereira the entire journey. I just noticed he was on the train, that's all. And when I read that he'd been murdered, I realized he must have been killed less than two hours after I left him at Penn Station."

There was a moment of silence before Bill Ogilvie spoke. "That's the first I heard that Pereira traveled by train from Washington to New York right before he was murdered."

It had never occurred to Summer that she would be revealing new information by mentioning that Fernando da Pereira had traveled to New York by train. "Surely you aren't telling me that the police didn't know da Pereira arrived from Washington, D.C., by train right before he was killed?"

"I have no idea what the police know. This investigation is sewn up so tight that nothing's getting out. Detective Sergeant Callahan is an old warhorse who's a master at making lengthy statements that don't reveal anything useful, and my usual sources inside the department swear they don't know anything that I don't."

"So what do the official statements say at this point?" Summer asked. "I don't even know that."

"The autopsy confirms Fernando da Pereira was killed instantaneously as a result of multiple gunshot wounds to the head and heart, and that the presence of an empty meal cart in his room suggests that the killer or killers gained access to the suite by pretending to have come from room service. As for motive, the official line is that the killer was probably motivated by opposition to Pereira's views on land development in Brazil."

"That's basically what Callahan was saying right from the start."

"Yes," Ogilvie agreed. "It's also logical and quite possibly true—"

"But?"

"But I'd be more willing to believe it was the whole truth if everyone didn't seem so damned anxious to stop the media sniffing around this story."

Was that nervousness because the FBI and the CIA already knew that there was a family link between Joe Malone and Fernando da Pereira? Summer wondered. If so, the government's investigators seemed to have reached the same conclusion she had, namely that the disappearance of one cousin and the death of another might well be related events. Still, she wasn't at liberty to reveal that linkage to Bill Ogilvie. On the contrary, she'd been threatened with prosecution if she breathed a word about her kidnapping for any reason.

"The police department may be so uptight about avoiding leaks for the simple reason that Pereira is one of the richest and most powerful men in Brazil," she suggested.

Ogilvie grunted. "True. But I've been investigating crime and murder in this city for twenty years and my thumbs are pricking on this one. You're the daughter of the secretary of state, so you must have realized by now that when the administration heavies want to keep a story under wraps they have enough power to keep everything sewn up so tight that nobody sneezes in public without permission."

Did Olivia have the power to keep the investigation sewn up this tight? Summer didn't think so. Her step-mother was presumably sweating bullets in case her connection to Fernando was revealed, but it didn't seem likely that she could influence the course of a murder investigation without revealing facts that she'd much rather keep hidden. As secretary of state, Gordon Shepherd wielded real power. His wife had social prestige to spare, but no practical power whatsoever.

"I'm not questioning your instincts as a journalist," Summer said. "But sometimes the obvious explanation is also the true one. Maybe the police are being so careful simply because Pereira was an important man and they don't want to offend the Brazilian government by blowing the investigation."

"You're doing a great job of downplaying the strangeness of this case, Ms. Shepherd, but right now I have to tell you I'm wondering if it's pure coincidence that the person who's calling me to inquire about the status of my investigation just happens to be the daughter of our illustrious secretary of state."

Summer gave a rueful laugh, relieved to be totally honest at last. "Trust me on this one. I'm making these inquiries strictly as a private citizen. My father would most likely be more annoyed with me than with you if he knew the two of us were talking."

"So far, I wouldn't say we were talking," Ogilvie said dryly. "Not about anything significant, at least. But I'm waiting in hope."

Until she knew for sure that there was a family connection between Joe and Fernando, she really had nothing to tell him, tempting as it was to set him loose on Olivia's trail. "Give me a bit more time and I'll get back to you," she said.

"And if you don't call me, I'll call you. Count on it."

"Before you hang up, there's one other thing," Summer said. "Have the police produced any theories about why Pereira was killed here in the States? If his murderers were Brazilians who opposed his efforts to control development in Amazonia, wouldn't it have been easier to kill him in Brazil? I was in Manaus last year, and officials there admitted they can't even get accurate numbers on how many people are murdered each year in the Amazon region, much less find the killers.''

"According to my research," Ogilvie replied, "Pereira lived in houses that were armed fortresses, and he never moved anywhere inside Brazil without a small army of bodyguards. And when I say small army, I'm talking literally. Anyone who wanted to kill Pereira and didn't want to stage a pitched battle would know that their best chance of success was likely to come when he was traveling overseas with only a couple of bodyguards to protect him.''

Summer thought of the man she'd watched on the train with her stepmother and frowned in puzzlement. There hadn't been a bodyguard anywhere near Fernando that night, she was sure of it. "One minute he's so paranoid he's protected by an army, and the next minute he travels by public train from Washington, D.C., to New York, and then crowns his carelessness by opening the door of his hotel room to an assassin disguised as a waiter. That doesn't sound believable.''

"I couldn't agree more," Bill Ogilvie said. "I talked to one of the reservationists at the hotel and she let slip that the suite was only reserved for Senhor da Pereira late that afternoon, which makes it even more difficult to believe that he was killed by people who opposed his views on development policies for the Amazon—''

"Because they wouldn't know where he was staying in New York to arrange the hit—"

"Exactly. But according to the police, that's what happened." Bill Ogilvie sounded beyond cynical. "In fact, according to yesterday's official statement, they're optimistic that they're shortly going to make an arrest."

"Does your sarcastic tone of voice mean that you think they're going to arrest the wrong man?"

"That depends on what you mean by the wrong man. I expect they're going to arrest some naive scumbag who was paid to pull the trigger and then got hung out to dry by his employers. The police will get their murderer, and the public will lose what little interest in this story they ever had. In the meantime, whoever is working so hard to keep this case under wraps will heave a giant sigh of relief, and everyone will be happy except for a couple of people like me who really want to know who ordered and paid for the killing, not whose finger pulled the trigger."

Summer realized that a heavy stone had settled in the pit of her stomach, so heavy that it made her whole body hurt. Olivia seemed to be one of very few people in the world who had known exactly where Fernando was going to be the night of his murder. She had known there were no bodyguards on the train. She would have been in a perfect position to inform a hired assassin that Fernando was alone in his suite and vulnerable to attack....

Summer pulled herself up short, shaking her head. Olivia was a stuck-up pain in the ass, but to suspect her of murder was carrying dislike way too far. It was plain crazy to accuse Olivia of involvement in a murder plot, even if she was only making the accusations in the privacy of her own mind.

To compensate for the wayward direction of her thoughts, Summer spoke with redoubled fervor. "Bill, I swear I don't have a clue about who was behind da Pereira's murder. The only thing I might have is a vague lead that would tie this killing to another crime—"

"Give me your lead. Let me track down the connection if there is one."

"I can't." Summer's hand tightened around the phone. "I'll get back to you, I promise, but there's something I have to check out before I can say anything more."

"I'll call you next week." Bill reluctantly accepted the finality in her voice. "And, Summer—"

"Yes?"

"This case stinks. Be careful who you confide in, and don't ask questions unless you already know the answers."

She laughed doubtfully. "There's not much point in only asking questions when you already know the answers."

"But it's a hell of a lot safer," Bill said. "Before you turn over too many rocks, you want to be sure there aren't any reptiles living under them. You'd make a very tasty meal."

The call to Bill was so unsettling that Summer felt an urgent need for reassurance. She dialed Duncan's number, then slammed down the phone when she realized what she'd done. She brewed herself some iced tea, getting a better grip on her unruly emotions as she went through the familiar procedure. She didn't need to call Duncan, Summer told herself. The person she needed to talk with was her father. Not only was he the logical person to provide some emotional support, he was secretary of state and would be far more informed about all the latest details concerning her kidnapping and Joe's disappearance.

Fortunately, her father picked up the phone, not Olivia. He greeted her warmly and immediately reiterated his concern about her being alone in New York and vulnerable to a renewed kidnapping attempt.

Summer insisted that she was fine. "Dad, face it. Unless I become a hermit, I'm always going to be a target for terrorists who want to make a point with you—"

He spoke in the dry voice she loved, even though it had always been such a contrast to her mother's bubbling effervescence. "If you're trying to reassure me, Summer, I have to report that your ploy isn't working."

She smiled. "Dad, truly, I'm okay. I even managed to sleep last night without taking a pill."

"That's great. But if you need help, don't hesitate to ask for it. There's no shame in feeling shaken up by what's happened to you, and there are plenty of doctors on staff at the CIA who've dealt with the physical and emotional consequences of kidnappings—"

"Dad, I'm fine. The only thing that would make me more fine is if we could find out what's happened to Joe Malone."

"We all want that, but I'm afraid there's nothing concrete to report at this stage. I wish there was. The FBI director believes that Malone and the other Justice League members left the country by a regularly scheduled flight going from Orlando airport to Mexico City. They're assuming he traveled onward from there to

Brazil. But, as you know, it's always a delicate matter when we have to coordinate our investigations with those of a foreign country, and officials in Mexico aren't falling over themselves to search their flight records. And we have to assume that Malone is traveling with a false passport by now, so I'm afraid this isn't going to be easy. Julian Stein isn't saying as much, but it's my belief we're most likely to find out where Malone went when he chooses to come forward."

"If he *can* come forward. Dad, the FBI is never going to find Joe if they persist in treating him as a criminal instead of a victim. I'm absolutely sure Joe is a prisoner of the Justice League, not their ally, and Mr. Stein obviously doesn't believe me."

"Be that as it may, my dear, you can rest assured that the finest agents in the FBI, using the best and most modern technology, are searching for Joseph Malone. We have to wait for them to be successful."

"But what if they are never successful?"

"That's unlikely. Julian Stein isn't a man I would call my friend, and our political views are quite diverse. However, I believe he has one of the most brilliant investigative minds in this country, and I'm confident he will ultimately find the answer to all our questions."

Summer wished she shared her father's confidence. "I'd be more likely to agree with you if I thought Julian Stein was directing his brilliant mind down the right path. Joe's an American citizen, after all. He deserves protection if he's being held against his will. What's all that stuff about the right to be considered innocent until you're proven guilty? Doesn't that apply to Joe?"

"That, my dear, is a legal right, not a practical

guideline for an FBI investigation. If they thought everyone was innocent, they wouldn't get very far pursuing criminals.''

''You think Joe orchestrated his release from jail, don't you?''

''Not necessarily...''

Her father's voice tailed away and Summer drew in a deep breath, asking the question that had worried her for the past several days. ''Tell me the truth, Dad. Do you think I helped him?''

''My dear, I'm sure you didn't.'' Gordon sounded entirely sincere, a useful quality for a diplomat lying through his teeth. This was her own father, Summer reflected painfully, and she had no idea whether or not he was telling her the truth. A sad commentary on the state of their relationship.

''I know Malone is a very special friend of yours,'' Gordon continued. ''And I understand why you're worried, but one of the ways I've learned to cope with my workload since I came to Washington is by delegating and compartmentalizing. The FBI and the CIA employ thousands of trained professionals to solve mysteries like this one. My role is to assist the president in conducting the foreign policy of the United States. I can't fulfill my duties effectively if I'm constantly trying to do Bram Cooper's job, and Julian Stein's, along with my own.''

''I understand.''

Her father's voice softened. ''No, Summer, I'm not sure that you do. You've always wanted me to react with my heart, and I always let you down because I've trained myself to react with my head. But in this instance, I didn't mean to imply for a moment that your safety and well-being are less important to me than my official duties. Of course that's not true. I simply wanted to convey the message that we have a lot of very competent people working to find Joseph Malone. We can speculate all we want, my dear, but the fact is, we—meaning you and I—don't have the resources at our disposal to make intelligent judgments. This is truly a case where leaving the investigation to the professionals is not only the right thing to do, it's also the smart thing. This case requires cool heads, not warm and impulsive hearts.''

''Yes, of course. I can see that, Dad, truly I can. It's just very hard to switch off my natural curiosity when I'm the person who spent three days blindfolded, tied up and drugged.''

Her father's voice thickened. ''My dear, it was a horrible experience and you came through it with amazing courage, thank God. But in my opinion, you're trying to tough this out alone when you really need help. Why won't you let me arrange for a Secret Service guard on your apartment for the next little while? Wouldn't that give you the boost to your sense of personal safety that you need? Please say yes. I'm sure we'll have some word about Malone's whereabouts within a couple of weeks, so you wouldn't be afflicted with a bodyguard for long. Better yet, why don't you come back to Washington and stay with me and Olivia till the FBI have a firm handle on what's really going on.''

''I can't, Dad, but thanks for the offer. I appreciate your concern, really. But this is a busy time for me at work, and sharing my apartment with a Secret Service agent wouldn't reassure me. It would be a sure-fire method of giving me round-the-clock insomnia.''

Her father gave a brief chuckle. ''Why am I not in

the least surprised by that answer?'' His voice suddenly changed, becoming brisk and efficient. "Summer, I have another call coming in, one I have to take. Look after yourself, honey. I'll call tomorrow to see how you're doing.''

Summer ought to have found her father's words comforting. Instead, she hung up the phone feeling vaguely depressed. Shaking off her gloom, she sublimated her multiple frustrations in an orgy of administrative clean-up and left her office around four-thirty, feeling virtuous for having cleared her in-tray and answered all her E-mail.

By the time she got back to her apartment, some of the smug glow had dissipated and she realized that a long evening stretched ahead with nothing much to fill it. Her hand reached for the phone, and her fingers had dialed the start of Duncan's number again before she slammed down the receiver and shoved her hands into the pockets of her slacks.

Determined not to sit at her desk and stare at the phone, she opened her freezer and rummaged inside, wondering if she could work up the energy to cook a real meal from scratch. Maybe, if she got really motivated, she could even call a couple of friends and see if they were free to join her for dinner.

Her gaze fixed on a package of frozen chicken breasts, which sat on top of a TV dinner. The trademark symbol of its manufacturer leapt out at her.

The copyright symbol, she thought, stunned into immobility. The copyright symbol for the obscure Save The Rain Forest Fund. My God, maybe that was the clue Joe had expected her to find! Slamming the freezer door, she upended her satchel over the sofa and found the box of transparencies she'd picked up that morning at Varsity Printing. Holding one up to the light, she checked for the copyright symbol. It wasn't there. The transparencies she'd collected this morning carried the same headers as the charts on Joe's disk, but they weren't identified as being prepared by the Save The Rain Forest Fund.

She had no idea what her discovery meant, but surely it meant something. All fingers and thumbs, she turned on her computer, then loaded Joe's disk. She clicked onto the first chart, dated 1973, and held the corresponding transparency up to the screen to check for differences. Other than the missing copyright symbol, the charts seemed identical. Just to be absolutely sure, she held the transparency right over the screen.

The screen image and the transparency image weren't the same size, but even so, her gut told her that the two charts didn't quite match. The differences were subtle, but undoubtedly there. Twitching with impatience, Summer gave the print command, adjusting the size. She then had to sit and watch while her painfully slow color printer churned out copies of all twenty-five charts from Joe's disk. Carrying her printouts to the coffee table in the living room, she covered each printed sheet with its counterpart from her pile of copy-shop transparencies.

As she'd suspected, now that they were exactly the same size, she could see that every transparency was slightly different from the corresponding printout. In 1973, the minuscule differences were centered on the Manaus area. With each subsequent year, the differences spread farther west, but it was impossible to see any particular pattern, or to understand what message Joe was trying to convey to her.

Summer stared at the charts until her eyes burned

and her head ached. The differences between the two charts revolved around tiny strips of dark brown that, according to the key code, meant barren land. Was Joe trying to tell her something about illegal cutting of primeval forest? That seemed unlikely. In an age when satellite reconnaissance enabled CIA spooks to tell when hostile governments moved a tank from one army base to another, it seemed unlikely that Joe would have discovered a pattern of rain forest destruction that was unknown to the authorities. Besides, he would have no reason to keep such a discovery secret. Given his passion for environmental causes, he would want to blaze that knowledge to any media outlet willing to carry pictures of the destruction. He wouldn't waste time sending her a disk that carried a high risk of his message never being deciphered by her or anyone else.

Even with hard copy of both sets of charts to work from, it was really difficult to get an accurate fix on precisely what the differences between the two sets were. With a flash of inspiration, Summer realized she could download the charts from Joe's disk onto her hard drive, scan the transparencies, and then run a computer-generated comparison of the two sets of documents. It took her a while to complete the mechanics, but an hour later she was looking at an astonishing image on her computer screen.

After comparing each document with its partner and telling the computer to draw a composite chart of all the differences, she was left with a line of brown that headed a thousand miles west of Manaus, into the hinterland of the Amazon rain forest, and culminated in a brown dot on the chart in the center of an area that was entirely surrounded by a patch of dark green.

Which, according to the original key, indicated an area of virgin, unexplored rain forest.

It was impossible to believe she was looking at a graph of deforestation, Summer decided. What Joe had sent her was a map. A map that led to a tiny village, deep in the rain forest, where a tribe of Indians conducted some sort of religious ceremony that involved the use of a beautiful, mauve-tinted orchid.

She had finally decoded Joe's message. Now all she had to do was work out what in the world it meant.

# *Thirteen*

Until he was actually standing inside the cubicle that masqueraded as a lobby in Summer's shabby apartment building, Duncan had managed to convince himself that he'd traveled to New York in order to take care of urgent business with the Peruvian delegation at the United Nations. But feeling his heart pound and his pulse race as he pressed the buzzer for Summer's apartment, he acknowledged the obvious. His three-hour meeting this afternoon with the Peruvian commercial counselor had been his excuse to visit New York, not the reason.

The truth was, he'd come to New York because he couldn't stand to be away from Summer any longer. Ever since the moment last Sunday when he realized she'd been kidnapped, his usual defense mechanisms had been blown away, exposing his vulnerability. Which was why he was shuffling from foot to foot in her lobby, doing a first-rate imitation of a lovesick teenager, on the slim chance that a woman as beautiful, intelligent and sexy as Summer Shepherd might be hanging around in her apartment on a Saturday night with no plans. Yeah, right.

"Hello?" Summer answered the buzzer, her voice distracted.

"It's Duncan." Famous within the State Department for his witty one-liners, his mind went blank at the sound of her voice. He not only couldn't think of anything witty to say, he couldn't think, period.

"Duncan! Isn't it Saturday? I could have sworn it was Saturday." At least she didn't seem annoyed to hear from him, only confused by his turning up a day early for their date.

"It is Saturday, but I have some news for you that couldn't wait."

"About Joe?" Her distraction vanished instantly at the possibility of hearing something about her beloved Joe.

Duncan gave a mental sigh. "Yes, I have the information about Malone's family that you wanted. Let me in, Summer, okay? This isn't the best way to pass on the details of his family tree."

"Of course. Sorry, I wasn't thinking."

That sure made two of them. The door-locking mechanism buzzed and he went inside quickly, bypassing the clanky, old-fashioned elevator and climbing the dusty stairs to Summer's fourth-floor apartment. She was waiting for him when he arrived, standing in the doorway and looking as if she was actually pleased to see him. A definite first, for which he could no doubt thank Joe Malone.

"Come in." She stepped back, holding the door open. "Your timing's great. How'd you know I'd be home from the office by now?"

Since his brain and his vocal chords remained equally nonfunctioning, he followed her into the apartment without speaking, although he looked around with interest. The eclectic decor of the living room suited her complex personality perfectly, Duncan thought, from the stark white walls and functional window blinds, all the way through the comically ornate fireplace and the sofa decorated with a life-size chimpanzee who wore wire-rimmed glasses and had been propped up against the cushions so that he appeared to be reading a copy of *National Geographic* magazine.

"Who's your friend?" he asked, pointing to the chimp. Not exactly a quip to go down in history, but at least it was words, coming out of his mouth and sounding almost like normal conversation.

"That's Algernon," she said. She stroked the chimp's head affectionately. "Joe gave him to me for Christmas a couple of years ago. Isn't he wonderful?"

Duncan repressed an unworthy desire to dismember either Joe or Algernon. Or better yet, both. "He's a very handsome fellow," he said. He glanced at his watch and looked up again without the faintest idea what time it was. "I won't keep you long if you're going out tonight."

"I wasn't going anywhere." Summer's fingers wove affectionately through Algernon's hair. Duncan wondered if it was possible for a sane human being to be jealous of a stuffed toy.

"You said you had news about Joe—" Summer prompted.

Duncan snapped out of a daydream that involved him and Summer engaged in activities that would have caused even Algernon to glance up from his *National Geographic*. "Oh, yes, I do. I found the information you asked for yesterday about his family background."

"That's great, Duncan! You worked really fast. Thank you."

"I called a friend in Brazil and he came through for

me.'' He'd called in every favor he was owed by half a dozen friends and colleagues before getting what he needed. ''Malone's father was a professor at Duke University. I guess you knew that?''

She nodded. ''He must have been in his late forties when Joe was born because he died about three years ago and he was at least eighty. Joe's mother was his second wife, I'm pretty sure of that.''

''Yes, Professor Malone married twice, and Joe's mother was much younger than her husband. She was a Brazilian woman named Anna Constanza Ribeiro.''

''And she's dead, too. I don't think it was much of a surprise to Joe when they lost her, although he was devastated, anyway. She'd had rheumatic fever when she was a child and she was always a bit of an invalid.''

''His mother's gone, but fortunately, she wasn't the end of the trail. It took a bit of scratching to unearth the details, but the Pereira family is so prominent that there's a wealth of information available about them if you look hard enough. Anyway, to cut a long story short, it turns out that Joe's maternal grandmother, Anna Constanza's mother, was a member of the da Pereira family.''

Summer exhaled sharply. ''I knew it,'' she said, almost to herself. She looked at him, her attention so focused that he felt scorched by the fierceness of it. It was merely one more example of his hopeless state of infatuation that he was more interested in the astonishingly brilliant blue of her eyes and the luminous glow of her complexion than he was in the reason for her strong reaction.

''Did you manage to find out the exact relationship

between Joe's mother and Fernando da Pereira?'' she asked.

"Joe's grandmother, Maria Constanza, and Fernando's father, Ernesto, were brother and sister."

Summer's forehead wrinkled in calculation. "So that makes Joe and Fernando cousins," she said.

"First cousins once removed, to be precise. But Ernesto and Maria had five other brothers and sisters, and if you traced all the grandchildren from those seven da Pereira siblings, I bet you'd be looking at forty or fifty people who can claim some reasonably close degree of cousinhood with Fernando da Pereira."

"But only one of those fifty Pereira descendants was murdered last weekend and only one of them was whisked off by the Justice League last Tuesday morning—"

"True," Duncan conceded. "But bigger coincidences than that happen every day."

Her gaze turned savage. "I don't believe Fernando's death and my kidnapping happened within twelve hours of each other by sheer coincidence. Do you?"

"I don't know." Duncan decided not to point out that if Fernando's murder really was linked to her kidnapping and Joe's disappearance, it was just as likely that Joseph Malone had been the mastermind of the whole operation as the victim. While part of him wished that Summer wouldn't be so blindly loyal to Malone, another part of him wished that he could be on the receiving end of even a small part of such passionate and steadfast devotion.

He walked over to her side and unwound her hand from Algernon's arm. "Supposing I say that I agree with you that Fernando's death and Joe's disappearance seem likely to be linked. What explanation can you come up with that ties the two events together?"

Her gaze shuttered, although she didn't move away from him. "I don't know," she said.

He'd been expecting her to say exactly that, so he was surprised by the flash of hurt he felt. He crooked his forefinger under her chin and tilted her head back so that she was forced to look straight at him. "Don't lie to me, Summer," he said tightly. "Tell me to get the hell out of here. Tell me that you don't trust me and that you're not going to share a damn thing that you know or suspect about Fernando's murder and Joe's disappearance. But don't lie to me."

A wave of hot color stained her cheeks. She pushed his hand away and walked to the window, wrapping her arms around her waist in an unconscious gesture of self-protection. "I can't tell you what I really think. You're a government employee. Doesn't that mean you're obligated to report whatever I say to the FBI?"

"No," he said. "I have no official role in the investigation of your kidnapping. I'm here as your friend, nothing more and nothing less."

"Even so, it's not easy for me to confide in you." She kept her back turned and talked to his reflection in the window. "When I look at you, I still see a man who's first and foremost Olivia's brother."

"That should be easy enough to take care of." Duncan often thought how ironic it was that the family member he felt least close to should stand as such an impenetrable barrier between himself and Summer. He crossed the tiny living room in a couple of strides, taking her into his arms and once more twisting her around to face him. A tide of desire washed over him, all the more powerful because he had kept his feelings for her suppressed for so long. "Make love to me," he said huskily, "and I guarantee you'll forget that I'm Olivia's brother."

The look she directed at him was incredulous, but at least she didn't push him away. "Are you that good in bed, Duncan? Or are you just terminally arrogant?"

"With you, I would be that good in bed."

She laughed softly. "Ah, I see. Arrogant for sure, and possibly talented, but I have to have sex with you to find out. At which point, if you haven't lived up to your promises, I guess I'm out of luck."

When she laughed like that she was so damn sexy that he had trouble remembering the basic rules of civilized behavior. His breath came fast and choppy, matching her heartbeat, which thudded against his chest, quick and heavy. She wasn't quite as calm and controlled as she seemed, Duncan realized. Taking a chance, he did what he'd been longing to do and kissed her, holding nothing back. She clung to him, responding hotly and only attempting to draw away when he started to undress her.

With a surge of need, primitive and forceful enough to take him by surprise, he put his hands on her hips and held her immobilized, not attempting to conceal his state of arousal. "If you're going to say no, Summer, now would be a really good time."

"Would you leave if I asked you to?"

He closed his eyes, opening them again when he had sufficient control to give her the answer she deserved. "Yes."

She splayed her hands across his chest, her fingers fidgeting with the buttons of his shirt. He wondered if she had the faintest clue what she was doing to him each time her fingernails scraped against his bare skin.

"Sex makes everything about a relationship messy and complicated," she said.

"Not always. Sometimes it makes things simple."

"Not with me. Trust me, Duncan, we're both going to regret it if I go to bed with you. We're just starting to be good friends—"

"What I feel for you right now has got nothing to do with friendship."

"You said you were here tonight as my friend—"

"Different subject, different context." Amazingly, if he concentrated really hard, he could talk almost like a normal person. "First rule of diplomacy, always put every statement in context."

She touched his cheek, flushing when she felt the instant, involuntary response of his body. "What context does me having sex with you fit into?"

"Mutual pleasure." She'd run a thousand miles if he mentioned the word *love*.

Her fingers finally stopped twiddling with his shirt buttons. He wasn't sure whether to feel relieved or sorry. "But would it be pleasurable?" she asked, looking up at him, her gaze unsettled. "Supposing it doesn't work out and we're left trying to find excuses for a disaster? The honest truth is that you might be great at this sexual stuff, Duncan, but I'm not. You may as well know that up front."

"I'll take my chances."

"But why?"

"Because I've wanted you for a long time now." That, God knew, was the stark truth. "Because I think there's chemistry between us that neither of us quite knows how to handle."

"The fact that a person of the opposite sex sets your teeth on edge doesn't mean that there's chemistry between the two of—"

"You could be right. Let's find out." Holding her head still, he lowered his mouth to hers, parting her lips with his tongue before she could analyze herself into a state of total rejection.

She gave a tiny murmur of protest, but instead of pulling away as he'd half expected, she hesitated for a split second, then locked her hands behind the nape of his neck and responded to his kiss with a passion that rocked him back on his heels.

He had always known that making love to Summer would be something unique and wonderful. Even so, he had never realized that it would take only a couple of deep kisses with her to bring him almost to the brink of orgasm. Usually he devoted a lot of time and effort to making sure his partner was totally aroused. With Summer, the woman he wanted to please more than any other, he was reduced to a state of basic lust that left no room for sophisticated sexual games.

Panting, fingers shaking with the urgency of his need, he ripped open the fastening of her shirt with all the finesse of Algernon's prototypes swinging through the jungle. He seared a line of kisses down the length of her throat and over her breasts, no longer fighting the primitive urge to stamp his brand on her, determined to blot out any comparisons she might be tempted to make with Joe Malone.

When he thought he might explode if he didn't break off the kisses, he tore his mouth away from her, and stood, arms clasped loosely around her, gasping for air. Summer stared at him, stunned and wide-eyed, not moving. Scarcely seeming to breathe.

No wonder she looked as if she'd been poleaxed. He had to go slower, Duncan told himself. Except that while going slower would be great for Summer, it would surely kill him. While he was still fighting to regain some control, she leaned toward him, reaching for the buckle of his belt and then for the zipper of his fly. When her hand slipped inside and encircled him, any lingering hope of leisurely lovemaking vanished.

Muttering various incoherent phrases intended to convey God knows what, he unfastened her slacks and swung her up into his arms, letting her slacks drag to the floor and then tugging them over her feet after he carried her over to the sofa. She landed with her head in the middle of Algernon's plump belly, with one of the chimp's feet poking out from beneath her ear and a yellow felt hand flopping over her forehead.

Duncan, who prided himself on the elegance of his seductions, barely noticed Algernon. Clothes had disappeared, Summer was flushed with desire, her body damp with sweat, and he found her disheveled state erotic in the extreme. He concentrated his gaze on her face as he skimmed his hand down her rib cage and over her belly, mostly because he wanted to watch the moment when she climaxed. He half expected her to look away, but she kept her eyes locked with his as he slipped his hand between their bodies and eased his finger inside her, moving with insistent rhythm. She writhed beneath his hand, her hips rising off the sofa, their bodies sliding against each other, slick with sweat, pulsing with mutual desire. He saw the exact moment when her gaze lost its focus and she toppled over the edge into orgasm. With a tiny cry of astonished pleasure that pierced him to his core, she shattered beneath his hands.

After a few seconds, she closed her eyes and went limp, but he didn't give her time to come down slowly. He drove into her, hard and deep, and her body arched convulsively beneath him, already gathering fire again. Her nails raked down his back and his control broke, desire rushing over him in a wave that swamped reason. He dug his fingers into her hips with bruising power, opening her to the full force of his thrusts. Seconds later, he climaxed—much too soon, and yet at the outer limits of his endurance. Clinging to him, Summer moaned softly and followed him over the brink.

When her mind finally reconnected with her body, Summer's first coherent thought was to wonder why she had run so hard and fast to avoid something as wonderful as what had just happened between her and Duncan. The answer came without too much searching. She'd run from him because she was a smart woman who didn't want to get her heart split in pieces, and Duncan was guaranteed heartbreaker material, prime grade. Unfortunately, she was remembering all her excellent reasons for avoiding involvement with him much too late. Making love to Duncan had been exactly the dangerous event her subconscious had always anticipated. The sex had been wildly exciting, but what she'd discovered about her feelings for Duncan could best be described as terrifying. She didn't want to be in love with him. She refused to be in love with him. Why couldn't she have fallen in love with somebody who shared her view of life? Why did she have to have all these inconvenient and completely overwhelming feelings for Duncan Ryder?

She watched covertly as Duncan sat up and moved toward the end of the sofa, leaving her excruciatingly aware of her nakedness. She spotted her slacks on the floor and her shirt crumpled on a chair, but her bra and panties had disappeared into the ether. As she made to get off the sofa, she realized Algernon's glasses were caught in her hair, and his magazine was stuck under her, making ripping noises as she moved.

This was why having sex with someone was such a high-risk proposition, she thought gloomily, untangling Algernon's glasses. It wasn't the actual sex that left you so horribly exposed and vulnerable, it was the aftermath. There was no graceful way to ask a man if he happened to remember where he'd tossed your underwear.

Duncan took her hands and pulled her to her feet, putting his arms around her waist and holding her loosely against him. With a complete lack of logic, she immediately felt less naked. "That was incredible," he said softly. "You're the most amazingly sexy woman, Summer Shepherd."

Standing in the circle of his arms, the smell and taste of sex all around them, she could momentarily convince herself that he was telling the truth. "It's never been like that for me before," she admitted. Common sense briefly returned and she glared at him in frustration. "Dammit, wouldn't you just know that you're every bit as good at this sexual stuff as you claimed?"

His eyes darkened with a flash of amusement. "Er...is that a problem?"

"Of course it is! It's infuriating to have great sex with a man you've spent the past ten years actively disliking!"

As soon as she'd spoken, Summer wished she could call her words back. For a moment, she could have sworn Duncan looked almost despairing, but he recovered himself quickly and gave her one of his usual cool smiles. "There seem to be two solutions to that problem," he said. "You can enjoy the sex and ignore the fact that you dislike me. Or you could reconsider and see if maybe you could learn not to dislike me so much after all."

How had she ever deceived herself into imagining that Duncan was controlled and unfeeling? Summer wondered. Her heart actually gave a twinge of physical pain as she saw the effort he was expending not to reveal how badly her flippant comment had hurt him. She stood on tiptoe and pressed a gentle kiss against his mouth. "I've already wasted ten years," she said. "I don't plan to waste any more time."

Duncan directed one of his most ironic glances at her. A sure sign, she now realized, that he was disguising intense emotion. "As a mere male, I need help from time to time in understanding statements that women would consider crystal clear. What, exactly, do you mean when you say that you've already wasted ten years?"

"I mean this," she said, and kissed him.

Stepping out of the shower, Summer realized that she was deliriously happy—and ravenously hungry. She wrapped herself in a towel and padded back into the bedroom.

"Duncan?"

"I'm dead," he said politely. "Please go away."

She held her hand over his head and shook a shower

of cold water droplets onto his face. "That's no way to treat a corpse," he said, opening one eye.

"I was planning to cook my world-famous ravioli, but since you're dead, I guess you won't be interested."

Duncan slowly pulled himself into a sitting position. "It's possible that ravioli might bring me back to life."

"I'll start cooking. Join me when you've decided you're alive again."

Twenty minutes later, Summer dropped crushed basil leaves into the pan of sauce and stirred, humming under her breath. Showered and dressed in pants and an unbuttoned shirt, Duncan put place mats on her table and added cutlery, a bowl of Parmesan cheese, a pepper grinder and paper napkins. With only a small sense of shock, Summer realized that although she was much too physically aware of him to say that she felt relaxed, his presence in her apartment didn't feel intrusive. If he wanted to spend the night, she had to admit that she would be glad. Not just because the sex would be out of this world, but because it would be nice to fall asleep knowing that Duncan was lying next to her.

"Why are you frowning?" he asked, coming up behind her and putting a glass of white wine on the counter next to the stove.

"I was wondering if there was enough salt in the sauce—" She broke off. The protective lie had been automatic. Ten years of deception died hard. She drew in a deep breath. "Actually, I was thinking how odd it was that it felt so comfortable to have you around."

"Comfortable?" He quirked an eyebrow, then grinned. "I guess I should take that as a compliment."

"The best." She held out the wooden spoon. "What do you think about the sauce? Does it need more salt?"

"No, it's perfect." He leaned against the counter, watching her, sipping wine. "I'm starving. How long before dinner's ready?"

She stuck a fork into one of the ravioli. "Two minutes."

"I guess I can wait that long." The oven timer pinged. "I'll get the bread," he offered.

When she carried their plates over to the table, she discovered that Duncan had lit the yellow candles she'd had sitting as a centerpiece since Easter. He'd turned off the lamps so that her computer desk faded into the shadows and her fireplace took on the magical glow of its glory days at the turn of the century. She'd eaten lots of other candlelit meals, often with people she liked, but Summer couldn't remember a meal she'd enjoyed more. Even the prepared ravioli— straight out of the freezer—tasted delicious.

They lingered over a dessert of lemon sherbet, talking about Duncan's most recent trip to Brazil, the progress of her atmospheric studies, and even managing to discuss politics without destroying their unusual harmony.

"How do you feel about your father's decision to make a run for the presidency next election?" Duncan asked, getting up to bring the coffeepot to the table.

She didn't even feel alarmed. "Whatever gave you the idea he's going to do that?" she asked, clearing away their dessert dishes. "Dad told me when he was appointed secretary of state that this was his last job and that he was getting really tired of politics, especially party politics. As soon as the next president is sworn in, he's going to retire to his cottage in Maryland and write his memoirs.''

There was an infinitesimal pause before Duncan replied. "Sounds like a good plan." He smiled. "Will he hire a ghostwriter, do you think?"

Summer felt her stomach knot. "Your recovery was almost perfect, Duncan, but I heard that crucial split-second hesitation before you answered me. My father has told you he's going to run for the presidency, hasn't he."

"He and Olivia have mentioned it a couple of times," Duncan admitted. "I'm sorry. I assumed you already knew."

"No, but it doesn't matter. Running a presidential campaign isn't something my father could keep secret, is it?"

"Not for long, anyway. He'll have to announce publicly by the end of the year if he's going to have any serious chance of getting the nomination."

"Right. By breaking the news to me, you've saved him a job I'm sure he was avoiding." Summer managed to smile, aware that it was petty of her to feel betrayed. In her heart of hearts, she had never expected her father to keep his promise to retire. And, if you got right down to it, she didn't have any right to expect him to limit his ambitions to suit her life-style preferences. She was an adult, living an independent life. Just as her father had no right to determine her choices, she had no right to resent his.

Duncan leaned forward and took her hand. "I'm not going to insult your intelligence by saying that it will make no difference to your life if Gordon campaigns for the presidency. But win or lose, once the campaign is over, you should be able to keep out of the limelight and lead your own life.''

''I guess. And it would be awesome to spend the occasional night in the White House. I just hate the idea of all that media attention, though.'' No wonder her father had been so uptight about her kidnapping, Summer thought. The party bigwigs still played a huge part in deciding who got given enough money to be a serious presidential contender, and they'd never have handed over precious campaign funds to a man whose daughter had staged her own abduction.

Duncan's thoughts had apparently switched back to her kidnapping, too. ''This seems like a good moment to change the subject and ask why you think Joe's disappearance might be linked to Fernando's murder,'' he said, pouring coffee for both of them.

She was surprised by how much she wanted to tell him how her interest had first been sparked by the fact that she'd seen Olivia and Fernando traveling together. But somehow, everything that had happened tonight made it more difficult than ever to tell him that she suspected his sister and Fernando of having an affair. She stirred cream into her coffee, buying a few extra moments to think. In view of what she'd just learned about her father's presidential ambitions, she was no longer sure exactly what she'd observed on the train journey from Washington to New York. Olivia was a woman of clawing, vaulting ambition. It was almost impossible to believe that she would have risked her marriage to Gordon Shepherd and her shot at playing the role of First Lady, just to enjoy a night or two of hot sex with Fernando da Pereira. In fact, even to think about Olivia and hot sex in the same sentence seemed like an oxymoron.

There was absolutely no point in mentioning that troubling train journey, Summer decided. It would merely make her sound spiteful and would throw no light whatsoever on Fernando's murder. Better that she should stick to explaining her theory about the link between Joe and his billionaire cousin.

"You're going to wear out the cup if you keep stirring much longer," Duncan said.

She put down the spoon. "Sorry, I was trying to think how to be brief and to the point. To put everything in a nutshell, I believe that Joe discovered some plant in the rain forest that can be used as the basic ingredient in a valuable new drug. I think he must have approached Fernando, his cousin, and asked him for help in bringing this drug into production on a large scale."

"That sounds quite likely in view of Malone's past successes and his relationship with Fernando," Duncan said. "But the fact that the two of them might have been working together on a new drug doesn't begin to explain why one of them got killed and the other abducted."

"I've been thinking about that for days," Summer said. "The only way it makes sense is if the profit potential from this drug was…is…so enormous that it got Fernando killed and Joe kidnapped. I know that the cash flow generated by some widely used drugs can run into multiple millions. Usually pharmaceutical companies have a burdensome investment in research that they have to recoup, so they don't make quite as much profit as you'd expect. But just think how much profit there would be if a company could put an important and effective new drug on the market with no research costs other than the clinical trials you would need in order to get it approved by the FDA.''

"You're right. That would be enough money to interest a lot of people.'' Duncan frowned. "Are you just guessing that Joe and Fernando were working together? Or did Joe tell you he was working on a project like this with his cousin?''

"Joe never mentioned Fernando. But when we were together last fall, Joe was very excited about the positive results he'd achieved with some preliminary tests he was running for a powerful new drug he'd developed. He was more elated than I'd ever seen him. He said that it wasn't often you had the chance to save the lives of thousands of people, and that's what he thought he might be able to do.''

"What sort of a powerful new drug are we talking about? A broad-spectrum antibiotic? A cure for cancer? The answer to Alzheimer's?''

"He didn't tell me. In fact, looking back, I realize now that he avoided giving me any details, almost as if he wanted to protect me from having dangerous knowledge.''

"That sounds like the wisdom of hindsight,'' Duncan protested.

"It's true that I didn't have a clear impression of danger at the time,'' she conceded. "But it was there, and my subconscious picked up on it. Basically, I've connected a lot of tiny pieces over the last couple of days since I realized Fernando was murdered, and the assembled picture is pretty amazing.'' She walked over to her desk and unlocked the drawer, taking out the charts and transparencies Joe had sent her.

"Come and look at these,'' she said, switching on the lights and spreading the charts over her coffee table. "Joe sent me an encoded computer disk from the Manaus Airport right before he left Brazil. I think he sent me the disk because he was afraid something would happen to him, and we've known each other for so long that he trusted me to interpret clues that would be meaningless to most other people."

Duncan came and sat next to her on the sofa and looked through the stacks of charts and transparencies. "All of this material was on the disk Joe sent you?" he asked.

"Not exactly." Summer explained how she'd picked up the transparencies at the copy shop, then prepared the final computerized comparison that she believed actually worked as a map. Duncan listened in silence, turning over the slides of flowers and plants as she talked.

"Your detective work was brilliant," he said when she finished. "And I'm sure you're right. This final chart is definitely a map."

"I still haven't worked out why Joe sent me pictures of so many different plants. Maybe they're nothing but cover for the charts in case the disk fell into the wrong hands—"

"I don't believe there are that many different plants pictured in these photos," Duncan said. "My father is a keen wildlife photographer, and one of the things I've learned from looking at his pictures is how radically different animals and plants can look according to the season, or the angle of the picture."

"But there aren't any real seasons in the rain forest," Summer pointed out. "There's just damp, wet and wetter."

He grinned. "Even so, I think all these photos are of only two different plants. One orchid and one tree.

You see this picture of leaves? I think it belongs with this picture of buds, and this picture of an orchid in full bloom. And this picture of insects is really a close-up of the underside of the orchid's leaf, and so on, and so on. The same thing with the tree.'' He picked up a transparency. ''This picture is a long shot of a stand of trees in the rain forest. They all look identical—''

''That's highly unlikely,'' Summer interjected. ''The rain forest is the most diverse ecosystem on the planet. The trees may look alike at first glance, with tall trunks and spearlike leaves, but you'll find that there are lots of different species in the one stand of trees if you look closer.''

''Exactly my point. Look, this next picture is a close-up of one of those trees. Now we move on to closer views of the trunk and the bark. And here's the leaves, then the tree in full bloom, with a hummingbird hovering. And these red gourdlike objects are most likely the mature fruit of the tree, so that there can be no doubt about identifying it.''

''How did I miss that?'' Summer said, studying the pictures with renewed interest. ''You're almost certainly right. Joe wanted to be sure I could recognize a specific orchid and a specific type of tree.''

''In which case, what Joe has sent you is a map to get to the place in the rain forest where we can find this tree and this orchid, plus an exquisitely detailed photo record of what they look like.''

Summer traced the outline of a tree branch, heavy with gourds. ''The tree and the orchid must both be vitally important if Joe has gone to so much trouble to identify them. Which probably means they're the source of the drug he was working on, wouldn't you agree?''

"Yes, I agree. Although we still don't have the vaguest idea what kind of drug we're dealing with, or how it's made."

"Joe gave us a clue as to how it's made, at least in the crude form used by the tribe." Excitedly, Summer pulled out the photo of the tribal ceremony. "Look, one of the men in this picture is carrying orchid blossoms, another man is holding one of those red gourd thingies, and the man stirring the pot looks as if he's using a strip of bark. Doesn't that suggest Joe attended some tribal ceremony where the elders brewed up this concoction and then Joe discovered that the mixture had a real, measurable effect on blood pressure, or heart rate, or brain function, or something?''

"Yes, it sure does. Hot damn, now we've got the location, the plants and the basic method of production. Mix, add water, heat.''

Summer grinned. "So you see, I was right. Fernando's death and Joe's disappearance are not only related, they're tied up to Joe's discovery of a valuable new drug.''

"Wait a minute!" Duncan protested. "You've leaped several steps ahead of me. I still don't see how we get from Joe's discovery of a wonder drug to the fact that Fernando has been murdered, you were kidnapped, and Joe has disappeared.''

"Easily." Summer felt increasing confidence as she expounded on her theory. "Fernando's rivals heard about this fabulous drug with massive profit potential. They decided to steal the formula and get all the profits for themselves. Unfortunately, they don't know where the village is located, or what plants are used as the basic ingredients to make the drug. Fernando is protecting Joe, so they have to murder him and kidnap Joe in order to force him to cooperate with them and reveal the secret formula.''

For a minute, Duncan looked intrigued. Then he shook his head. ''It's an interesting theory, Summer, but it doesn't fit the facts.''

''Why not? With Fernando dead, his rivals can move in and steal the formula for the drug from Joe and reap all the profits—''

''Sure they can,'' Duncan agreed. ''But why didn't they kidnap Joe in Manaus? Or in Recife before he boarded his flight to the United States? Unless Fernando's rivals are completely insane, why would they wait for Joe to land in America before they took action against him?''

''Because they couldn't get at him while he was in Brazil. Fernando had him protected, remember.''

''It's unlikely that even a man as powerful as Fernando could keep Joe safe in the middle of the Amazon rain forest. But let's imagine that Joe is untouchable in Brazil for some reason. So he flies to the States where the bad guys can pick him off. And now we're faced with the same old question. Why not kidnap him from Miami Airport and beat him until he coughs up the formula?''

''Because the bad guys didn't know he was coming in time to make the arrangements?'' Summer suggested.

''Sure they did. They not only knew when he was coming, they had an elaborate plan in place to get him seized by U.S. Customs officials the minute he landed. Unless he really was smuggling cocaine and it's sheer coincidence he got busted.''

Summer shook her head. "No, that's not possible. There's no chance that Joe was smuggling cocaine or any other illegal drug."

"So, under your theory, we have to accept that he's been set up by the bad guys and tossed into jail. Then these mysterious and definitely wacko bad guys decided to make their lives really difficult by kidnapping you and threatening to kill you unless Joe got released from jail into their custody. A sure-fire way to bring the entire weight of the United States government right onto their backs." Duncan looked at her with rueful inquiry. "And their reason for doing this was...?"

"To get hold of Joe—"

"Which they could have done without ever bringing you into the equation."

Summer sighed. "Okay, I have no way to explain why they didn't just grab Joe the minute he landed in Miami. What's your theory?"

"I wish I had one. Apparently, because they wanted to go through all the hassle of kidnapping you and forcing the government to spring Joseph Malone from jail. Which obviously makes no sense at all."

"Maybe they've seen too many bad movies and they like to make their lives difficult." Summer threw up her hands. "All right, we can neither of us provide a logical reason why they did what they did. Maybe they're plain old dumb."

"They were smart enough to arrange an exchange of you for Joe Malone without leaving a single clue as to who they are. Which would suggest that they're not dumb—and that they have enough money to handle plenty of up-front bribes and miscellaneous expenses."

"Let's assume they'd already tried to get Joe to

cooperate with them and he refused." Summer shuffled through the charts as if they would provide enlightenment. "So now the bad guys are desperate to persuade him to give them the formula, and they can't just shoot him, like they did Fernando, so they kidnapped me to pressure him into giving up the formula."

"They have a hundred ways they can coerce Joe's cooperation. Kidnap him in Manaus and break his kneecaps. Starve him. Beat him."

Summer shuddered. "Perhaps they were afraid he'd resist so strongly that they'd end up killing him before he agreed to cooperate. So the bad guys decided it would be easier to force his cooperation if he was afraid for my safety rather than for his own."

Duncan thought about that for a few moments before shaking his head again. "The only reason we knew you'd been abducted on Sunday morning was because the kidnappers called me and told me they'd taken you. If they'd kept quiet, the kidnappers could have had you out of the country and in some remote stronghold in the Brazilian hinterland before anyone even realized that you were missing. Again, why drag in the U.S. government? If these inscrutable rivals of Fernando's wanted to force Joe's cooperation, it would be much more effective to have you as their prisoner and compel him to watch while they tortured you."

She shivered and Duncan rested his hand lightly on her knee. "I'm sorry. I didn't mean to upset you. I was just playing with scenarios."

"But they aren't just scenarios," Summer said. "That's the problem. While we're sitting here, congratulating ourselves on how clever we are to have worked out what these charts most likely mean, Joe's life is on the line.''

Duncan didn't say anything and Summer blinked back a sudden, unexpected rush of tears. "You think Joe is already dead, don't you?"

"Not necessarily. A lot of people went to a lot of trouble to get him out of jail alive."

"Then he's being tortured for information. You said it yourself."

"Maybe not." Duncan brushed his thumbs across her eyelids, wiping away her tears. "Summer, we have no idea who the kidnappers were, why they kidnapped you, or why they exchanged you for Joe. For good or ill, you have to face the fact that we still don't really know whether Joe is their prisoner or whether he went with them willingly."

"We do know that," Summer said tautly. "I'm telling you that Joe would never have allied himself with the people who kidnapped me."

"Okay, but we still can't ignore the fact that although we've discussed some interesting theories here tonight, there's absolutely nothing we've come up with that explains why you would have been kidnapped and then set free in exchange for Joseph Malone. And until we understand that, we're blundering around blindfolded without knowing where we are. Which is a pretty damn dangerous thing to do."

Summer jumped up, carried a stack of dishes over to the sink and began a noisy clean-up. Duncan followed her. He turned off the hot water and swung her around to face him, ignoring the trail of soap bubbles that landed on his chest. "Summer, you need to talk to Julian Stein. If you're right...if we're right and Fernando's murder is linked to Joe's disappearance, then the FBI needs to know that. There's no way the FBI can make the connection themselves.''

"Julian Stein won't listen to me. He thinks I'm a flake, or a criminal, or both. Besides, if Joe had wanted to involve the FBI, he'd have spoken directly with Julian Stein. They met face-to-face while Joe was still in jail—''

"True, but they met along with a roomful of people Joe had no reason to trust.''

"Joe could have asked for a private meeting with the director. I'm sure Stein would have agreed to that.''

"I'm sure he would. But we can't begin to guess what was going through Joe's mind at that meeting,'' Duncan said.

"And we don't know now, either. But he sent that disk to me, not to the FBI. That must mean something.''

"But what? In practical terms, we don't have many choices, Summer. If you don't tell Stein about your theories, what are you going to do next? Charter a plane and fly off into the jungle?''

"Why not? Joe sent me a map. Presumably he won't be surprised if I use it.''

"I'm damn sure Joe doesn't expect you to fly off to Manaus and use his map to sail down the Amazon in search of his precious plants. Because short of blowing up the map and sticking it on a billboard in Times Square, I can't imagine a better way of revealing to the world exactly where that village is located.''

"Then what am I supposed to do?'' Summer demanded. "Sit twiddling my thumbs and waiting for news of Joe's death to filter back up north?''

"You know what I think you should do. Call your

father right now and ask him to arrange an emergency meeting for you with Julian Stein. And then tell Stein everything you've told me."

She probably would have to talk to the FBI director in the end. But first she ought to talk to Olivia. It was suddenly so clear to Summer what she needed to do that she couldn't imagine why it had taken her so long to reach such an obvious conclusion. Of course she had to talk to Olivia and explain how she'd seen her on the train with Fernando. Knowing Olivia, even if she had been involved in an illicit affair, she'd probably come up with an explanation for her presence on the train that sounded convincing to most people, but Summer didn't think she'd be easily deceived.

"I guess you're right," she said, relieved that she'd finally resolved the issue of what to do about her stepmother, at least in her own mind. "I'll try to arrange a meeting with Julian Stein. I just have to hope that he recognizes the truth when he hears it."

"He will. He's a smart guy." Duncan gave her an encouraging squeeze and held out the phone. "Call Gordon," he said. "Trust me, Summer, it's the right thing to do if you want to have the best possible chance of rescuing Joe."

# Fourteen

She had forgotten to close the blinds when they went to bed, and the early-morning sun streamed in through the window, tickling Summer's eyelids and warming her cheeks. She surfaced gradually, even though she was instantly aware that she wasn't alone in bed. Duncan's legs were sprawled over hers and one of his hands rested possessively on her hip. She was amazed that she'd slept so well and that his presence in her bed felt so natural. In the past, even the prospect of sharing her sleeping space had been enough to give her raging insomnia, but last night, with Duncan, she'd apparently dropped off to sleep the second they finished making love.

Duncan was still sleeping, and she turned onto her side so that she could look at him. With his eyes closed, he appeared far less cynical, although his features were still strong, and his jawline was broad enough to save him from mere handsomeness. His skin was unexpectedly dark. Everywhere. Summer trailed her hand lightly across his stomach. Either he spent a lot of time naked on tanning beds, or he had quite a few southern Mediterranean ancestors along with those pallid WASP *Mayflower* pioneers Olivia liked to boast about. Summer smiled. It was always a pleasure to pierce her stepmother's armor-plated snobbery, even if only in her thoughts.

Duncan's hand shot out and snagged her roaming fingers. "Care to explain the Cheshire cat grin?"

"Nope." She kissed his forehead. "Want coffee?"

"Not right now."

"Okay. See you later." She made to get up, but in two swift moves he'd straddled her and held her under him with her hands pinned over her head.

"It's Sunday," he said. "We need to start the morning right."

"I agree." She managed, with considerable difficulty, to look straight into his eyes and continue breathing. "And that means drinking a leisurely mug of steaming coffee as soon as possible after waking."

"Wrong answer," Duncan said softly. "Try again." He began at her throat and trailed kisses in a line straight down the center of her body.

Summer decided coffee could wait.

In the movie *Groundhog Day,* the hero gets trapped in a time warp. Stuck in a small Pennsylvania town, he is condemned to repeat the mundane events of a cold, snowy February 2 until he has learned enough about himself to move on to February 3 and the rest of his life.

If she was ever going to get caught in a time warp, Summer thought, she would want the day she lived over and over again to be this Sunday with Duncan. Everything about their time together was perfect: the sunny skies while they walked through Central Park, the lunch they ate at a French bistro on Third Avenue, and the off-Broadway comedy they saw in the evening that kept her laughing for two hours straight. Best of all was the magic sheen ordinary events took on just because she shared them with Duncan. His presence was a shining thread woven through the plain cloth of the day, transforming it from dull gray to gleaming silver. Even the obligatory phone call to her father seemed less stressful than she'd anticipated. He agreed to arrange for her to meet with Julian Stein as soon as possible, and since he was on his way out the door to attend a function at the White House, he had no time to ask any probing questions that might have been difficult to answer.

Reality set in on Monday morning. Duncan left at six to prepare for a seven-thirty breakfast meeting across town near the United Nations. Half an hour later, her father called to give her the news that Julian Stein would be able to fit her into his schedule at four o'clock that afternoon.

"How difficult is it going to be for you to get time off from work?" Gordon asked.

"It should be quite easy, since everyone thinks I've been in the hospital," Summer said. "As long as I'm back at work by Wednesday, I'll have time enough to prepare for the seminar I'm scheduled to give at the end of the month. There's a lot of tricky analyses still to be done, but I already have most of the raw data I need."

"Good. Then I'll let the director know that you'll be at his office by four. Oh, by the way, do you want me to come to the meeting? Moral support and all that."

"Thanks for the offer, Dad, but there's no need for you to come. I know how busy you are and this isn't a big deal. I just want to go over a few things with the director." Summer realized she was sounding evasive, which she hadn't intended.

Her father picked up on her hesitation. "Summer, what's going on? Please don't spring any surprises without warning me first. What are you going to say to Julian Stein that's so urgent? And I have to ask if you've considered the fact that you might need a lawyer with you at the meeting."

"I don't need lawyers, Dad." At some point over the weekend she had stopped worrying about the fact that her father obviously still suspected that she might have cooperated with her kidnappers. "The only reason I need to see Mr. Stein is to let him know that I've come up with a possible reason why the Justice League was so anxious to spring Joe from jail."

"Well, if you've come up with an explanation for that mystery, Julian Stein will bless you. Me, too. What's your theory?"

"I believe Joe discovered an important new drug while he was researching native healing plants in Amazonia, and I'm guessing that the Justice League plans to keep Joe a prisoner until he agrees to cooperate with them and hand over the formula."

"Hmm...is this all speculation? Or do you have some hard evidence that Malone has discovered a new drug?"

"Not exactly hard evidence. Just a couple of things Joe mentioned to me when we were in Brazil last year. It's a bit complicated to explain, which is why I need a face-to-face meeting with the director."

"I don't want to pour cold water on your ideas, Summer." Her father sounded very dubious. "But even if you're right, why wouldn't Malone cooperate willingly with the Justice League? He was their leader for at least two years, and according to the CIA, the current members of the League are all old friends of his. If I recall, Bram Cooper mentioned during one of our briefing sessions that Malone donated half the profits from one of his earlier discoveries to the League.''

"Even if he did, that doesn't mean he would automatically be willing to hand over the profits from this new drug to the League.''

"A falling-out among old partners, is that what you're suggesting?''

"It happens," she said, realizing that a lifetime of guarded conversations with her father made it impossible for her just to open up and tell him everything she suspected.

"It sure does, and I should know." Her father gave a wry laugh. "There are no enemies more bitter than former friends. That's a lesson you learn early in politics. Anyway, in view of Malone's past success in developing profitable new drugs, I agree with you that it's more than possible he's discovered another potential moneymaker—''

"Something profitable enough that people are willing to go to great lengths to steal the formula," Summer put in.

"Yes, that would make it difficult for him, wouldn't it? A man working alone in the jungle, no powerful supporters to scare away competitors... Hmm... Although, once Malone found himself face-to-face with the director of the FBI, why didn't he explain his problems? If he wanted protection for himself and his formula, the director of the FBI is the perfect man to provide it.''

"I don't have a clue why Joe said nothing to Mr. Stein—''

"And why did he agree to be ransomed in exchange for you?"

Her father was asking all the same questions Duncan had asked, and the same ones she'd asked herself a dozen times. Summer sighed. "Dad, I have no idea why Joe agreed to be ransomed in exchange for me. Unless he was afraid the Justice League would kill me if he didn't agree to give himself up."

"Does he care about you that much?" Her father sounded discomfited by this step into personal waters. "Do you care about him that much?"

"Joe would never let anyone else get hurt if he could prevent it so, yes, in a way he cares about me that much," Summer said. "And of course I care about him. We're old friends. But it seems to me that Joe's motives are a bit irrelevant at this point. The FBI director needs to know that there might be a huge financial incentive for a group of terrorists to get their hands on Joseph Malone even if I can't explain exactly how that information ties in to the fact that I was kidnapped."

"You'll get no arguments from me on that one. You're quite right to tell the director what you're thinking, even if your theories turn out to be wrong in the end. Every scrap of new information helps bring Stein's team a bit closer to making an arrest."

"I hope so."

Her father drew in an audible breath. "I'm sorry, Summer, I get so angry when I think about this that I can feel my blood pressure start to skyrocket. It not only infuriates me to think those scum who kidnapped you got away, quite frankly, it terrifies me. Until we have the people who abducted you safely behind bars, I'm never going to feel easy in my mind."

She was touched by his concern. "Dad, you don't have to worry. If the kidnappers had wanted to harm me, they've had plenty of time to do it already."

"Unfortunately, I would feel much more confident that you are out of danger if we only knew exactly what it was the kidnappers hoped to achieve by involving you in their schemes. For the next couple of weeks, I think you're going to have to endure daily phone calls from me."

He cleared his throat, harrumphing in embarrassment. Boston Brahmin to the core, emotion always flustered him. "I know how fiercely independent you are, my dear, and how much you hate the feeling that I'm checking up on you, but I'm not going to sleep easily at night unless I've spoken to you and know that you're safely tucked up in your own bed."

Hearing the worry and suppressed emotion in her father's voice, Summer felt guilty for not telling him about Joe's charts, and the map, and the fact that she actually had pictures of the plants that probably formed the natural basis of the drug Joe had developed. But there was no easy way to make her explanation more detailed without mentioning Fernando's name, which was precisely what she wanted to avoid, at least until she managed to speak with Olivia.

That delayed journey she'd made from Washington to New York sure was causing major trouble, she reflected. She would never have expected a chance sighting of her stepmother on a train to cause so many problems.

"I'll call you tonight once I'm back in New York," she said. "I'll leave a message on the answering machine if you're not there."

"Thank you, my dear. I appreciate that. Olivia and

I have yet another diplomatic reception to attend tonight, so I doubt if I'll be here to take your call, but
I'd like to come home and hear your voice."

"You sound a bit tired, Dad, which isn't like you
at all."

"It's just been an especially hectic few weeks, quite
apart from the horror of your kidnapping." He gave a
sigh. "You know, sometimes I wish we could declare
a ban on official entertainment for a year and see
whether the world still keeps turning."

Summer smiled. "The world would keep turning,
but diplomacy would screech to an ugly halt. Anyway,
you can't really complain. You and Olivia secretly relish all the high-powered entertaining that comes with
your job."

"You know us too well, I'm afraid." Gordon gave
an apologetic murmur. "The truth is, with all you've
been through recently, I feel terrible that I'm not offering more support. I feel so guilty that I can't just
drop everything and take you to the cottage in Maryland for a week of R and R. I ought to be available
to offer more help, lend you a shoulder when you need
it, but this is a troubled world and I'm responsible for
keeping our country on a safe path...."

Summer pulled a wry face. She and her father
seemed to do a great job of inspiring mutual guilt,
which wasn't what she'd intended. She reassured him
that she was feeling fine and told him that she'd slept
really well the previous night without the aid of sleeping pills, gliding smoothly over any mention of Duncan. She thought it might be a while before she would
be ready to expose her relationship with Duncan to
scrutiny by her father and stepmother.

They hung up as her father's limo arrived to take

him to the office, and she waited half an hour before calling the house again. Her stepmother didn't answer, so she left a message on the answering machine, asking her to call as soon as possible. At eight-fifteen she called again and left another message. At the airport, waiting to board the shuttle, she called for the third time. Olivia finally picked up the phone.

"Yes, Summer, what is it?" Her stepmother sounded as she usually did when there was nobody to overhear—impatient and hostile.

"I'm boarding the shuttle in ten minutes. I have a four o'clock meeting this afternoon with the FBI director. I need to see you some time between landing at National and meeting with Julian Stein. You can name the time and the place, providing it's somewhere I can reach by taxi."

"Summer, I'm much too busy to take time out of my day—"

"Trust me, this is one meeting you need to keep. Name the time and place, Olivia. They're boarding my flight and I have to go."

"This is ridiculous—"

"No, it's important."

"Very well, then. Eleven-thirty at Primavera. It's in Georgetown, on M Street—"

"I know where it is. I'll see you there, Olivia. Don't forget."

The Primavera was one of the year's in places for intimate power luncheons that you wanted to have observed by half of Washington. It was typical of Olivia's need to be recognized as a social leader that, even when forced to make a date with her despised stepdaughter, she couldn't bring herself to arrange their encounter anywhere that was less than supremely fashionable. Summer arrived at the restaurant a minute early and the maître d' greeted her with all the indifference that he could afford given the four-week waiting list for tables.

"I'm meeting Olivia Shepherd," she said. "We have a reservation for eleven-thirty."

"Ah, yes, *signorina*." The maître d's manner underwent a subtle transformation. He acknowledged Olivia's position at the pinnacle of Washington's social pyramid by cracking a smile and bowing slightly. "If you will follow me, *signorina*. Madam Secretary has not yet arrived, but you might care for a glass of wine while you wait?"

Madam Secretary was a title reserved exclusively for women who held office, not for wives of male office-holders. Summer was amused. She bet the maître d' knew that as well as she did. "I'll just have water, thanks. I have a long afternoon ahead of me."

"Of course, *signorina*." The maître d' clicked his fingers. Water and a basket of bread appeared with magic speed, but her stepmother didn't follow. Olivia arrived at twelve, late enough to make sure Summer realized how incredibly lucky she was to have been squeezed into her stepmother's hectic schedule.

Olivia sat down at the table, elegant in a dove gray linen suit, pulling off her gloves and setting them neatly on her narrow envelope purse. Jackie Kennedy was Olivia's icon, and she mimicked the details of Jackie's wardrobe with considerable flair and a knack for subtle updates. The maître d' clearly adored Olivia, or at least her job title. He flattered her with a discreet compliment on her appearance. In return, she called him Franco and inquired after his wife.

A little hum of recognition buzzed through the res-

302     Jasmine Cresswell

taurant as other people congratulated themselves on
choosing to eat lunch in the same place as a political
celebrity—in Washington, the only sort that counted.
Olivia, exquisitely conscious of every murmur, pretended supreme unawareness. She ordered San Pelli-
grino to drink and a mixed green salad with fresh artichoke hearts and no dressing as her meal. In
comparison to her usual lunchtime fare, the artichoke
hearts were a reckless caloric indulgence. Summer figured that she must have worked off a few thousand
calories making love to Duncan over the weekend, so
she ordered mushroom caps stuffed with crab and
cheese, smiling blandly at her stepmother's raised eye-
brows.

When the entourage of maître d' and waiters had
withdrawn, Olivia directed a sharp glance toward her
stepdaughter. "I canceled lunch with Jardine
Ormsby," she said. "This had better be good, Summer."

Lady Jardine was the wife of the British ambassador
and the daughter of a duke. The only people Olivia
admired more than descendants of the Pilgrim Fathers
were foreign aristocrats, and British aristocrats were at
the absolute top of her scale.

In view of her stepmother's attitude, Summer decided to abandon any attempt at tact and get straight
to the point. "I saw you on the train a week ago Saturday with Fernando Autunes da Pereira."

Olivia displayed no reaction other than to look
mildly puzzled. "Were you on the train, too? I didn't
notice you. How odd."

"Your back was turned toward me. Besides, you
seemed very fully occupied."

"Is that remark supposed to mean something, Summer?'' Olivia took a small, graceful sip of sparkling water.

"Only that Fernando was murdered less than two hours after the train arrived at Penn Station, and I wondered if you'd informed the police that he made the journey from Washington in your company."

"Forgive me if I seem obtuse, but am I to understand that you caused me to cancel my luncheon appointment with Jardine Ormsby so that you could inform me that you traveled on the same train as I did to New York, at which time you saw me with my very old friend Fernando da Pereira? Who, I might add, is also a good friend of my husband's."

"Yes, Olivia, that's exactly what I did." In the past, her stepmother's sarcasm would have reduced her to melting Jell-O. Perhaps her being kidnapped, or the afterglow of Duncan's lovemaking, or both, had inserted some steel into Summer's previously pliant backbone. "Another way to look at it is to say that I asked you to meet with me before I see the FBI director this afternoon. At which point, among other things, I plan to tell Mr. Stein that I saw you on the train with Fernando da Pereira and that I know the two of you checked into the Carlyle at the same time, and that Fernando was planning to share an intimate dinner with you in his suite—except he got himself rather messily murdered before the food arrived."

Olivia leaned forward. "I know you dislike me, Summer, but can you possibly be suggesting that I had something to do with Fernando's dea—" She broke off, and turned to greet a distinguished-looking man in uniform, with three stars on his shoulder flashing. "Douglas, how delightful to see you. I thought you were in Rome...."

The general shook hands. "Helen and I got back last week." He smiled at Summer, holding out his hand. "I don't believe we've ever met. I'm Douglas Collins."

"And I'm Summer Shepherd—"

"Are you stationed in Washington now?" Olivia didn't give Summer the chance to finish her sentence. "I saw Helen at the Kennedy Center last month and she mentioned that your tour of duty in Bosnia was over."

"Yes, it is. I've been assigned to a large desk in a small office over at the Pentagon. It's good to be back, although I'm not a man with a lot of patience for pushing paper."

Olivia laughed. "I know that! Gordon and I will have to find a way to put your knowledge of Europe to good use at some of those endless diplomatic parties we throw." She smiled with subtle flattery. "To be honest, now that Eastern Europe keeps breaking itself up into smaller and smaller countries, I need all the smart guests I can get if I'm not going to embarrass everyone with a horrid faux pas."

"It's impossible to imagine you ever embarrassing anyone," the general said. "Your reputation as a hostess is the envy of everyone in Washington."

Olivia inclined her head with a modesty as false as it was charming. "Thank you," she said, leaning back in a gesture of dismissal. "It was good to see you, Douglas. I'll be in touch with you very soon."

"Helen and I will look forward to hearing from you. Goodbye, Olivia." The general nodded courteously to Summer. "Miss Shepherd, I'm very sorry to have interrupted your lunch. It was a pleasure to have met you."

The waiter arrived with their meals as the general left. The interruptions had clearly given Olivia time to regain her composure. She ate a sprig of arugula and a morsel of artichoke heart, assured the hovering waiter that her meal was delicious, and sent him away. When she and Summer were alone again, she put down her fork and pushed her plate to one side.

"Summer, it's obviously past time for us to speak frankly. I don't intend to be rude, merely honest, and I hope you'll take what I say in that spirit. You and I have nothing in common except your father. The fact that we both love Gordon means that although you find my life-style shallow and I find your goals naive, we are compelled to search for some way to live with each other."

"I understand that," Summer said quietly. "It's why I'm here."

"Then, although I find it extraordinary that I have to say this, let me assure you that I didn't murder Fernando da Pereira. We were working together on a major international benefit event, an auction of contemporary art that we hoped would raise several million dollars to provide medical care for the victims of various civil wars. Brazil has some of the most exciting painters in the world today, and Fernando has a stunning collection of twentieth-century art. Just prior to his death, he had not only agreed to donate one of his most valuable paintings to the auction, he was also on the brink of agreeing to organize a committee to raise contributions of art from all his friends in Brazil."

Olivia had had plenty of time since Fernando's death to invent a plausible explanation for their presence together on the train. Nevertheless, her account of their plans for that night had the ring of truth, Summer thought. Is that what she'd seen on the train? Not two people romantically wrapped up in each other, but two dynamic and efficient people organizing an event that would attract enormous amounts of favorable publicity for both of them? God knew, it was easier to imagine her stepmother getting excited about a high-profile international charity event than it was to imagine her risking her marriage for the sake of an affair with Fernando. In fact, it was such a believable explanation that Summer couldn't understand why she didn't instantly accept it.

"Why were the two of you traveling by train?" she asked. "Doesn't Fernando go everywhere with bodyguards? And you always order a limo to take you to New York for your shopping trips."

"For heaven's sake, Summer, you really do ask the oddest questions. As it happens, Fernando had arranged for us to travel in his limo. We were heading out of town when we were involved in a minor accident. Fernando's chauffeur broke his thumb, and the bodyguard who was sitting in the front passenger seat was cut badly enough to need stitches. The paramedics took them to the hospital and assured us we would merely be in the way if we went, too. Fernando and I decided to continue our journey to New York, at which point we realized we were close to Union Station and that taking the train would be quicker than waiting for a limo service to send us a replacement car."

Summer wondered if she was paranoid to think that the accident that removed Fernando from his bodyguards might not have been an accident at all.

Olivia shook her head, misinterpreting Summer's silence. "For heaven's sake, Summer! The mere fact that we were on a train together should have told you that we weren't involved in a clandestine affair. Half of Washington shuttles backward and forward to New York on that train. If you hadn't seen us, any one of a thousand other acquaintances might have done so."

"Yes, I thought at the time that it was very high-risk behavior on your part."

Olivia clicked her tongue in irritation. "It wasn't high risk at all because there was nothing whatsoever to hide! Which you would have found out for yourself if you'd had the common courtesy to come and speak to us."

"I'm sorry. It was an awkward situation."

"Only in your overheated imagination."

"I understand that now." Her stepmother was haughty and cold, except when she was kissing ass, but Summer didn't think she was usually a liar. "Have you told the police in New York that you were on the train with Fernando?"

"I haven't told 'the police' in general. I've spoken with Captain Halley, who's in charge of the case."

"And Captain Halley is sitting on the information. Keeping it quiet."

"Why would he report it?" Olivia shrugged. "It has no relevance to Fernando's murder."

"So you weren't the person Fernando planned to have dinner with in his suite?"

"Of course I was that person." Olivia was becoming visibly more impatient with Summer's questions. "Fernando and I intended to settle the details of our plans for the charity auction over a quiet meal. Then I planned to travel up to Connecticut to spend Sunday with some old friends. Fernando...to be honest, I've no idea what his plans were for the rest of the weekend. I do know I was devastated when I went along to his suite, expecting a pleasant meal and a successful wrap-up to our conversations, and discovered instead that Fernando had been shot. It was a shocking, terrible experience...."

"What did you do?" Summer asked. "Were you the first person on the scene after the room service waiter who found his body?"

"No, the hotel manager was already there, along with a swarm of staff. I went back to my suite and called Gordon. I told him what had happened, and he pointed out to me that if I could avoid publicity, it would be a very good thing. He pulled some strings and arranged for me to speak with Captain Halley, rather than the detectives on the spot. I told the captain what little I knew, and then went straight back to Washington in the limo that Gordon had arranged for me. For obvious reasons, I didn't feel in the mood to continue with my original plan of spending the rest of the weekend with friends in Connecticut."

"It must have been a dreadful experience," Summer said, feeling a reluctant and surprising sympathy.

"It was worse than dreadful." Olivia's face showed more emotion than Summer could ever remember seeing. "I never want to live through another weekend like that one. I'd barely returned to Washington when Duncan called with the news that you'd been kidnapped. I was exhausted, your father seemed on the verge of a heart attack, and for a couple of days it seemed quite likely that when we did see you again, you were going to be dead. Annoying as I find you, that wasn't an eventuality that I looked forward to."

The waiter returned to their table. Summer hadn't

eaten much more of her stuffed mushrooms than Olivia had of her lettuce leaves. "I hope everything was satisfactory with your meals," the waiter said.

"Everything was excellent," Olivia said, with total disregard for the piles of food left on their plates. "Would you like dessert, Summer?"

She shook her head. "Just coffee, please. Cappuccino, if you have it."

Olivia ordered decaffeinated espresso, and the waiter left. "I've been extremely frank with you, Summer, and I'd appreciate it if you would return the favor. Why are you back in Washington so soon after you left? Did you make the trip just so that you could tell Julian Stein that I was having an affair with Fernando da Pereira?"

"No," Summer said. "I came because I had the chance to do some thinking over the weekend and I came up with an idea about why the Justice League might have wanted to get their hands on Joseph Malone."

"Apparently you think Malone has discovered an important new drug," Olivia said. "Gordon mentioned something about that when I called to tell him we were meeting for lunch."

"Yes. Mr. Stein kept pressing me to come up with a motive for the Justice League to have gone to so much trouble to get their hands on Joe, and over the weekend it occurred to me that maybe the motive was the oldest and most reliable one in the world. Money."

The waiter returned with their coffee. "An espresso for you, *signora*. Decaffeinated. And a cappuccino for you, *signorina*. Enjoy."

"Thank you." Olivia carefully removed the twist of lemon peel and placed it in her saucer. "Everything comes down to money in the end, even politics," she said. "If you listen hard enough when our government talks about foreign policy, the issues that command serious attention are always the ones where some interest group in this country stands to make or lose a lot of money."

Surprised, Summer looked at her stepmother. "That sounds more like me talking than you."

"Yes, it does. I'm being indiscreet. The last couple of weeks have been stressful and I'm feeling tired." Olivia almost visibly shook off her mood of unusual frankness. "What I don't understand is why you think Julian Stein would be interested in hearing that I'd traveled to New York with Fernando. As far as I know, the investigation into his murder is being handled strictly by the New York City police."

There was no reason for her to continue to be evasive, Summer realized. Olivia's relationship with Gordon wasn't going to be damaged by the revelation that she had traveled to New York with Fernando, because even if Olivia was lying, her lies were entirely convincing.

"I don't think anyone connected to the investigation of my kidnapping realizes that Fernando and Joe Malone are...were...cousins," Summer said. "I can't imagine how the two events tie together, but I think it's strange that Fernando was murdered in New York only a scant few hours before I was kidnapped. Apparently just so that I could be ransomed for his cousin three days later."

Olivia put down her cup, spilling coffee into the saucer. She turned so pale that Summer was alarmed. "What is it? What did I say?"

"Are you telling me that Fernando and Joseph Malone were cousins?'' Olivia spat out the final word as if it were an epithet.

''Well, yes. Joe's grandmother and Fernando's father were brother and sister—''

Olivia closed her eyes briefly. When she opened them again, she appeared calmer. ''I'm sorry, I over-reacted. It was just so horrible to imagine Fernando being murdered and then, only a few days later, his cousin disappearing into the hands of some hideous terrorist group....''

It was a bold attempt to cover up, but it didn't deceive Summer. For some reason, her stepmother was shattered by the news that Fernando da Pereira and Joe Malone were related. Surprisingly, she felt the faint stirrings of an emotion that felt almost like sympathy. ''Look, Olivia, I came to Washington in order to warn Julian Stein that there may be a link between my kidnapping and Fernando's death. But I don't have to pass on that suspicion of mine. I don't want to cause trouble or send Stein searching in the wrong direction, especially if he's going to embarrass members of my family in the process.''

Olivia had already recovered her poise. ''Naturally you should pass on to the director any and all information that you believe might be relevant.'' She glanced at the plain gold Movado watch that she always wore in the daytime. ''Good heavens, one o'clock already. I'm afraid I'm already very late for my next appointment. Will you be able to catch a cab to FBI headquarters?''

''The director is sending a car.''

''Good. Don't rush finishing your cappuccino. I'll

take care of the bill on the way out.'' Olivia walked away, looking neither to the left nor the right.

For once Summer had the impression that her stepmother genuinely didn't hear the buzz of admiring comments that followed her departure.

# *Fifteen*

It was past eight o'clock when Summer got back to her apartment building. She felt tired and dispirited, not just because the day had been long and exhausting, but also because her sessions in Washington had been so unproductive. Deep down, she'd expected something momentous to result from her meetings with Olivia and Julian Stein. Instead, Olivia had been her usual withering self, which wouldn't have been so bad if she hadn't also been quite convincing in her explanation of why she'd been traveling by train in Fernando's company. Summer had a strong suspicion that the relationship between her stepmother and Fernando had been more sexual and flirtatious than Olivia cared to remember. But so what? It was fairly safe to conclude that Joseph Malone hadn't disappeared into the clutches of the Justice League because Olivia and Fernando had rubbed against each other and created a few sparks.

Julian Stein had also been his usual self: cool, competent and politely skeptical of her theories. The marble halls and Formica work cubicles of the FBI building seemed specifically designed to dampen emotions and remind excitable citizens that the FBI dealt in facts and forensic science, not wild theories. Summer had felt suitably chastised.

She couldn't complain that the director had been uncooperative or openly dismissive. He expressed interest when she handed over the charts and photos Joe had sent to her, and even complimented her on her ingenuity in constructing a map from such unpromising basic material. He promised to be in touch with the New York police and to get a full report on Fernando's murder. If there were any links connecting the two men beyond their family relationship he would find it, he promised Summer. And, yes, absolutely he agreed that Dr. Malone might have discovered a new drug, and, if so, it was quite possible he had talked to his cousin Fernando da Pereira about production rights. The director's voice had tailed away at this point, leaving Summer with the distinct impression that he saw no compelling reason why anyone sensible would connect Joe's business dealings with his disappearance into the grasping hands of the Justice League.

Instead of reassuring her, the director's calm, measured tones had swamped Summer with a panic-stricken feeling that Joe's chances of survival were fading as fast as Julian Stein outlined his logical, methodical steps for finding him.

During the flight home she tried to reassure herself that she'd done everything she could to save Joe. If it would help to find him, she would willingly have caught a plane to Brazil and trekked into the rain forest to locate the tribal village on the secret map that Joe had been at such pains to deliver to her. But such a journey would take at least two or three weeks, even if everything went as smoothly as possible, and once she arrived at the village, there seemed zero chance that she would find Joe waiting there.

On the contrary, if her theories were correct, the reason he'd been sought so eagerly by the Justice League was precisely because they didn't know where that village was located and wanted to force the information out of him. In fact, her trip through the rain forest might actually provide the Justice League with the exact information Joe was trying to conceal—the location of the plants that formed the basis of his new drug.

Resolved to put a stop to her unproductive thoughts, which she'd been rehashing ever since she left the FBI director's office, Summer paid off the cabdriver and walked briskly across the sidewalk to her apartment building. At least she was back in Manhattan, a definite plus. Washington always left her borderline depressed, perhaps because she associated it with miserable trips to visit her father when she was growing up. Her mother had found the Washington social scene ridiculous and she hadn't made much effort to conceal her opinions. As an adolescent, Summer had laughed and joked with her mother about the farcical antics of politicians desperate for reelection. In retrospect, she could see that her father had some justification for his angry tirades about his wife's blatant mockery of the political system. As a congressman and then a senator, he had deserved more from her than ridicule laced with resentment and a flat refusal to appear at fundraisers. Still, at the time, Summer's sympathy had been overwhelmingly with her mother, and the bitter fights between her parents had been ugly to witness, especially when her father's anger spilled over onto her.

Shaking off a whole bunch of unpleasant memories, Summer searched in the recesses of her purse for her keys, which had performed their inevitable vanishing act. Her gloomy mood wasn't improved by the knowledge that she was coming home to an empty apartment. She'd always relished the freedom of living alone, and it was disconcerting to discover that a single night of Duncan's company was enough to make the prospect of solitude seem lonely rather than restorative.

A husky male voice spoke from very close behind her. "Pizza delivery for Ms. Summer Shepherd. Double cheese and pepperoni. Sexual favors accepted in lieu of a tip."

"Duncan!" She swung around, laughing when she saw that he really was carrying pizza. "Where did you come from?"

"The café across the street, where I just paid a fortune to gain possession of this gourmet meal from a group of starving students."

"They'll probably fail their finals."

"Because I bought their pizza?"

"It's a proven scientific fact that you can't study for an exam unless your stomach is lined with pizza. Surely you knew that?" She unlocked the door and they walked inside. "I thought you were supposed to be back in Washington by now?"

"I managed to persuade the Chilean ambassador to the UN that he needs to meet with me tomorrow afternoon, so I'm in New York for another twenty-four hours." He pressed the elevator button for the top floor, then leaned across the pizza box and kissed her.

She kissed him back with an enthusiasm that surprised both of them. How did he manage to send her from dejected to exhilarated with the mere touch of his mouth against hers? Sexual attraction was really the weirdest thing, Summer reflected. Confused, she hurried out of the elevator, putting some physical space between herself and Duncan while she tried to sort out her capricious emotions.

He followed her into the apartment and dropped the pizza box onto the kitchen counter, putting his arms around her waist with a confident familiarity that both intrigued and flustered her. "Rough day?" he asked, tucking a strand of hair behind her ear.

She nodded. "Really rough. I have this gnawing fear that something terrible is going to happen if we don't find Joe soon, but nobody else seems to feel that there's the slightest urgency. It's been almost a week since he vanished into that damn Humvee, and while the FBI is screwing around, working through channels, making sure they don't offend the Brazilian government, the people who took Joe are doing God knows what."

"The FBI isn't going to share details of their investigation with you, Summer. They almost certainly know a lot more than they're saying."

"But they haven't found Joe and that's all I care about." Summer swallowed over a lump in her throat, dismayed to discover that her volatile mood had swung back to gloom and she was fighting tears. "I don't want Joe to die," she said.

She started to cry in earnest, and once she started, she couldn't stop. Duncan didn't say anything, just held her tight until she finally sobbed herself into silence. Embarrassed, she scrubbed her eyes with the heel of her hand, trying to regain her composure. "I'm sorry, I don't quite know what that was about."

He handed her a wad of tissues. "Fear. Frustration. Anger that you can't do more to find Joe."

"You're right. I can stand most things, but not this awful feeling of helplessness."

"I recommend that you stop worrying about it for an hour or two—"

"I can't." She walked around the kitchen, straightening the lid on her pasta jar and putting away the morning's coffee mugs that stood on the draining board. "I'm sorry, Duncan, but I'm going to be lousy company tonight. Maybe you should go—"

"Not a chance, unless you throw me out. And even then I may stage a protest and sleep on your doorstep." He brought her hands up to his mouth and kissed her knuckles. "The pizza's getting cold. Come and eat."

She wasn't willing to be cajoled out of the blues. "Thanks, Duncan, you go ahead, but I'm really not hungry."

He popped the top on a can of ice-cold Dr Pepper and handed it to her. "Then sit with me while I eat, okay?"

She took a swig of soda and followed him into the living room because it seemed churlish to keep refusing. Duncan was still wearing a formal dark business suit, and he tossed the jacket over Algernon's shoulders and loosened his tie, unfastening the top button of his shirt before sitting on the sofa and helping himself to a large slice of pizza. The fact that he looked eminently desirable made her grouchier than ever. It was alarming to discover that you could be worried sick about something really important like Joe's disappearance, and still have half your mind thinking how great it would be to fall into bed and make love.

"This is prime quality pizza," Duncan said, licking tomato sauce from his thumb.

"Is it? I've never bought pizza from that café, but they make good sandwiches."

He sent her a quizzical look. "Sure you won't change your mind and have a piece?"

She shook her head, pulling Algernon off the sofa and burying her nose in the soft artificial fur on his belly. His big eyes stared up at her sadly, reproaching her for abandoning Joe to the Justice League. She got up and paced across the room. "Duncan, it's no use. I can't sit here and toss around conversational knick-knacks when I have no idea where Joe is or what's happening to him. I'm sorry. I know I'm being a pain."

"That's nothing to apologize for." Duncan put down his can of soda. "Look, this might not lead us anywhere, but I got stuck in traffic coming across town tonight, which gave me time to think some more about those charts Joe sent you. You know, by the time you finished putting all the clues together and creating that map, you'd used every scrap of information that Joe had included on the disk. Except for one thing."

"What was that?"

"The copyright symbol with the logo of the Save The Rain Forest Fund appeared on one set of charts and not the other—"

"But I utilized that information, remember? That's how I realized the charts weren't identical. Joe had to provide some clue to make me recognize that I wasn't looking at two sets of exact duplicates, and the copyright notice was it."

"That's true. Except that to clue you in to the fact that the two sets of charts were different, all he needed to do was write *Copyright, Save The Rain Forest Fund* on one set of charts and not the other. Joe did more.

He gave you their address, too. And I seem to remember it was somewhere right here in the city."

She whirled around so fast Algernon's glasses fell off. "Good grief! How did I miss that?" She was at her desk, turning on her computer as she spoke. "I left the hard copies of the charts with Julian Stein, but I still have Joe's disk." She slipped the disk into the drive and keyed in the password. As soon as the first chart came up on the screen, she read off the address. "Okay, here it is—2299 Broadway."

She gave the command to turn off the computer and swiveled around on her chair. "Duncan, that must be near the Children's Museum. It's only a few blocks from here...."

He sent her a long-suffering look and closed the lid on the pizza box. "Let me guess. You'd like us to take an immediate stroll down Broadway."

"Would you mind? I know we're clutching at straws and we're not likely to find out anything important, but it's a lovely night and I can't just mooch around at home doing nothing. Not when there's a chance that we might find out something that will save Joe."

He stood up, pausing only to sit Algernon down in front of the pizza box. "Enjoy," he said, patting the chimp on the head. He held out his hand to Summer. "Let's go."

"This is it," Duncan said, "2299 Broadway."

"It's a restaurant," Summer said, stating the obvious. She read the name from the small sign alongside the door. "*Alegria*. That's Portuguese for happiness, isn't it?"

"Yes, and since it's a Brazilian restaurant, I guess

there's—" He didn't have time to say any more because Summer was already making her way inside.
The aroma of black beans simmered with onions, ham
hocks and garlic sausage wafted out from the packed
dining room. Some form of *feijoada completa,* the
Brazilian national dish, was apparently on tonight's
menu. A tall dark man in his early forties, holding a
wine bottle in each hand, greeted them. "Do you have
reservations?"

"No—"

"Then I'm sorry, we won't have a table free for
another hour."

"That's okay," Summer said. "Actually, we didn't
come here to eat. A friend sent us, and we were hoping
to speak with the owner."

"Just let me deliver this wine to the table." The
man took off at maximum warp, presented the bottles
of wine for inspection, whisked out the corks, offered
a taste and filled glasses with such a well-practised
flourish that it almost disguised the speed at which he
was working. By the time he returned three minutes
later, a new group of diners had arrived and were
crowded around the entrance area, all talking at once
in Portuguese.

Smiling, sharing a joke in the same language, the
man greeted one of the couples by name and led the
party to a reserved corner table and swiftly got them
settled with menus and a basket of bread sticks. Duncan was impressed. No wonder the restaurant was so
crowded.

"Sorry to have kept you waiting," the man said
when he came back. "Do you want to sit at the bar
until I have a table for you?"

"We don't actually want to eat dinner," Summer reminded him. "I was hoping to speak to the owner."

The man shook his head. "Sorry, that won't be possible. The owner isn't here tonight."

Duncan decided it was time to intervene. "Funny," he said in Portuguese. "I got the distinct impression when you were speaking to those other people just now that you were the owner of this place."

The man's head snapped back. "You speak Portuguese?"

Duncan grinned. "I do my best."

"It's a pretty good best." The man shrugged his shoulders, then returned the grin. "All right, you caught me out, *senhor*. But we're busy as hell tonight, and I'm a line cook and a waiter short. I can spare you three minutes, maybe five if we get lucky."

Duncan switched to English so that Summer would be able to understand what was being said. "We were hoping to talk to you about a good friend of ours, a man called Joseph Malone. He's been working in Brazil for almost three years now, but we believe you know him."

The restaurant owner showed little reaction. "I know Joe," he said. "But I haven't seen him since he was here in the States last spring. He came to give a series of seminars at the university, and I saw him then. What's this about, anyway? Why come to me?"

"Joe sent us," Summer said. "I spent some time with him in Brazil last fall. We took a vacation together." She held out her hand. "I'm Summer Shepherd. Joe and I have been friends since college."

He sent her a long, assessing look. "Nice to meet you, Summer Shepherd. I'm Antonio Joao Silva. Tony to my American friends."

Summer blinked when she heard his name, but she quickly held out her hand and met his gaze steadily. "Hello, Tony. I'm glad we had this chance to meet."

"Likewise," Tony said, taking her hand. Duncan saw a flash of mutual understanding and acknowledgment pass between the two of them.

"What did you want to see me about?" Tony asked.

"I had a message from Joe a couple of weeks ago. The message was urgent, but it wasn't very clear—"

"Why not?"

"That's complicated to explain, but it didn't come directly and we're afraid that he's run into some trouble. I think he might have sent me to you for help."

"What sort of trouble could Joe run into?" Tony took a bill from one of his waiters and rang it up while he spoke. "Last I heard, he was stashed away safely in some hellhole village in the jungle."

"He's made some powerful enemies since he started working in Amazonia," Summer said. "But to be honest, I'm not sure why he sent me to you, or what he expects us to do next. He just gave me your address and said I should come. Like I said, the message I received didn't come directly from him, and didn't even mention your name. I'm operating totally in the dark as to why he wanted the two of us to hook up."

Tony questioned the waiter about a couple of items on the bill, but Duncan was sure that the questions were simply an excuse to give himself time to decide how he was going to respond to Summer. When he'd finished ringing up the bill, he turned and gave Summer another quick, assessing look. "Are you and Joe planning to get married?"

She didn't seem to find the question nearly as odd as Duncan did. "No." She didn't elaborate.

Tony's flashing dark eyes narrowed assessingly. "Your decision or his?"

"It was mutual."

Tony seemed to find that information as interesting as Duncan did.

"Wait here," Tony said.

He was back in less than five minutes, carrying a small sealed envelope. "Here," he said, handing it to Summer. "This came in the mail from Joe about a month ago. He wrote a covering letter that said if you ever came to the restaurant, I was to give you this and tell you never to file it in the same place as the charts and photos. So here it is, and I've given you his message. I figure I owe him that much since he gave me half the money I needed to start this place. Now, if you don't mind, I'd appreciate it if you would get the hell out of here. I've got a business to run and I don't need to waste the evening worrying about Joe Malone. Been there, done that, and it's time to move on."

"Thanks, Tony." Summer turned the envelope over without opening it. She held out her hand. "Next time I see Joe, should I tell him to be in touch?"

Tony looked at her consideringly. "I don't know. You tell me."

"I think he should call you," she said.

Tony walked away without saying goodbye, and Summer stuffed the letter into the pocket of her slacks. "Come on, Duncan. Let's go home."

"Would you mind telling me what just happened in there?" Duncan said as soon as they were outside.

"You know what happened. Joe sent me to that address—"

"No, not that. What was going on between you and Tony? What do you both know that I don't?"

She hesitated for so long that he said her name again. "Summer?"

"Joe and Tony were lovers for a couple of years off and on," she said at last. "It was pretty serious, but Joe broke up with Tony last spring because he wanted to marry me."

Two simple sentences that explained so much, Duncan thought. But they also raised a host of new questions, including how long Summer had known that her best friend was gay, and how she could be so sure that Tony had been Joe's lover when she had obviously never met the man before tonight. "How do you know that Joe and Tony were lovers?" he asked.

"Because Joe told me the name of the man he'd been in love with." Summer was walking fast, as if she wanted to outdistance her own thoughts.

"Was that before or after he asked you to marry him?" Duncan discovered that his hands were balled into fists. He shoved them into his pockets. A very unsatisfactory substitute for shoving them into Joe's face.

Summer stopped in the middle of the sidewalk. "Joe never asked me to marry him," she said. "He told me about his affair with Tony to explain to me why he couldn't...why we couldn't manage to make love..." She floundered to a halt, drew in a shallow breath and tried again.

"Duncan, I'm not ready to talk about this. There's no valid reason for me to discuss Joe's sexual history with you, or my relationship with him."

"Yes, there is. I'm in love with you, Summer. I've been in love with you for years. But I'm not willing to be the guy you go to bed with because you need some sex and the man you love can't give you what you need.''

She stared at him, appalled. "Is that what you think happened? That I'm emotionally pining for Joe, but I got overwhelmed by a few sexual urges, so I hopped into bed and let you take care of them?''

He gritted his teeth. "It sounds possible. In the circumstances.''

"Not if you understood the first thing about me!'' she said hotly.

"If I don't understand you, it's because you do a damn fine job of making sure that I don't! It's easier to get the inside scoop on Donald Duck's love life than it is to prise any information about your feelings out of you.''

"That's ridiculous! I've never hidden—'' Summer stopped, and when she spoke again her voice was a lot quieter. "You're right. I don't talk about emotional things very easily.'' She crossed her arms in front of her chest and marched on.

"That's it?'' He caught up with her and swung her around to face him. "This is the sum total of insight into your feelings that I'm going to get from you?''

"I'm not having sex with you because Joe can't give it to me,'' she said through clenched teeth. "There, does that satisfy you?''

"Not even close. Why are you having sex with me, Summer?''

"Because I...want you.'' She sucked in an unsteady breath. "Because I've realized that I like...being with you.''

It was more than he'd expected to hear, less than he wanted. A couple of the knots tied in his gut untwisted themselves. He held her face between his hands and kissed her lightly on the mouth. "I like being with you, too."

Her smile was a bit unsteady. "Even when I'm being a royal pain in the butt?"

"Especially then." He grinned. "It's such a familiar role for you, it's become almost endearing."

She scowled, then laughed. "If that's an example of your diplomatic skills, then I can't imagine why you weren't booted out of the State Department years ago."

"Diplomats aren't supposed to be suave liars," he said. "That's a misconception."

"You're supposed to be tactful at least."

He considered her statement for a moment, then shook his head. "Not even that. Our job is to understand foreign cultures so that we can discover what the other side really wants. Whether we're negotiating trade agreements or brokering peace treaties, we can only make the best possible deal if we know what's really at stake. For the other side, as well as for us."

He spoke lightly, but Summer was sensitive enough to pick up on his underlying frustration. "You must get really tired of people assuming that being a diplomat means you're a smooth guy who does great at cocktail parties," she said.

He turned to look at her. "Yeah, it can be frustrating. Depending on how much you care about the person misjudging you."

She squeezed his hand briefly before reaching into the pocket of her slacks to pull out Joe's letter. "Okay, let's direct your diplomatic skills to interpreting this latest message from Joe. What's really at stake here, and what does he want from us?" She ripped open

the envelope and extracted a single sheet of graph paper, covered with symbols and equations. She stared
at it intently, her forehead wrinkling in concentration.

Duncan peered over her shoulder. "I guess I've
blown my first chance to shine. I haven't a clue. If
you can understand what that's all about, then I'm
really impressed."

"This isn't my area of scientific expertise, far from
it. But it's obviously a chemical formula, and I'm
guessing these equations show you how to get from
what you start with in line one to what you finish up
with in line twenty-two."

Duncan studied the lines of figures and symbols
with renewed interest, but still no comprehension. "I'd
say it's all Greek to me, except that Greek would be
a hell of a lot easier to understand. Do you think we're
looking at the formula for Joe's wonder drug?"

"What else could it be?" Summer carefully folded
the piece of paper and returned it to the envelope. She
held it out to Duncan. "Will you look after it for me?
Joe specifically asked me not to keep it in the same
place as the charts and the photos. Presumably that's
because if the wrong people get their hands on that
map and this piece of paper, they'd have everything
they need to start making the drug. Maybe you could
take it to your office? Would that be a safe place to
hide it?"

"I have a steel filing cabinet with a secure lock. It
should be safe enough there."

He hadn't been aware of exactly what he was thinking until Summer called him on it. "I'm beginning to
recognize that absentminded-professor look. What's
bothering you, Duncan?"

They were back at her apartment building, and he

waited until they were inside before he answered her. "Joe sent you that disk because he was afraid he wouldn't be around to see his discovery launched onto the marketplace. If the drug he discovered has the potential to save lives, we shouldn't keep this information to ourselves. At some point quite soon, we're going to have to decide if we should take everything we have to an experienced biochemist and ask him to analyze what Joe has given us."

"The only reason to do that would be if we thought Joe wasn't going to come back. If he was dead."

"Yes."

The single word hung in the air, bleak and threatening, but he suspected Summer wouldn't thank him for sugarcoating his reply.

"He's not dead yet," she said, her voice low and passionate.

"Probably not," Duncan agreed, taking the key from her and opening the door to her apartment.

"I've let Joe down," Summer said, walking into the living room. "He's sent me the formula because he trusts me to find him. He gave himself up to the Justice League to save me—"

"You have no way of knowing that for sure, so don't torture yourself imagining a sacrifice on Joe's part that may not be true."

"What other explanation is there?"

"Let it go, Summer, at least for tonight." Duncan took her face between his hands, feeling the tension radiate out from her. "Julian Stein probably wouldn't talk to me, but as soon as I get back to Washington, I'll try to get the inside scoop about the FBI investigation from Gordon. Maybe the FBI has made major breakthroughs in their investigation that we don't know about.''

"That would be great. My father will talk to you.'' Summer felt some of the weight lift from her shoulders. Increasingly over the past few days, she'd felt as if Joe's life rested exclusively in her hands, which seemed pretty small for the size of the task. Duncan's offers of help managed to relieve her of at least some of that burden.

Duncan brushed his knuckles over her cheek in a caress that was so tender it set her heart beating in double time. Earlier tonight he'd told her that he loved her. She wanted to give him something back, to tell him that she loved him in return, but the words stuck stubbornly in her throat. Not because they weren't true, but because they scared her. She and Duncan were such different people. Not quite as different as her mother and father had been in their view of the world and what was important in life, but different enough to frighten her. She'd always resented the way government and politics had consumed her father's life, and although Duncan's career was in international diplomacy rather than the rough-and-tumble of elective politics, she wasn't sure she could handle a long-term relationship with a man who seemed destined to become part of the same Washington power elite she'd spent most of her adult life running away from.

But the trouble was, her emotions weren't in sync with her brain. How did you resist a man who made your bones melt when he looked at you?

There was no good answer to that question, so she didn't even try to resist when he tipped her face up to his. "You think too much," he said softly. "Sometimes you just have to go with the flow.''

"What happens if I'm afraid I won't like the destination?"

"Then enjoy the ride." He kissed her lightly. "Who knows, maybe you'll change your mind when you finally get there. If not, at least the journey was great."

She raised her hand to his cheek. "I do lo..." She swallowed. Not yet. She couldn't say it yet. "Make love to me, Duncan."

For a moment she thought he was going to refuse. Then his mouth came down on hers, hungry and demanding. Electricity jolted through her as their lips met. The feeling of instant meltdown was almost familiar by now, but she couldn't say she was used to it. Maybe she would never get used to it.

Summer turned her head away, not quite ready to surrender, even though she was the one who'd initiated the kiss and asked him to make love. He didn't say anything, just scattered more kisses on her face and throat, tantalizing her, teasing her slowly forward. She realized suddenly that she was resisting because she liked what he was doing too much, not because she wanted him to stop.

Amused, she decided that was a bit too neurotic even for her. She shifted against him, letting her body warm to his touch. The second she let down her mental fire walls, drowsy warmth turned to scorching heat.

She consigned the future to the devil and let the blaze consume her.

# Sixteen

When Joe awoke from his drug-induced sleep, the clock beside the bed indicated that it was 6:00 a.m. on Tuesday morning. His brain still fuzzy, it took a while for him to calculate that the plane must have touched down more than twelve hours previously. He was hooked up to a monitor that showed pulse, respiration, heartbeat and blood pressure. No way he could feign unconsciousness when the electronic data were clearly signaling that he was awake.

Sure enough, Alonzo and one of his favored henchmen came into the room within minutes. "How are you feeling?" Alonzo asked.

"Like shit." Joe tore off the monitor leads and swung his feet out of bed.

"Take a shower. Jango can come in with you if you're afraid of passing out."

"I'll manage."

"We're leaving to pick up the drug samples as soon as you're dressed."

"Okay." Joe walked into the bathroom and slammed the door. He looked carefully, but he couldn't see any sign of a video camera monitoring his actions. Unfortunately, that might mean nothing except that he hadn't spotted the camera. He unwrapped a toothbrush and tried to focus his thoughts while he cleaned his teeth. What he needed was five minutes with a phone so that he could call the FBI. Which he was about as likely to get as a round-trip ticket on the next space shuttle. Failing that, twenty seconds alone with a clerk at the mailbox facility might do the trick. If he could get a note written before they left.

He walked back into the bedroom, staggering a couple of times to indicate weakness, and pretended to look through the clothes Alonzo had provided for him. He found the pencil and paper that were the real objects of his search on the nightstand. Whoever had cleaned the room for his arrival had apparently removed the phone but not the message pad. He sat down on the bed, resting his head in his hands, then abruptly jumped up and made a dash for the bathroom.

He stuck his head over the toilet and made retching noises. Flushing the toilet, he wove an unsteady course back to the bed and collapsed on to it, sweeping the notepad and pencil under the sheet as he fell. So far, so good.

It was incredibly difficult to write without looking, but he managed to scrawl a note that he hoped to God would be legible.

*Do not make any sound.* The men near me have guns. I am Dr. Joseph Malone. I've been kidnapped by Alonzo da Pereira. Take this note to the FBI.

Anyone observing him on a video monitor would attribute the squirming movements as he wrote to pain or nausea. He hoped.

Joe tore off the page, and tucked it into the waistband of his pajamas seconds before Alonzo came back into the room, this time accompanied by the doctor who'd flown with them from Manaus.

"What's the matter?" Alonzo asked. "If you think you're going to avoid taking us to your supply of drugs by pretending to be sick, think again."

"I'm not pretending," Joe said sourly. "You should have checked with me before you let Dr. Frankenstein shoot me full of crap. I could have told you that heavy doses of sedative don't agree with me."

Accepting Joe's self-diagnosis, the doctor hurried forward, stethoscope at the ready. Joe pushed him aside—his disgust was genuine—and turned to speak to Alonzo. "Get this asshole away from me before I puke all over him. You don't have to persuade me to hurry. I'm as anxious to pick up the drug samples as you are."

He got up, keeping his elbow pressed against the waistband of his pants. "I've accepted that there's no way I'm going to get out of this situation alive except by cooperating. The sooner you have the samples, the sooner you'll realize that I've given up fighting you."

Alonzo sent him a look that suggested he'd believe Joe was cooperating when his company was counting the profits on the initial production run. "Out," he said to the doctor, jerking his head toward the door. The doctor scurried out, head bowed.

"Alcoholic prick," Alonzo said.

"You shouldn't have kept me sedated and then you wouldn't have needed him."

"If you'd cooperate with me, then I wouldn't be obliged to keep you sedated." Alonzo sat down on the bed, propping his feet up on a chair. "You know, Joe, you could save yourself a lot of grief if you would just provide me with a precise statement of how your drug works to slow the onset of AIDS.''

"You know the basic mechanism by which my drug works. You must have seen the results of the preliminary trials that I conducted in Manaus and São Paulo, or you wouldn't have been so determined to get your hands on me and my formula. You know that my drug is more effective than protease inhibitors in restoring T-cell count in patients with full-blown AIDS, and that its side effects are limited to mild nausea and leg cramps. For people infected with HIV, my drug seems to delay the onset of AIDS, perhaps for several years. We've been conducting clinical trials in Manaus for two years. So far, nobody infected with HIV has developed AIDS.''

"Yes, you're right, I do know that. Your drug isn't a silver bullet, but it's pretty damn close. So work with me, Joe, instead of against me. Our goals are the same. We want to save lives. Let's get this miracle drug out to the world. Let's take it to the FDA and ask for fast-track approval.''

Joe stood up, unable to tolerate such close proximity to Alonzo. "We've been over this so many times. I'm not a fool. The moment I give you that formula, I'm a dead man. You know it. I know it.''

Alonzo looked mournful. "Joe, Joe, Joe, you're so wrong. It's not in my best interests to have you dead, of course it isn't. I look forward to a long future of cooperation." He shook his head. "I can see you do not believe me. It's written in every line of your body. So, give it to me straight. What would it take for you to start trusting me?''

An interesting question, Joe thought. Right now, if angels appeared on either side of Alonzo and testified to his honesty, Joe would look for the devil hiding behind the curtain. Still, two people could play at the game of friendly lying. "Set me free," he said. "I would consider that a pretty convincing demonstration of your sincerity."

"That, my dear Joe, would be an example of sheer stupidity, not sincerity. However, I am willing to discuss financial terms with you as evidence of the fact that we don't intend to steal the formula for your drug."

Joe shrugged. "You can promise me any financial terms you please at no cost to yourself, since you're quite sure I won't be here to collect. I'm not going to discuss finances with you until I've devised some method whereby I can deliver the formula into your hands without signing my own death warrant. At that point, be warned. I intend to take you for every penny I can get."

Alonzo got off the bed, his expression showing grudging admiration rather than annoyance. As far as he was concerned, money and power were the root of all transactions, and when Joe talked money, he understood what was being said. He clapped Joe on the shoulder. "You know, it's possible we may be able to work together after all."

"Believe it, Alonzo. You want profits, I want this drug on the market—and maybe a Nobel prize for discovering it. Now all I need is some convincing evidence that I'm not going to die and we have the basis for a good solid deal here."

"First we will collect these samples so that my biochemist can take a look at them."

"I'm warning you now, Alonzo. He's not going to be able to run a chemical analysis and give you the magic formula. There are plant-based ingredients in my drug that he won't be able to quantify because they've never before been taken out of the rain forest."

"Fine. At least when I have these samples in my possession I am no longer dealing with a total unknown." Alonzo marched to the door, his stride impatient. "I plan to leave this apartment in fifteen minutes. If you want to shower before we go, you'd better be quick."

Since Joe was the one who knew where they were going, there was no point in blindfolding him for the drive, and so he discovered when they took him down to the limo that they'd been staying in Fernando's giant penthouse atop the Watergate complex—now, presumably, Alonzo's giant penthouse, since Fernando was dead. Unfortunately, there was no way for Joe to add that information to the scrawled note that he was carrying tucked into the cuff of his sport shirt.

He tried not to let his extreme nervousness show, but it was hard when he was staking his life on the outcome of this trip. Months ago, he had rented this storage space and filled it with samples of a drug he'd been working on to prevent indigestion. The basic ingredients of the drug were plants found only in the Amazon rain forest, so they were unfamiliar to Western science, just as he'd claimed. With luck, it would take Alonzo's biochemists weeks of testing before they could be certain of the precise properties of the drug. It would certainly take months more before they could complete trials that demonstrated the drug had no effect on people infected with HIV or AIDS, except possibly a very minor degree of help in preventing nausea and keeping down food.

The chauffeur didn't attempt to find a parking space for the limo when they reached Packages Unlimited, their destination in Roslyn. Joe was escorted out of the car with a bodyguard on either side and Alonzo bringing up the rear, while the chauffeur drove around the block. That made one less watchdog to contend with, at least.

Joe had originally chosen Packages Unlimited to store his samples because the lockboxes were controlled by electronic codes, not keys, and he'd figured it was much easier to remember a code—his father's birthday—than to keep a key safe in the Amazon rain forest. In view of the fact that anybody could open the box once they had the code, he was incredibly relieved that Alonzo hadn't decided simply to torture the combination out of him.

He was so damn tense he was afraid he might hyperventilate and pass out. Blinking nervously, he wiped the sweat off his forehead with the sleeve of his shirt and felt the crinkle of paper. Jesus! For a second, he'd forgotten that his note was stuffed into the cuff. He dropped his hand down against his side and sneaked a covert glance at Alonzo. Thank God, he didn't seem to have noticed that betraying slither of white paper poking out of Joe's sleeve.

"Which number box are we looking for?" Alonzo demanded.

Joe drew in a steadying breath. And then another. "Number forty-three. It's over there, on the right." He looked around, desperate for a clerk, but both of them were behind the counter, helping customers.

They had arrived at box number forty-three. "Okay, Joe. Open the box." Alonzo's voice was hoarse with tension.

His window of opportunity for rescue was vanishing at high speed. Joe slowly keyed in the release code and the lock clicked audibly open. Alonzo pulled open the metal drawer, his breath sucking in on a sigh of surprise and pleasure when he saw two dozen small vials of oatmeal-colored powder stacked inside.

Alonzo clicked his fingers. "Bag," he said to his entourage.

The bodyguards exchanged uneasy glances. "We don't have one, *senhor*."

The fact that nobody had thought to bring a container to carry the samples gave Joe his first piece of luck in three weeks. For a few crucial moments, Alonzo wasted time berating the guards. Then their attention was focused on scooping out the vials and transferring them to their trouser pockets. Since neither Alonzo nor the guards were wearing jackets, they were seriously short of carrying space.

While the three men squabbled and organized samples, Joe scanned the room in search of a potential rescuer. The clerks were still behind the counter, but a middle-aged woman, smartly dressed in a navy blue linen suit, was clearing mail out of her post-office box only a few feet away. She shut the box and turned to leave.

Stomach churning, Joe pulled his note out of its hiding place and held it clasped between the middle and index fingers of his left hand. Using that hand made his movements clumsier, but less easy for Alonzo to see. The woman started to walk toward the door. She would pass within a foot of where he was standing, which meant that he was within easy physical distance of slipping the note to her. But would she take his warning about keeping quiet seriously? If she started to scream, there was a horrible chance that Alonzo and the other two would open fire and blast their way out of the storage facility, leaving God knows how many dead bodies behind them.

His potential rescuer was right beside him. Joe had no more time to ponder ethical dilemmas, only to breathe a swift prayer and shove the note into her hand. The woman looked up, startled, and glanced quickly from Joe to the note before dropping it on the floor. Holy shit! His worst nightmare was coming true. Joe slid his foot over the note, hiding it, but some sixth sense must have alerted Alonzo to the possibility of trouble. He stopped what he was doing and swung around, his gaze dark with suspicion when he saw the woman looking at them.

Joe closed his eyes—as if that would make the danger less! He opened them again, silently begging the woman to move on, to get the hell out of here.

"Is there a problem, ma'am?" Alonzo's voice was thick with suspicion.

"No," she said uncertainly. "No, I guess not." Unaware that she was dooming him, the woman's gaze slid to the floor where the note had fallen and then moved upward to look again at Joe.

Alonzo's gaze followed the woman's. "We're almost finished here if you need anything," he said to the woman, scooping up the three remaining vials.

"Thanks, but I've already collected my mail." Aware that there was some sort of a problem but not wanting to get involved, she hurried out of the store.

"Take him outside," Alonzo hissed to the bodyguards in Portuguese. "Get him in the car." Alonzo pushed Joe from behind, so hard that he would have fallen if the bodyguards hadn't been holding him up.

There was no way to conceal the note as he stumbled forward. Alonzo picked it up, read it and shoved it into his pocket, his face twisted with rage.

The street was crowded, but Joe didn't have a chance to scream, even if he'd dared to risk it. One of the guards punched him hard in the gut, doubling him over. The other guard bundled him into the limo, and the chauffeur accelerated away from the store at high speed.

His attention was pretty much concentrated on not puking, but even so, Joe could see that Alonzo was almost apoplectic with rage, and that he was holding himself under control with difficulty. Joe had a dismal suspicion that Alonzo's unusual self-discipline boded ill for him.

He was right. The second they were back at the penthouse, Alonzo rounded on him, bringing his arm crashing down in a backhanded swipe that knocked Joe to the floor. The bodyguards picked him up and Alonzo hit him again across the mouth. The pain was bad enough to render him unconscious.

He came to when cold water was thrown into his face. Another punch broke his nose and made him wish that he hadn't regained consciousness. "Fucking asshole." Alonzo didn't scream. He pushed his face right up close to Joe's and spoke scarcely above a whisper. He punched him in the gut, right where the bodyguards had already hit him. Joe would have fallen except that the bodyguards were holding him upright.

"So you're cooperating with me, is that right? Is this how you cooperate?" Alonzo punctuated his questions with more blows.

Joe didn't answer. He didn't know what to say, and

anyway, his mouth was so swollen he wasn't sure he could speak.

"Yeah, you're cooperating with me, all right. Sending notes to the FBI." Alonzo delivered another series of punishing blows. "Fucking asshole."

He hurt too much to think. Joe closed his eyes as a wave of scarlet washed over his eyes. Humiliatingly, he vomited right before he passed out.

He woke up to water in his face and the sound of Alonzo's voice. "If you think the FBI is going to come running to your rescue, you can fucking think again." Alonzo was so angry that he was hitting Joe without any obvious purpose other than to relieve his frustration. He obviously didn't like the experience of being defied by one of his victims.

"Stop that, Alonzo. You're going to kill him and we can't afford to have him dead." A cool patrician voice interrupted Alonzo's muttered obscenities. Mercifully, the pounding on Joe's ribs also stopped.

With an effort of will that almost caused him to black out for the third time, Joe lifted his head to see who had spoken. He recognized the newcomer with a jolt of horrified surprise—and a sense of inevitable recognition.

The newcomer spoke. "Good evening, Joseph. I wish we could have met again under more pleasant circumstances. You really should give your cousin the formula, you know."

Joe shaped his puffy lips into a few slurred words that took all his remaining strength. "Fernando warned me…'bout…you. I wouldn't…believe him…."

"Believe it, Joseph. And now that you know who and what you're up against, shall we talk terms?"

# Seventeen

By four-thirty on Tuesday afternoon, Summer had exhausted her supply of information concerning the causes, symptoms and treatment of appendicitis. When her colleagues discovered she was back on the job, they showered her with sympathy and shared their stories of friends and relatives who had undergone similar surgery. Her boss arranged for a pot of multicolored tulips to be delivered as a welcome-back-to-work gift and the chairman of the Meteorology Department actually took her to lunch. Everyone wanted to hear details of her supposedly dramatic rush to the hospital, and Summer discovered that the cover story invented for her by the FBI was seriously lacking in several vital respects. If she'd been a spy, she'd have been lined up in front of a firing squad long before mid-morning, she decided wryly.

Although she'd planned to work late, Summer felt oppressed by the need to fudge answers to inquiries that she couldn't answer truthfully, and she leaped at the chance to get away when Bill Ogilvie called from his office at the *New York Times*. He told her that the police had made an arrest in the da Pereira murder case and indicated that he didn't believe the arrest was the end of the story.

Summer was eager to hear the specifics, even

though she was beginning to accept that if the FBI couldn't find Joe, she didn't have a prayer of discovering what had happened to him. Still, learning more about who killed Fernando was too good an opportunity to miss, and she agreed to meet Bill at Finnegan's, a bar on Third Avenue that was a favorite hangout for journalists.

Wrapping up a few essentials, Summer managed to get across town by six o'clock, as arranged. "I'm meeting Bill Ogilvie from the *Times,*" she said to one of the bartenders. "Do you know him? Is he here yet?"

"I sure am, and I'm right here." A red-haired man in his early forties joined her at the bar. He shook her hand, his smile relaxed and friendly. "Rita Marcil told me you look like your father, but a lot prettier. She's right on both counts." His smile widened into a grin. "Fortunately, I can say that since you don't work for me."

If Bill Ogilvie wanted to convince her that he was a laid-back kind of a guy, he should remember not to rake her over with such swift and penetrating appraisal, Summer thought. Fortunately, now that she wasn't worried about Olivia, she had nothing to hide that related specifically to Fernando's murder, so she found his scrutiny easy to tolerate. "Did you order a drink yet?" she asked. "If not, what can I buy you?"

"Thanks, but I'm halfway through my one bourbon of the night." Bill nodded his head to indicate a table in the corner of the room. "I'm sitting over there. Tell me what you want to drink and I'll bring it over. My tab."

"Then thank you. I'll have a glass of white wine,

please. A sauterne, if they have it, otherwise chardonnay is fine."

Bill carried her drink over to the table. "Sauterne as ordered. I have to be back at work in an hour, so let's get right to the point. I'll tell you what's going to be printed in the paper tomorrow about the murder. Buried deep inside, of course, because it's not very newsworthy. The police have arrested a man named Arturo Branco and charged him with first-degree murder in the shooting death of Fernando da Pereira."

"That's quick work," Summer commented. "How did they find him?"

"They got a tip-off that led them straight to Arturo. He's a Brazilian citizen, living in Brooklyn on an expired tourist visa, with a record as long as your arm back in his native country."

"Did the police say what they think this Arturo person's motive for the shooting was?"

"Money," Bill said succinctly. "They claim this was a contract killing."

"If it was murder for hire, who paid him?"

"Ah, the $64,000 question." Bill took a swallow of bourbon and leaned back against the wall. "I had one source inside the police department who told me that Arturo was turned in by the same people who hired him to do the killing, but I've no idea how they know that. According to my source, Arturo's employers didn't like the direction the investigation was taking so they ended the investigation by turning Arturo in."

"Not the kind of employer you want to work for when you kill for a living," Summer said.

Bill gave a brief chuckle. "You're right."

"Are the police going after the people who hired

him? Or are they going to let their investigation drop now that they have the man who pulled the trigger?''

"They aren't saying."

"But do you know what they're planning to do?"

Bill stirred the ice cubes in his drink. "Okay, Summer, let's inject a note of reality here, shall we? Rita's a good friend, and I'd like to help you out, but I've got a job to do, and a year-end bonus that will look a lot healthier if I break an important story. So here's where we're at, from my perspective. A very important foreign millionaire gets murdered. The daughter of the secretary of state is interested in the case and tells me she might have some insider information to pass on to me, but she needs some time. Now, in the news business, taking some time means a couple of hours, maybe a couple of days. It sure as hell doesn't mean a couple of weeks. So when time passes and I get no call from the secretary of state's daughter—"

"I wish you wouldn't call me that," Summer said. "I'm a person in my own right, not an appendage to my father."

"Sorry, Summer." Bill didn't look even marginally contrite. "This may be strictly un-PC, but from my point of view, where this story is concerned, I look at you, I see Gordon Shepherd's daughter."

"Then your vision is skewed. My interest in this case has got nothing to do with my father." That was almost true, Summer thought, hoping it was too dark for Bill Ogilvie to see her guilty flush.

"So you've said, but I don't believe you. I've never seen an investigation buttoned down so tight, which means there's a lot more to it than meets the eye. And I think the daughter of our much-admired secretary of state knows a hell of a lot more about this case than she's letting on.''

Summer gritted her teeth and decided to overlook Bill's pointed refusal to see beyond her relationship to her father. "Fernando da Pereira was a multimillionaire, and a very important figure in his own country. Of course the investigation is a top priority for the police department, with strict control over possible leaks. We discussed this before. I'm sure the State Department has been on top of them from day one, threatening dire consequences if they blow the investigation. But, trust me, none of that State Department pressure has got anything to do with why I'm here.''

"Have you noticed that when people say *trust me*, you'd be real smart to hang on to your wallet? Anyway, I've now told you that the police have made an arrest in the case. I've told you the suspect's name, and I've told you he has a criminal record. You know what? It's time for you to tell me something I don't know.''

Summer had come prepared, knowing she would have to give some explanation for her interest in the case. "All right, how about this? I told you that I had a friend who'd negotiated a deal with Fernando. I implied this friend was a woman. It wasn't. It was a man, and he'd discovered something big." Summer drew in a quick breath. "I believe that right before he died, Fernando da Pereira was getting ready to announce that his company was gearing up to produce a drug that is both a huge improvement over existing products on the market, and a correspondingly huge source of profit.''

Bill looked at her askance. "That's your big revelation? That Industria Agricola do Norte, which has one of the largest pharmaceutical operations in Brazil, was about to produce a new drug?''

''Yes, that's it. But this is a wonder drug. Something that will truly make news and bring huge profits to the company that's making it.'' As she spoke, Summer realized that she was drawing amazingly firm conclusions from information that had been remarkable chiefly for its ambiguity.

''What sort of a drug?'' Bill sounded skeptical. ''A cure for male-pattern baldness? A diet pill that really works? Something that makes cancer go away?''

''I don't know.''

He rolled his eyes and she shook her head. ''No, really, I don't know, Bill, and that's the truth. I wish I did know what we're dealing with. But whatever this drug is, it has the potential to make a lot of money. A diet pill that really curbs people's appetites would make millions. Or maybe it's a new antibiotic to replace all the ones that bacteria have become resistant to. The one thing I'm sure of is that this drug fills a real need and will also make the person or company that owns the production rights very, very rich.''

''Pereira was already very rich.''

''Yes, but he has plenty of rivals who bitterly resented his success. One of those rivals may have decided to even the score a little. A drug as valuable as the one we're talking about could cause a lot of unscrupulous people to start thinking about how much money they could make if only Fernando were dead.''

Bill kept stirring his drink, although it was mostly melted ice by now. ''You're suggesting that Pereira was killed before he could get the deal for this new wonder drug all sewn up with legally binding contracts.''

"It seems a logical and convincing motive for killing him, don't you think? Pereira gets bumped off before he's signed the deal that gives him exclusive manufacturing rights, so the person who discovered the drug has to go elsewhere to get it produced. Millions of dollars in annual income is enough to tempt anyone, especially a rival who was already annoyed by Fernando's success."

"Maybe one of those rival Amazon developers the police were talking about as suspects when the case first broke..." Bill suggested.

"Yes." Summer nodded. "The ones who were afraid of losing scads of money if Fernando's legislation limiting rain forest development actually made it all the way through the Brazilian congress. With Fernando dead, the person who murdered him reaps a double revenge. The legislation stalls, and they get to make a gazillion dollars with the new wonder drug."

"You paint a convincing picture. Which I guess leaves us with just two interesting questions. How do you know so much about Pereira and this wonder drug, and who is the mysterious person who discovered it? You must know that since you claim he's your friend."

Summer was silent for a moment. Then she realized that the only way she was going to get Bill's cooperation was to tell him nothing but the truth, even if she couldn't tell him all of the truth. "I'm going to answer you indirectly, but that's the best I can do. Fernando da Pereira was one of the wealthiest and most powerful men in the world. Despite that, he couldn't provide sufficient protection to keep himself alive. He never went anywhere without bodyguards, and yet on the night that he was killed, his limo was involved in a minor accident that sent his chauffeur and his most trusted, longtime bodyguard to the hospital. So he traveled to New York by train and checked into the Carlyle hotel by himself, where Arturo was waiting for him. He was killed less than an hour after he checked into his room. That's how easy it was for the people behind Fernando's murder to cut a giant hole in his safety net.''

She saw that Bill was about to interrupt with questions and she shook her head, silencing him. She leaned forward across the table, her gaze locking with his. ''I can't give you honest answers to some of your questions, so I'm keeping quiet rather than inventing lies. There are still a lot of answers I don't have, and people's lives may be at risk if I say the wrong thing.''

''Now you're losing me,'' Bill said dryly. ''I don't go much for melodrama.''

''Neither do I. And my suggestion that people's lives were at risk wasn't melodrama, it was unpleasant fact.'' She looked at him appealingly. ''When we first talked, I asked you for more time, and I'm still asking you for the same thing. Give me some more time, Bill, and in the end I'll give you your story. I promise you it's a big one.''

Bill shook his head in disbelief. ''Rita warned me that on a good day, you could charm a snake into giving up its rattle. She didn't know the half.''

There was enough laughter in his voice that she smiled back at him. ''I'm going to take that as a compliment. The thing is, Bill, I still need your help. I need to know who Fernando's most powerful rivals are, because that's probably where we're going to find the names of the people who paid for his murder. I could do the research myself, but you've probably done it already, and there seems no point in reinventing the wheel."

"You're right, I did do some preliminary research on the people who've been loudest in their opposition to Pereira. He was a man with plenty of powerful enemies." Bill reached down by his chair and retrieved a slender leather portfolio, which he put on the table between their drinks. Unzipping it, he reached inside for a manila folder. Balancing the folder on top of the portfolio to avoid patches of damp left by their drinks was a difficult task, and a photograph and a sheet of typed text fell out of the folder, landing on the floor by Summer's feet.

"I'll get them," she said, bending down.

"Thanks." He indicated the photo she now held. "This was taken at Pereira's funeral. It was supposed to run in tomorrow's paper, but it got axed because of space considerations. It's the president of Brazil with Mrs. da Pereira leaving the cemetery after Fernando's funeral. I guess those four girls are his daughters."

Summer glanced at the picture, curious to see what Fernando's wife and children looked like. The light in their corner of the bar was dim, but the photo had been taken by a professional, and the faces of the five women were surprisingly clear. Senhora da Pereira was as slim and elegant as most wives of wealthy Brazilians. Her daughters were teenagers, or perhaps in their early twenties, their tears hidden behind dark sunglasses. All five women were standing by a stretch limo of monstrous proportions, with the president of Brazil getting ready to hand them into their car, and a muscular chauffeur posed rigidly at attention as he held open the door for them to get in.

Summer looked at the chauffeur and felt her entire

body freeze. The chauffeur had a chillingly familiar face. Broad forehead, snub nose, full-lipped mouth. She'd spent several agonizing minutes staring at that face from the back of a minivan and she recognized it instantly.

Senhora da Pereira's chauffeur had been one of her kidnappers.

A shout of laughter went up from the next table. She barely heard it. Bill Ogilvie touched her hand and she realized that he'd spoken to her, but she couldn't reply because she hadn't the remotest idea what he'd said.

"I need this photo," she said. "Can you lend it to me for a few days?"

"Why?"

"I can't tell you, but it's really important."

"Jesus, Summer, I'm a reporter, not a Boy Scout. You have to give me something in exchange for the photo. What did you see in it that's got you all fired up?"

She hesitated for a second, then pointed to the chauffeur. "I recognize that man. I need to find out who he is, and whether he's really an employee of the Pereira family. If he is, then Fernando's murder may be an inside job."

"You can have the photo." Bill shoved it across the table. "But only because it's available on all the wires and you could get it from a dozen other places if not from me."

She realized that he was angry with her because he thought she was lying. That she was really interested in something else in the photo, not the chauffeur. "There's no way I can prove this to you, Bill, but I've told you nothing but the truth."

She stood up, tucking the photo into her own bulging portfolio. "Thanks for the drink. I'm grateful for your help and I'll be in touch. You probably don't believe me, but I wish I could have told you more."

"Yeah, sure. Have a nice day, Ms. Shepherd, and give my regards to Daddy."

There was no answer she could make to that. She walked out of the bar before Bill could say anything more, barely waiting for the door to swing shut behind her before breaking into a run. She wasn't even going to waste time going back to her apartment and packing a bag.

She was going to head for the airport and hope that she would be in time to catch the last shuttle to Washington. Now that she could show Julian Stein the face of one of her kidnappers, the search for Joe could be narrowed to a point where there was a real chance of finding him.

She hailed a passing cab. "La Guardia," she said as she climbed in. "And please hurry."

# *Eighteen*

Summer ran up the small flight of steps that led to her father's town house and rang the bell. She hadn't called ahead from the airport, since she figured that even if Gordon and Olivia weren't home, the housekeeper would be. But she was in luck and her father opened the door himself.

"Summer, what a nice surprise! Come on in." His smile turned to a frown as she stepped into the narrow, high-ceilinged hallway. "But what are you doing in Washington? I thought you were in New York and back at work already. I hope there's nothing wrong? No new problems?"

"No, I'm fine, but I uncovered a piece of information that seemed too important to wait until the morning to share. About my kidnapping."

"I can't wait to hear what it is. But why are we standing in the hall? I was catching up on my reading in the living room, so let's go in there. Would you like a drink? I have a really fine brandy that was given to me by the French ambassador—"

"No, thanks, Dad. Nothing for me." Summer followed her father into the living room and took a seat by the empty fireplace, trying not to fidget while her father refreshed his drink. All the chairs in this room were uncomfortable, presumably because they'd been chosen by Olivia for their antique elegance, but this one seemed even more uncomfortable than most. For the first time, Summer paused to wonder what fundamental insecurity drove her stepmother to sacrifice comfort in her own home for the sake of impressing visitors with her sense of style.

"Where is Olivia?" she asked.

"She's gone to bed already," her father said, sitting down opposite her. "We've had such an exhausting schedule these past few weeks, and then with all the added stress of Fernando's death and your kidnapping, I'm afraid she's succumbed to the strain."

"I'm sorry to hear that—"

"Yes, and to make matters worse, we only have temporary help in the house at the moment." He wafted the brandy glass under his nose before taking an appreciative sip. "Our housekeeper had to go back to Michigan to put her mother in a nursing home...the poor woman has Alzheimer's...so Olivia has been inundated with all the extra work of running the house. We've hired a cleaning service, of course, but there's only so much they can do without supervision."

"You must be tired, too," Summer said. "I know it's getting late, and I won't keep you up any longer than I have to, but I wanted to fill you in before I talk to the FBI—"

"My dear, I'm a night owl, so you're not keeping me up at all. And if you were, it wouldn't matter. I don't remember how long it's been since you and I last spent any time alone together, but I do know it's been far too long."

"It's really been about eleven years," Summer said, suddenly not willing to foster the illusion that their relationship was something that it wasn't, and probably never would be. "We haven't spent an evening alone together since the week after my mother died."

Her father winced and swirled his cognac. "There's nothing much I can say in answer to that rebuke except that I'm sorry. You don't become secretary of state for the most powerful nation in the world without sacrificing some of your personal life." He cleared his throat. "A lot of your personal life, in fact."

"I understand." He started to say more and she shook her head, not willing to get bogged down in another conversation about the amazing pressure of his work, a subject which he never seemed to tire of. "No, really, I do understand, Dad. Anyway, let me tell you why I'm here. I'm sure Olivia mentioned that we had lunch together—"

Her father nodded. "She explained that you wanted to let her know that you'd seen her and Fernando on the train together right before Fernando was killed. We both found it very strange that you didn't speak to her at the time instead of waiting for days. I know your relationship with your stepmother has always been difficult, but—"

"Dad, I really have a lot of explaining to do, and it's quite urgent, so could we please stick to the point?"

Her father looked startled, as well he might. Summer wasn't in the habit of interrupting him, and she'd just done it for the second time. "Very well. What is it you want to tell me?" he asked.

"I met with Bill Ogilvie earlier tonight. I don't expect you'll recognize the name. He's the senior crime reporter for the *New York Times,* and he phoned me just as I was leaving work to tell me that the police have arrested a man named Arturo Branco and charged him with murdering Fernando da Pereira.''

"Olivia and I heard the same news earlier this evening. Knowing how upset Olivia had been, the chief of police was kind enough to call and let us know personally. I must say I'm very pleased they found the perpetrator so quickly. Fernando was a good man, despite a rather swashbuckling start to his business empire, and his death leaves a big hole in Brazil's commercial and industrial leadership.''

"Bill Ogilvie isn't convinced that the police have uncovered the real story behind Fernando's murder. He doesn't think the arrest of this Branco person is the end of the story, and since I feel the same way, we agreed to have a drink together and share a few ideas.''

Gordon looked alarmed. "Goodness, Summer, that was risky. I hope you were extremely careful about what you said to him. These reporters have all sorts of underhanded methods for tricking information out of you—"

"Bill didn't try to trick me, Dad. He's not that sort of journalist.''

"Trust me," Gordon said dryly. "They're all that sort of journalist. My dear, I don't want to sound alarmist, but if any leaks get out about your kidnapping and they can be traced back to you, Julian Stein won't hesitate to prosecute you for breaching the Official Secrets Act, and I won't be able to protect you from him. He isn't the sort of man to cut you any slack just because you're a civilian, much less because you're my daughter.''

"Dad, you don't have to worry. I promise I chose what I said to Bill Ogilvie very carefully. In fact, I only brought up the fact that I'd met him to explain how I came into possession of this picture. Which is why I'm here." Summer drew the photograph taken at Fernando's funeral out of her portfolio and handed it to her father. "This is a wire service photo, taken at Fernando's memorial service, and the *Times* was considering running it tomorrow to accompany their article about the arrest of Arturo Branco."

Her father put on his reading glasses and looked at the photo. "I recognize the Brazilian president," he said. "And I assume these women are members of the Pereira family? I seem to remember that Fernando had several daughters but no son."

"Yes, that's Senhora da Pereira and her daughters, but from my point of view, they aren't the interesting people in the photo. Do you see the man standing by the car?"

"Do you mean the chauffeur?"

"Yes." Summer drew in a deep breath. "He was one of my kidnappers."

"Good God!" Gordon appeared stunned. "Are you sure?"

"Absolutely. Remember I told you that I got a really good look at the man sitting in the front seat of the minivan when the kidnappers were driving me to Florida? Well, this chauffeur is the same man who was in the minivan. I spent fifteen minutes staring straight at him and I'd recognize him anywhere."

"I know you said at the time that you had a very clear mental picture of him. But still, you were in a dark car...."

"Yes, but the headlights of the oncoming traffic highlighted his face every couple of seconds. It's not that any one of his features is so memorable, but the combination is pretty striking, especially that unusually broad forehead contrasted with a small snub nose.''

Gordon pulled the lamp on the side table closer and tilted the shade so that light shone directly onto the picture. "I can see what you mean," he said at last. "That isn't a face you would forget once you'd seen it in the circumstances you've just described."

Summer was relieved that her father didn't doubt her identification. That was the first hurdle crossed. Now she only had to convince the FBI director. "I'm absolutely certain he was one of the kidnappers, and I'm confident I would be able to pick him out of a police lineup."

"Yes, I can see that you're very sure of yourself and that's good, because I expect Julian Stein will press you hard before he accepts that this is the man you saw in the minivan."

"Dad, don't worry so much." In an odd role reversal, she seemed to have been repeating that phrase like a mantra ever since she arrived. "Apart from the fact that we're close to having a name for one of my kidnappers, the fact that the man I've identified also works for the Pereira family confirms my suspicion that there's a strong link between Fernando's murder and my kidnapping, don't you agree?"

"I certainly do." Gordon took off his glasses and rested them on top of the pile of papers he'd been working on when she arrived. "To be honest, I still can't grasp what the link is, precisely, but obviously it's there."

"I don't know what the connection is, either. But once this chauffeur is in custody, then the FBI should be able to get answers to all of our questions. Most important of all, we have a really good chance of finding out where Joe has been taken to.''

"Don't get your hopes up too high," Gordon said. "I wish it was that easy. The FBI should have no trouble locating this chauffeur, but unfortunately that doesn't mean we'll be able to question him, much less extradite him to this country. You've no idea how difficult it is to persuade foreign governments to surrender their citizens to U.S. law enforcement agencies. And, if my memory serves me correctly, there's no extradition treaty between our country and Brazil."

He got up and paced the length of the room, shaking his head as he talked. "Latin American countries have bad memories of U.S. intervention in their internal political affairs, and these days they're very sensitive to anything that smacks of neocolonialism on our part."

Summer stood up as well, too angry to remain seated. "That man is part of a terrorist group that kidnapped me, starved me, and kept me blindfolded and tied up for more than three days. They held the United States government to ransom and threatened national security in the process. They also abducted my friend Joe, and probably ordered the murder of Fernando da Pereira. Bringing that chauffeur back to this country to stand trial has got absolutely nothing to do with neocolonialism or neo-anything else. It's simple justice. Julian Stein needs to see that photo and the FBI needs to get its butt in gear and haul that man back here."

Her father stopped his pacing, turned to look at her, then smiled, albeit a touch wryly. "My dear, I think you just put me very effectively in my place. Sometimes I'm so busy being a diplomat that I forget about being a man. Not to mention a father."

"I didn't mean to be rude—"

"You weren't in the least rude, merely forceful. Wait here, my dear. I have Julian Stein's emergency phone number in my study. I'll go and call him right now. We need to show him this photo immediately, because I believe we're looking at the lead that will crack this case wide open."

Her father left the room, and the frustration Summer had been feeling for the past week gave way to a heart-racing sense of urgency. Knowing that there was finally a realistic chance of finding out what had happened to Joe, the control she'd exerted over herself for the past several hours broke and she started to shake so hard that she had to sit down. She tried to imagine what would happen next, but her head was swimming with hopes and fears, leaving no room for coherent thoughts.

"I managed to reach the director," Gordon said, coming back into the living room.

"He was sleeping and not at all pleased to be disturbed, but I convinced him this was a major breakthrough and that he needed to speak with you as soon as possible. To cut a long story short, he's agreed to meet you right now, in his office at FBI headquarters. I suggested that he should come here, but he pointed out that he's going to need secure communications equipment and experts who know how to use it, if we're going to pin a firm identity onto the man in the photo. So if you're not too tired, my dear, we need to leave as soon as possible. Get the ball rolling, so to speak."

"I'm not tired at all. Just relieved that we're finally getting closer to finding Joe." Summer gave her father a quick, awkward kiss on the cheek. "Thanks, Dad. I really appreciate your help in getting Julian Stein to see me at this hour of the night.''

"You don't owe me any thanks," her father said. "I'm just glad that you decided to come to me first and ask for my help.''

Olivia had taken a prescription sleeping pill, and although she hadn't fallen asleep, she was—thank God—feeling drowsy, and for a long time the distant murmur of voices registered as nothing more than a tiresome background hum that barely intruded on her consciousness. Eventually, though, she came sufficiently awake to realize that Gordon was talking to someone. Who? Bette, the housekeeper, was back in Michigan coping with her mother's failing health, and there wasn't supposed to be anyone else in the house.

Olivia squinted at the luminous dial of the clock. Eleven-thirty. She sat up, drowsiness vanishing, and put on her robe and slippers. She crept to the head of the stairs, not wanting to be seen if Gordon was entertaining some official visitor. But he wasn't; the woman with him was Summer. Olivia could recognize her stepdaughter's voice at a thousand paces, even if she couldn't actually distinguish enough individual words to understand what was being said.

She crept down a few more steps so that she could hear better and realized that Summer and her husband were planning to go out somewhere together. At this hour of the night she couldn't imagine where they would be going.

Amend that thought. She couldn't imagine anywhere safe and harmless that they could be going.

Olivia debated whether or not to continue on downstairs or whether she should take the easy way out and return to bed. Over the years of her marriage, she had developed the talent of knowing when not to ask questions into a high art form. But tonight, the fear of speaking up was balanced by the fear of the consequences if she kept silent. Tonight, she didn't think she could turn her back and hide away upstairs.

It was really hard to make herself walk down the remaining stairs. Almost in a trance, she put one foot in front of the other, her slippers making no sound on the carpeted steps. She turned left in the hallway and walked through the open double doors into the living room. Once inside, she didn't look at Summer, just stared at Gordon.

Dry mouthed, she asked the question she didn't want him to answer. "Where are you taking Summer?"

Gordon smiled. "Olivia, my dear, I thought you were sleeping."

His answer terrified her, because it wasn't an answer at all, and that was always a bad sign with her husband. She closed her eyes, wishing herself a thousand miles—a million miles—away from here.

"Olivia, are you all right?" Summer's voice. So pretty, so soft. So infuriatingly appealing.

Olivia opened her eyes. She still didn't look at her stepdaughter. Why bother? Summer was undoubtedly wearing some bargain-basement outfit and looking gorgeous, just as she always did. She repeated her question. "Where are you going with your daughter, Gordon?"

"To see Julian Stein. He's waiting for us at FBI headquarters." She recognized the anger gathering behind his smile. "Now, my dear, let me take you upstairs and see you settled. Summer, I'll be with you in a minute.''

Olivia hesitated. Should she just turn tail and go upstairs with him? It would be so easy to pretend that she believed her husband. That's what she'd been doing for the whole of the past year, pretending that she believed him. Stomach churning, she admitted to herself that it was finally time to call a halt.

"Julian Stein is in Chicago," she said flatly.

"You must be mistaken," Summer protested. "Dad called him only a few minutes ago—"

Olivia cut in as if Summer hadn't spoken. "For the last time, Gordon, where were you really planning to take your daughter?"

Her husband put on his concerned and benevolent voice. "Olivia, my dear, I'm afraid you're not in an entirely rational state of mind. Those sleeping pills you took must be affecting you more than we either of us realized—"

"It's no good, Gordon. I'm not going to let you get away with this any longer." Her fingers were digging so hard into the back of her favorite Louis XIV chair that she felt the silk rip. "We've passed way beyond the point where I can pretend to myself that the end justifies the means. However much you want to be president, however much I want to be first lady, I'm calling a halt. This stops right here. Now, before Summer gets hurt."

"Dad, for God's sake, what is Olivia talking about?"

"I have no idea," Gordon said, tight-lipped with suppressed rage. "As I told you, the stress has been acute these past several weeks—"

"Maybe the sleeping pill is affecting me," Olivia

said. "Maybe it's blunted the edges enough that it's given me the courage to speak up about what you're doing. What you've been doing for the whole of the past year."

Her stepdaughter spoke again. "Olivia, please, clue me in on what's happening here. Would you at least look at me, dammit?"

Summer sounded desperate. Olivia finally brought herself to glance at her stepdaughter, who was indeed looking her usual fabulous self in casual navy linen slacks and a white cotton sweater that had probably come from the sale rack at some discount chain store. She appeared pale and tired. And more beautiful than ever since she was one of those utterly loathsome and infuriating women who simply turned exquisitely vulnerable-looking when they were worried.

The trouble was, much as she disliked Summer, Olivia couldn't convince herself that jealousy of her stepdaughter's annoying good looks was adequate grounds for letting something really bad happen to her.

"Answer me one question," she said to Summer. "Why did you want to speak to Julian Stein?"

"Leave it, Olivia," Gordon snapped.

Summer's glance flashed from her father back to Olivia. "I want to see Julian Stein because I've identified one of my kidnappers," she said.

Olivia's breath exhaled in an involuntary gasp. "Who is he?" she asked, holding herself very still, preparing for the worst.

"I don't know his name, but he's one of the chauffeurs working for the Pereira family."

Hearing her stepdaughter's reply, Olivia felt herself shatter, even though she didn't move. There was no longer any wiggle room left for hope. The coincidences were too great, and she could no longer pretend Gordon was simply an innocent man, caught in the center of a damaging storm. She looked at her husband, forcing him to meet her eyes. Strange how deeply she still loved him, even though she knew that he was fundamentally a flawed and corrupt human being. "Did you arrange for Summer to be kidnapped?" she asked.

"No!" He sounded genuinely outraged, although his shoulders slumped and he dropped his gaze. "For God's sake, Olivia, what do you think I am? Only a monster would agree to put his daughter through the nightmare Summer endured! I was as upset and horrified as you when I got the news that she'd been kidnapped."

Her attention was so strongly focused on her husband, trying to decide if he was telling the truth, that Olivia momentarily forgot about Summer's presence in the room. She jumped when Summer grabbed her by the shoulders and swung her around so that they were face-to-face.

"Olivia, answer me! What in the name of God are you suggesting? Are you saying that Dad..." Summer's voice broke for a moment, but she quickly regained possession of herself. "Are you accusing my father of arranging to have me kidnapped?"

There was no point in pretending or prevaricating. "I thought it was possible," Olivia said dully. "I was suspicious from the moment I heard that the kidnappers wanted to exchange you for Joe Malone."

Summer walked to the center of the room, her anger almost palpable. "Dad, either you or Olivia had better start explaining what's been going on or I'm going to call the FBI and you can do your explaining to them.

Or maybe I'll just call Bill Ogilvie and tell him that scoop he's aiming for is waiting right here, at Gordon Shepherd's stately Georgetown home.''

"You see what you've done?" Gordon said bitterly to Olivia. "I was only going to drive Summer to the cottage in Maryland and keep her there until I managed to get things under control with Alonzo. No harm would have been done—''

"And what if you didn't get things under control with Alonzo?" Olivia asked acidly. "He's been tying you up in knots ever since you first got involved with him. When are you going to accept that he doesn't play by civilized rules—''

"Okay, that's it. I've had enough." Summer walked over to the corner of the room and picked up the phone. "I'm calling 911. First, I'll ask them to send some men in white coats to take you both away—''

Gordon snatched the phone out of her hand, grabbed her roughly and shoved her into a chair. He loomed over her, his patrician features contorted with fear and rage. "Unless you want to see me impeached and jailed, you'd better keep your mouth shut tight.''

Olivia felt a surge of despair, mingled with disgust. "That's right, Gordon. Yell at Summer because you've single-handedly destroyed your chance at becoming president. That's what you do best, isn't it? Blame other people for your own mistakes.''

"You were the one who told me that we needed money so that we didn't have to waste all our energies trying to raise funds to support my campaign.''

Olivia didn't even care that he was doing it again. Blaming her for his criminal decisions. At this moment all she wanted to know was the extent of his betrayal. "Tell me one thing, Gordon. It's been bothering me for two weeks now, even more since I had lunch with Summer. When you sent me off to New York with Fernando da Pereira, did you know that he was going to be murdered?''

"No, of course not!" Gordon shouted his denial, and for once Olivia couldn't decide whether it was guilt or outrage fueling his anger. "Alonzo set me up. Just like he did with Summer's kidnapping."

"Then explain to your daughter what this is all about," Olivia said. "And to me, too, while you're at it. Explain to both of us why you're so deeply involved with a despicable man like Alonzo da Pereira that you daren't let your daughter inform the FBI that she's identified one of the men who kidnapped her."

Gordon sat down abruptly. "Summer, I was trying to protect you. But since you've insisted on poking and prying into affairs you'd have done better to leave alone, I can see there's no way to avoid telling you this anymore. The fact is that Alonzo da Pereira loaned me a great deal of money, seven million dollars, in fact."

"Who, exactly, is Alonzo da Pereira?" Summer asked.

"Fernando's cousin, and the new president of Industria Agricola do Norte. Alonzo had big plans for marketing Joseph Malone's AIDS drug—''

"AIDS drug!" Summer exclaimed, her eyes growing wide. "Is that what Joe has been working on? Oh my God, no wonder he was so frantic to get the drug into production. Has he found a cure?"

"We don't know," Gordon said. "The tests Fernando conducted weren't on a large enough scale and they didn't last long enough to know for sure. But they did prove that Malone's drug will restore immune function over limited periods of time. For at least a year, in fact.''

Summer frowned. ''This is wonderful news, but I don't understand what it's got to do with you. How and why does the marketing of Joe's AIDS drug affect you so closely?''

Gordon cleared his throat. ''Alonzo agreed to cut me in as a silent partner in the company. I intended to pay him back for the seven-million-dollar loan with the profits we would make when the company went public on the New York Stock Exchange. Alonzo plans to spin off the pharmaceutical arm of Industria Agricola as soon as Malone's drug is in preliminary production. All the partners in the company will make millions.''

The wonder on Summer's face was replaced by revulsion, and Gordon spread his hands in a gesture of appeal. ''You have to understand what's at stake here. I needed a source of funds to float the initial stages of my presidential campaign. A presidential candidate can spend as much money as he wants, provided it's from his own pocket. This country can't afford to have another ineffective president, and I realized it was my duty to find a source of funds so that I can save Americans from another four years of ridiculous sex scandals and dirty party politics.''

Summer's mouth turned down in distaste. ''Party politics have their sleazier moments, but they sure beat dictatorship by the deluded.''

Olivia cut off an instinctive rebuke to her stepdaughter. After so many years, it was hard not to spring instantly to Gordon's defense. ''I went along with your rationalizations about why you needed a source of private campaign funds,'' she said to her husband. "But ever since Fernando was murdered, I've known you were more involved with Alonzo da Pereira than you ever told me. Just how far have you waded into the muck, Gordon? Are you going to end up in jail?" She swallowed hard. "Are *we* going to end up in jail?"

"My dear, as if I would allow such a thing to happen. Of course we won't go to jail."

When he spoke in that gentle voice, Olivia's resistance always melted. But not tonight. "Sweet words aren't enough to prevent what's about to happen, Gordon. We've been hurtling downhill to disaster ever since Summer was kidnapped, and now we're going too fast to stop."

"We can stop," Gordon said confidently. "In fact, it's probably better that Summer finally knows the truth. There's no need for what we've discussed to go any further than the four walls of this room." He swung around, his eyes feverish. "Summer, you understand that you can't go to Julian Stein with this story about recognizing the Pereiras' chauffeur as one of your kidnappers, don't you? A piece of information like that would tie your kidnapping right into Fernando's murder, and before you know it, everything I've worked so hard to achieve would start unraveling."

Trembling with shock, Summer stepped back so that she wouldn't accidentally touch her father. "You might not have planned my kidnapping, but you must know why it happened. Explain that to me, please."

"It's very complicated—"

"I have a mind that's been educated at great expense to handle complexity. Try me."

Gordon sighed, as if he found her request both tiresome and unreasonable. "Alonzo's personal financial interests have always been heavily centered in the Amazon region, and he was threatened with ruin by Fernando's campaign to preserve the rain forest. Alonzo cheered up a bit when he learned that Joseph Malone had discovered this amazing new drug that produced a dramatic slowdown in the onset of full-blown AIDS among people infected with HIV. But to Alonzo's horror, your friend Malone persuaded Fernando to sell the drug virtually at cost, throwing away almost unimaginable profits." Gordon shrugged. "That was probably when Alonzo decided that his cousin Fernando had to die."

Olivia was white around her lips, clinging to the embroidered back of the chair as if she would keel over without its support. How ironic it was, Summer thought, that her despised stepmother was obviously a moral and humanitarian giant in comparison to Gordon. Her father bent down and pried his wife's hand from the chair. He carried it to his lips in elegant supplication. "Livvy, I didn't know that Fernando was going to be killed that night, I swear."

Olivia looked up at him despairingly. "But you knew something was going to happen, Gordon, didn't you? You used me."

Annoyed, he dropped her hand. "Alonzo asked me to make sure that Fernando went to New York with you. But I only realized that he was planning murder after you called to tell me Fernando was dead."

"What about my kidnapping?" Summer asked. "Did you only realize Alonzo was planning that after it happened, too?"

"I knew nothing about it," Gordon said harshly. "Even after we got the ransom note I still couldn't believe that Alonzo was behind your disappearance."

With an effort, Summer steadied her breathing. "The fact that the kidnappers wanted to ransom me in exchange for Joe should have clued you in."

"Well, yes, it did, of course, in a way. But until that moment, I had never realized how ruthless and without heart Alonzo actually is. It's difficult to believe that someone you've considered an ally and friend could betray you so badly."

"Why did he decide to betray you, as you put it? It seems to me the two of you had a very cozy relationship."

Emotion flickered across Gordon's patrician features. Evasiveness, Summer realized, and a repellent touch of cunning. "Alonzo wanted to shift the balance of power between the two of us," he said. "I realize now that Alonzo's plan is to funnel the profits from Malone's AIDS drug into my campaign. Then, when I'm elected, Alonzo will have the president of the United States in his hip pocket. I'll never be able to thwart him or oppose his stand on issues because he will always be able to threaten to reveal something that will bring down my presidency."

Summer noticed that her father was talking in the present tense. Gordon, it seemed, was crazy enough to believe she would stand by in silence while he campaigned for the office of president. Not in this lifetime, she thought fiercely.

She didn't express her disgust because she still needed information. "Nothing you've said so far explains why Alonzo kidnapped me," she said.

"To keep me in line, of course." Gordon sounded quite gratified that he was important enough to force Alonzo to take such a risk. "He knew I would guess right away that he was responsible for Fernando's death, and he didn't want me to turn him in to the police. And then, with your kidnapping, he achieved two goals at once. He kept me quiet about Fernando's murder, and he got his hands on Malone."

"There must have been a hundred easier ways for Alonzo to capture Joe," Summer said.

"Plenty of easier ways," Gordon agreed. "But most of them carried a high risk that Malone would resist and end up dead. This way, in one fell swoop, Alonzo got Malone alive and he trapped me into complicity in a crime. It was really important to Alonzo for Malone to be on U.S. soil, in U.S. custody, when you were kidnapped. That way I was bound to get drawn right into the middle of all the negotiations."

"Thereby digging yourself into a deeper and deeper legal pit if you kept quiet."

Gordon looked at her with earnest blue eyes. "I kept quiet for your sake, Summer. I knew Alonzo would kill you if I spoke up and fingered him for Fernando's murder. So in a way, the mess we're in now is all your fault."

The American people were missing out on the chance to elect a president whose capacity for shifting blame was literally breathtaking. They'd never know how lucky they were. Summer walked over to the glossy cherry-wood desk set in an alcove in front of one of the bay windows. Cream vellum writing paper was stacked in the pigeonholes, and a Mont Blanc pen rested on a pewter stand, along with a bottle of old-fashioned ink. Only the best for Olivia. Except in husbands, where she seemed to have got stuck with something pretty close to the worst.

Summer held up a piece of paper and a pen. "You have a letter to write," she said. She couldn't call him Dad anymore. The word stuck in her throat.

"I have no idea what you're talking about, Summer. You always did have a birdbrain, just like your mother's, hopping from one idea to the next without ever settling."

More blame-shifting, but she didn't even bother to feel angry. Gordon Shepherd no longer had that much power over her. "You have a simple choice," she said. "Write a letter of resignation to the president, effective immediately, or I'll call Julian Stein and tell him everything you've just told me."

He blustered and spluttered. He protested, he swore, he called her foul names. In the end, it was Olivia who put a stop to the tawdry performance. "Stop it, Gordon," she said, her voice thready with weariness. "The dream is over. You killed it the day you took an illegal seven-million-dollar campaign donation from Alonzo da Pereira. Just be thankful that Summer is willing to keep quiet and you're not going to end up in jail."

Protesting to the end, Gordon sat down at the desk and wrote his letter of resignation to the president. He got up, leaving the letter and a hand-addressed envelope on the blotter. "Take the letter and leave," he said to Summer. "In the circumstances, I'm sure you won't be surprised to hear that I don't ever want to see you again."

"I can't leave yet," Summer said. "There's one subject we haven't even touched on."

"I can't imagine what. You seem to have done a comprehensive job of destroying everything I've ever worked for...."

Shaking with rage, Summer braced herself against the desk. She couldn't afford to lose her temper. Not yet. "Where's Joe? Is he still alive?"

Her father's response was smooth and immediate. "I don't know where he is, but Alonzo assures me he's alive and well."

"Why would you believe Alonzo? According to you, he's lied consistently in the past. More to the point, why should I believe you?"

"Because it obviously isn't in anyone's interest to kill Malone. We need him to give us the formula for his drug."

"I have a deal to suggest to you," Summer said. "How about if you help me get Joe out of Alonzo's clutches, and in exchange, I'll give you the formula for Joe's new AIDS drug?"

Gordon's head jerked up, his eyes suddenly sparkling. "Are you telling me that you've had the formula for the drug all along?" He gave a short laugh. "How ironic."

Summer pressed her lips together and waited for her stomach to settle. Sickened, she realized that Gordon had lied right up to the end. He knew exactly where Joe was being kept prisoner and would never have told her unless she had produced the key that unlocked the door to his self-interest.

Hunched into herself, Olivia sat silently twiddling her thumbs, with sad eyes fixed glassily on her hus-

band's face. Summer suspected that her stepmother
understood as well as she did that Gordon's explanations over the past half hour had been highly selective
and self-serving. The true version of his activities over
the past few months would most likely reveal far
greater complicity in Alonzo's various crimes and mis-
demeanors. For starters, it would take a lot more than
suave assurances from Gordon before Summer would
believe that he hadn't deliberately tricked his own wife
into setting Fernando up for murder. He and Alonzo
both seemed to have million-dollar reasons for wanting Fernando dead so that Alonzo could take over the
running of Industria Agricola do Norte.

When she could trust herself to speak, Summer
turned to face the man she was now reluctant to acknowledge as her father. ''You're lucky that I want to
rescue Joe a lot more than I want to see you and
Alonzo da Pereira punished. Are you ready to do a
deal, or shall I go straight to Alonzo and offer him the
formula? I'm sure with only a very little effort I could
find out where to reach him.''

''For your own sake, Summer, don't try to deal with
Alonzo direct. You can't trust him, and he wouldn't
hesitate to kill. It's much better if you deal through
me. That way, Alonzo has some incentive to keep his
word.''

Nothing that Gordon had revealed tonight suggested
that Alonzo was the type of man to keep his promises
for any reason except that it suited him to do so, but
Summer was willing to go along with Gordon's suggestions, at least for the time being. He obviously
knew where Joe was being held, and she would do
almost anything to extract that information from him.

With a bit more information, and just a little time, she could set up a deal—Joe for the formula—in such a way that there was at least a good chance of Joe coming out of the transaction alive.

"All right," she said, forcing herself to turn and meet her father's eyes. "Let's start talking terms."

# Nineteen

Summer had been waiting on tenterhooks for Duncan's arrival ever since she'd phoned and asked him to bring Joe's formula over to her father's house. When the doorbell rang, she jumped up from the sofa before Olivia or Gordon had time to react. "I'll get that."

She drew back the bolt on the heavy front door and pulled it open, close to tears at the sheer relief of seeing Duncan standing on the other side. She gave him a wobbly smile. "As my granny used to say, you're a sight for sore eyes."

He smiled back. "You're looking pretty delectable yourself, which is a huge compliment coming from a man who was dragged from his bed at two in the morning."

"I'm sorry I woke you up. I needed you."

"Then I'm glad I'm here."

She wanted to cry again, which was ridiculous. Too overwhelmed by the night's events to pay attention to her usual inhibitions, she tumbled into Duncan's arms, grateful when his hold tightened, making her feel not only safe but wanted.

Unconditional love. That was what had been lacking all her life with Gordon, Summer thought, nuzzling her cheek against Duncan's chest. Since earliest childhood, she had recognized that although she might win her father's approval from time to time, his love was unavailable to her. Growing up, watching her mother get hurt over and over again, she'd absorbed the lesson that the only safe way to deal with powerful and charismatic men was to keep your emotions tamped down, locked up and safely guarded. She'd resisted falling in love with Duncan because she'd expected him to reject and hurt her.

Belatedly, she recognized how misplaced her fears had been. Duncan's easy charm sprang from a warm heart and covered a rock-solid core of integrity that would prevent him from ever deliberately wounding her. Gordon's cold charm covered a hollow center that drove him to bolster his own sense of worth by starving the emotional needs of the people around him.

Poor Olivia, Summer thought. No wonder she's always trying so damned hard to be perfect.

Duncan tucked a strand of hair behind her ear and kissed her. "Not that I don't appreciate the warm welcome, but do you want to tell me what I've done to deserve it?" He grinned. "That way, I'll be sure to do it again."

Yesterday it had been impossible to say the words. Tonight the world was a different place, and it seemed important that she should no longer hide the truth. "I love you," she said gruffly. "And I'm grateful that you came right away when I said that I needed you."

It still wasn't easy for her to express her emotions, and her hands balled into fists as she spoke. Duncan gently unclenched them. "I love you, too," he said. "And I was happy to know that you needed me." He tipped her face up to kiss her but didn't get that far. "What's happened?" he asked, brushing away the tears that clogged the ends of her lashes. "You don't cry easily, so what's happened to upset you?"

She was going to have to tell him about Gordon, Summer thought gloomily. How horrible to have to admit that your father was a thief, a political conspirator, and possibly worse. The churning in her stomach started up again, along with the panicked sense of time running out. "The long version takes more time than we have—"

"Okay, try the short version."

"The short version is that Gordon has known all along who kidnapped me. He knows where Joe is being held prisoner, too. He's always known."

"Gordon knew?" Duncan's face darkened. "I hope you're going to tell me there's some absolutely staggering life-or-death reason why he didn't tell anyone before now."

"He claims that if he'd spoken up, I would have been killed."

Duncan relaxed a little. 'That's a valid reason to remain silent."

"Yes, if you believe him. Personally, I think his major worry was that he'd be arrested if he told the FBI what he knew."

"You're taking too many verbal shortcuts here. I'm lost. Explain to me in simple terms why Gordon is in danger of being arrested."

"In simple terms?" She drew in a ragged breath. "Okay. Gordon has taken millions of dollars in illegal campaign contributions from Alonzo da Pereira, who is the new president of Industria Agricola do Norte. And although he won't admit it, I think he was an accessory before the fact in Fernando da Pereira's murder."

Duncan's jaw dropped and he shook his head. "I'm not taking this in. You're claiming that your father knew about Fernando's murder? You can't be serious!"

"I'm very serious. I always knew Gordon had a hunger for power that's almost insatiable, but I never realized until tonight what lengths he would go to in order to appease that hunger." She looked at Duncan and sighed. "You don't believe me, do you."

"Yes," he said slowly. "It's terrible, but I do believe you. In fact, while you were talking, I was wondering how I could accept such shocking accusations with relative ease once the first surprise had passed. And then I realized that Gordon is not only one of the most driven men I've ever met, he's also one of the most elusive. Despite the fact that he's my brother-in-law, we've never been friends, only polite acquaintances. Same thing at work. He leads competently, but he doesn't inspire because he's too closed in on himself. His passions are all turned inward."

"Not only turned inward, but twisted. That's been made horribly clear tonight." Summer paused outside the open doorway leading into the living room, not caring if Gordon and Olivia could hear what she said. "I've just worked out a plan that might get Joe safely out of Alonzo da Pereira's clutches, but I'm counting on you to point out all the holes so we can fix them before we put the plan into operation. The first thing we need is the formula for Joe's drug. Did you bring it?"

"Sure did." Duncan patted his jacket pocket. "It's in here. I made three extra copies on my fax machine before I left home and then hid them in various obscure spots. Since this is the only copy of the formula for a supposedly life-saving drug, that seemed like a smart move.''

"Very smart," Summer said, walking into the living room. "If something goes wrong with this rescue plan, we don't want everything Joe has worked for to be lost. According to Gordon, Joe's drug slows the transformation of HIV into full-blown AIDS by several years, and without most of the unpleasant side effects of the protease inhibitors that are on the market now.''

"My God! That's why everyone is fighting to get their hands on the formula!" Duncan had no chance to say anything more before Gordon saw them. He stood up and greeted Duncan as if he'd come to join a pleasant social event. "It's good to see you," he said, sliding his hand into his pocket with feigned casualness. He was smart enough not to risk rejection by holding out his hand. "Well, I heard Summer catching you up on the latest developments in this nasty Pereira situation. This is truly a miracle drug that our friend Malone has discovered, isn't it? There are almost no side effects, you know. Nothing but a mild buzz, followed by an even milder headache. And I understand you're the man who is lucky enough to have the formula for this wonder drug in your possession.''

"Yes." Duncan sent him a level, assessing look, and Gordon had the grace to drop his gaze. Duncan turned away without saying another word, walking over to the chair where his sister was sitting. "Livvy, honey, how are you feeling?''

"Sick," she said.

He took her hand, cradling it in his. "Would you like a glass of sherry? You always say that's the most civilized aid to digestion there is.''

Olivia gave him a smile that cracked in the middle. "Thanks, Duncan, but I think this particular bout of sickness will require more drastic measures than sherry."

"Perhaps you should go and lie down?"

"No, I want to hear what you think about Summer's idea for rescuing Joseph Malone." Olivia straightened in her chair, visibly trying to get a firmer grip on herself. "I really want us to save him," she said. "It would make me feel a bit better for having been such a gullible fool over Fernando. But I don't want Gordon to go to jail, Duncan. I couldn't stand the shame of that."

"We'll try to find a way to save Joe without involving the police," Duncan said. "Summer, let's get started. What's your plan?"

"It's pretty basic." Summer rubbed at the headache pounding ferociously between her eyes. "First, you need to know that Gordon has agreed to step down as secretary of state. He's already written his letter of resignation, and it's sitting over there on the desk, waiting to be hand-delivered to the president as early tomorrow as Gordon can arrange a meeting."

"I think I was too hasty in writing that letter," Gordon said plaintively. He cast a sidelong glance at Duncan, hoping to find an ally. "It's not going to be easy to explain why I have to step down. In fact, the president will probably refuse to accept my resignation—"

"Then persuade him that he must," Duncan said coolly and with absolute finality. "Your career is over, Gordon, I'll make sure of that. Now, Summer, you were saying?"

She smiled at him, grateful beyond words for his support. "Just before you arrived, Gordon admitted that Alonzo da Pereira is here in Washington with Joe. He told me they're staying in Fernando's old penthouse apartment, which is where the kidnappers were holding me, apparently. The fact that they're here in D.C. makes things a bit easier to arrange from a logistical point of view. I'm suggesting that Gordon should phone Alonzo and tell him that I have the formula for Joe's drug, and that I'm willing to exchange it for Joe. Then we'll arrange a neutral meeting place. Alonzo can bring Joe, Gordon and I will take the formula, and we'll do a swap.''

In other circumstances, Duncan would have laughed. The plan was breathtaking in its inadequacy, and Duncan was sure Gordon must recognize its many shortcomings even if Summer didn't. He felt a burst of murderous rage toward Gordon, who seemed totally indifferent to the extreme danger of what Summer proposed. Didn't he care that his daughter was virtually inviting Alonzo to kill her?

Fighting for calm, he took her in his arms. ''Summer, honey, you don't have to present yourself to Alonzo as a living sacrifice to make up for the fact that your father is morally bankrupt.''

''No, that's not what I'm doing. I won't be in any danger. Besides, we have to get Joe—''

''Think about it, honey, and you'll realize there's no way you can get Joe back safely just by offering to hand over the formula. Whatever he promises, Alonzo won't keep his word. He'll come to the rendezvous with an army of bodyguards, and once he figures out you haven't brought the feds, he'll use force to steal the formula. Even if by some miracle Alonzo allows you to escape with your life, Joe wouldn't stand a chance. Alonzo simply can't afford to let Joe live." And, if Duncan were placing bets, he wouldn't put very high odds on Gordon making much of an effort to keep his daughter alive.

"Then help me come up with a better idea," Summer said. Her lips quivered, then managed to hold a smile. "I'm feeling overwhelmed, Duncan, I admit it. Not to mention plain old-fashioned exhausted."

Gordon started to speak and Duncan rounded on him. "If you're half as smart as I once thought you were, you'll sit down and shut up."

Gordon sat.

Fine, Duncan thought. I've beaten up on Gordon, but where the hell do we go from here? As fast as he thought of plans, he rejected them. Alonzo couldn't be trusted, but Gordon wasn't much better, so how was he going to rescue Joe, protect the formula and keep Gordon out of jail? Not that he cared a rat's ass about Gordon, but he didn't want Olivia and Summer to suffer because Gordon was publicly identified as Grade A slime.

Go back to basic diplomatic negotiating principles, he told himself. To make a deal, you always needed a stick as well as a carrot. They had the carrot—Joe's formula—but it wasn't a very good one because it was too easy for Alonzo to steal. And they didn't have a stick at all. What could they use as a stick? The threat of jail didn't work. Exposing Alonzo automatically exposed Gordon. Same for the FBI. Threatening to hand Alonzo over to the FBI would scare the shit out of him, but he would turn the threat right back and expose Gordon's criminal behavior. If only there was some way to use the threat of the FBI without involving Gordon. Maybe they could threaten Alonzo with the FBI at the same time as they promised to save him....

That's it! Duncan thought. We can lie. The only proviso was that they had to make their lies credible to Alonzo, who might be criminal but was certainly not a fool. There was absolutely no margin for error here.

"Okay, Gordon," he said, pacing and plotting. "This is what we're going to do. You need to call Alonzo da Pereira and warn him that you've just this minute learned that the FBI is planning a full-scale raid on his penthouse at five this morning. No, that gives Alonzo too much time to think. Say the FBI is planning the raid for 4:00 a.m. Tell him there are going to be thirty agents swarming over the place and that he needs to get Joe out of the apartment, right now, the second you hang up. Oh, and get the guards out of there, too." *The stick.*

Gordon poured himself another cognac. "The most likely result of such a phone call is that Alonzo will lose his nerve and kill your friend Malone."

"Not if you do this right. Remind him that you still don't have the formula and that you need Joe alive. You have to persuade Alonzo to smuggle Joe out of the penthouse right away, before the FBI agents have supposedly surrounded the building. Then you have to convince him that the only safe place for him to hide Joe is here, in your house. Sound reluctant. Tell him to get rid of the bodyguards. Agree to let Joe stay here until tomorrow nightfall, but no longer. Stress that Alonzo has to make arrangements to transport Joe somewhere else within eighteen hours." *The carrot.*

"My God," Summer breathed. "That's brilliant, Duncan."

"Alonzo will smell a trap." Gordon took a nervous sip of his cognac. "He knows me too well to believe that I'd put myself and my career so much at risk."

Duncan reached over and removed Gordon's brandy snifter.

"Make him believe it," he said flatly. "Find a way to make this happen. Because if Joseph Malone dies, you're going to be contemplating your failure to save him from a prison cell."

Gordon had made the phone call to Alonzo da Pereira and it seemed to have worked. Alonzo would be arriving shortly with Joseph Malone. Olivia sat in her chair listening to the discussion but contributing nothing. Her brain felt too full, and she couldn't find a way to pull any single thought out of the tangle and put it into words. Duncan was instructing Gordon on how he was to greet Alonzo to maximize the chance of avoiding violence. Bring Alonzo into this room, Duncan was saying. Summer and Olivia would wait upstairs, out of harm's way. Summer protested. Duncan was adamant. Nobody bothered to ask her opinion.

Watching her brother, Olivia felt an acute stab of jealousy. The chemistry between Duncan and Summer sizzled, even under these tense circumstances. It seemed that she was never going to be free of the knife blade of Summer's presence in her life. First as the smart, beautiful daughter of the man she loved. Now as the smart, beautiful wife of her brother. Olivia shuddered at the horrible vision of future Christmas holidays, with Summer dropping names of eminent scientists and casually tossing around scientific concepts that Olivia couldn't even begin to grasp. And there would be children, too, clambering on Summer's lap and getting swung up on Duncan's shoulders. The children she had always wanted and Gordon had refused to have.

Olivia felt a grief so sharp that for a moment it was a physical pain. She blinked and brought her wandering attention back to Gordon and Duncan. They were discussing the precautions they would take in view of the fact that Alonzo would almost certainly be carrying a gun. Or two. Duncan paced out the diagram of exactly where and how he would spring out from behind the door and bring down a heavy silver candlestick on Alonzo's head.

The candlestick her brother planned to use was one of Olivia's favorite pieces, a neoclassical wonder from the late eighteenth century, similar to a pair in the John Quincy Adams State Drawing Room. She had been thrilled the day she found those candlesticks in a little antique store in Virginia. She wondered if she should find Duncan something less valuable to use as a head-basher, then decided she didn't have the energy to get up from her chair.

At this time of night it would take less than thirty minutes for Alonzo da Pereira to get from his penthouse to Georgetown. She looked at the clock on the mantelpiece, which was a perfect reproduction of a seventeenth-century design by watchmaker John Harrison. Just looking at the exquisite workmanship calmed her somewhat. Her life couldn't be worthless if she'd acquired so many lovely things. Maybe she wasn't smart like Summer, but at least she had perfect taste.

It was three-fifteen. Twenty minutes since Gordon had hung up the phone. Alonzo should be arriving at any moment.

Over the past four years, since he became consumed by the lust to become president, her husband had gradually turned into a man she didn't recognize. Listening to him with a mixture of love and hatred, Olivia realized that what she feared most was that Gordon wouldn't keep to his side of the bargain he was making with Duncan. And she couldn't think of any way that Gordon could double-cross Duncan without dead bodies ending up on the drawing room carpet.

It was a tragic commentary on the man she had chosen to marry that she was no longer sure if Gordon would worry about the death of his daughter, much less the death of Duncan, a mere brother-in-law. But since the maintenance of any political influence would be seriously threatened by having to explain the presence of dead bodies in his living room, Olivia was cautiously optimistic that her husband was being sincere in his promises to help free Joseph Malone.

"Time to go upstairs, Livvy." Duncan came and helped her to her feet. She felt disoriented, but Summer's pitying glances helped to put at least a touch of steel in her backbone. The link between her brain and her voice unlocked and she could speak again. She looked at her husband, forcing him to meet her gaze.

"The plan my brother has outlined seems very simple and also effective. Are you sure you've understood all the finer points, Gordon?"

"I'm perfectly capable of understanding plain English." Gordon was icily controlled, barriers so firmly in place that she couldn't tell what he was feeling, much less what he was thinking.

"Olivia, we'd better get out of the way," Summer said. "We'll only be a dangerous distraction for Duncan if we stay down here."

The fact that she could speak again didn't mean that she had to answer her stepdaughter. With the rest of her life coming unglued, dislike of her stepdaughter remained a valuable constant. Olivia swept out of the room without a backward glance. When they got upstairs, she gestured to the guest room. "You can wait in there," she said. Reluctantly, she added an explanation. "It's better if we're not in the same room. We'll be tempted to talk, and we'll only make each other more tense."

"You're right," Summer said. She hesitated for a moment. "Olivia, I'm sorry that things have always been so difficult between us. I didn't realize... I didn't understand..."

"I'm quite sure you didn't," Olivia said. "You still don't understand." She went into her bedroom before Summer could dish out any more of her unwelcome pity. How could Summer possibly understand what it was like to fall fathoms deep in love with a man who was incapable of returning your feelings? A man in whom the lust for power dominated all his other emotions?

The doorbell rang less than five minutes later. Ear pressed to the crack of her bedroom door, Olivia listened as Gordon greeted Alonzo da Pereira.

"Come in quickly, for God's sake. Where's Malone?"

"In the car. He's drugged. I need help to move him!"

"Okay. I'll help you. We need to get him inside and out of sight. Jesus! What have you done to him this time? Is he still alive?"

"He's alive. I gave him a shot to knock him out, that's all. There wasn't time to arrange transportation, so I had to drive over here in my Mercedes. I didn't want him screaming for help every time we stopped at a traffic light.''

"Take him into the living room," Gordon said. "This way. We need to work a few things out to make sure we have our stories straight for the FBI."

"I don't understand why Julian Stein is suddenly interested in me—'' Alonzo's reply was cut off by the sounds of a muffled blow, followed by a body falling to the floor.

"We did it!" Duncan said a second or two later. "Gordon, help me tie Alonzo's wrists." He sounded excited, relieved. Fatally trusting. Olivia knew she had to hurry or disaster would strike. She ran out of the bedroom and heard Summer following hard on her heels.

"Gordon, what happened to that tape we were going to use?" Duncan sounded breathless, as if he was heaving Alonzo's inert body around. "We need to get him out of here as quickly as possible. I'll drive him somewhere and dump him. He'll be furious, but he's not going to complain to the police."

She'd been right to panic, Olivia realized as she ran into the living room. In a lightning glance she took in the whole scene. Duncan absorbed in taping Alonzo's wrists behind his back. Joe lying unconscious on the sofa. And Gordon opening the drawer of her marquetry desk.

"No!" In her mind the word was a giant scream, a repudiation of everything that her husband had done and become over the last few years. But nobody seemed to hear her.

Except Gordon. Her husband swung around. The gun was in his hand just as she feared. God, no! She wouldn't be able to get there in time. The explosion of the shot echoed and reechoed in the room, and inside Olivia's head. She screamed.

Duncan stood up, blood on his hands, white to the lips. Behind her, Olivia heard Summer's running footsteps clatter to a halt.

"God Almighty, Gordon, what have you done?" Duncan asked hoarsely, feeling for Alonzo's pulse.

"I couldn't let him live," Gordon said. "You're a fool if you think he'd have kept quiet. The moment the feds got their hands on him, he would have been shouting to make a deal and that would have been the end of me."

Summer went and stood next to Duncan, clinging to his arm, despite the blood. She looked down at Alonzo. "Is he dead?"

"Yes. The shot went straight into his heart." Duncan drew in a choked breath and then another. "We have to call the police."

"Don't be ridiculous," Gordon said. "I didn't kill Alonzo da Pereira just so that you could inform the police and give them something else to charge me with." He walked over to the sofa and pointed the gun straight at Joe Malone's head, but he directed his gaze to Duncan. "Give me the copy of the formula for the drug, Duncan, or your friend Malone dies. If I can't be president, at least I'm going to retire from public life a very rich man."

"You know I'm not going to give you the formula," Duncan said. "It's time to end this, Gordon, and you've made it impossible for us to help you retire with dignity. All we can do now is make a phone call to your lawyer and advise you not to say anything more until he gets here."

For answer, Gordon shot Joseph through the arm. "Your friend Malone has been having a rough few days," he said, twirling the gun in his hands. "Without prompt medical treatment, he's going to die. Give me the formula, Duncan, or I'll put another bullet in his other arm."

"Give him the formula," Summer said feverishly, trying to staunch the blood gushing from Joe's arm. "Jesus, Duncan, I think he's shattered the bone. Just give it to him or he'll kill Joe."

"She's right, you know." Gordon took aim. "I'm not much of a shot, but at this distance, even I can't miss. On the count of three…"

"No, don't! Here, take the formula, for all the good it will do you." Duncan reached into his jacket pocket.

Olivia screamed, and this time the sound came out, loud and piercing. Didn't they realize what would happen as soon as her husband had the formula in his possession? Not only Joseph Malone would die, that was for sure.

For a split second Gordon was disoriented by her scream, and she flung herself at him, wrestling the gun from his grasp. She was inches away from him, so she didn't stop to take aim, just pulled hard on the trigger. Once, twice, three times. The recoil threw her back. It was nowhere near as easy to fire a gun as it looked in the movies, she thought dazedly.

Gordon made a gurgling sound. He stared at her in utter and complete amazement before he crumpled and fell to the floor.

It was a moment before anyone moved. Then Duncan and Summer both ran and knelt next to Gordon. Olivia let the gun drop to the ground, but she didn't approach her husband.

"I can't find a pulse," Summer said. "Duncan, help me!"

"He's dead," Duncan said a few moments later. He ran his hand over Gordon's face, closing his eyes. He took Summer's hands and pulled her away from her father's body, taking her over to the window and rocking her in his arms until she started to cry.

It was finished, Olivia thought, weak with relief and bitter regret. Duncan and Summer were safe. Gordon was dead.

Her husband's quest for ultimate power was finally over.

# Epilogue

Tony had barely seated Summer and Duncan at a secluded corner table in his newly expanded restaurant when Joe arrived. Grinning from ear to ear, Joe pushed through the crowd of lunchtime patrons and sat down opposite them, looking tanned and surprisingly fit for a man who had spent two weeks in the hospital hovering near death only three months earlier.

Joe set a folder of papers in the center of the table. "Read 'em and cheer, folks," he said.

Summer opened the file, beaming as she saw the official seals and signatures. She pushed the folder across to Duncan. "This is terrific," she said. "Congratulations, Joe. You've achieved everything you were working for."

"Yes." Joe's face was flushed with excitement. "We're still working on the basic science of growing the plants in mass quantities, which isn't my area of expertise, to put it mildly, so for the next couple of years, the company is going to follow Fernando's original plans and rely on harvesting indigenous plants that grow right around Manaus. That should produce enough of the basic ingredients to get wide-scale clinical trials under way.''

"This is really great," Duncan said. "Utilizing Brazilian labor and land to produce the basic ingredients means that you're not only responsible for finding a drug that helps in the fight against AIDS, but you've found work for displaced laborers and peasants in Amazonia. Not to mention you've provided the best possible commercial incentive for developers to stop chopping down the rain forest in the name of progress.''

"Yeah." Joe smiled cheerfully. "There's nothing like the whiff of windfall profits to have international corporations suddenly deciding that conservation is cool." He crunched on a bread stick, opening the menu. "Jeez, I'm hungry enough to eat everything on here. Did Tony say what was good today?''

Summer chuckled. "What do you think? According to Tony, every dish is perfection, as always.''

"Ah, yes, foolish question. Did you two decide on your particular piece of perfection?''

"I'm having grouper," Duncan said.

"And I'm going to have the hearts of palm salad.'' Summer exchanged a self-conscious glance with Duncan and cleared her throat, suddenly shy. "If Tony talks me into eating any more of his *feijoadas*, I'll have to waddle down the aisle next month.''

Joe looked up from the menu, his gaze flicking between the two of them. "Wait...waddle down the aisle... Does that mean you and Duncan have finally set the date?''

Summer nodded. "Yes, the fifteenth of next month.''

"For obvious reasons we're keeping the ceremony

small and very informal," Duncan said. "But we both hope very much that you can come."

"Of course I can. Wouldn't miss it for the world." For a moment, Summer thought she saw a hint of regret for might-have-beens in Joe's eyes, but if regret was there, he banished it instantly and got up to walk around the table to pump Duncan's hand and give her a convincing hug. "Thank God you've finally put the man out of his misery," he said. "The poor guy was getting desperate the last time we talked. Muttering about kidnapping you and making for Las Vegas."

"Lucky for him he didn't try it." Summer pulled a face at her fiancé. "You know, kidnapping is not the very best way to win my heart."

"Joe pointed that out to me," Duncan said.

"And I'm real glad he listened, even though he had all my sympathy. What took you so long to say yes?"

Dropping her joking manner, Summer laid her hand alongside Duncan's. "I wanted to have everything connected to my father's death behind us before we got married. It seemed important not to have the start of our future tangled too deeply in the past."

"I can certainly understand that." Joe put down his bread stick. "Speaking of tangled pasts, how is Olivia doing?" he asked quietly.

"She has good days and bad," Duncan said. "To be honest, more bad than good, despite all the medication that's supposed to keep her happy."

Summer looked sad. "What bothers her most is the fact that she's lost Gordon. Despite everything, she's still in love with him. I guess at one level that doesn't surprise me, but at another level, I find it really shocking."

"You, of all people, should understand where she's

coming from," Joe said. "Gordon Shepherd was a charismatic man. Look at how hard you and your mother worked to win his approval."

"That's true—"

"And it's only to be expected that Olivia feels terribly conflicted about the fact that she was the person who fired the shot that killed Gordon," Duncan pointed out.

"Poor woman." Summer shivered. "I guess we all have to be grateful that Julian Stein was willing to accept our claim that Olivia killed Gordon in self-defense. Thank God we didn't have to put Olivia through the trauma of a trial."

Duncan frowned. "She wouldn't have survived a trial, I'm sure. Not mentally, and maybe not physically. As it was, the media attention was enough to send even a strong-minded person around the bend."

Joe grimaced. "Just thank your lucky stars, your guardian angels and anyone else you can think of that it was in the government's best interest to pretend that Gordon Shepherd died protecting his family from Alonzo da Pereira's murderous schemes. I'm really impressed with how Julian Stein has managed to keep the details of the FBI investigation under wraps."

Summer nodded. "That's because the investigation was given the highest security classification—"

"I realize that," Joe said. "But it sure helped that Alonzo da Pereira was a Brazilian citizen and your father was secretary of state. Those two facts gave the administration a fig leaf to hide behind when they were stonewalling the media on the grounds of national security."

Summer took a swig of water and shook off her gloomy mood. "There are a few bright spots. Julian

Stein groveling to you and me and apologizing because he hadn't believed either of our stories will always remain one of my more gratifying memories."

Joe laughed. "Mine, too. Groveling was obviously a novel experience for him."

"But in the end, we managed to make him do it so well." They grinned at each other, covering pain with laughter.

Tony came across to their table, carrying a bottle of champagne and four flutes. He rested an arm affectionately around Joe's shoulders. "You're all looking mighty pleased with yourselves. Do we have a signed agreement to celebrate?" he asked.

"We sure do," Joe said. "My agreement with Boettcher Pharmaceuticals has been officially signed, sealed and delivered as of ten o'clock this morning. And there's more good news—Summer and Duncan have set a date for their wedding."

"Congratulations." Tony popped the cork. "You're a lucky man, Duncan," he said, pouring champagne into the four glasses. "Get married in New York, Summer darling, and have the reception here. I owe you both for saving Joe, and I'll throw you the party of a lifetime."

"It's a deal," Summer said promptly. "Thank you, Tony."

Joe raised an eyebrow. "Hey, let's show a little tact here, kiddo. Don't you have to at least pretend to consult with Duncan?"

"No." Duncan grinned. "We have a great decision-making system already in place in our relationship. I focus on world-shattering decisions like how the United States will keep the peace in Bosnia, and Summer decides the trivial stuff like where we'll have our wedding reception.''

Joe laughed and Tony lifted his glass in a toast. "I predict a great future for this marriage," he said. "Summer and Duncan, *felicidades!*"

From the critically acclaimed author of
*Iron Lace* and *Rising Tides*

# EMILIE RICHARDS

**Comes an unforgettable novel about
two families ruled for generations by a
flawless but deadly treasure.**

# Beautiful Lies

It's a pearl so flawless, it has no price, but those who
possess it pay dearly. For generations it has cursed the
Robeson and Llewellyn families, unleashing a legacy of
rivalry, greed and murder.

Now Liana Robeson and Cullen Llewellyn embark on a
heart-pounding odyssey to find their son and the
missing pearl. Swept into the wild beauty of Australia,
they are plunged into a deadly game with a rival who
will go to any lengths to possess a treasure as fatal as it
is flawless.

On sale mid-March 1999
where paperbacks are sold!

Look us up on-line at: http://www.romance.net

MER492

New York Times **bestselling author**

# LINDA LAEL MILLER

## *Escape from Cabriz*

Kristen Meyers's impulsive decision to marry the exotic prince of Cabriz is beginning to seem like a very bad idea. On the eve of their wedding, the palace is under attack by angry rebels, and her fiancé has suddenly become a coldhearted stranger. There doesn't appear to be any escape from the complicated mess.

Then Zachary Harmon arrives. Kristen and the secret agent were once lovers. Now he's risking his life to rescue her. All the old chemistry is still there, but now they must survive something even more explosive—escaping from Cabriz alive.

> "Linda Lael Miller is one of the hottest romance authors writing today."
> –*Romantic Times*

*On sale in mid-March 1999 wherever paperbacks are sold!*

**MIRA**

# MURDER AT THE MOVIES

## CHARLENE WEIR
## GEORGE BAXT
## MAXINE O'CALLAGHAN

### MURDER TAKE TWO
### by Charlene Weir

Hollywood comes to Hampstead, Kansas, with the filming of a
new picture starring sexy actress Laura Edwards. But murder
steals the scene when a stunt double is impaled on a pitchfork.

### THE HUMPHREY BOGART MURDER CASE
### by George Baxt

Hollywood in its heyday is brought to life in this witty caper
featuring a surprise sleuth—Humphrey Bogart. While filming
*The Maltese Falcon*, he searches for a real-life treasure, dodging
a killer on a murder trail through Hollywood.

### SOMEWHERE SOUTH OF MELROSE
### by Maxine O'Callaghan

P.I. Delilah West is hired to search for an old high school
classmate. The path takes her through the underbelly of broken
dreams and into the caprices of fate, where secrets are born and
sometimes kept....

*Available March 1999 at your favorite retail outlet.*

If you enjoyed this intriguing
story by

# JASMINE CRESSWELL

Order now to receive more great tales by one of
MIRA's bestselling authors: